LIBRA'S LIBERATION

BOOK 7 OF THE ZODIAC

PAUL SATING

PAUL SATING

THREE FREE NOVELLAS

Free Fantasy!

Sign up for Paul Sating's newsletter at
paulsating.com and receive THREE novellas for free!

THE ZODIAC SERIES

Book 1 - Bitter Aries
Book 2 - The Horn of Taurus
Book 3 - The Gemini Paradox
Book 4 - Cancer's Curse
Book 5 - The Pride of Leo
Book 6 - Virgo's Vigilantes
Book 7 - Libra's Liberation

SAVE A DEMON

If you enjoy this book, do the right thing for Zeke and the gang and leave a Rating and Review.

Your time is valuable, but so is your review. Thank you for being a good mortal by leaving a review!

To Baylee, you have the heart of a bulldog and the attitude of a bear... all in a nine-pound body. All the world's heroes could take lessons from you! Love you, grandpups!

1

UNDERWORLD, ISLE OF DREAD

MINUTES AFTER VIRGO

TANG. TANG.

Through the fog that stretched from the lips of the waters of the Acheron Ocean to the impenetrable mists above, where demonic sky lurked behind the bright azure of the Hellfire, the metallic sound of a dock bell rippled toward our raft.

"That's creepy," Bilba said as he fidgeted with the backpack between his legs.

"As if this fog isn't." Ralrek adjusted, still laid out on his back to catch Hellfire rays for a better base. As if the dude needed a rich tan. What? Was he not already attracting enough eyeballs? "We've been drifting through it for hours."

"Not hours," Azazel said from the cushioned chair at the rear of the raft. "Though I can understand why it would feel that way. The Isle has an ability to change the perception of time."

Bilba turned, squinting. "But we're not at the Isle yet."

Azazel stared above Bilba's head, into the fog. When he flicked his finger, we all turned.

My breath caught.

Behind the veil, a dark shape loomed on the near horizon.

A pillar cutting through the sky. Immense enough that even this never-ending fog couldn't obscure it, the cliff had to be a thousand feet high and more than a mile wide. Even through the curtain of gray, its plateau was conspicuous. I imagined the view from atop that mesa. I bet it would be stunning to stand atop the rock and look out over the ocean—well, if I could see anything through the stupid blanket of white that clung to the waters the Acheron, suffocating us and choking out the rest of the Underworld.

Oddly placed, it was as if Lucifer, or One, or whatever—you get my point—dropped a massive slab of squared rock right in the middle of the vast body of water. How long had we drifted on the raft? Nothing to either side, in front or behind. An endless stretch of ocean blue that provided no hints of what was to come, but gave us plenty of time to reflect on our actions and question our life decisions. Then this wall of fog, from sea to sky, drew all attention.

"How close are we?" I asked, suddenly feeling a creeping anxiety about seeing the Isle of Dread, a place unknown to your everyday demon. A destination the powerful sent those they could control. Where the wayward were sent to rot.

"Not long now," Azazel said, watching us. After a moment, he continued in a friendly, almost fatherly way. "If you incubi have anything you'd like to ask, now would be the time. I'm afraid when we reach the dock, my departure will be swift."

"Why?" Bilba asked. The fog gripped the air in a chill that kept even the tips of his ears from turning a light shade of pink.

Azazel rolled his lips, making his long, flowing goatee bob forward. "Let's just say that as a Founder, the residents of the Isle aren't exactly enamored with me."

Ralrek scoffed.

I understood.

We were being shuffled off to yet another location. Location number... well, let's see. I'm losing count. Cities far and wide throughout the Overworld and Underworld to deal with the likes of Aries, Taurus, and Gemini. More adventures as those missions and our bumbling brought Cancer, Leo, and Virgo into our lives. We were essentially world travelers at this point. No one in my old life, before the Council saw something in me that led them to task me with inconceivable jobs, had left the Fifth Circle.

The Isle of Dread was just the latest in a long line of destinations where Lucifer's Council tossed me, hoping I'd meet my end. I'm sure they hoped this was my last. But if Azazel was being truthful, and I had no reason to think he wasn't, we wouldn't be restricted to the island—if we were smart. Azazel was helpful like that. He had been for years. Sadly, that was something I hadn't seen until recently.

Turning from the sight of the towering mesa, I tapped my forehead with a finger at a sudden epiphany about Azazel, his helpfulness, and my time in the Overworld. "Was it you who gave me that bag of mortal currency when I was Abandoned?"

The ancient demon's lips curled in an all-knowing smile. "Why, young Ezekial, I wondered how long it would take you to figure that out."

"He's not the brightest," Ralrek said, his eyes still closed, hands still behind his head, as if he was stretching out on a beach.

I extended my leg, planted my foot against his hip, and shoved. Not hard enough to send him over the edge of the raft, but enough to make his heart skip a few beats.

Ralrek's arms flailed, slapping against the wood.

Everyone got a chuckle, including Azazel's guards.

"Careful with that," Azazel said, tipping his head toward the water. "There are things under the surface you don't want to meet."

Bilba's head whipped around. "Like what?"

The Founder shrugged as if Bilba had asked who would win the Underworld Blazeball League's championship four hundred years from now. "Things best left under the waters of the Acheron. Things that protect the Underworld from the island's residents, and the island's residents from the rest of the Underworld."

"Doesn't the ocean already do that?" I had to ask. I mean, come on, we'd been sailing and rocking across it for what felt like the better part of my best years—that's an exaggeration, but I'm bored and prone to being hyperbolic when I've got nothing to do, if for no other reason than to entertain myself. Maybe it felt like that because we'd been shoved off to the wasteland of the demonic realm without our loved ones or the comforts of home. A reward for standing up to the unscrupulous rulers of Hell. Yes, I might still be sour.

"It does," Azazel said. "But it does not. There are ways to travel... for the smart demon. As to your question, Ezekial. Yes, it was me. I wanted to help. Lucifer knows you needed it. Plus, I figured it'd serve as a deserved nudge in the right direction."

Ralrek adjusted again, cocking his head with the most minimal of movements.

"Didn't think I had friends besides these two ugly bastards," I said with a tip of my thumb at Bilba and the prone Ralrek. "Good to know I did. Wish I'd been smarter about seeing the signs earlier."

Azazel wagged a finger. "No need for that. I was careful, young Ezekial. Well, I tried to be. The others on the Council can be... conniving, as you've discovered far too many times."

"You don't say?"

"Caution is the key. Always exercise it when surrounded by those who'd do harm. Unfortunately, circumstances force me to operate in that manner," he continued, as if I hadn't interrupted him. "Then or now. Especially now."

"You know I appreciate it, Azazel. At least, I hope you do. But I am curious why."

"Why what?"

The guards at Azazel's side rocked along with the motion of the raft as if this were nothing more than a fancy cruise instead of what it was—the end of our lives as legal residents of the Underworld.

"The help. Why would you put yourself at risk? All three of us have seen what the other Founders are willing to do. I'm sure your muscle heads are privy to a thing or two as well. You definitely know how devious they can be."

"I do," Azazel replied after flicking a smile at his guards.

"So then, why risk it? Beelzebub tried to kill all of us in Olympia. What's to say he wouldn't, isn't, plotting something similar for you?"

My skin tingled at the memory of Beelzebub's attack on a women's clinic in the Overworld. An attack we stopped with help from a small band of vigilantes and a smoking hot angel—almost literally. The Prince of Demons had rained terror on a segment of the small city without mercy. Even though he targeted a vulnerable population, they weren't his aim. Though it never came out during the Council's in-fighting, it was pretty obvious Beelzebub had more nefarious goals in mind.

I almost stopped him too, just coming up short.

During the battle, I'd come face to face with the bleached-sideburns bastard and he'd almost killed me. Only Creed's super-mysterious power, its ability to call on the Hellfire, saved my ass.

Now, I chuckled at the memory of Beelzebub diving head-first into a Rift to escape death at my hands.

"What's so funny?" Ralrek asked, an eye cracked open, eyeball aimed at me.

I told them. We shared a good laugh over the image of the big bully scrambling to save his skin. Even when you're immortal, life is short and there's always time to find humor in demons like that getting their comeuppance.

"Oh, how I wish I could have been there," Azazel said.

"Would have been dangerous, but you'd have loved it."

"Zeke was badass," Bilba said with a beaming smile.

"So were you. Everyone was. Heavens, Ralrek took the top of a building off."

"Not without Cassie's help," he said, still from his back.

"Yes. Yes." Azazel lowered his head, shaking it. "That caused quite the problem for us. Thankfully, no innocents were injured from the falling debris. Though..." He smacked his lips and wagged a finger in our direction, even though he still hung his head. "The entire mess occupied a lot of resources. Both ours and the angels'. Had to call in favors to repair the damage before the morning and wipe more witnesses' minds than I care to think about. So many of them. So many resources and time. You wouldn't believe how hard it is to change what was once reality for hundreds of mortals, especially with so many having their own experiences and biases."

"How so?" Bilba asked.

"Some believe in aliens and inter-dimensional travel. Like... like that..." The Founder's face scrunched before his face brightened with recollection. He snapped his fingers. "String theory! That's it! Very useful for our purposes, let me tell you. Anyway, wiping witness memories was quite the project and a half, but as far as everyone involved, those privy to the situation, it's as if it never happened."

Bilba whistled. Ralrek grunted.

"Well, except for that whole Beelzebub-trying-to-kill-me-thing," I said. "That definitely happened."

"Good thing it didn't," Azazel said with a chuckle. "All of my help would have gone to waste. Not a good thing. Something I'd most like to avoid, if possible." His voice waned as we drifted closer to the clanging dock bell. "Well, anyway.

There is no point honking my horn. Let's just say you've been worth the investment, young Ezekial. All of you have, of course. I only mention him because of his history with my peers."

Ralrek's growl sounded as though it came from somewhere near his abdomen. Though he kept his posture prone, I noticed his hands clench.

I flicked at the raft with my fingernail. Each pass rubbed a nano-sized layer from the wood. "Not sure I could have got through this without the assists. So I appreciate it."

"As I said, you're worth it," Azazel said, his tone flattening.

Ralrek didn't bother to cover or hide his snort this time.

"Don't underestimate your friend, Mr. Burning. He's destined for amazing things, as I feel you all are." The Founder stopped, turning his aged face to me. I couldn't look away. I wanted to. I... just couldn't. "Each of you is important to the future of the Underworld. How it's run. Who runs it. Making sure you're able to help is the challenge we now face. Not just me and my allies. Like Dialphio." He paused. I still wouldn't look. "Bilba, you may be the Rebel Mage, but that's just a name. Something they'll use now that you've been exiled to diminish your achievements. Learn from Ezekial's experience as the Segregate. Names, titles, even pejorative, are just words. They can hurt, but they cannot stop you unless you allow them. No matter how they're used to disparage you and your work, past and future." Another pause. This time, he drew my attention. Azazel tipped his head from side to side as if the placid current was rocking the raft. "If I had a cool name like that, I'd embrace it. And you, Mr. Burning, are young and brimming with the type of confidence that will drive enemies away while also drawing in those who need a powerful beacon to direct them. Don't overlook either of those aspects of your personality. Trying times lay ahead of us and if Ezekial is going to challenge the very structure of the Underworld, we all need to do our part, or they win."

There was no need to remind everyone who 'they' were. Waves lapping against the migrant raft were the only answer to the Founder's comments. Ahead, the pillar of rock widened across the horizon as we neared the Isle of Dread.

So close now.

What was living here going to be like? How hard was it going to do what needed to be done? To check in on Virgo's Vigilantes? To make sure Dialphio was okay? How could I make sure my mother was doing better than simply surviving now that she knew my father was a key element in us being banished? Was she suffering as she tried to reconcile the fact that the incubus she loved had directly contributed to her son's expulsion to the fringes of the world, never to return? What about Cassie? Was I going to see her again? Lucifer, how I wanted that to happen. To challenge the Council. To finish my business with Beelzebub.

Tang. Tang.

Louder now.

A moment of clarity with the cacophony of the island's bell; we were going to find out soon.

"The dock we left from and the dock we'll land act like ley lines," Azazel said in a hard shift of topic, pulling me out of my spiraling thoughts. "There isn't much possibility of drifting off into the ocean. The two points are magically connected to prevent that."

"You mean to prevent exiles from escaping," Ralrek said in a grumble.

Without missing a beat, Azazel continued, "The ocean is treacherous. A defensive tactic that is also quite convenient for traveling to the Isle when needed."

"Who would travel to the Isle? Especially on purpose?" Ralrek asked. A legitimate question considering the risk of being on the island posed to an immortal.

"Those with permission from Lucifer. The danger is for anyone who attempts unapproved crossing."

Bilba rang his hands. "How so?"

"If the ocean, or the creatures it's hiding, doesn't kill them, the guards waiting at the Underworld dock will. It's under constant surveillance. A requirement the Council is only too happy to support. They'll be even more diligent now that the three of you are residents. The last thing they'll want is you to cross into the Underworld. This is a perfect opportunity to focus their efforts on a very specific area to target you, should it present itself. Don't worry about being sent adrift should you try to cross the Acheron. Just, and always remember this, stay on the raft when you do, and you'll have nothing to worry about until you near the dock. Don't forget that. Above all else. If you go into that water, you may never come back out. That's not how your stories need to end."

"I've got to ask," Ralrek said from his back, throwing an arm up, forming a long, lean-yet-muscular L-shape with his body.

"Yes, Mr. Burning?"

"Exactly what's in the water that'll turn a relaxing day floating on a raft into a miserable one?"

Azazel mumbled. "Well, a kraken, of course. A large one, though if I'm being honest, no one has read the oceanography reports in ages. The last time I did, it was well over two hundred feet from the tip of its head to its longest tentacle."

"Two hundred feet?" Bilba asked, his mouth hanging open.

The guards to Azazel's sides cast glances at the water surrounding us.

The Founder's face scrunched. "Not something you want to encounter, no matter how strong you think your Abilities are. Do a favor for the hopes of everyone who wants a free Underworld. Stay away from any silliness when crossing."

"Second question," Ralrek threw the other arm up, now looking like a mummy from an early Hollywood movie when mortal Technology Abilities weren't sophisticated. A dated monster that was now more comical than anything capable of striking fear into the hearts of the young and old. This time, Ralrek didn't wait for Azazel to acknowledge him. "If there's a raft on the island, and some magical pulley system between it and the mainland Underworld, why can't everyone stuck here just hop on and sail away?"

Azazel twitched his mouth. The movement made his long goatee sway slightly. "There's a narrow band around the island, where the fog clears and the waters are perpetually calm. Great fishing in that zone, I've heard. They use the raft for that. Not for crossing the ocean. Anyone who tried?"

"Would know about the kraken?" Bilba concluded.

"Exactly, my boy." Azazel looked about to say something, and then stopped to shake his head. His long beard swayed from armpit to armpit. "No, no, no. They wouldn't have the fortitude. The kraken has terrorized the waters for eons and the long-term residents know that."

Bilba snapped his fingers. "Because they didn't have permission?"

The Founder nodded. "The stories are bred so deeply in their psyche, they're one of the first lessons parents teach their young. But the three of you? You will be safe to cross. Even if you face the kraken, you just might survive."

"Might?" Bilba said with a noticeable bulge in his Adam's Apple.

Azazel's shoulders bobbed as he chuckled. "You'll be fine. If you're careful and follow the rules."

"We will," Bilba said at once. "Of course we will. Though, if I'm being honest, I'd rather not meet it."

Ralrek shuffled his shoulders into a more comfortable position.

"I know," the Founder said with an air of... what was that? Reflection? "You are vulnerable. On the island and when you cross back to the mainland. The Council, or those who represent their interests, lay in wait. It might not be a month or even a century, but they have time to wait for the right opportunity. I want the three of you to be very careful and understand what you put at risk if you act without care. Use your demonic notebooks and communicate travel plans with our common friend."

He didn't have to say Dialphio's name. We all knew who he was talking about, and I was more than happy to have an excuse to chat with her again. That taskmaster would make slow days here pass in the batting of fairies' wings.

"She has ways to contact me securely. Keep me in the loop, but don't abuse the ocean crossing."

I leaned closer. "Meaning?"

Azazel dipped his head at my two magic-loving friends. "They need to work on those Gateways and Rifts."

"They'll work on the Isle?" Bilba asked, eliciting a twitch of Azazel's lips.

"All the Underworld needs you to not sit around the Isle, working on your tans." He paused long enough for one, just one, of Ralrek's eyes to pop open. The handsome devil—see what I did there?—groaned before sitting up to face Azazel. "In order to open your Rifts and Gateways, get back to the Underworld's dock. There's a block on the island."

"But I thought we could use Abilities there?" The pink at the tips of Bilba's ears was spreading around to his lobes. "If there's a block—"

"The block prevents Rifts and Gateways." Azazel shrugged. "A safety mechanism installed by Lucifer at the Isle's inception. Abilities are accessible, but to travel, you'll first have to get back to the Underworld dock." I think he could see the frustration and confusion in our faces because his shoulders slumped, and when he spoke, his words came out softer. "Get to the Overworld and take care of what you need to. Ensure there are good relations with the vigilante group. See your lady friend, Ezekial."

"She's not my—"

"Don't try it, Zeke," Bilba and Ralrek said, sounding like they'd been practicing the line.

Azazel didn't look interested in ribbing me. His tone was ominous. "Use those confusing coordinates I gave you to find the Horn. I'm afraid its location is becoming more and more important."

"Do you think—" I started to ask about his thoughts on whether or not Seraph was the one behind its disappearance.

Azazel waved a hand. "We'll explore that another time. When you're settled and able to focus energy on the matter. For now, use your notebooks to keep communication open. The Horn is important. But whoever possesses it is not in a position to use it. Yet. That time may be coming. It may never arrive. We can't know that for sure. Not now. But you three are much like them, unprepared for the final push. That can change now that you're residents of the Isle of Dread. A masterstroke, if I say so myself." He lifted a hand, one finger extended. "But if you don't get settled and focused, you won't be of much help."

TANG. TANG.

The ocean's depths were black. If any fish or a kraken swam below us, I wouldn't spot them. But the fog was evaporating. More of the vast pillar of rock darkened behind the white veil, pushing it away and allowing the island to take a stronger hold.

The pillar dominated this new world, slowly sloping to the base of the island. The edges of this new home stretched away, disappearing into the ring of fog. The front of the island met the Acheron, becoming clearer with every foot we drifted closer. Soon, details took shape.

A long slope of obscured trees reached down toward a wide clearing of brown beach. The clearing wasn't symmetrical, which would have really ticked off Kanthor Sunstone. My father believed in everything having its place and having a place for everything. This beach clearing wasn't like that at all. There was a fluidity to the way the clearing reached into the depths of the island forest in wide, curving branches, only to pull back toward the beach and allow the green to curve its way through the sands. Rounded knobs of tall weeds pushed the beach back before the sands arched in the forest's direction a few feet later. Not so different from the rest of life; two forces, opposing one another, seeking vulnerabilities with subtle shifts.

"Wow," Bilba said, looking up the slope of the mesa.

I seconded that.

"Welcome to the Isle of Dread," Azazel said behind us.

Sand. Trees. Ridiculously large mesa. Forest. Dock. Annoying bell. But no other demons.

I spun. "Before we get too close?"

"Yes, young Ezekial?"

"I need to know about Cancer. I can't thank you enough for making sure I knew at the fighting pit." When the Council tried to rub me out of existence by forcing me to fight to the death against a trained fighter and blessed good demon in Leo Neto, I only knew that Cancer Nijal, another beloved friend and confidant, had supposedly died in the world war. A nurse by trade, a saint if a demon ever could be, she positioned herself to be sent to the war zone to give medical care to civilians affected by the fighting. Months later, I had no idea if she was alive or Abolished. I needed to know. Now.

"As soon as I get specifics about her situation, you'll be the first one to know."

Bless it. If I couldn't get a definitive status, I'd take a simple nod. "Thank you."

Azazel gave it freely.

We drifted in silence through the last wafting strands of misty fog. The Isle of Dread, our new home, greeted us with eerie silence. No welcoming party. No festive island music. But hey, at least the fog fell behind us, ringing the island as

Azazel had said it would. From above, the rays of the Hellfire once again warmed the day. That had to be worth something. Right? To know that, if nothing else, at least sunny days would fill life here? You cling to that kind of stuff when the rest of your life is a tumultuous mess.

TANG! TANG! TANG!

For whom the bell tolls and all that.

2

UNDERWORLD, ISLE OF DREAD

THE RAFT DRIFTED TO THE DOCK. AZAZEL'S GUARDS MOVED TO stations at the bow as we neared. We had to shift around on the raft so the weight change didn't result in us being dumped into the water. This close to the dock, the water was shallow. Well, I mean, it was deep enough that my under-five-foot-eight frame would fit nicely beneath its depths, but the rippled sand of the ocean floor was clearly visible. Seeing the sand carved into neat rows of waving lines also assured me that the kraken wasn't waiting to sniff out a Zeke-sized snack if I toppled off the vessel.

As it was, we denied snack time for any creature of the deep. Docked, it only took minutes to unload our gear. The guards were a big help. Azazel wasn't. Not that I expected him to lug around our bags and those chests of goodies he provided to see us on our way to our new life. Instead, the ancient Founder remained on the raft and watched the tree line.

The dock bell stopped its racket when we moored, casting a thick silence all around the area of the dock, the beach, and this entire freakin' side of the Isle of Dread. The beach was empty. Just us, a Founder, and a soft wind lazily cross-cutting the brown sands.

Hmmm. "So, this is it?" I looked around. Where to start? "Where is everyone? Are the stories of the hundreds and hundreds of demons shoved off to the Isle another exaggeration of Hell's elite?"

"Sadly, plenty of demons call the Isle of Dread 'home,' Ezekial," Azazel said. I noted a shake of his head that he tried to hide. "Many, many, demons. Too many, if you ask me. But such is the way of the Council. Just because you don't see them doesn't mean they're not here." He gripped the bars of the ladder leading to the upper dock and dragged himself up. The guards moved to his sides when he reached the last run, readied to catch him should he slip. "Now, I cannot stay long, but I must get off this Lucifer-forsaken raft and onto something solid for a few moments. I'm too old for seafaring, I'm afraid."

Bless it, it was so cool to hear a Founder use our Lord's name in vain.

We lugged our belongings and the trunks to the end of the dock, taking a moment to soak in this new reality, which helped me ignore how much I was sweating from the work.

"It's really quiet," Bilba said, his hands on his hips as he looked around. "Does everyone live on the other side of the island? I'm guessing so. If they were dispersed, surely we'd have seen some signs of civilization even before we landed, but especially now."

Azazel tipped his head, his mouth opening. The cracking of a branch in the nearby grove of palmetto trees cut him off. We turned, me warily, Ralrek nonplussed, and Bilba excitedly, as the guards slid in front of Azazel without a word spoken between them.

A cluster of demons emerged from the forest's shadows cast by the clutter of red-leafed branches. They inched forward, remaining close. Incubi, succubi; young and old;

every shape and size; every ethnicity imaginable. A microcosm of Hell's population. The Isle of Dread did not discriminate, it appeared.

Bilba leaned back, closer to the Founder. "Who are they?"

"The residents of the Isle," Azazel said in a firm tone devoid of his usual personality.

I noticed he didn't move from his spot between the guards. Interesting. By the expressions I saw in the crowd, I understood. We were facing down a swath of demons not bothering to hide grim, harrowed looks. Faces twisted in outright scorn. Heat created by revenge filled hundreds of sets of eyes.

"Is there some kind of problem we need to know about?" Ralrek asked without turning to the Founder.

"We're among those exiled to this place by the Council. As the sole representative of the very body who took them away from their homes and families, I'm not welcome."

"Makes sense."

"Ralrek!" Bilba looked shocked. He could be so adorably naïve sometimes.

On the right, movement in the trees caught my attention long before I saw the outlines of forms. More demons. Stepping into the clearing, this group was roughly the same number as the other. Same demographics.

"More friends?"

"I'll be honest. I don't know how the Isle works." Azazel tipped his chin toward the first and second groups of exiles. "But if my instincts are correct, I'd say they're two groups who not only don't like me being here, but they don't like each other. See how they glance at each other? Tread carefully."

He started to lift a finger like he was about to make another observation, but he didn't get a chance. Half a blazeball field away, a third group emerged from the thickest part of the forest rimming the beach. A fourth one was hot in their heels, just from the opposite corner of the cove.

Bilba whistled. "How many groups are there?"

Azazel mumbled something unintelligible. "I'm not sure. I wish I could advise you better."

Once the last group halted at the beach's edge, unspoken, the four groups moved out of the forest. Their ranks were so deep I couldn't tell if we were looking at all of their numbers. They just kept coming. At least a hundred belonged to each.

Bilba must have recognized the same thing. He whistled again, this time low and raspy. His gulp was even more audible. "I had no idea so many had been exiled."

"Not the Council's accomplishment I'm most proud of," Azazel said, his tone restricted.

"Shouldn't be," Ralrek grumbled, and I couldn't disagree. "On top of Abandoning demons in the Overworld," he said, only stopping to swing his arm in a horizontal arc to include each of the four groups of the island's fragmented population, "exiling a few hundred to this Isle is a shitty thing to do. Even for the Council."

I shifted uneasily, not sure how to proceed. Noone in any of the groups, even those who appeared to be the more senior members, spoke. Demons crossed arms, staring at Azazel as if they would roast him with Angelfire if they could cast the blessed magic. Spanning the four groups, heads bent closer together, whispered messages shared. Fingers stabbed in the Founder's direction, as if they wanted to poke his eyes out with a single gesture.

Azazel quietly cleared his throat. "Well, I best be on my way. Don't want to overstay the welcome and..." He had half-turned back toward the dock. The slight breeze grabbed his long goatee and was pulling it toward the water as if an invisible hand meant to tug him to a watery grave. "Well, remember what I said. No time to rest. Get settled, and then get to work. Everyone needs you. I'll check in soon."

Without a word, the Founder staggered down the dock

with more energy than I'd seen him display in years. His sneakers thunked on the planks.

Azazel was very good at playing the 'old incubus' game when he needed to project a certain image. Now, though, he didn't dally. His guards, to their credit, occupied the line of the junction between wood and sand. A demarcation. If any of the Isle's unfriendly residents wanted at the Founder, they would have to go through those two muscle heads. The guards had his back, just like he'd had mine. I didn't know these demons. I couldn't trust them. Not saying I trusted Azazel, but I wouldn't turn away if this was a moment of need.

I took a single step back. Ralrek eyed me, following my lead.

"So, what do you guys think?" Bilba asked, his jaw hanging halfway open. Noticing we were now behind him, he turned away from the Isle's exiles.

I restricted my sigh and looked toward the end of the dock. The guards were helping Azazel down the ladder, one from above, the other standing on the lower dock we'd moored the raft to. When he was on the vessel, they pushed off, back to the Underworld. The fog pulled them into its embrace not long after.

My attention swayed between him and those ringing the brown beach until the stirring sea fret obscured the Founder. Only then did I turn back, partially surprised to see the exiles in the same spot they'd been in before, still watching us.

Finally, Ralrek answered Bilba's question. "I'm not sure. Do you feel anything, Zeke?"

Ever since Aries gave me the most kick-ass halberd in all creation, my senses had been heightened. Like, to a ridiculous level. Beyond anything anyone before claimed to feel. One of the increased capabilities I'd enjoyed from that moment was the ability to tell when someone not only cast a spell, but even the moment they tapped into their Ability. It's not a perfect science—trust me, nothing about me is perfect—but I haven't met a demon, or angel, yet who can draw on their magical Abilities without me picking up on it. Well, except for the Big Man who ruled Hell—I assume His counterpart in the Upperworld is pretty much the same. Exception to the rule and all that. No one among the four or five hundred sharing this broad swath of beach with us was preparing a spell.

"We're good."

"Mmm, hmmm," Ralrek said, before bending to pick up one of our trunks. He held it as if it was nothing more than an oversized loaf of bread. The bastard. Height. Gorgeous hair so thick I'm sure some of his lovers' fingers had taken minutes to untangle from it. Strong, masculine features. Magic so powerful he couldn't be trusted to experiment. Ralrek had it all.

He started off toward the middle of the clearing.

"Where are you going?" Bilba called out.

"To start a conversation," he said over his shoulder without a hint of strain, as if he wasn't carrying eighty pounds of belongings.

"Come on," I said to my best friend. "Let's not leave him on his own. Who knows what trouble he'll kick up?"

Ralrek moved to about the central point between the four silent groups. I watched them watching him. His maneuver seemed to tickle a fair number. They flashed more than a few smiles when he set the trunk in the sand—a little harder than it needed—and stood up straight, clapping non-existent dirt from his hands. "Which one of you is the leader?"

Heads swiveled among the groups, just not in between them. Murmurs. Grumbled complaints. Caustic snickers and grunts aimed at my friend. Their animosity toward Ralrek was the only interaction between the disparate groups. Strange stuff. Did these demons always revert to grade seventy-three when the Isle received a new exile? Did they also pull each other's hair when the teacher wasn't looking? Island life was about to get interesting.

No one answered.

"Can someone at least tell us where we can set ourselves up?" This time, he waved his arms out to his sides, waist level, and palms up.

Crickets. Not literally—I don't think the island has them. If it does, they were as unhelpful as these fellow exiles. Though, to be honest, I'm not sure I could think of these demons as fellows in any sort of way. Entertainment value at our discomfort aside, they didn't appear interested in anything to do with the island's three new arrivals.

"We could really use help. Anyone?" I said, moving beside the tall incubus, trying to show a united front on the off-chance they thought we were just three blokes who'd pissed off the wrong elite. The faces staring back told me exactly what I could do with that request.

Bilba followed suit, standing to Ralrek's other side. "You'd be doing us a favor." Maybe he thought chiming in and showing a three-incubus front would encourage at least someone to speak up. He was as wrong as my father is about the Council's assertion about having the moral high ground.

I don't know if you've ever been somewhere, maybe giving a speech to classmates or a report to a bunch of important people in a conference room or something, and you lose your train of thought. Where a lifetime of uncomfortable silence seems to pass. Everyone staring at you. Time plods forward. Silence thickens. Your pulse races. Clamminess coats your skin. No one in the crowd seems interested in helping? Fun stuff like that? Yeah, that's how this introduction to the Isle of Dread felt.

Just when I'd all but given up hope that we'd elicit even a harsh welcome, an incubus from the group decked out in brown furs sneered at those at his side. This gaggle looked like they'd just fallen out of a turnip carriage. He spun without further consideration and headed toward the forest. Almost as one, the rest of the brown-furred group turned and disappeared back to wherever it was they came from.

The group of well-groomed demons, these looking like they'd just stepped out of a Sunday service in a demonic temple, watched the departing demons. One succubus tapped the shoulder of a much older succubus dressed in a black wool dress that stretched around her endowed frame. The older one turned, her head and body swiveling as one, and allowed the younger to hook her arm. The younger, her auburn hair reminding me of Dialphio's, laid her free hand on the older's arm in a gesture of comfort. The demons in that clump waited for the pair of succubi to disappear into the trees before following.

Not long after, the last two tribes departed. Not a word spoken. To us or between the groups. Alone on this foreign sand, we watched the strange demons shuffle back into the protective murk of the forest.

In the end, one incubus lingered. He had turned with the rest of his clique, but had stopped before disappearing. Half-cocked, he stared. His eyes, narrow and lined by age wrinkles, were as soft as a loving mother's. He analyzed us a moment longer. Long braids of brown hair were wrapped in a loose bun behind his head. His skin matched the hair.

The incubus opened his mouth. His chest swelled like he'd taken a deep, rapid breath. And then he snapped it closed, spun and trotted into the trees.

"Well, that wasn't an encouraging start," Ralrek said.

"What do we do now?" Bilba asked.

I looked around the beach, seeing nothing of utility. "I'm not sure we should go chasing off into the forest. None of them looked pleased about us being here. Except for that last guy, no one looked like they wanted to give us a chance to earn our meals. We're going to need to make our own way, so we should probably get started."

"With what?" Ralrek asked.

"Finding shelter. Food. Water." I turned to the empty dock, more than tempted to take my chances and jump on the fishing raft to flee back to the mainland. How many guards would the Council station around the Underworld dock? It's not like these exiles were of any help. I'd have better luck facing a squad of Council guards, right? A quick death versus slowly fading away from dehydration. A sigh was at my lips before I realized I was a little frustrated and a lot ticked off by our reception from the hundreds the Council had also crapped on. "I don't imagine the Isle has a hotel, and none of them are going to open their towns, or villages, or whatever they have, to us. We're on our own boys."

The tips of Bilba's ears turned pink.

Something in Ralrek's chest rumbled. "Guess you're right. So, what? Do we make camp in the trees? I love beach life as much as the next incubus, but I'm not sure I'm okay being out in the open. Something tells me those groups might have someone watching us. At least for a while. Let's at least make it a challenge for them."

"Agreed."

"I don't want to be too far from the shore, though," Bilba said. I gave him a questioning look, and he followed up on his reasoning. "Until we find fresh water, we're going to need to draw it from the ocean. So we'll have to find a way to carry it, and none of us brought a bucket. We'll have to improvise, and that means we're going to lose more water than we can carry to our site. Thus, we need to stay close. Unless one of you wants to spend all day hoofing it back and forth between our camp and the ocean."

I swung my arm up, finger touching the tip of my nose. "Not it."

One corner of Ralrek's mouth curled in a smile as he snorted. "I might be last, but I'm still not it." He pointed to a spot near where the second group made their appearance.

"Let's at least get our stuff lugged over there. We can check our trunks and see if Azazel provided anything we can use to collect water. Then we can scout for a suitable site to set up whatever we can build that will pass as a camp, I guess."

"Sounds good."

It didn't take long to lug our trunks under the protection of the palmettos stretching from the slope of the intimidating mesa to the lip of the Acheron. It took a bit longer than expected to search through our trunks without scattering everything to the winds.

"Look at this," Bilba said excitedly, holding up a pot that was bigger than his head. Even if I hadn't noticed that it was a cast-iron pot, the way my friend's cheeks took on a pink hue of exertion would have betrayed its weight.

"Where'd you find that?"

"In the bottom of my trunk. No wonder it was so heavy."

"Or because you're a wimp," Ralrek said, not missing a beat.

Even a flash of the old Ralrek couldn't sour my mood after finding the pot. Not that he was trying to. Ralrek loved giving both of us a hard time. We loved dishing it back. It's an incubi thing. You wouldn't understand if you're not one. So while he headed off to fill the pot, Bilba and I scoured the ground for kindling and dried bark and branches. Clearing a wide circle so we didn't burn the entire island down on our first day as residents, we soon had a fire going... well, after a decent time. I'd love to tell you we made it as expediently as contestants do on my favorite television survival show, but I am a lousy liar. We had to wait for Ralrek to use his Fire Ability. Side note: it was nice to see Azazel proven right, that the guys could use their magic on the Isle.

We spent the rest of the Hellfire light hours eating enough grapes to dissolve our intestines and fell into an early sleep. Well, at least they did. I couldn't sleep.

After growing bored with the dissonant concert created by

Bilba's snoring, I decided to have a go at a romantic beach stroll in the dark—just without all the romance.

Is there any sound as calming and good for your mental health as ocean waves rolling to shore? Especially at night? I mean, it's creepy too, don't get me wrong. All that unstoppable water just pushing, pushing, pushing toward you. Like, there could be a tsunami out in that darkness with this beach in its sights, and I'd be none-the-wiser until the wall of water slammed into me. That's just not cool to think about. So I tried not to as I plopped down and kicked off my sneakers containing more sand than the cooling beach I now sat on. Hooking my arms over my bent knees, I tried to relax. Possibly, I could have spent the rest of my immortal life like this. Listening to the rhythmic whoosh of the Isle's small waves. Thinking about the demons, mortals, and places I already missed and wondering if I could fill those yearnings here among a population that clearly planned to avoid us. Pondering next moves against Hell's decrepit rulers. You know, the small stuff.

I can be slow on the up-take at times, learning plenty of life's harsher lessons, well, the hard way. One of my areas of needed improvement was staying in contact with the demons I cared for and who cared for me. During my Abandonment, I'd been lousy about writing to my mother. Mostly, it felt like a chore. Even worse was when I didn't write to my ex-boss whenever she checked in on me. Dialphio Tywald is the owner of The Book Abyss, and the first business owner to give me a fair shake after Beelzebub's grotesque murder of Aries that I was somehow punished for not taking part in. Shunned by every other place of employment, she gave me a job and a chance. She was there for me when I thought I was on the right track, and she was even more stubbornly supportive when life started going real bad, real quick. Far too often in my Abandonment, I forgot to write her back from time to time, and she let me know what she thought at every occurrence. I learned a lesson about reciprocity.

Smiling, I pushed my feet out, carving two neat troughs through the sand, and plopped the notebook on my legs, opening it and putting the quill to paper. Demonic notebooks are neat devices that allow the holders to communicate to one another over vast distances, even between the Overworld and Hell. Even further.

Having already written to Dialphio and my mother, tonight's letter was for someone demons weren't supposed to commune or communicate with. I had done both in the recent past, and wanted to again. Soon.

ZEKE: Cassie, hey! Yes, I can be eloquent. I wanted to let you know we're safe and sound on the Isle of Dread. Not so dreadful. I could get used to beach life once I have a roof over my head. Movies and restaurants would be nice too, but an incubus can't have everything, am I—

CASSIE: Hi, Zeke! I'm so glad to hear from you! You've got to tell me all about the trip.

The world changed every time I spoke to the angel, one who was supposed to be the eternal enemy of my kind. The air smelled cleaner. Birds' songs were no longer annoying. Hell's food wasn't so bland. Beer had more body. That was Cassie's true Ability, not the Angelfire she'd used to save my life in Olympia when I was knocking on the Grim Reaper's door and begging to come in.

Suddenly, the Isle of Dread wasn't so bad. How did she do this?

We caught up for a while. How long? No clue. I yawned a few dozen times. I didn't care. This was good. This was the Isle of Dread. My home for the foreseeable future, as long as I didn't die at the hands of an assassin or Founder. I planned to enjoy it for what it was and talk to this angelic beauty for as long as she gave me time. Which, for those of you counting at home, was quite a lot.

It was all fun and games until I asked about Virgo and his group of vigilantes.

CASSIE: They're okay. As you can imagine, they're still mourning. They lost people and immortals. My heart is broken for them. Our two Councils did what we could. Repaired the damages instantly. Wiped witnesses' memories away and replaced them. Of course, that does nothing for those who were lost and those who loved them, but maybe it'll help everyone heal.

ZEKE: They don't remember the attack? At all? The demons? Beelzebub?

Azazel had briefed us, of course. I knew the mortals and the city were taken care of. I didn't expect Virgo's Vigilantes to have their memories erased like a whiteboard. That could be a problem.

Turns out, it wasn't.

CASSIE: There was a special dispensation for Virgo. The rest of the Vigilantes won't remember what happened. Not accurately. But it was in the interest of peace that Virgo be allowed to recall what transpired. From what we heard, your Council had quite the argument about allowing Beelzebub's involvement to remain in Virgo's memory. Sort of funny, I think.

ZEKE: Interesting. And I agree. That's funny. I paused, wondering how much she knew about Lucifer's Third Council. Sharing what Azazel said about its problems with an angel might be a step too far in my blossoming relationship with the Founder, no matter how much trust I had for the angel on the other end of this message. How about your kind? Are they behaving?

CASSIE: Behaving?

ZEKE: No power grabs or anything?

CASSIE: No. Nothing like that. I swear.

Her promise carried weight. Cassie was unbelievably— not because of her age, but because of who she was and what she meant to me—serving on Yahweh's Council. Meaning I received straight-intel from the supposed enemy.

ZEKE: They've got to stay in their lane.

CASSIE: They will.

ZEKE: Good. Thank you, Cassie. That helps give me peace of mind while I'm here. Serious street cred goes to your side for being so cool throughout this. Long may it last.

CASSIE: I'm laughing over here. Let's hope it stays this way for a long, long time. Listen, I've got to run. It's late. You should probably sleep too. Bet you haven't yet. Check in again? Soon? Like, only a day or two?

ZEKE: Why, if I didn't know better, I'd say you're stalking me.

CARRIE: Oh, Zeke. You're funny.

I was trying to be serious, not funny. Probably best to leave that unsaid.

ZEKE: I promise. I'll check in tomorrow so you can know we're not dead.

CASSIE: Gee, so sweet. Always the charmer.

We said our farewells, and I set the notebook down, wrapping my arms around my knees and pulling them in. As the night grew late, the blue of the Hellfire faded well past a deep purple, a chill flitted across my skin.

I rubbed my arms and tried to get comfortable.

Well, that was, until I felt a slight tingling inside my skull. So slight, if I'd been in almost any other situation, I might have missed it. But here I was, sitting on a quiet beach in the dark, all alone, enjoying the music of the ocean. Easy to pick up on a threat in those circumstances.

The voice of Crazy Zeke in my head didn't hurt, either.

"He comes."

So sudden, so unexpected. I jolted when it pierced my serenity. The breeze suddenly held a chill—fabricated or not, I couldn't be sure. Ocean waves sounded choppy. Sand felt scratchy. I know it was my overactive imagination at hearing the disembodied voice, but still, these things matter.

Since coming back to Hell after my Abandonment, I'd been hearing voices. Well, not plural. A single voice. One that made sporadic, unpredictable appearances. Every time I heard it, something was happening or about to happen. A new, clairvoyant trait I'd picked up coming through Azazel's Rift, or evidence of an impending mental breakdown, was still unclear.

So it goes with little surprise that my hand slipped to the sand beside me, reaching for Creed. The magical halberd was in a fisted hand before the 's' sound of Crazy Zeke's warning faded. I didn't activate it yet, but that's only because Creed can be a nasty—yet advantageous—tool in a fight and I didn't feel like giving the cloaked presence any hints of my capabilities.

The tingling sensation vanished.

I blinked. And waited. Nothing.

I peered into the dark. Whoever had been lingering no longer was.

I was alone again.

Just me, my thoughts, and my handy dandy halberd.

"Please don't make me use you. We're new here," I told the halberd. "And you're terrible at making friends."

Creed buzzed three times and went as cold as the night.

3

UNDERWORLD, ISLE OF DREAD

SLEEP. IF YOU'RE GETTING ENOUGH, BE THANKFUL AND NEVER take it for granted. If I could turn back my life clock to the time before the Isle of Dread, that saying would be something I'd live by. Trust me. Three days of lousy sleep is a perfect elixir for ungrateful demons who take their slumber for granted.

Three nights. Was that really all it had been? Three nights that might have been a week. Two?

You'd think with the way I'm whining that we were sleeping out under the open sky. We weren't. Though it had taken most of the time we weren't searching for something to eat and drink, washing the stink off in the Acheron Ocean, or doing other bodily things, we learned how to build a survival shelter straight out of bushcraft. Let's not get carried away. It's an A-frame with a six-foot wide bed of the smallest logs we could scrounge from the forest. Half the wood we found, mostly old growth, was rotted. It took way too long to find the right toppled trees, and just as long to build a bed and a roof.

The lack of sleep and nutrition had exhausted Bilba, and couldn't hold his conjured ax for more than an hour at a time.

Honestly, good thing we got as much of it done as we did. The first night we slept on loose logs, and as miserable as that sounds, it was better than the logs splitting apart, sending us down to embrace the moist forest floor. Talk about motivation. By night two, we'd secured the wide bed. By night three, the A-frame roof was in place. Ralrek and I did the transporting of wood and securing of the shelter, but Bilba was the true champ. Since the ax was a manifestation of his Abilities, he was the only one who could use it, so he did all the chopping. What a hero, that guy.

The lesson I learned? An easier way to defeat those with magical Abilities in a fight? Just keep them tired and starve them. A very effective strategy. One I hoped the Council wasn't using against me and my friends at this very minute.

Ralrek wasn't faring much better, but thankfully, we only needed his berry and water gathering skills once the shelter was up. Though we weren't living fat like kings, we got enough nutrition and hydration to not die. I'm calling that a win.

All in all, we were three miserable incubi. The Isle was winning.

So imagine my annoyance when I finally got a night of relatively undisturbed sleep—meaning two or three continuous hours—and was woken in quite a painful way.

I don't know if your body has ever betrayed you good sleep, like those times when you stretch while asleep and your foot cramps up like it's being squeezed in a vice? You're suddenly no longer sleeping, your heart is skipping like you'd just been plopped down in the middle of a rave, and your stupid foot will just not unlock? Seconds of your life, but impactful enough for you to remember how your sleep was ruined when you woke? On this fourth night, I thought I was going to get some much needed rest. It was promising. I was cold, hungry, and exhausted. Even during the later hours of the day, I fell asleep any time we stopped working. So this night's sleep was going to be epic.

Except that it wasn't.

At one point, while the sky was still a mixture of deep purple and black that only college students and shift workers typically explored, I was stone cold crazy asleep. The deep kind. The kind that, when you wake from it, makes the following day brighter and the world's assholes less bothersome. And pain shredded that wonderland.

Sharp. A pebble-sized pain in my skull.

Wincing out of my sleep, my hand to my head, I rolled over, thinking I'd slammed my head against a rock in the middle of an awesome dream—details of which I will not go into. It's personal. But as I drifted back to the wondrous lands of make believe inside my meat container, I felt it again. This was no rock but a legitimate pebble, and it had come from above, not below.

Wincing for a second time, I looked for the source of my rude awakening—get it? Through squinted eyes, I noticed Bilba and Ralrek were still fast asleep. The camp was quiet. Our fire had burned down to a faint, almost pink, glow. The night was dark, its silence only disturbed by the monotonous crashing of waves against the beach a few hundred yards away.

My eyes slowly adjusted to the purple-black darkness. Beyond the camp, the palmetto tree trunks reached up into the night, their long fan-like leaves barely visible to my sleepy mind.

Whack.

Another pebble. Whatever little forest creature was tormenting me with pebbles had blessed good aim. Not once had a pebble struck the roof of our shelter, the ground in front of my feet, or—gasp—my personal bits.

Shifting to my side, I surveyed the darkness, not yet

wanting to slink away from the dying firelight to discover my tormenter.

Nothing. The palmettos were silent, giving away none of the night's secrets. The lack of light did me no favors either.

Whack.

The next pebble hurt. A lot.

"What the fuck?" I whispered harshly into the night.

Bilba's cacophonous snoring halted sharply. He breathed in a momentary burst and then started snoring again. So helpful, that one. Ralrek mumbled.

Whack. Whack.

Two more found my skull. The dots of light I saw reminded me of the stars in the Overworld sky in that immense tapestry of black.

No pebble or stone found the roof. I put my hands up to ward off another shot. Whoever was torturing me was one heaven of a shot. I'd have to recruit them for any future intramural blazeball team I might join if I ever got off the island.

"Stop it!" I whined the next time a pebble met my forehead. The stars I had previously seen multiplied. Leaving my head partially unprotected, I whispered to my halberd. "Creed!"

The foot-long truncheon form of the collapsed halberd tunk'ed against something and slapped against my skin a second later.

I scooted off the end of the bed. On my feet, with Creed in my hand, I circled the makeshift shelter and raced through the open strand of trees. It took seconds, but even my speed couldn't get me to where someone was screwing with me. All I found was sand, flora, and palmettos.

Whack.

From above.

I looked up and groaned. "Son of a bitch."

Floating above just within my sight, its wings flapping rapidly, a harpy grinned down at me. A big one. With a wingspan of a good two feet, it was the largest harpy I'd ever seen. The first I'd heard of being outside Lucifer's headquarters. In the dark, she may have been green. Could have been blue. Who knows? All that mattered was that this four-foot tall, sharp-taloned green—or blue—feathered harpy ruined my night of sleep and I was pissed.

Then she had the gall to chirp at me. Can you believe that? Me, getting chirped at, with attitude, because she woke me up. Tell you what; it was almost enough to make me activate Creed.

"What's your problem?"

She chirped again, her tiny face drawn in a scowl, raising her tiny clawed hand filled with a single pebble that was boulder-sized to someone with her dimensions.

I wanted to look away—there's just something weird about how a harpy's feathers don't cover their entire bodies. Weird and very awkward. Feathers wrapped from wing-tip to wing-tip, across her torso, but barely covered her intimate, feminine parts. So here I was, trying to stare her down to intimidate her enough that she'd leave me alone, while also trying not to look at her. Trust me, it was as difficult to pull off as it sounds.

When I swatted at her, she dodged. When I jumped to snag a leg—without realizing her talons were as long as my fingers and would carve me open—she floated out of reach. I could blast her with Creed, but the problem is that I can't control when it allows me to tap into its magic. If, and that's a big if, Creed allowed me, I could end up setting the entire island on fire.

The halberd was not an option. Basically, I'm saying I was about to give in to the fact that the harpy could screw with me all night if she wanted.

I dropped my hands to my sides, keeping Creed pinned to my leg, but ready to activate if required to save my neck. "Listen, I'm tired. I'm new to the island. I just want to sleep. Okay? How about you leave me alone?"

"You trespassed," the harpy said. Her words fluttered, like she was speaking through the blades of a fan. Then she made a sound like when someone spits water through their teeth.

"Where? Here? Our camp?"

"Yes," she said, and then made a *pfft* sound I was pretty sure had nothing to do with her wings.

After tucking Creed into my armpit, I raised my hands in the universal sign of surrender. "I'm sorry. We've only been on the island for a few days. Had we known this was your territory, we wouldn't have camped here. I swear."

"Ours." Pfft.

"Yes, I get that." Now she was testing my patience. "But when we were dropped off, no one on the island helped us. We don't know where we are or what belongs to who."

"Isle. Not island. Isle." Pfft.

"Sorry. The Isle." Man, I was doing a lot of apologizing to this overgrown mosquito. "Give us tonight. Okay? Tomorrow, we'll search for a new location. We'll need a few days, but we'll move off your territory. Is that cool?"

It was most definitely not cool with me. I didn't want to tear down this camp and start over again. Neither did I want to lug what we had built halfway across the island—err, Isle. But I also wasn't hot about sleepless nights for the rest of my eternity because we'd unintentionally traipsed into some harpy's love shack.

She crossed her wings—thankfully, because that meant she covered herself—and dropped to the ground, landing without shuffling a grain of sand.

"Three days." She held up a wing—thankfully the other still covered her—and uncurled three talons, one after the other. She only had three on each hand. Probably why we were on limited time. "Then." Pfft.

I craned my head closer. "Then what?"

Pfft. She unfurled her wings. I looked away out of instinct until I heard the flapping. Half afraid I'd turn to see her clawed feet inches from my eyes and not willing to go sightless for the sake of someone else's dignity, I was relieved to see her lifting away into the darkness.

"Bless it."

Imagine how easily I fell asleep after that? I think I set a record for crappiest sleep ever.

THE DAY GOT OFF TO A KICKER WHEN CRAZY ZEKE WOKE ME. "Mend the wild."

My eyes snapped open. I gasped at the sudden sound of the voice in my head and bolted upright. The dulled Hellfire told me it was too early to be awake. My ruckus woke my partners.

Bilba was all sunshine and roses. Ralrek was Ralrek. He's not a morning demon. I woke, cold, sore, tired, and hungry. Great start to another eighteen-hour day.

"What's up? You're wincing?" Bilba asked when he saw me stretch, catching myself with a hitch, and adjusting when I lost breath.

"Slept like crap."

"So much for awesome healing abilities, huh?" Ralrek poked at the fire as he tried to breathe life into it without having to call on his magic.

"Man, island life has been lousy enough. I don't need it screwing with that." I stretched. Something popped. I bent to retrieve Creed. A sharp pain in my lower back stopped me. Maybe Ralrek was onto something. Maybe the Isle was affecting my self-healing abilities. Instead of risking blowing out my back, I raised my hand over the collapsed halberd and called it. "Creed."

It responded, tipping up on its end and jumping up to my hand.

"Where are you going?" Ralrek asked without looking away from the fire as he continued poking.

"To stretch out and practice my forms." I intended to do just that, and then I was going to come back and tell them about the stupid harpy and the somewhat disturbing suspicion I had that we also shared the beach with a mysterious demon. That could wait. Maybe my small mind-tingle experience was nothing more than a flash of paranoia. The harpy's need for us to leave might not wait. We'd have that chat after I worked out my sleep kinks.

"Have fun." Poke. Poke.

"Don't kill yourself," Bilba called out, with too much joy in his voice.

The warm beach presented an excellent opportunity to work on my forms. Rising Dawn, my slow warm-up, got things unhinged. My back stopped twitching every time I tried to rotate to my left. I started feeling better. By the time I made it to my last form, Shadows Fall, I was jumping and rotating in the air like an early pubescent incubus—just with all the stretching and warm-ups of someone not an early pubescent incubus. I hear it gets worse as you get older. I doubted the Isle or the Council would give me a chance to discover that for myself.

Mend the wild? What in the world did that mean? What was Crazy Zeke trying to tell me? A task? If so, what needed mending? What was the wild? The Isle itself? The groups of demons, at least four, populating this expanse of land on the far edge of the Acheron Ocean? The stupid harpy—she seemed pretty untamed if first impressions count for anything. Was the 'wild' something outside the Isle?

My story didn't end in exile. I knew that. Azazel would make sure, with all his contacts, it wouldn't. Creed still worked—though I hadn't tried to cast yet—and my two buds back at camp had already proven the Isle hadn't stripped away their Abilities. We were going nowhere except the places the Council didn't want us to go.

We needed to be ready.

I had no worries about either Bilba or Ralrek doing their part. Less than a week into our island life, they'd used their magic on multiple occasions. I imagined that wouldn't slow down, especially if we were a threat to harpies and demons alike, until—if—we found our own place to call home. Plus, with Bilba and Ralrek's ability, if not skill, in opening Rifts and Gateways, with Azazel arming us with intel so we could understand the risk of traveling off the Isle, we had reasons to wake up and continue the fight. It would come, whether we wanted it to or not. What mattered now was if Beelzebub and Apopis or any of their henchmen stole to the Isle to slit our throats in our sleep, or if they waited at the Underworld dock to do it. They might lie in waiting for us to travel to the Overworld to meet up with Virgo's Vigilantes. Heavens, they might try to pull a slick maneuver during our first trip.

No, a fight was coming, and we had to be ready. Maybe that's what Crazy Zeke was trying to tell me.

If the All granted me one wish, it'd be that the halberd was a little more loquacious.

Finished with my forms, I scouted the beach for any presence, demon, harpy, or otherwise. I saw nothing and no one. I had to stay sharp. Lucifer, bless it, I needed to get sharp again. Neglecting my precious Creed wasn't something the halberd would let me get away with, not for long.

Running the forms felt good. I was tired, but in a 'just had a heaven of a workout' sort of way. On a better day, I might have run through them one more time. But there was something else I needed in order to knock the rust off, and it required quiet focus. Without an obvious sign that I was being watched, it was time to try to birth Creed's magic.

I lifted the halberd in a single hand until it was eye-level. "You ready, buddy?"

Creed didn't answer.

"Don't be a jackass. More demons than just me are counting on you."

Hard, unresponsive dark cherry sat idly in my open palm, balanced perfectly.

I gripped the haft in a fist and turned toward the ocean. Over the past few years, I'd called on Creed's power. The first time, in an Overworld apartment in Germany while being attacked by an assassin, I hadn't realized what I was doing. Since then, I'd tapped into increasingly higher levels of Hellfire from the halberd, the last coming when Beelzebub and his minions were killing mortals at a woman's health clinic. In a moment of blind fury, I'd unleash an attack. The beam of Hellfire totaled six cars and blew out nearly a hundred windows in the surrounding buildings.

All that power, and still the halberd refused me in all but the most essential times. That needed to change if I had a snowball's chance in Hell of surviving this inevitable struggle.

I lowered Creed, aiming the double-ax heads at the rolling waters of the Acheron, and willed the halberd to come alive.

Cold steel bobbed in my view.

I pushed again. "Come on, dude. This is important."

Nothing.

Sighing, I pulled it upright, fully shoving the wavy dagger into the beach sands deep enough that the halberd remained standing when I let go.

I'd felt nothing, not even a spark of a connection. Maybe Creed couldn't touch the Hellfire here. Maybe I was just exhausted and slowly starving to death, depriving me of the energy to focus enough to tap into the weapon's innate powers. Maybe Creed was just being an ass, stubbornly enjoying island time.

"Screw you," I said to my weapon, gifted from Aries, the

last First of His Name, and walked toward the waters of the Acheron. I kicked off my shoes and stepped into the ocean. The water was lukewarm, lapping at my ankles.

"Mend the wild," Crazy Zeke said for a second time, somewhere behind me. Between the annoying voice, the insufferable halberd, and the terrorist harpy, I had half a mind to sea if I could swim the Acheron and take my chances with the kraken.

4

UNDERWORLD, ISLE OF DREAD

"How was it?" Ralrek asked. Squatting next to our firepit, he blew on a fledgling flame. Whether by his Ability or by good old-fashioned chemistry, the flame reached skyward, leaned sideways like it wanted to smash its face into the ash from yesterday's fire, and then flicked upright again.

I pointed at the base of the fire. "Why don't you just use your Fire Ability to start an inferno? Would save you time and energy."

"To do what with? We're isolated on an already isolated island, in case you hadn't noticed. Not much going on."

"I noticed. But if you weren't spending time with that, how much ocean water could you have lugged back to camp?"

Ralrek, still squatting, straightened his back, looking at me like he was about to deliver a smartass comment. "And do what with the water? Without a fire, retrieving pots of salt water would have been pointless. Anyway. Were you able to tap into Creed's magic?"

"Nope. Deader than my romantic prospects."

"Oh, did you and Cassie break up already?"

I made a fist and shook it at him jokingly before raising a finger. "First, we were never going out. We're not like that."

"Sure."

I added another finger. "Second, you're one to talk. How long did your relationship with Torlan last? Couple weeks?"

"A little longer." He looked back at the struggling flame, holding his smirk.

"Mmmm, not so sure."

"I'm impressed you remember his name."

"Why wouldn't I?" I said, moving to our shelter and setting Creed on the log bed. "He was important to you, so he's important to me."

"Not that important."

"Oh?"

"He was needy."

"And you're a slut. We all have our faults."

Ralrek chuckled. "You're alright, Zeke."

We'd come a long way, baby.

Only my friends got to call me Zeke. Everyone else referred to me by my full name, Ezekial. I can be stubborn like that. Over the past few years, though, things with the tall, sort of dark, and handsome incubi had swayed from an adversarial relationship to one where we no longer hid our shame at actually liking each other. It was frightening how easily I referred to him as 'friend.'

"You're not so bad yourself."

"Get a room, you two," a squeaky voice said from behind a tree twenty feet away. Bilba leaned back, grinning.

"What are you doing?"

"Going to the bathroom, if you don't mind?"

Gross. "Can you not talk to me when you are emptying yourself, if you don't mind?"

My best friend finished his business and then joined us. Stretching, he rubbed his stomach. "I'm so glad you had a nightmare and woke us up, Zeke. Without Callers floating around to get the day going, we could have slept late."

"And that's a problem, why?" Ralrek asked.

"Because we have a lot of tasks today," Bilba said, sliding closer to the fire, coughing when the wind shifted and the gray smoke shrouded him. He continued explaining his rationale as he swatted at the column that followed he slowly circled the pit. "Get the fire going. We've got to collect a lot more firewood. Have you seen how much we've gone through? Then there's the water. Collecting it, getting it on the fire to purify it, letting it cool enough to be drinkable. At some point, we'll have to find something besides berries to eat. We're going to finish what we've got before tomorrow, and I'm not sure it's healthy to sustain on berries alone. Then, there's—"

I held my hands up. "Okay. Okay. Enough already, ol' Bringer of Doom. We know. We have a ton of chores. And, no, I hadn't thought about Callers. Now that you mention it, it's weird to not hear them make their morning and evening calls. Can't say I miss them."

"I always thought they were creepy," Ralrek said, getting on all fours to provide oxygen to the fire now.

"Something else we agree on."

"Miracles never cease."

"Why don't you just light it yourself? Why are you doing it the hard way?" Bilba asked, repeating my question from earlier.

I flipped a hand in the air. "That's what I said."

"He's stubborn."

"Yes, he is."

"Like you're one to talk, Zeke," Ralrek said, drew a deep breath, and slowly exhaled into the base of the flame. The red glow brightened to orange, and for a second, I thought the incubi had finally caught momentum. Sadly, for his efforts and our ability to stave off the morning chill, the flame died down as soon as he ran out of breath.

"He's right," Bilba said, piling on.

"Since when did this become about me? The last time I—"

A distant shout cut me off.

Bilba's eyes widened. "What was that?"

I cocked my head in the shout's direction. "Not sure. Could have been anything. Animal or demon."

"Definitely demon," Bilba said, getting a far-away look in his eyes. I opened my mouth, and even without looking my way, he held up a hand. "Shhh. Listen." He pointed off into the forest. "Voices. Multiple voices. Maybe ten. Maybe more."

Ralrek had given up on the fire, at least for now, and joined us. "Coming from where?"

When Bilba didn't answer, I pointed toward the south slope of the mesa. I couldn't really see it through the vast rows of trees, but its rock face provided an obvious hint of its presence. You couldn't miss something so big it threatened to sink the island under its sheer weight. "That's where I heard the first shout."

"What are we—" Ralrek didn't finish before two things happened simultaneously. Another shout, masculine, cut through the forest just as Bilba's hand cut through the air.

"See? Shhhh. I told you," the pink-eared Deception user said. "Now I missed it." His head swiveled, and then his arm shot straight out toward a split in the forest about two bodies' width wide. "There. From over there. Let's see what it's about."

"Bilba, wait," I said as he scurried along the open path I'd been clearing with Creed. When he didn't turn to acknowledge my request, didn't slow or stop, I nudged Ralrek with an arm. "Feel like chasing him down?"

Ralrek squinted at me. I winked at him. We turned to look at Bilba's back. This version of my best bud was a slimmed-down version from his younger, unhealthy self. Still adorably chunky—he simply had the body type that would never be conducive to male swimsuit magazine covers succubi secretly loved—Bilba wasn't athletic or coordinated. Catching him wouldn't force the first bead of sweat to pop on my forehead.

I swatted Ralrek's arm. "Let's go, before he exposes all of our secrets to someone who doesn't need to know them."

"And you're going to help stop that? I've got to see this."

As predictable as rain in the Pacific Northwest, we caught Bilba within fifty yards and moved through the thickening underbrush together. The bushes and weeds grew thicker the farther we ventured from camp and away from the ocean. With the increasing vegetation, I also noted the increase in not only the number of voices but also the volume of outrage. Whatever was going down, this might be a tricky situation to get involved in, especially for the Isle's newest residents.

"Hang on," I said, stopping and turning toward the camp that was now a quarter-mile behind us. "Creed."

I didn't have to shout. No bellowing. No cupping-hands-around-mouth and howling into the wind either. With a single name spoken, I connected with my magical halberd, still relaxing on our bed of logs back at the camp.

In the old days of our relationship, especially our first few months together, I wouldn't have made it this far from the weapon. Creed and I had an interesting connection. Back then, I couldn't be more than a few feet away from the halberd. Literally. Over time, I worked with the halberd until an entire room separated us. Then a full floor. Building trust, or jadedness from spending too much time together, Creed allowed me a greater and greater distance before enforcing quality Zeke and magical halberd time.

At speaking Creed's name, the forest filled with the noise of shouting, birds cawing in treetops, and the distant smashing of ocean waves against the sand, the halberd zipped in my direction. It dodged trees, split ferns that were too tall to avoid the halberd's rush, and only slowed as it approached. Instead of smacking into my palm, Creed hampered its charge and slid into my open hand.

"Still so cool, every time I see it," Bilba said with transparent admiration.

I wasn't wearing jeans and a belt, so I didn't have a frog to slide the weapon into. Instead, I'd have to carry it in my palm —or let it float alongside me. The latter wasn't really an option. If we were walking into a mess, I didn't want to give away any advantage, especially since no one on the island had made a single friendly gesture to us yet. I glanced down at the halberd. "Yeah, he's 'aight."

Ralrek had slunk ahead while I waited on Creed. In the mere seconds that reconnection took, the dark-haired incubus hadn't gotten far. At almost six-and-a-half feet tall, he would have stood out anywhere. Surrounded by the tall palmettos that concealed his height, he took careful steps. Without turning away, he asked, "Zeke, do you sense anything?"

"Give me a second." I no longer had to close my eyes. My skills at Sensing another demon using magic had improved to where I could do it while eating a batch of the Overworld's hottest chicken wings—side note, damn, I missed chicken wings. Slinking through the foliage, I pushed my Sensing out. The shimmering wave, invisible to all but me, rippled away, flowing over the bushes and ferns, around the thick tree trunks, deeper into the forest toward the angry voices. I felt nothing, but gave my Sensing a few more seconds to stretch deeper, and confirmed my suspicions. "If anyone is holding their Ability, they're out of range. Whoever is doing all that griping is doing just that; griping."

"You sure?"

"As sure as I can be. I'd still be ready." I lifted Creed, which was stupid because Ralrek's back was still to me. "I know I am."

Another three hundred yards into the forest—distance is so difficult to gauge in the wild—the voices rang clear and loud. Underneath them, and in between shouts and cries of 'foul' and 'unfair,' water roared over rock.

We crept forward, each of us in a crouch, until our view opened to a wide natural pool tucked in a crevice at the base of the mesa. From our vantage point, the pool was thirty feet below our location. Opposite, the terrain rose to meet the rock of the mesa, its height blocked by branches above.

Demons crowded the nearest corner of the pool. Just like with our arrival on the island, they stood in distinct groups. Unlike that time, though, they weren't so ominously quiet.

Between them, they shouted, jabbed fingers, shook fists and heads so aggressively I'm surprised they didn't twist them off. More than a few times, I heard the popular 'goose neck sow's tongue' insult hurled.

"What's going on?" Bilba asked.

"No idea. Should we find out?"

Ralrek grunted. "And get involved? I vote for us staying here for a second to make sure we aren't walking into a trap."

"You think this is a setup?" Bilba asked.

"Convenient that this is happening close to our camp when they've got an entire island to argue, don't you think?"

My rounder friend shrugged.

"I'm with Ralrek. Let's wait a minute and see what goes down."

So we did.

Time only increased tensions. The shouting never diminished. The heat carried in the words only intensified. Insults grew more personal. Bodies drifted together.

I was about to mention that it looked like fists were about to be thrown when, in fact, they were.

"What do we do now?" Bilba asked as incubi tussled, succubi scratched and clawed, and even imps played tug-of-war with each other's wool shirts or ponytails.

"We get involved," I said, now on my feet and rushing toward the fracas before either of my friends could stop me, argue, or try to convince me this was my dumbest decision since my last dumb decision.

Even outside the protective shelter of trees, none of the combatants noticed me. Older siblings shuffled implings away, and the elderly hung back from the fighting, protecting themselves and others who didn't have anyone to protect them. Some spotted me, and I saw a few pointed fingers in my direction. To them, I might have been a savior who could stop this ridiculous aggression, or I might be the unknown aggressor. If they saw me as the latter, it was well within reason to suspect the entire horde of battling demons to turn on me. What else could I do? Let hundreds of demons tear each other apart?

In the thicket of bodies pressed together, shoving, pulling hair and swinging fists, someone yelled out. A string of expletives followed. Splashing water gave away the fact that bodies were falling or being tossed into the natural pool.

You'd think that'd stop the fighting, but nope. Two succubi, their clothes sticking to them, sprang out of the pool and resumed smacking each other and pulling hair. No one was above the violence. Older incubi helped ramp up the tension. On the edge of the scuffle-turning-into-full-fledged-battle, two older guys shook liver-spotted fists at each other before engaging in one of the slowest shoving matches you'd ever see. It would have been funny if it wasn't so pathetic.

"Stop it!" Bilba shouted behind me.

No one listened.

I pulled up outside the line of fighting. If I was getting involved, it'd be in the name of self-defense. I waited and watched alone for a few moments before, first, Ralrek stopped at my side, joined twenty seconds later by Bilba.

"We've got to stop them," my best friend said between pants.

"How? If you've got any ideas, I'm all ears."

Ralrek grunted, watching the fighting. The way he stood

with a slight forward lean told me he wasn't taking our safety for granted. His hands held a slight glow to accompany the scratching feeling I felt seconds before I looked down.

"Think you'll need your Fire?"

He blinked as if questioning whether or not he heard me correctly. "This is escalating." He glanced down at my hand. At Creed. "I'd feel a lot better if you showed off your stick."

I was about to make an inappropriate joke when Bilba stepped forward. "I don't know, guys. We've got to be careful."

Ralrek lifted a glowing hand. "I am being careful. If you—"

"Stop!" I said, sensing magic beyond my handsome pal's Fire. "Someone is about to cast."

"This could get ugly."

"Listen, everyone," Bilba said over the din. "If you stop for a second, we can talk through this."

My skin warmed in a flush. Manipulative magic. Shit.

A column of water rose from the pool, collapsing back down in a crash. The result was a three-foot-tall wave that pushed toward the embankment in all directions—impressive considering that the body of water was less than two hundred feet across.

It hit land, smashing into anyone nearby and sending them tumbling. Before I had the wherewithal to think to check on the injured, the water was sucked back to the middle of the pool and reformed into a column.

The tower grew to thirty feet and bent toward a group of combatants on the far edge of the fighting. There were at least two dozen demons in its path.

"Someone could get hurt," Bilba said, his voice pinched in a whine.

"Someone could get killed," Ralrek rightfully growled.

"Not if I can help it," I said, giving my hand a shake. The silent gesture was a command to my magical halberd, the most powerful weapon in all creation—at least as far as anyone in Hell was concerned.

The column of water bent lower and fell faster, as if the caster couldn't contain its momentum as gravity pulled it toward the ground.

"Zeke, don't!" Bilba yelled behind me as I sprinted forward.

I dashed around an old incubus, dodged a punk throwing fists, held Creed laterally and bowled over two succubi doing their best to scratch each other's eyeballs out—don't judge me, I'm utilitarian in times like these. I made sure Creed's blades wouldn't nick an arm hair on either of them.

On the periphery, Bilba and Ralrek yelled orders, trying to draw everyone away from the collapsing column. Water was still being drawn into it. Whoever was casting this towering death trap was making it abundantly clear they planned on doing real damage. This wasn't about getting your opponent's attention so you could talk them into seeing your side. This move wasn't even about bullying them into your way of thinking. By channeling this much water to send crashing down, this was nothing more than bludgeoning an already defeated foe. This was a career-ending knockout blow.

Except this punch wouldn't land.

One guy swiped at me with something. It might have been a flat bat; I couldn't tell because I was moving too fast. I was around him before he started his forward swing.

"Get out of the way," I shouted to the combatants, who were seconds away from no longer having anything to fight over. "Move! Move!"

My shouts drew attention from a smattering of those nearest, but did nothing to get the others to stop this shit show.

The water column was almost horizontal now.

"Don't be a jerk," I whispered to my halberd, pushing my will into it as I sprinted the last few yards separating me from the future victims of this tidal column. There was no time to get into position or think through my approach.

I looked up at the column, no longer hanging over my head, but plummeting down to make me a permanent fixture; one with the Isle. Crystal clear water. A strange thought to have right before being crushed. Lifting Creed above my head, I spun it, letting my fear of dying feed the weapon.

In a flash, the double-ax heads and wavy dagger burst with the power of the Hellfire—the source of all life in the Underworld. The magic that fueled Lucifer. Mine to tap into through Creed.

Creed's reaction went beyond tapping, though. The azure glory of Hell's most powerful magic washed out the rest of the world. I no longer saw demons fighting all around me. The dominating mesa that rose behind the towering column of water disappeared into obscurity. All I made out was the blur of Creed's spinning haft, my hands moving faster and faster until they, too, became a blur, and the growing intensity of the shield of Hellfire.

I'd never been able to create a shield of this magnitude. It stretched well beyond the boundaries of the halberd's haft. Way beyond a bubble that would protect me and the closest demons from the crashing tidal force. Creed's shield blasted outward around me. Faster than you could bat your eyes, the force field encompassed every single demon around the pool in a U-shape. The only area not protected was the spot in the pool where the column took root, and the rising mesa in the background. Stunned as I was, I couldn't even worry about looking cool—no one has confidence in a hero who doesn't look like they know what they're doing—as I focused on keeping Creed's momentum going.

The column slammed into my barrier. My knees threatened to buckle, but I pushed back. It was a brief struggle. I'm not a big guy, and puberty was a distant memory, so I never would be. The demon who was Zeke in this moment of time was the best physical version of Zeke there ever would be. Older demons always told me to enjoy my youth, because it was fleeting. Yes, even for immortals. I'm on the wrong side of six-feet tall, and will never be a romance book cover model. Yet I held the most powerful weapon in creation, and I'd always felt a sense of calm when Creed was in my hands. As the column of water pummeled my shield, none of that changed.

The attack was over in a flash. Creed's shield had pushed the torrent to the periphery, sending small tributaries flowing off into the forest.

I stopped spinning my halberd, and the shield evaporated.

Tired, starving, and feeling half as healthy as someone my age should feel, I'd stunned myself with the size and strength of the shield. Where had that come from?

Silence fell over the area around the pool. Every single stranger who'd been willing to tear each other apart moments ago stood staring at me as if I'd suddenly grown a horn in the middle of my head.

"What the heaven did you do?" a succubus, with enough extra skin around her neck to make a new demon, said.

"Angels' work, that!" An incubus who looked like all his energy went into strengthening his muscles instead of his mind pounded a fist into his palm.

"Calm down," I said, directing my comment at him but meaning it for everyone. I've found through my time dealing with assassins and the bullies on Lucifer's Third Council that you had to come at bullies with direct and equal hostility or they'd sense vulnerability. Those types shied away from confident demons. "Or I'll use this on you and see if we can't take a little muscle off your... muscle."

"Oh? Yeah?" came the brute's not-so-intelligent response.

I looked him dead in the eye. "Try me."

He started forward, proving my suspicions about his intelligence, but stopped when a dark hand grabbed his wrist. The brute looked about to yank away when he saw who held him.

The incubus was older, his chin covered in a gray goatee. No rival to Azazel's, it still blocked the view of his neck. His mouth was barely wider than his broad nose, and his eyes drooped as if the weight of supporting those two features pulled them down into slits.

"There's no need, Jazep. See to your father," the older incubus said, nodding to his side. "He's okay, but he's injured."

Jazep gave me one more look and then his face lost its antagonistic, cocky hue. "Okay, Sethel." With that, he stepped away.

The incubus approached. I analyzed him, as did those who had been fighting each other until I saved their skins.

Bilba and Ralrek shuffled through the crowd gathering around us.

The dark-skinned incubus tipped his chin at Creed, which I still hadn't collapsed into its truncheon form, and wouldn't until these dolts proved they wouldn't try to kill each other again. "That was impressive. Thank you for saving my people."

"What was the fighting about?" Ralrek said before I responded.

The incubus Jazep had called Sethel looked the tall demon up and down before answering. "We have a long-standing agreement over usage of the pool. But that has been violated."

"We held to the accord until your lot broke the rules first," someone, a young someone by the sound of their voice, called out from the crowd.

He slowly turned to address everyone flooding toward the cluster from all around the lake. These demons didn't seem as interested in fighting each other as they did witnessing what was about to happen between Sethel and us three.

"We did," he answered everyone at once, "and we apologized for that."

"Apologies don't replace water," said an elderly succubus with so many wrinkles her skin looked like a crumpled piece of paper. Even her top lip had ripples of wrinkles.

"No, it doesn't, Cantrell, and for that, we're sorry. But this?" Sethel turned, extending his dark arms and taking in everyone with a slow examination. "This is not how we settled disagreements."

"If I may," Bilba said, squeezing forward and standing directly between me and Sethel. "Why is there a need for an agreement about the pool?"

"It's the only clean water on the island," Sethel said, looking almost apologetic.

"Else we're doing like you knobs and purifying ocean water," a hostile voice called out, sounding distinctly like Jazep.

"All of this over water, when we're surrounded by it, inconvenient as it is?" I asked.

"Are you enjoying collecting and desalinating water every day?" Sethel said, still watching the circle of islanders while answering. "Tedious, isn't it? Imagine ten thousand, twenty thousand more years of it. Imagine a growing population that requires an ever-increasing collection. Were you to have lived that experience, you'd understand why the pool is so important."

"Shocking," Ralrek grumbled, crossing his arms. "Another group working just for themselves." He shook his head and then looked at me and Bilba. "We should just head back to the camp."

Bilba crooked his mouth, murmuring, "And not help?"

"They're going to steal water now that they know the location of the pool," a fiery redhead said.

"We're not stealing crap. We live here too," I answered, pilfering Ralrek's thunder, I'm sure.

"We can come to an agreement," Bilba said, stepping forward. He pointed at the pool that was now distinctly lower than it had been at the outset of the argument. "Look at what your actions have done. One of you used a spell that wasted enough water to have supported everyone for a few months."

"And an act of aggression," the wrinkled woman named Cantrell said. "One that will be met."

Sethel held up his hands, pleading. "Please. Please. You know what will happen."

"Justice," said a thin woman standing at Cantrell's side.

"Violence!" an incubus of no more than five thousand years said from the opposite side of the circle. He donned filthy overalls and looked like he could bench press a chimera. Three of his buddies at his side nodded.

"Stop this!" a voice cut through the threats and counter-threats. Eyes widened, hands went to mouths. Parents pulled their children closer. I was equally shocked because it wasn't a native calling for ceasing tensions, but my best friend. Bilba stepped around Sethel as he spoke to the throng of exiled demons. "I know we just arrived, but none of you have extended a hand to help us. We could have died out there and it wouldn't have mattered to a single one of you."

"It would'ta had," someone said in a cracked voice. Snickers greeted the insult.

"I don't doubt that," Bilba said as he continued his slow circular walk, staying just out of reach. Maybe the fact I still held Creed in its halberd form helped. Maybe it was my buddy's air of confidence. Either way, no one looked ready to challenge him, not even Sethel. "The way you've treated us, combined with what I've seen here today, says everything I need to know about what kind of demons you are."

That got a reaction. These exiles fired a fair share of growls, insults, and even a few globs of spit in his direction.

Ralrek stepped toward Bilba, a snarl pulling up one side of his mouth.

"Complain all you want," Bilba said, doing well to hide the slight waver in his voice. "But you can't look yourselves in the mirror and honestly think you don't have a part to play. None of you are innocent." He jabbed a finger in my direction. "If it wasn't for Zeke, someone would have killed thirty, forty, demons. Maybe more. Over the use of bountiful water! Murder." He paused, allowing the word to sink in. "Over a resource that could outlast all of you if managed appropriately. You should be ashamed."

"You should shut up," the farm incubus said, crossing his thick arms, featuring fine slashes of injuries in the middle of healing.

If he was trying to antagonize Bilba, he was bitterly disappointed when my friend didn't rise to the taunt. Instead of focusing on someone who probably drank goat urine for fun, Bilba kept his tone even and his voice calm. "All of us are here because the Council or your Circle's Administrators saw fit to kick us out. We are the lesser. We don't deserve the right to live. Not in their eyes." He kept walking, but there was something different this time. I noticed he slowed his already gentle pace each time he moved in front of a young imp or fragile elder. "I can't speak for your experience, but I can tell you mine. The Council has employed me. I've been to the Overworld. I've overheard their meetings, been part of them, and I've been in a fight against Beelzebub and his minions. I know what the Council thinks of demons like me." This time, he stopped in front of the succubus named Cantrell, reached out slowly, and took her hand. "Like you." He held her hand and her gaze, drawing not only her focus, but that of everyone observing this moment. I was drawn in, too. My friend was doing what he did best. He was speaking from the heart. When he released Cantrell's hand, he turned toward the inner circle but kept his gaze moving so every demon knew he was including them. "I know their hearts, and I promise you; none of the Underworld's rulers care about you.

Just as I promise they hope we tear each other apart. They don't value us. They don't care about us. And if we fight and kill each other, we're one less thing for them to worry about. But I feel all of you are worth more than that." He drew a nasally breath. "At least I hope you see yourself and those you love in that way."

"He's right," Sethel said. "The stranger speaks with wisdom."

"His name is Bilba," Ralrek said, not releasing his snarl.

"We're new," Bilba said to the circle. "We have no biases. If you're willing, I'm willing to sit down with everyone to mediate and hash out an agreement so that something like this never happens again."

"Oh yeah? And what do you want out of it?" a tall incubus said, not sounding like Bilba's gentle approach had swayed him.

"Fair use of the pool for me and my two friends," Bilba said. "Three of us won't make a dent in its volume. More than fair."

"Fat chance, fat boy," the farmer said.

Ralrek growled. I hefted Creed. The slight movement drew a few dozen yelps, one wail, and a sudden uneasy flinch from the farmer.

"We won't sit. I'm sorry," the white hair woman in wool said, and turned away. The wall of demons split and wrapped back around her once she'd departed.

Sethel sighed.

"Giving up?" I asked.

"Cantrell is central to any agreement. If she won't take part in talks, nothing your friend does will make a difference. I'm sorry." He started away, back to the people dressed in the same brown furs he wore.

"So you're not even going to try?" I said to his back.

His head dropped. Without turning, he said, "Won't do us any good. A waste of time, and survival on the Isle is hard enough. Better learn that before you find yourself in trouble." Sethel's group split apart as Cantrell's had, but before he joined them, he looked at Bilba. "Thank you for trying."

Bilba watched the elderly succubus sink into his tribe. Even before the incubus was gone, the tips of my friend's ears went pink, and his cheeks flushed. I felt for him and waved him over.

When he joined, I nodded at the rest of the demons now making their way back to wherever they hid. "Valiant effort, bud."

"I don't understand why they wouldn't want to come to an agreement. Nothing is worthless until you think it is."

I gripped his shoulder. "Wise words from a wise demon. But we don't know their struggles, and we've got to be careful or we're going to become targets too."

The crowd continued to thin. Though stragglers stayed back, watching us as much as they watched others to make sure no one was taking an unfair share of water from the pool. Putting my neck on the line and Bilba trying to help them reach a peaceful resolution had done nothing to ease tensions. Now that most of the natives had moved on, we'd benefit from doing the same. Staying behind would only cause more headaches if another round of fighting kicked off over an extra bucket of water.

"Come on," I said, wrapping my arm around his shoulder and urging him toward the trees. "Let's get back to camp and get our pot. It's a longer walk than the ocean, but at least we won't have to treat this water. We can use the extra time to find something to eat, since we won't get their help."

I'd ignored the handful of demons spread around the pool in small clumps from the instant they'd proven uninterested in coming to an agreement or even thanking me for not letting them or their loved ones die. I'm over ungrateful demons, to be honest. I didn't bother scanning the remnants of the crowd. Had I been, I might have noticed the succubus before Ralrek laughed at the same time I heard someone clapping slowly, with more than a bit of sarcasm.

"Well, well, will you look at that?" he said, jerking his head at a figure standing apart from all the others.

I did a double-take.

This wasn't a blast from the past. This was a face of disgrace. Someone I never thought I'd see again. Someone the younger me swore he'd get vengeance on. I was tired of being used and abused by my fellow demons. This succubus had been the first to make me feel like that, the first to break my naïve trust in others. The first to teach me that Creed could be stolen. The succubus directly responsible for helping us acquire the Horn of Taurus, and equally responsible for nearly getting us killed after handing it off to Seraph.

"Hi guys," Marijon Hausu said with a tentative wave once she stopped clapping. "Fancy meeting you here."

5

UNDERWORLD, ISLE OF DREAD

"WHAT IN THE HEAVEN ARE YOU DOING HERE?" BILBA ASKED Marijon, his tone as light as if we were at a family reunion, seeing a long-estranged but still-loved relative. I wanted to remind him that her betrayal had led to him receiving one of the worst ass kickings he'd ever had the pleasure of receiving.

"Marijon?" To me, my voice sounded like it came from someone outside my head.

She held her hands up. "Peace?"

"My friend asked you a question," Ralrek said, subtle as a kidney punch.

I still held Creed, extended in halberd form. The last time this succubus was anywhere near me and my weapon, she'd cast a spell that nearly knocked me unconscious. I was trying to stop Taurus Hammerwulf and his thugs from beating the Hellfire out of Bilba and Ralrek. She'd intervened for the bad guys. Not only had she tipped the scales by betraying us, but she'd used an implement to steal Creed. It was the first and only time someone else had held the weapon since I took ownership of it.

I tightened my grip on its haft.

Marijon hadn't dropped her hands. Smart move.

She looked the same as she had three years ago. Same rich brown skin. Those enticing hazel eyes and perfect teeth that went with a smile that could have you happily handing over the keys to your house.

Whereas I'd felt an affinity to her before, that had changed. Betrayal does that—even to thick-skulled incubi like me. Turns even the most beautiful to hideous by peeling away the veneer they want the world to see and exposes their true nature.

"I'm not the same succubus, guys," she said. Her hands drifted down to her sides. A sheepish expression passed over her face. "Let me start by saying how sorry I am for what I did to you. I can explain, if you'd like."

"That would be fair," Bilba said.

At the same time, Ralrek answered, "It wouldn't matter."

"I'd like a second chance. Zeke?"

Words were hard to form. This wasn't about my youthful exuberance at her beauty. I didn't see her like that, not anymore. Besides, there was only one female I was interested in and that wasn't happening, thanks to the taboo nature of demons and angels courting, talking, dating—however the kids were referring to it nowadays. No, my reason for being sluggish had more to do with trust. Bilba could be too forgiving; Ralrek, too harsh. Usually, I'd try to find middle ground. Doing that required motivation I couldn't find at the moment. Not for Marijon. "Why would we, after what you did?"

One corner of her mouth twitched like she was going to smile. "I have food. Proper food. I can share. How long have you guys been exiled?"

"Not even a week yet." Bilba blurted out the information before I could determine how much to share with her.

"What about you?" I asked.

"Little over a year," she said after taking a long breath. "It's been a long one, too. Only being here for a few days, I don't imagine any of the tribes have taken you in? Not after that little display of yours." She looked at Bilba. "Nice try at politics, but the tribes won't respond to that. This is a lawless land. They govern themselves. None of the tribes allow the others to dictate their actions. I think you've seen that now. My gut tells me none of them have allowed you guys into their community, so they're not going to listen to you, no matter how practical your solution." Now she turned to me. "And that was a powerful shield. The last time I saw you, the only thing you could do with your stick was whip it around and wag it at demons." She chuckled. When it was obvious we weren't going to join her, not even Bilba, she cleared her throat. "Sorry. I understand you guys being guarded. Let me tell you, what you did with that shield, protecting those demons even though you didn't have a devildog in the fight, will go a ways. A good first step. Maybe nothing more than that, but at least it's a start. You'll need more than that to get any help around here, though."

"Oh? Why's that?"

Marijon shrugged. When she was in the Eighth Circle misleading us about her ambitions, she decked herself out in tight leather pants, a leather half-shirt that exposed a flat stomach, and opal-painted pauldrons which made her look like a total badass. Apparel from her past. Now, her lime t-shirt was stained and held small holes like it'd served as a buffet to the Isle's insects. Her jean shorts probably had once been a pair of pants, sacrificed in the name of practicality. She wasn't even carrying her staff. "They only help their kind."

"So, if you're not one of them, you're not getting crap?"

"You saw how they fought over this water. It's fed by a ground spring. We aren't going to run out, but you wouldn't know that by listening to them. I've never seen them duke it out like they did today, but they come close all the time. Basically, any time they trip across each other. Which, by the way, isn't difficult to do on an island, no matter how big."

"Which one do you belong to?" I asked.

"I don't. None of them have accepted me." She looked away and swallowed hard.

My question had hit a nerve. But this was Marijon the Betrayer, not someone I wanted to sit down over beer and chicken wings with to explore a troubled mind. "Why not?"

She watched the last few demons around the pool, collecting water for their respective tribes. Her chest heaved with a sigh. "Because I've got nothing to offer that any of them want."

"On an island where demons nearly killed each other over access to water, you have nothing to offer?" Ralrek asked, crossing his arms. "Call me skeptical, but that's hard to believe, and it's not like we have a reason to believe you."

"Ralrek!" Bilba chastised.

"No. No. He's right. Heavens, if I were you, I wouldn't trust me either. But I swear it; I'm on my own here. Have been. And I could really use some friends."

Ralrek snorted.

"So you apologized to us because you're lonely and need help to survive on the island?" I gave Creed a shake, collapsing it back into its truncheon form. Marijon was armed with nothing more than ragged clothes and a bucket fashioned from splints of bark. It was leaking in small springs and would be empty before she got a couple hundred yards away if we carried on trying to clarify her situation.

"I'm apologizing because I am sorry, Zeke."

"Ezekial," Ralrek and I said at the same time.

"Guys," Bilba said softly, giving us 'that' look. With widened eyes, I knew he was trying to tell us to give her a few minutes of our day. He was concerned with how we were going to make it on the Isle. Now that we had further proof the other exiles weren't the slightest bit interested in helping us, figuring out how to survive was of even greater importance. My blasted best friend was a lot more rational than me. He's smarter too. I'd defer to him this time. But that didn't mean I'd let my guard down around her. Though, if she could give us a boost in the right direction, I'd take it. She owed us that much, at least. "Let's hear her out."

Ralrek grumbled.

"Fine," I said.

"Let me make a peace offering," Marijon said.

"Peace? How?" Ralrek said. Always an incubus of many words.

She tipped when she pointed across her body with her free hand. "My camp is over that way. About a mile. It's isolated, but I've managed decently. I have a garden and a tiny farm. Goats and chickens. And I caught a boar yesterday and I haven't salted it yet. You're welcome to it. Went fishing this morning and brought in a small catch. I can share what I have. It won't be the best meal you've ever had, but it's something."

"Better than what we've been eating," Bilba said. His rosy cheeks bulged as he smiled.

"If I eat one more berry, I swear I'll turn into one," Ralrek said. "I'm down. You, Zeke?"

The guys didn't look ready to change their minds. My stomach growled. Against my better judgment, I said, "Let's go."

"THIS IS AN IMPRESSIVE SETUP," BILBA SAID. SQUATTING ON A log, he picked the remaining scraps of meat from his fish.

Impressive was right. Each of us had a fish, thick slices of gamey boar, small salad, and as many potatoes as we could eat. The air smelled of smoke and charred meat. Gorging like this knew no limits beyond the expanding boundaries of our guts. The next bowel movement wouldn't be pleasant, but the cost was well worth this experience. Coconuts waited for us as dessert. Marijon had been correct; it wasn't the best meal I'd ever eaten, but after days of only eating berries and drinking boiled ocean water, this was a feast fit for Lucifer's Council.

Her camp wasn't half-bad either. The shelter looked far more permanent and secure than our small A-frame. Her home was a small hut. Who knew she had engineering chops? Somehow, she'd cultivated a wide garden that pushed the forest back. She not only grew potatoes, but spinach and tomatoes as well. Marijon said she was trying and failing with a crop of zucchini. On the other side of her small wood-frame home, a second field, this one growing wheat, was half the size of the garden, but healthy in its own right.

"Thank you," Marijon said with a reserved smile. "It's been a struggle. The Isle isn't exactly forgiving."

Ralrek snorted. "No lie. How'd you do it, then?"

"What? Build all this on my own?"

"Yeah."

Marijon lowered her handcrafted bowl, setting it on the ground at her feet and leaning her elbows on her knees. "Getting exiled was traumatizing. You guys know that. At least you guys came together."

"Doesn't mean this is easy," Ralrek said.

"No, it doesn't. And it isn't," she replied. "Exile isn't easy for anyone. I've tried to help a couple who came after me. One guy, he had to be at least forty thousand years old, ran into the forest at night after about a month. I never saw him again. I doubt he made it, but who knows? Most likely fell off a bluff or into a canyon. Or a creepy island creature ate him. Or tried to swim the Acheron home and drowned." She finished with a bob of her shoulders, like the unnamed succubus's fate didn't matter.

"And the others you helped? What about them?"

"Other," she corrected. "She didn't run off, but got sick. I don't know if she ate or drank something that was the cause, but when I went to check on her one day, she was curled into a ball and screaming through cramps that never ended. In pain the entire time. I sat with her, but I don't think it helped. She passed." Marijon paused, looking down at her cupped hands. "When I saw you running through the crowd, Zeke... Ezekial, I thought I'd lost my mind. No way that could be you, I told myself. Not someone I knew. A friendly face. Well, a familiar one. I thought my luck was about to change, that I'd somehow missed you guys in one of the tribes, and you'd help me get in. I didn't know you were new exiles." She grunted. "I've done a lot of soul-searching since the last time you guys saw me, but I understand why you'd want nothing to do with me. Still, for a moment, when I first saw you, I thought I was saved."

"How'd you get exiled?" I asked, not really caring, but knowing the longer the conversation went on, the more I'd eat. The more I ate, the stronger I'd feel. The more energy I'd have. Then, maybe we could build something like what Marijon had and finally focus on getting off the Isle to get a proper meal in the Overworld, move our camp before the terrorist harpy slaughtered us, find Libra, and check in with Dialphio. To see Cassie.

"What did I do?"

"Yes." I watched the top of her head since she still refused to look up. Her black hair was wrapped in rows that didn't move when she shook it.

"Things changed after Taurus died," she said after a pause that allowed the three of us to fill our bellies.

Bilba had a chunk of potato near his lips. It hovered in front of his open maw. "In the Eighth, you mean?"

"Yes." Marijon straightened.

It was then that I noticed she looked older. Maybe it was the diminishing daylight playing tricks on my eyes, but I swore the creases around her cheekbones were deeper and that she wore a single wrinkle across her forehead that hadn't been there the last time I saw her. Sure, a few years had passed, but as immortals, that's a blink of an eye.

"Everyone in my neighborhood was thrilled when the news about Taurus' death came out. I don't know how much you guys remember about my Circle, but—"

"Enough to get a feel for the type of demons who live there," Ralrek said.

"Fair enough," Marijon said without a hint of ferocity or defensiveness. "It's a hard Circle that creates hard demons. We had to be to survive under the Hammerwulf stranglehold. But the thing is; we thought it was bad when he was paying off our politicians and patrols. It only got worse after you..." She caught my eye, shook her head again, looking like she changed her mind on the fly. "Well, when he died."

"Worse? How? Why?" Bilba asked, finally shoving the potato into his waiting mouth.

"My mom was sick," Marijon said. "She had been for years, but it was manageable. She took a turn for the worse a few months after we stole the Horn. By then, things were far worse for everyone in the Circle. Even the wealthy people."

"Why them?"

She pinched her lips. "They became targets. There was less food, more crime, and no one to enforce the peace. The Council didn't send any help when the Circle administrators and sub-Council asked for help. Demons were hungry and getting more and more desperate as the supply chains broke down. Crime went through the roof. Wealthy demons hired security teams to protect what they had. Of course, they're the gung-ho type, so it wasn't long before there were incidents."

"Incidents? Like what?" I asked.

"Over-reactions. Civilians killed by these hired... whatever. For threats of violence. Harassment. Theft."

Ralrek grunted. "Doesn't sound like you buy that."

"I don't."

"Why not?"

"Because I know there's one truth above all others."

That stopped me in mid-bite. "What truth is that?"

"The rich and powerful play all of us off each other," Marijon said, and I heard for the first time during this reunification, conviction in her voice. "Race, gender, political identity. They use those things to divide us, to make us see each other as enemies. But classism is the true divider. Don't get me wrong; racism, sexism, and that stuff, it's chimera shit. But a lot of it is also manufactured, if you're paying attention. As long as we're distracted by not trusting each other, succubus against incubus, white against black, traditional against progressive, and so-on, we'll miss the telltale signs that we're being used by the rich. They span the spectrum just like the rest of us, but they have something we don't."

"What's that?" Ralrek asked. "Coin?"

"Power," Marijon said fiercely. "They control the supply chain and markets. Healthcare. Access. Opportunities. Sure, they'll divvy up some breaks to the lower classes, but only enough to keep us believing we have a fighting chance to get ahead in life. But we don't. We never have and they'll ensure we never do. After Taurus was removed, that became painfully obvious. Within a year, the Eighth was chaotic. The wealthy manipulated what and who they could to grab more for themselves. Scrambling to gobble up his leftovers even though they already had so much. By then, I didn't care. My mother was gone." Marijon pressed her lips together, draining their color. "Wasted away in pain because we couldn't get the medications and treatment she needed."

Marijon had a campfire going long before our dinner. Now the flames were fading. Bilba pushed himself up and grabbed a log to add. I gave him a quizzical look, thinking he meant to stay longer. He held my gaze for a second before tipping his chin in Marijon's direction.

She hung her head again, but this time it bobbed ever-so-slightly. She was crying. Dammit. I didn't want to feel for her, but what kind of demon would I be if I didn't? That'd been the end to her story, an unfair one. Hardly surprising. I knew when she betrayed us, she was doing so for selfish reasons. We already knew inequality was rampant in the Eighth Circle of Hell. None of us could be shocked with what became of the place after we high-tailed it home.

"I told you guys it got bad for my mother," Bilba said quietly. Then he softened his tone for Marijon. "I stayed there after our mission." Her head snapped up, and she wiped at her nose with the back of a finger. "I wanted to help my mother with her business, and..." His eyes narrowed as if he was now thinking about her for the first time in a long time. "I saw first-hand how quickly crime increased. She ended up losing her business because of it. No matter what I tried, I couldn't help her keep the shop open with all the theft and burglaries and stuff. It got bad. I'm sorry to hear about your mother."

"Thank you, Bilba," Marijon said between sniffles.

Man, life had broken this succubus. Until now, Marijon had been one of the toughest demons I knew. Not in the true sense. Dialphio was tough. That loveable bookstore owner was heading secret subversion groups, positioning them to resist against the Council. That's tough, right there. Marijon projected an image of toughness, and I'd learned throughout my trials that those who put so much effort into appearing tough were often the frailest of us all.

"You're welcome."

"I don't want to sound callous, but it sounds like the Eighth disintegrated. How did that get you exiled?" I asked.

"The unfairness got to me," she said, her eyes still wet. "I was bitter and angry. That led me to make poor decisions. With my mother gone, I didn't care about much anymore. I was disconsolate, I guess. Definitely disenfranchised. Until I found a purpose. I wanted to help those I could. Help them like the system should have helped my mother. The only way

I knew how was to fund treatments and medications for those in need."

"And the only way you could do that was by taking coin that wasn't yours?" I guessed.

Marijon nodded. "During a burglary of a succubus, one of the crew accidentally set a fire. The entire building caught. Everyone took off, but I stayed behind to help get the succubus out. She was old and frail. Had more valuables than any demon should have, but that didn't mean she needed to die. Especially not like that."

"Did you save her?"

"Yes. But by the time I got her outside, the authorities were there and took me into custody."

"You took the fall for everyone?" Bilba asked.

"Of course," Marijon said. "Most of them had sick families or children who needed to eat. I had... I have nothing. They didn't need to go down too. Had I squealed, their families would have been the ones to suffer."

We fell silent. What did you say to something like that? If it was true, and why would she lie now, it changed how I saw Marijon. Not completely, of course. I'm no longer naïve enough to give everyone the benefit of the doubt—well, outside of my two friends and Dialphio. Okay, and probably Cassie too, but she's an angel, and that's an entirely different set of circumstances. Someone being as vulnerable as Marijon was genuine or a master manipulator, and I didn't want to choose to see the world like the latter implied. Not anymore.

After a while, Marijon finished her story. "They informed the exiles I was a thief when they dropped me off. So, I never got a shot with any of the tribes. Can't blame them if they think I'm going to rob them blind in the middle of the night and set their camp on fire."

"I doubt their reasons for being exiled are much better," Bilba said, sounding as if he was offended for Marijon.

She scoffed. "Who knows? One thing's for sure; I'll never

find out. They'll never let me that close." Her gaze traveled across the three of us. "Enough about me. What happened to you guys? Why are the Council's golden boys on the Isle of Dread? Another mission?"

It was our turn to scoff now, but we took turns filling in our story. Bilba even sounded like he was bragging about being referred to as the Rebel Mage, a title he wasn't sure would stick on the Isle. Marijon said it might endear the tribes to him. When we finished, Marijon looked as impressed as she did that day, all those years ago, when she first discovered, through Bilba's blabbering, that we were working for Lucifer's Council.

"You guys never cease to amaze." Her gaze fell on me, then Creed, which I had leaned against the log I was sitting on. "I'm glad you got that back."

"Me too." Creed vibrated, and Marijon's eyes went wide.

"Does that thing… can it communicate?"

I tipped my head, unable to hide my smile about the halberd's personality, stubborn as it is. "I'm still trying to figure it out, honestly. Should have let you keep the blessed thing."

This time, Creed rattled so harshly that it tipped over into the sand. I left it there.

"Ezekial, I'm trying to make amends every single day of my life. I'm sorry I almost stole that."

"Technically, you did steal it," I said.

She pulled her lips back, exposing those wonderfully perfect teeth. "Yes, I did. I didn't know what I was doing. One of Taurus's henchmen gave me a clamp for my staff and told me I'd only get paid if I got it from you. No doubt it's a cool weapon, even before I knew you could create huge shields with it. Back then, I didn't understand why they wanted it so badly. Now, I think I do."

There was no way in heaven I was going to tell her about the true nature of Creed and what it could do. Plus, even I wasn't sure of its limits. "I'm just glad you were unsuccessful. It's a pain in my ass, but we've bonded. I won't throw it in a fire. Not yet. Not unless it drops to freezing on the Isle."

Our laughter covered Creed's vibrations.

"We need to head back to our camp before it gets dark," Ralrek said, looking up at the sky that was just now losing its azure luminosity.

"Let me escort you. I have a shortcut to the beach that will get you back with light to spare," Marijon said, standing. When we got up, she patted the air with both hands. "No, leave the bowls. I'll take care of them when I get back. It's... lonely here. I need the distraction."

We were near the familiar stretch of beach far quicker than I expected.

"That was a serious short-cut," Bilba said with a smile. "Thank you for the meal, Marijon."

"You're welcome. It's the least I could do."

Ralrek grunted. I stayed silent, distracted by how the Isle seemed to break Marijon in one short year.

"Guys, one piece of advice?"

"Yeah?" Ralrek said, half-turned toward the forest to take the trail back to our camp.

"Unless you want to end up alone like me, scavenging for your meals and hoping you never get sick so you can still plant food, tend the gardens, get water, and everything else it takes to survive, you need to show the tribes your value."

"What do you mean?" I asked.

"They won't take any of you on unless they see how you can help their society." She lifted her chin as she examined the line of trees. "No matter what I do, even having Water Abilities, I can't get any of them to accept me. My magic is diminishing more every single day. I can feel it. Doesn't feel the same. Once it's gone, I'll have absolutely nothing to offer them. My advice? Don't wait. What you did today was a wonderful start. You definitely got their attention. But you'll need to show them more if you want one of them to accept you. Life on the island is a lot easier when you can depend on an entire community. Don't take my path."

"Thanks," I said.

"Thank you, Marijon," Bilba said with a wave as she started away.

We watched her go. None of us said a thing until long after she was out of earshot.

Bilba blew out a breath, his lips flapping. "Wow. That was weird."

Ralrek patted his stomach. "That was good. I'm going into a food coma as soon as I hit our shelter."

The pair started toward the tree line. I hung back.

When he noticed I was dragging along behind, Bilba stopped. "You coming?"

I looked down the beach, seeing the tiny, distant form of Marijon slip into the trees. "Nah. You guys go ahead. I'm going to stay out here and think."

"You sure?"

"Yep."

Ralrek slapped Bilba on the back. "Let's go. I've got to shit and then I'm crashing out. 'Night, Zeke."

"Good night."

With them gone, I strolled toward the ocean. A roll of black hung on the horizon, a precursor to the rapidly approaching night. I found a safe place close to the water, but far enough to not have to worry about high tide.

I liked the beach. It was becoming a good thinking spot. Honestly, it was the only place on the island where I felt a sense of peace. Not contentment; I doubted I'd ever feel that here. At least I could rest my frustration and anger every time I dug my feet into the cool, wet sand. That was all I had, but it was something. I still had more than Marijon.

How hard was life for her? What about others like her? Others with fewer survival skills, ones not hardened by life in the Eighth? How miserable was the appropriately named Isle of Dread for those struggling with things like food and clean water that every demon in Hell took for granted back in the Circles? I felt bad for Marijon, having to escape the misery of the Eighth, only to find more of it on this isolated heaven.

Were there hundreds of other stories around the Isle like hers? Had other demons been screwed by Hell's rulers as she had been? As we had been?

I laid back in the sand, not caring that the coolness was probably because of my shirt soaking up the beach's dampness.

Exiling demons was wrong. Shoving so many to the Isle, to fend for themselves and let them die in agony if they couldn't, went beyond cruelty.

One day, if I ever got the chance, I'd figure out a way to get everyone home and then sink this blessed island.

6

UNDERWORLD, ISLE OF DREAD/FIFTH CIRCLE

"DON'T MOVE SO MUCH. IF YOU FALL IN, I'M NOT SAVING YOU," Ralrek said, once again stretched out on the deck of the raft.

"How much longer?" Bilba said. This time, his ears weren't pink. I think the constant rocking of the raft had a lot to do with keeping any color but green from his face.

"Not long. Right?" Ralrek said, scooting into a more comfortable position, and locking his hands behind his head again.

"We're almost there," I said to my nervous, sea-sick friend. "Are you sure you've got enough strength to open a Gateway as soon as we land? Azazel told us the Council has the dock guarded. I'll bet it'll be Beelzebub's lemmings. They won't give us any quarter. We've got to be ready."

Bilba swallowed hard. His cheeks puffed like he was seeing how long he could hold his breath. "I am. I just wish we could open one on the island because I don't like crossing the Acheron." He stretched taller, turning his head to the deep waters. "Especially with Azazel's warning about what's down there."

"We've got permission to cross. Stay on the raft and you don't have to worry about the kraken, remember?" I was half-tempted to give him a playful shove. Not enough to send him off the raft, of course, but to just screw with him and see if I could get him to sick-up. An empty stomach might help him focus on his important role.

"I don't plan on falling off, but how can you stay so calm now that we know about it?"

Hell doesn't have many large bodies of water. Reservoirs feed the towns and cities. The Second Circle is a miserable island of constant rain. Besides those, my only true experience was large bodies of water before floating across the Acheron was in the Overworld when I was deployed to the Middle East. They flew us across an ocean. Flew. Across. An. Ocean. The less I thought about that time, the better.

None of that helped my nerves at being on the open water. It didn't help me ignore the smell of salt in the air I was now trying to enjoy as we drifted about as swiftly as my father admitted his wrongdoing.

As if not sensing I was thinking up a devious plot, even if completely unwilling to act on it, Bilba pulled his legs up, spun on his butt, and faced me. "Did Dialphio say anything else in her message?"

He was talking about the note I'd received last night through the demonic notebook from my ex-boss. One that made me nervous that something was going down, even though Dialphio told me not to worry. "Other than that she wanted us to get to her as quickly as we could, and that it wouldn't take long because she knows we're still trying to not starve or freeze to death?"

Bilba rocked his head. "Well, yeah. Of course. Wait. She's not feeding us?"

"You want Dialphio to feed us?"

"Well, we are the ones traveling. We're taking a risk at the Underworld dock. She knows we're hungry. You told her, right?"

"Yep. Still, have you ever seen her cook?"

As if he didn't hear me, my friend sat back, pulled his knees up to his chest, and rocked. "Then I'm sure she'll feed us. Dialphio is good like that."

Yes, she really was. "Just focus on what you're going to do once we reach that." I pointed at the dock that had once seemed a day's floating away. Now, we were close enough to mark it on the shore. "Wake up, Ralrek."

The tall demon grumbled, but woke, rubbing his face. "Did Bilba get eaten by the kraken?" He did a double-take at our mutual friend. "Oh, hey."

"Uh, you're a little too relaxed about that very real possibility for my liking," Bilba said.

"Aw, don't tell me I hurt your feelings? I was just kidding."

"Were you though? When you fall asleep on the way back to the island, I'm pushing you overboard. Then we'll see how well your Fire works as the kraken is pulling you to the bottom of the ocean."

A black form shifted behind a rock outcropping about sixty yards from the dock. "Threaten each other later. Help me keep an eye on the dock. I think I just saw something move."

"A Founder?" Ralrek asked, suddenly sounding much more serious.

"Can't tell. Too far away."

"It could have been anything. Anyone. Even a civilian," Bilba said, squinting to make out what I'd seen.

"I'm not willing to take any chances. Are you?"

The pink rims of her ears, the first color he'd regained since we cleared the wall of mist surrounding the Isle, gave him away before he answered. "No."

Probably too unnerved to focus, we readied ourselves for arrival. Thankfully, what Dialphio was asking of us wouldn't require a ton of clothes or gear. We were traveling light, taking one of our trunks from the camp, keeping two pounds of berries and a jug of water in case the journey took longer than we remembered. We weren't even going to bring this much until Ralrek whined about needing to eat to maintain his metabolism. Bilba sealed the decision for increased substance we were going to carry when he hypothesized about the possibilities of being blown off-course.

When the dock came into clear detail, along with the outcropping of rocks to the left and a narrow, tall structure to the right, we prepared.

I didn't expect the Council's henchmen to use the tall building as a hideout. They'd know we'd know to expect that move. Plus, if they actually used it to conceal their presence, they'd have protection, but it'd limit their attacks. No, if their goons were here, they were hiding behind the small outcropping of rocks.

I felt better. The rocks were more like boulders. They'd provide cover, but there wasn't enough of it to hide a sufficient force. Not really one to trouble us.

"I don't remember the coast being this sparse," Ralrek said, his hands glowing with his Fire Ability.

I used Creed to point at his hands. "Won't that tire you, holding the Ability for so long?"

Ralrek didn't look away from the target beyond the dock. "I hope I don't have to use it. But if I do, I want the size and power of it to be directly proportional to the time I need it to buy for us so we can get through the Gateway."

"Speaking of," I said, looking to Bilba, "are you ready to open one?"

"Just get me close enough to place it on the dock."

"Will do."

The raft bobbed as we neared the dock. I kept my attention swiveling between the structure and the outcropping. More than one demon hid behind those natural shields. Three, I think. A fight we could manage. The closer we got, the slower the raft seemed to move, as if the supernatural forces that propelled the vessel were intentionally screwing with us.

Or making us sitting targets.

But I hadn't gone through days of feeling my stomach twist from hunger and dietary changes just to die on a floating collection of Lincoln Logs.

"Ready?" I asked when we were within two hundred yards. At least three demons hid behind the major outcropping, but then I spotted another two hiding away from the concentration of the Council's force. In a way, I was disappointed that they'd only brought five.

"I am." Ralrek fidgeted when he stood, legs spread in a boxing stance.

"I need to get a little closer to make sure I open it on the dock," Bilba said.

I gave Creed a shake, activating it. Within a breath, the weapon stretched to six-feet, featuring its customary double-ax heads on one end and wavy dagger jutting from the bottom. I spun it to create the shield that would protect us from any attack these loons might send our way.

"Closer," Bilba said, almost panting, but still looking in control. He'd come a long way from his failed Passage preparation tests. How many times had his mentor reminded him to keep his emotions out of his casting if he truly wanted to master his Abilities? In the end, Bilba had done exactly that and become a Major demon—a title bestowed on only the most adept casters. A title he had for about as long as I take to polish off a plate of chicken wings. Not his fault. That disgrace fell on the shoulders of my lying father and the conniving dirtbag politicians on the Council, who stripped him of the accomplishment at their first opportunity. Now referred to as the Rebel Mage, I think my buddy was coming into his own. It was a nice look.

Creed's shield extended in a greater circumference. Before we'd drifted another foot, the front of the raft was protected. If the demons in hiding wanted at us, they were going to have to move parallel to the dock for hundreds of yards to get a clear shot around the shield.

Fifty yards.

"Close enough to land it?" I said, noticing my breaths coming faster from the adrenaline pumping through me.

"Yes," Bilba said, and I noticed some hesitancy.

"But?"

I swore the tips of his ears wiggled. "But what if I open it and they get to it before we do? They'll know where we're headed."

"Good point. Just make sure you can get that thing open in time for us to jump from the raft. I don't want to be left standing around on the dock."

"Don't worry," he said with an encouraging air of confidence. "I'm ready."

The last twenty yards zipped by, as if the raft sensed the lurking presence of hidden demons just up the hill and wanted no part of anything that might transpire here.

Ten yards away, Bilba's hands started moving and the white border of his Gateway traced the air. At five yards, the Gateway was fully formed, the shimmering image of the Book Abyss, my home-away-from-home during the days when I wasn't a complete outlaw, came into view. My heart skipped, feeling an instant connection with the succubus on the other side of that magical portal.

"What's wrong with them?" Ralrek said as he reached for the dock piling while still keeping his eyes on the outcropping and nearly barren landscape. "Why aren't they attacking?"

"I think they're analyzing our approach," Bilba said with such clarity it was as if he wasn't focusing on holding the Gateway.

"Why would they do that? Why not try to fry us now and be done with it?"

"Ah, because they want to see how we planned our approach so they can find weaknesses in it and use those against us the next time?" I asked, seeing the sense in Bilba's rationale.

"Yep. Next time, they'll have a better understanding and more thugs," my Deception magic friend intoned.

"Well, crap."

"Don't worry about that now. There's nothing we can do," Bilba said with the wisdom of someone far beyond his years as Ralrek helped him onto the dock. I moved forward, keeping Creed spinning and the shield active, pushing it to cut off any attacks that might now be trained on the Gateway. "We'll reassess now that we know what they're up to. Between the three of us, I'm sure we can come up with something."

"Coming?" Ralrek asked an inch from the Gateway's entrance.

"You two first," I said, backing until I stood beside them. They stepped through. I backed to the mouth of the Gateway, and only stopped spinning my halberd when I was a hair's width away from crossing back into the Fifth Circle. I was inside before the shield dropped.

"Whew, that was fun. Feels sort of dangerous to be so rebellious," Bilba said with an adorable smirk.

"You're so edgy," Ralrek said, patting him on the shoulder before looking around the empty bookstore.

A closed sign hung in the window. Hard cover titles, mostly fiction, littered the circular tables. I was proud of Dialphio for putting her hair down a little and refusing to become a stuffy old lady—please don't tell her I said that. The place wasn't as dust-free as when I was in her employ, but whoever the less-persnickety demon that she was now paying to do what I'd done for her was, they still obviously cared for the store.

"Where is she?" Bilba said, moving toward the wide front window.

I slipped to the back office, which was really nothing more

than an alcove behind a stacked wall of old titles no one bought. Her desk was cluttered with paper, receipts, shipping labels, and books she still needed to inventory. An extra pair of red-rimmed glasses lay on top of a pile of bills.

"Not here," I called out, noting the desk parallel to hers was tidy, with not a single thing out of place. There wasn't even a picture of the employee's family or their devil dog.

Bilba and Ralrek stood together at the front window when I stepped back out onto the main floor. They were out of sight of the door and mostly blocked from view to anyone outside by the display books and the fact Dialphio had turned off the store lights.

"Be careful. Someone could still see you," I said.

Bilba took a slow step back. "I know. It just… it feels good to be back."

"We haven't been gone that long," I said with a chuckle.

Still facing the street, Bilba said, "I'm not used to being away, Zeke. Not like you. Besides the time in the army and when I stayed with my mom, I've been here. I wonder… I wonder if he's okay."

Ralrek put a hand in the middle of Bilba's back. I moved to them. "He's going to be fine, bud. If the Council was screwing with him, Dialphio would have said something."

"I know," he said with a distant stare out the window.

We watched life pass by in the Fifth. Outside on the cobblestone street, a district designed for shoppers and patrons of its restaurants and pubs. Not a place for chimera carriages or mounts of any kind. Demons of our home Circle moseyed from store to store without a care in the world. Even though the Underworld was falling apart right under their noses, they still shopped, probably for crap they didn't need, carrying bags from the shoe store, the clothes boutique, the sporting goods place, to prove they supported demonic capitalism like good, little demons. Across the way, three middle-aged incubi sat at a small white wrought-iron table. Three tall glasses of amber ale stood idly by in front of them in varying degrees of consumption. The three laughed.

I swatted Bilba's arm, no longer having any interest in watching my fellow demons pretend everything was fine. I sniffed the air. A meaty aroma wafted down from above us. "Come on. Let's go see what she called on us about. Plus, maybe there's food."

At the mention of a possible meal, Bilba and Ralrek nearly bowled me over to get to the stairs leading to the second floor.

Halfway up, Bilba inhaled. "Meatballs."

"What?"

He hustled up the remaining stairs. I swear, he was on the verge of taking two at a time.

"That's meatballs, Zeke. She cooked for us!"

"Shhhh. Do you want the Council's attention?" Ralrek said, though he was smirking.

We were on the unguarded landing. I pulled up.

"What's wrong?" Ralrek asked.

"Dialphio would have usually had someone sitting watch," I said.

Ralrek was stoic, but Bilba, who had been reaching for the door handle to the backroom where Dialphio hosted a rebel cell, paused.

"Do you think everything is okay?" he asked.

I slid forward. "Let me take the lead just in case it isn't, though. I can't see Dialphio not warning us somehow. Her message would have contained some sort of hint this visit wasn't all it was cracked up to be if this was a setup. Plus, if the Council suspects her, do you really think we'd have meatballs waiting for us? Unless your sniffer is off?"

"My sniffer works just fine." Bilba grinned, giving me a nudge. "Now, open the door. I'm starving."

I pushed down on the door handle when someone said, "It has begun."

I stopped and looked at my friends looking at me like I was crazy. Then, I remembered I was. Crazy Zeke and his unannounced drop-in visits. Neither of them had spoken. What I'd heard was the voice I'd been hearing since coming back through Azazel's Rift from my Overworld Abandonment. "Nothing. Ignore me. Sorry. Let's eat."

We walked into a surprise.

The meeting room Dialphio had tucked away on the second floor of The Book Abyss was as cluttered as always. A space of less than three hundred square feet that she used to hold meetings with the rebel cell she led was usually abuzz with activity. This room served as the place for demons to put together copies of The Histories of the Balance, one of the most important books in Hell—at least, if you're a masochist. Her efforts ensured the messages contained within the text survived the efforts of Lucifer's Third Council to eradicate it. Politicians tended to not be cool with the propagation of information that could spark the flames of inquisition among the populace and all that.

The tables Dialphio's charges used to copy the book and package it for distribution were cluttered with stacks of copies, but the room was empty of rebels except one. She wasn't alone.

"Ezekial!" Dialphio beamed over a crock pot. She had been stirring the contents, but stopped at our appearance, wiped her hands on a towel, and greeted us with her typical warm hug. Dialphio hugs rocked.

"Hi," I said as we embraced. She squeezed as if she was trying to make sure I was real. Considering everything that had happened in the time since I last saw her, I couldn't blame her. Not many face the Prince of Demons in a fight to the death, and live to tell everyone how they made him scramble to save his ass. In fact, I'm pretty sure I was the only one to fight Beelzebub and live to tell the truth. Which was why I was getting the type of hug that told you, without words, that the hugger never wanted to let go. "Smells great in here."

"It better," she said, stepping back to take me in. "I've been preparing them for hours. And you know I'm busy. But not too busy to feed the three of you." She looked me up and down, her hands still clasping my arms. "My, my. You look good. I'm very glad to see that."

Then she broke contact to deliver the same vivacious hugs to my two partners, leaving me to greet the Founder I hadn't seen since he dropped us off at the Isle of Dread.

"Ezekial," Azazel said, grunting and wincing as he pushed himself out of the deep-seat chair. "How was the crossing?"

"Uneventful. Sort of disappointing. I was hoping to see the kraken," I said as Dialphio ushered Bilba and Ralrek into the room, closing and locking the door behind them.

He wagged a slightly bent finger at me. "You say that now. But if you ever see it, I'm confident you'll change your mind. Nonetheless, I'm pleased to hear there were no problems. First crossings can always be interesting events. Good that yours wasn't, and that you made it without trouble."

"Not completely," Bilba said, moving closer.

"Oh?"

"Zeke spotted five guards at the dock. They didn't cause any trouble, but they were surveilling our crossing."

Azazel's mouth moved underneath his overgrown mustache and beard as he grumbled. "Yes, yes. I fear they're going to be a constant problem. Best be prepared and expect trouble every time you cross."

"That's what I'm worried about," Bilba said. "I'm sure they'll be waiting for our return."

"They will."

Azazel's immediate and confident response drew a hard swallow from my friend. "Well then, how can we be sure we'll be safe? What if they've sunk the raft and we're stranded at the dock? It's not like we can hide out here. Can we?"

"No, I'm afraid not," Azazel said, glancing at his cousin. Dialphio wore a mask, but I could tell she was bothered. "Don't worry about the raft. It is a feature of the island. They can obliterate it, torch it, sink it if their hearts desire, but the island will simply reanimate it. As much a part of the Isle as the wonderful smell of sulfur in the air. That is one problem we don't have to discuss."

"Hopefully one problem we don't have to discuss is Cancer," I said, wanting to get the issue of my missing friend out of the way first. A nagging worry. Her status would trouble me until I knew she was safe. Lucifer, please let her be safe.

"My sources haven't provided me with anything. I'm sorry," the Founder said, and sounded like he truly meant it. "The war has created chaos in that part of the world, as you can imagine. I promise, as soon as I know something, you'll hear about it."

I hung my head.

"Come, let's talk while we eat," Dialphio said, guiding Bilba by the arm toward the crock pot and bread bowl. "I'm sorry it's not the best meal in the world, but I've been distracted by events which have wreaked havoc on what the markets. You can never know what you'll be able to buy. So, I threw this together. Didn't think you'd mind."

"Not at all. Thank you," Ralrek said, sidling up to the pot ahead of Bilba. He looked down and shrugged. "Snooze, you lose."

With full plates, we sat. I pointed my barbeque-covered fork tongs at the stacks of books. "Looks like you're keeping the cell busy."

Dialphio looked at the stacks for a long time, longer than necessary if there wasn't trouble brewing in her mind. "Yes, I have. We're putting in as many hours as we can, but it's still not fast enough. By the way, do you still have your Fa' Hersei translation guide?"

I stopped in mid-bite of another juicy meatball, my neck craned forward over my plate.

She waved me away. "I can tell by your reaction that it's gone."

I sat up. I hated disappointing her. "I'm sorry, Dialphio. After the battle in the Overworld, the Council didn't give any of us freedom. The only things we took to the Isle of Dread came from Azazel. If not for him, we'd be in a bad spot. I didn't have time to grab my personal stuff."

"Not a worry, young Ezekial," the Founder said. "I made sure a trusted source sanitized your homes while you were on trial. Nothing any of the three of you had of value fell into the wrong hands, I promise. Everything is in safe hands for the time it can be transferred back. I imagine you'll want your belongings? It'll make your time on the Isle more tolerable. As soon as you're ready for them, we'll work out the details."

"Is the cell still just copying the book?" Ralrek asked without looking away from his plate, which was almost empty.

"We're still engaged in outreach, yes. But we're also engaged in community support," she answered.

He stopped chewing. "Community support? What's that mean? We need to prepare demons to stand by us, not get involved in social services."

"Supporting the community is part of preparing to stand against the Council, Ralrek," Dialphio said in a tone that implied she wouldn't tolerate nonsense. "I know the perceived lack of movement has frustrated you, but the cell is maturing in a responsible way. We can't add more members than I can safely manage, or we introduce unacceptable risk. We can't blatantly blare our message to the Underworld without the power to back it up against retributive actions, of which there would be many."

"Many heavy-handed ones," Azazel said, nodding his head.

"Fine. Fine." Ralrek held up his fork hand. Barbeque sauce started running down the fork handle. "I'm too hungry to have this argument again. But it would be nice to hear they're working on improving their spells or torching the Council's infrastructure at some point before we find ourselves on the wrong end of Lucifer's vengeance."

He had a point.

"Believe it or not, we are moving," Dialphio said stiffly. "For example, just the other day, Azazel had one of ours assigned to the Circle's Gateway monitoring station."

"One demon? What will that do?"

"It's a start," Bilba said kindly, "right, Dialphio?"

"Right." She reached across the table and laid a freckled hand on Ralrek's arm. In her eyes, I saw the toll of her work. She looked older, tired. "I know this is moving too slowly for the three of you. You're the ones taking the brunt of the changes. Please don't think that's not recognized. But if we're reckless, we're all dead, and then nothing changes."

"I understand where both of you are coming from," I said, holding up a meatball I'd stabbed with my fork, "but I don't understand why you called us. Obviously, it's something you didn't want to communicate in the notebook, and I doubt we're here just because you wanted us to eat something hearty. What's going on?"

Ralrek grunted and pushed back from the table. "I'm getting seconds."

I watched him saunter away. "Don't take all the meatballs."

He twirled his fork in the air as a response.

Even Bilba watched him warily.

The cousins looked at each other. Dialphio dipped her head, deferring to the Founder. Azazel clasped his hands and leaned forward. "This isn't a worry for you boys, but it will offer a context for why I will push you hard to find Libra."

"Okay," Bilba said slowly.

"During your recent trials, you've seen how dysfunctional the Council has become."

Bilba and I nodded. Ralrek continued eating, aggressively stabbing each meatball.

"What you haven't seen, because it's above your access to information, is that things are worse than they appear."

Dialphio cleared her throat. "The Council is disintegrating."

"What?" Bilba said, his fork clunking on the dish when he set it down just a little too hard.

From the table, dipping the ladle into the crock pot, Ralrek said, "You've got to be kidding me?"

"I'm afraid I'm not, "Azazel said, tapping a finger against the back of his opposite palm. "Faster than expected, too."

"Why? What changed?" I asked.

"Fractions. They're like hellhounds who've caught a scent. My peers have seen the Council's disintegration coming. They might have even manufactured much of it. And so, they're making their moves."

"What moves?" Bilba asked.

"To control more of the Underworld," Azazel said, sounding tired. He scanned us, registering our confusion. "From what I've seen, there are concerning variances in how the Circles are being administered."

"I'm confused. What does that mean?" I said, setting my fork down, meatballs forgotten.

"My fear," Azazel responded, stressing the second word, "is that my peers are digging their fingers into their personal circles of influence. Where they find a finger-hold, they cling and dig deeper."

"We think they're laying groundwork for independent councils," Dialphio said.

Bilba's jaw fell. "Independent states? Is that what you're talking about?"

"Possibly." Azazel nodded.

"Like, you mean Hell is splintering?" I said, stunned.

"It's within the realm of possibilities." Azazel stopped tapping the back of his hand with that thumping finger. "To be clear, a fractured Underworld is dangerous. I would hate to think what it would look like if the day comes that demons like Seraph, Beelzebub, and Apopis hold complete control of portions of our world."

A fractured Hell. Powerful demons controlling their own slices of it. Fighting each other for more power. Innocent demons falling under the unquestioned governance of someone like Beelzebub. Calling it disturbing didn't capture the essence of that potential future.

"What's Lucifer doing about this?" I asked.

Azazel finally unlocked his hands and opened them, as if he was holding something we couldn't see. "What he's been doing for hundreds of thousands of years."

"Absolutely nothing," I finished for the Founder.

Dialphio stood. "Let me get everyone dessert. This is a lot to think about, I know. We hate bringing you this news."

"Surely, you see why it's important, and why we must find the Horn," Azazel said, his mouth pinching. "If Libra can help us, then it's imperative you spend every free minute finding out what happened to him. I'll do what I can on my end, but the Underworld needs you. The Council misjudged by exiling you. Now, you have virtually free rein to move as you need, as the situation demands. That's our advantage. Maybe our only one."

Dialphio returned with smaller ceramic plates. Each held a fat slice of key lime pie that could have easily fed three. She set one plate in front of each of us. Ralrek came back, set his meatball-littered plate down, and slide the pie plate to the side. Baked crust and hints of vanilla cream made my mouth water. The bookstore owner's expression was grim. "Make no mistake; what we're talking about is civil war. We all know where this is headed. We just don't know how it ends."

7

UNDERWORLD, ISLE OF DREAD

THE NIGHT SKY HAD TURNED PURPLE LONG AGO. DARKNESS gripped Hell. Quite the double entendre, I know.

We'd returned from the Fifth Circle unscathed. The dock was quiet. Though twenty torches lined the dock and surrounding area, I couldn't make out any hidden threats, and no one tapped into their Abilities either. Maybe the Council's thugs couldn't be bothered. Maybe they were asleep on the job. Maybe they were simply keeping tabs on us the best they could. Regardless, it was uneventful enough that we slept through most of the return trip to the Isle.

Which was why, once home, I was wide awake and sitting alone on the beach. I had thinking to do.

Being back in the Fifth brought back a flood of feelings I wasn't ready to experience. Seeing Dialphio was great. Standing in The Book Abyss was a moment of reassuring sentiment. But we were prisoners in our own home Circle, not even free enough to get a coffee at Chilly Willy's and see if Gigi still worked there. Stepping outside Dialphio's bookstore would have meant taking unnecessary risks that could have doomed all of Hell, whether or not they appreciated or even knew of it.

But I would have liked to have strolled by my parents' home. Not to check in on them, but to see how easily they were moving on from my father's betrayal.

During our sentencing by the Council, the one that got us exiled to the Isle of Dread, my father had provided false testimony that condemned us and resulted in Bilba being stripped of the one life goal he had. How did you walk away from something like that? Forgiveness was out of the question— I'm no angel, I only try to be the best me I can be. His betrayal hurt. Forgive? No way. Could I forget?

I couldn't. Definitely not now. Maybe never.

Lilith Sunstone was a different story. She didn't share my father's blame. She was her own demon; a caring and tortured succubus. What was she thinking about her son's exilement to the Isle? How damaging was it to her spirit to think, maybe not incorrectly, that she'd never see me again? Did she have the fortitude to see this out, or would it crush her? Kanthor Sunstone would bear the weight of that.

How could she share a home with the man who'd betrayed his own son?

She deserved better, but I couldn't deliver 'better' for her any more than I could fly a humanitarian airlift operation and air drop hope for my fellow exiles.

My mother never wanted to see her family tearing apart. She played her role and demanded I play mine. But was she capable of making Kanthor turn his around? Once, she reminded me that not every demon gets a chance to say goodbye to loved ones. She'd begged me to 'not let that become our story.'

But sitting here alone, for the first time not worried about starving because Dialphio's meatballs were still slugging their way through my intestines, I didn't see any other outcome. Kanthor Sunstone had betrayed his only son, along with Bilba and Ralrek. He'd deprived Bilba of the title he deserved, the title he'd earned. The cost of his lies didn't stop with us. In a way, my father's actions deprived Akimon Ravenous of Bilba's company and love. Ralrek had no family, but his life had been turned upside down as well. My father's fingers were all over that mess.

Tonight, trying to relax to the rhythmic ocean waves, I wouldn't reach a conclusion about how I could satisfy my mother. I couldn't even make peace with my inability to make peace.

Crazy Zeke interrupted my troubling thoughts. "He comes. You arrive."

I bolted into a sitting position. My neck tingled. "Creed."

The halberd zipped into my open hand without me looking for it.

From the darkness, a form slowly emerged, drifting along the line between beach and ocean. In the poor light, I couldn't tell if it was an incubus or succubus. They were taller than me, that's for sure, but that's also not saying much. Their hair was longer. Shoulder length. I could tell because of how its light color contrasted with the night. Their gait was slow, as if each step needed to be deliberate.

The tingle bothered me. I'd felt it before, and it wasn't a pleasant experience. Crazy Zeke's message heightened my sense of wariness. What did it mean, 'he comes, you arrive?' That was crazy talk, but again, when you heard voices no one else heard, that was essentially the definition of the experience.

I swung around, risking taking my eyes off the approaching demon. There was no ambush. No tribe of fifty waiting to jump me from behind and drag me to their camp to make Zeke stew. The beach was empty of everything but sand crabs, me, and this approaching presence.

Friend or enemy? I was about to find out.

I pushed my Sense in the demon's direction. Nothing. Though the tingle was persistent, and my gut told me who to expect, my brain was trying to override the precautionary message. But that slow gait. The tall but bent frame. Closer now, I could see their hair was gray. All of it led to one conclusion that simultaneously was so obvious, but one I refused to accept.

I was sharing the beach with the ruler of Hell, and Bilba and Ralrek were nowhere to be found thanks to my insistence on getting some quiet Zeke-time.

Lucifer paused ten feet away. He stuffed his hands in his black overcoat pockets as if he meant to stave off a non-existent chill. Rings of his unwashed hair whipped about his neck. When he spoke, his voice sounded like animated rust. "Ezekial, may I approach?"

The lord of demons was asking for my permission? What madness was this? Had the island already broken me and this was nothing but a dream? In the list of fantastic dreams I wanted to come true, this was well below any involving Cassie.

A trap. This had to be a trap. The Council... But, wait. This was Lucifer, the king of demons, the big cheese, la mera mera. He didn't need the Council's permission or direction. He did what and went where He wanted, when He wanted.

"Yes," I said, sounding far less confident than I should have if I was serious about no longer being pushed around.

Hands still tucked in His pockets, Lucifer shuffled across the sand. A few feet away, He stopped. Under His thick eyebrows, His bantam eyes bore into me. I tried my hardest not to shuffle. Then He turned and faced the ocean, closing His eyes and tilting His head back, inhaling. "I love the smell of the ocean in the air. Have you gotten used to it yet?"

"Uh," I said, stumbling to think of something to say and facing the beach, so I wasn't awkwardly looking at His side profile. "It's growing on me. Yeah."

"The freshness. The way the breeze carries away the smell

of sulfur." He opened the flyspecks for eyes, head still tilted, and wagged a finger at the largest body of water in Hell. "But it's the waves. The sound. A constant reminder of their power. No matter how much any of us would like to think we control things, no matter how powerful we are or see ourselves becoming, the ocean waves are eternal and always mightier."

I watched the hull of the ocean, the few waves I could see, roll toward us, cresting and crashing in white froth against a somber background.

When He didn't elicit a response, the ruler of all demons, still watching the ocean, inhaled deeply again. It was a slow, lazy sound, as if even His body was tired of ignoring Him. "I imagine my presence has made you nervous. I can sense it."

"You could say that."

"I understand, and apologize."

Now Satan Himself was apologizing? Okay, this was officially nuts. In my time in the Overworld, I'd seen reality television shows enough to understand the concept of hidden camera comedy. More than a part of me wanted to turn back toward the forest to see if I could catch a glimmer of a reflection off a camera lens.

"For what?"

Lucifer side-eyed me. "For disturbing your reflection. Your introspection. Life on the Isle is difficult and takes some getting used to. You've been here for how long? Just about a week?"

"Yes." I wanted to ask why Lucifer cared. After all, He was ultimately responsible for us being here, even though we'd done nothing wrong. But when did doing the right thing, or at least not doing the wrong thing, matter?

"You'll get used to it," He said. "It gets easier, especially once you learn how to cultivate the land and have a reliable shelter. The weather is pleasant enough. The Isle doesn't have the storms of Overworld islands. That's a nice feature."

"Still not exactly easy living," I said. "I'd prefer my own place, with my TV, junk food, and booze."

Lucifer laughed. A jaded, half-hearted sound. But a laugh just the same. "I imagine you would."

"So would the hundreds exiled here."

A series of crashing waves filled our silence, the constant roar of moving water ensuring there was an auditory distraction.

Finally, Lucifer chuckled. I almost missed it under the boom of a fat roll of waves smashing against the sand.

"Did I say something funny?"

He shook His head. "No. No. It just hit me you haven't called me by name yet."

"You... you want me to?"

"No one has had the courage to refer to me as 'the big guy' before. Especially not in the face of my Council."

Oh, bless it. That name. "Uh, sorry about that."

"Are you?" Lucifer asked, aiming the question at the ocean. "Are you truly sorry about anything you've done?"

Ah, now we were getting somewhere. "We all have regrets, don't we? Of course, I'm sorry for a lot of crappy things I've said and done. Aren't you?"

Lucifer squinted, making His beady eyes almost disappear. "I don't believe in living with regrets. But if I had the power, I wouldn't be able to list all the things I'd do differently if I could do them over again. We'd be here for an eternity, and neither one of us has that much time."

"You do."

This time, Lucifer's laugh was heartier.

"Yes, yes, I imagine you'd see it like that. But even my time has limitations. That's one reason I don't believe in living with regrets. In a finite reality, spending time on regrets is pointless."

I shrugged, seeing the irony of the ruler of Hell taking my

precious thinking time for a baffling purpose. "You have that luxury."

Me and my big mouth.

"What do you mean?" Lucifer didn't sound pissed or even agitated. Instead, His question sounded genuinely curious.

When you're already balls to the wall, you might as well go out with a bang and slap it around a little. "Leo Neto was a good demon. A good guy in a shitty situation. Someone who did everything to take care of his family. An excellent servant to you. And look what it got him."

"The name doesn't sound familiar. Should it?"

Okay, now He was pissing me off. The conversation had been benign up to this point, and I really shouldn't have expected someone of His station to know everyone in Hell, or even those the Council brought to His attention. But Leo had a special place in my heart. Even though we'd started off on the wrong foot—I had that tendency with a lot of demons, it seems—in the end, I saw his true heart. He was someone who'd do whatever he could for those he loved. And he, like far too many, got screwed by the Council. Lucifer had approved my fight to the death against Leo. The fight that earned me my freedom, but one that had taken a good guy from the world. Lucifer was in the stadium stands that day. A recent event. Yet, Leo was so insignificant Lucifer couldn't put a name with a face at the end of its life?

"Guess not. Just someone you sentenced to death and stole from his family. With the way Hell is running, I'm not surprised. I learned that early on when your boy toy, Beelzebub, killed Aries."

Both guns blazing.

Lucifer groaned.

I remained silently seething. Even the rhythmic cadence of the ocean couldn't settle what churned inside me.

"We were friends," Lucifer said after a long while.

I blinked. "Who?"

"Aries and me." Lucifer adjusted, hands still stuffed in His pockets. The only sign I hadn't pushed Him far enough to roast me where I stood. He was the only immortal I'd ever met who could hide His Ability. In my fight against Leo, the ruler of the Underworld had cast against us to ensure we carried out His sentence, and I'd never felt it coming. I hated that. Hated that it was in the back of my mind that I'd always be on the back foot with Him.

"I didn't think you'd have friends."

Another chuckle, as incongruous as ketchup on chicken wings. "My best friend. I still miss him."

Now I faced Lucifer. Screw it. Let him fry me. "Then why let a piece of shit like Beelzebub assassinate him? Do you know what Aries was involved in? What he was actually doing? Do you know how he helped mortals? Do you know he wasn't doing anything subversive against You or the stupid Council?"

Lucifer's response was so even, so calm, He could have stilled the Acheron Ocean. "I know everything about Aries."

I saw His monotony and raised it with a layer of ice. "Yet you let Beelzebub murder him."

"Aries was there from the beginning," Lucifer said after a while, as if he hadn't heard me—or that my comment didn't matter. "When the duties of the realm became overwhelming, he was the first to help. When I couldn't wrangle all the ember cats, if you will, he settled me." Lucifer paused, squinting a few more times, as if he was trying to make out something in the night sky. "Did you know he was integral in forming the Council, the Circles? That he was the first Major demon?"

"I didn't."

"Quite an incubus, Aries. I miss him."

Sorry, but it was too obvious, like a bully thrusting their jaw forward, tapping it, and daring you to punch them. "Then why allow him to be murdered? Why allow that walking sack of muscles to continue walking around free to terrorize whoever he wants?"

To say it shocked me when Lucifer dropped his head would be an overstatement, but I hadn't expected that reaction.

"There are many things you cannot yet see, Ezekial."

I didn't like the fact that Lucifer was so comfortable using my name. As if we had anything approaching the loosest definition of a friendship. Over the past months and years, I'd collected shoves toward a destiny I didn't want. Rebel cells were popping up all over the Underworld, becoming more vociferous with every passing day. They drove efforts forward under the auspices that one day I would challenge Lucifer for His title. With those undercurrents, it was unnerving to have Him use my name. What was His endgame?

"Enlighten me."

"In time," He said, exhaling slowly.

I stepped away. I had to. Punching the lord of demons in the face was hardly a mechanism toward finding peace, serenity, and comfort. Running my hands through my ragged hair, I spun. "What's this about then? Why are you here? What do you want?"

I couldn't help it. Sorry-not-sorry. Had Dialphio or Azazel, Bilba or Ralrek been here, I'm sure my short rant would have resulted in dropped jaws and my name being spoken in chastising tones. Alone with the big boss man, I didn't have that concern. Of course, His presence gave me enough of those as it was.

Since I'd stepped toward the ocean, I was a few feet in front of Lucifer. His gaze fell on me. The night was too dark to make out much detail, but I could see His eyes narrow. "I wanted to meet you. Away from the Council. Away from your family and friends. From anything that might influence our discussion."

"Why?"

"To see what sort of demon you are."

Oh, boy. How many smartass responses did I have lined up?

Lucifer didn't give me a chance to fire them. He pulled His hands out of His pockets. I would have snagged Creed if it'd given me a warning, but the collapsed halberd was as dormant as my love life. Without being able to sense Lucifer tapping into His Ability, I had no idea if He was readying a spell or not.

"Do you have questions you'd like to ask of me?" He said.

"In what way?"

"Anyway. Anything you'd like to know or ask?"

"Anything?"

"Yes."

Oh gee, let me see where I could start. Could He reincarnate Aries and make him exactly the same incubus I knew for far too short of a time? How about imprisoning Seraph, Beelzebub, and Apopis in an isolated prison in the middle of the All, where they'd never ruin anyone's life? How about teaching my father what the unconditional love of a parent was supposed to look like? Heavens, at this point in my despondency, I'd take a lifetime supply of chicken wings.

None of those things, Lucifer would grant me. I'm not the brightest demon in Hell, but I knew that much. I'd test His offer with something reasonable that would also allow other wheels to remain in motion. So, I said, "Bring Leo's family to the Isle."

His expression was unreadable, as if I'd said something in a foreign language he didn't care to decipher. "Why?"

"Because I don't trust those you put in charge of Hell," I said as honestly, and maybe a little too rawly, as possible. "In case you're unaware, they're as dysfunctional as dysfunctional gets, and you did his family no favors when you forced

Leo to fight me in the pit. Doing this will protect them from your unscrupulous Council."

"Life on the Isle is difficult. You would want that for them?"

"They'd be safe," I answered immediately. "Safe from powerful demons who'd want to harm them. Plus, they're good demons, and one of the tribes would take them in, I'm sure."

"They have free will. What if they don't wish to be exiled?"

"I could talk to them."

For a fraction of a miniscule portion of a second, I swear Lucifer's lips moved like He was about to smile. "How? You're exiled. A prisoner of the Isle."

Well, shit.

"Though I can't force them to come to the Isle, I can ensure those discussions happen." He stuffed His hands back in His overcoat pockets. "Though I make no promises. They would make an interesting addition to your already interesting circles, Ezekial."

"Meaning?" Was Lucifer aware of our ability to get off the Isle? He knew who I was spending time with? Did that extend to Dialphio and the rebel cell? Did He know Azazel was wrapped up in this? Could I stop Lucifer if He was aware? Even to protect those I cared about and those working to change a corrupt government? Could I kill Satan Himself to make sure all of them lived to see another rebellious day?

The tingle was still there, subtly raking my skin. But I didn't feel the first hint of an invasive push into my thoughts. The Council had tried that numerous times in their chamber. Creed cock blocked them at each turn. But before it, they could invade thoughts there. Could Lucifer do it here or anywhere He chose, even if I held the magical halberd that was supposedly pooped out of the All?

"Well, your two friends have quite interesting stories," He said. "They've already accomplished so much, and I cannot foresee them not continuing on their paths. Rebel mage and a wayward son."

He didn't sound bothered by Bilba's new title, even though he'd gotten it because he broke multiple laws. And just what in the heaven was a wayward son, and what did it have to do with Ralrek? Would my friend know? If so, why wouldn't he have shared it before? No, there was something more there.

I was about to ask for clarification when Lucifer said, "You have close friends and associates, and many around the Circles who know your story, even if it's a folklore version. Few achieve that, especially in the days of the Third Council. Of course, that doesn't include Cassie."

My breath stopped. He knew about her? How? And how much? Shit and double shit.

"Does her father know about the time the two of you have spent together, I wonder?" He said without a devious smile or threatening smirk. "Maybe. Maybe not. Sadly, I don't have the time or inclination to inquire. It doesn't matter to me that you do, by the way."

I didn't dare say a word, worried my mouth would betray me, the aims set for me by others, and the secrets shared between us.

Lucifer didn't appear bothered by my silence. "Well, I will take my leave." The pocket of his overcoat bulged with a hand movement, and a Gateway opened instantly within arm's reach, perpendicular to my position and blocked what waited on the other side.

I set myself, sure He meant to zap me out of existence and head home for a nap.

Lucifer turned to the Gateway, stopping before stepping through. He didn't look my way, but stared into the other realm. "You seek answers, Ezekial? Start asking questions. Cassie would be a superb source."

Then Lucifer, the ruler of Hell, the king of demons, the yin to the Council's yang, stepped into the Gateway. It collapsed as soon as His lagging foot disappeared, leaving me alone again on the beach. Just me, the cathartic waves, and the cool night air. Just as my night started, it ended. Now, though, instead of the smell of salt air, a buzz of questions and the implications of their answers rumbled inside my head.

8

ACHERON OCEAN

I didn't tell the guys about Lucifer opening a Gateway on the Isle. I probably should have, but I didn't get the chance. As we sailed across the Acheron, I ran through the interaction with the ruler of this domain. The retelling was choppier than the ocean's waves. We needed to prepare for anything the Council's hidden forces would throw at us once we reached the dock. Bilba didn't need distractions, so I left out the part about Lucifer's Isle Gateway. I'd tell him when we got back in one piece. Then he could test his capabilities all he wanted and Ralrek could try his hand at them too, and probably take the entire island with him.

Halfway across the ocean, Ralrek proposed using his Fire Ability to propel the raft. His argument was that the Council was already aware of and watching our actions, so it wouldn't matter if he cast or not. A solid position. Neither Bilba nor I disagreed, and we were soon hanging onto the mast for dear life while the raft skimmed across the water's surface.

I won't lie. Besides saving time, it was childishly fun, and if I needed anything in my life to compliment the answers I sought and the chicken wings I desired, it was a bit of levity.

But it's hard to laugh when your clumsy friend topples overboard into the Acheron Ocean.

"Stop!" I shouted, even as Ralrek cut off his spell.

He'd used such force that our momentum carried us too far from Bilba, whose pale head bobbed in the water.

"We've got to grab him!" Ralrek said, as I adjusted, ready for the Fire user to reverse our position.

Bilba's voice barely reached us; his words were indecipherable.

The raft, designed to traverse the ocean in a straight line from the island to mainland Underworld, wasn't constructed to stop. We were drifting farther from our friend, and there was no way in all of Hell Bilba could catch the raft.

"Look," Ralrek said, his face falling.

Behind Bilba's floating head, the ocean roiled. A circle of frothy waves pulsed outward around a central point.

"What's that?"

"The kraken," I answered, scrambling to think of a way to save our friend.

Bilba had noticed the way the water moved even before the first tentacle broke the surface. Lunging into awkward kicks and strokes, his head rocked side to side as he did his best to cut through the water.

We were moving away and the implications of the first viewable part of the kraken's anatomy were clear. It unrolled, and the tentacle reached sixty feet in the air. As soon as the full creature emerged and spotted my buddy, he was a goner. Heavens, if it picked him out from below, he was doomed. No matter how fast he could swim, even muscles driven by panic, he wouldn't be able to outrace the reach of that single tentacle—and who knew how many tentacles a kraken had?

"Get to the front and use your Fire to propel us back to him," I said. Ralrek stood, stunned, looking up at the tentacle still rising from the ocean's depths. "Now!"

Ralrek blinked and shook his head, but bolted for the

opposite end of the raft. Even before he was in place, I felt the familiar scratching sensation of his Fire spell.

I couldn't do anything to help him move the raft, but I could help Bilba as long as Creed participated in this rescue operation.

I activated the halberd, feeling relief at the metallic clink of the three blades snapping from the haft once Creed extended to its full length. "Don't screw around unless you want to become driftwood," I warned the halberd. "That's my friend."

Already, the raft was rocking, partially from Ralrek's beam of Fire thrusting us to Bilba's position, but also from the competing force of the kraken's waves now reaching us. As they hit Bilba from behind, he was lifted. Panic painted his expression. When he disappeared behind the next roll, my fear matched his.

Three more tentacles shot skyward, each as long as the first. The kraken's fin pierced the air above the Acheron, broader than any ship I'd ever seen on television or in the ports around Seattle.

A deep moaning sound reverberated from underneath the water as the creature's trunk slowly slid out of the depths. Up, it crept into the sky.

"Holy Lucifer." I groaned. I'm sure Ralrek said something behind me, but I couldn't make it out over my own near-apoplexy and his stream of fire pushing the raft toward not only Bilba, but the goliath coming out of the ocean deep.

Thank Lucifer for us being in the middle of the Acheron. The constant ocean breeze probably carried away the smell of Bilba crapping his pants at the aquatic horror.

Bilba paddled, splashing small sprays that paled compared to the creature's. His mouth opened so wide I'm sure he drank more than his fill of salt water. A tentacle that could have pulled the stalactites from the roof of the Under-world crashed down so slowly I could have warned Bilba if he could have heard me. I don't think I breathed until I saw the appendage, as thick as a Circle's clock tower, smash thirty yards from him.

I couldn't even exhale in relief, because the resulting wave lifted Bilba and sent him careening out of our path.

"Can you move the raft off-course?" I shouted to Ralrek, pointing in our friend's digressive path.

"I don't know, but hold on." Ralrek growled before squatting and extending both hands. He pulled them back to his sides before shooting them forward. His beam of fire thickened. The raft surged forward.

"Careful you don't run over him!"

"Take care of the kraken," he responded, winning the tit-for-tat. He would; all he had to do was blow hot air. I had to fight something that was bigger than the Isle's beach.

What the heaven could I do to a kraken? I still hadn't seen the full size of the thing, but the portion that stuck out of the water was taller than the Space Needle in Seattle.

I heard the roar right before I found myself on my backside when Ralrek put more oomph into his spell. The bow of the raft pulled skyward, and for a moment I worried he was about to dump us into the water. I couldn't tell because I was too busy scrambling for the mast, but it felt like the stern was the only part of the vessel still in contact with the ocean.

"Slow down!"

Ralrek couldn't hide his astonishment. "I can't. Have. To. Get. To. Bilba."

"We'll run over him if you're not careful, and I can't do a thing to the kraken at this speed." Heaven, I couldn't even stand. Squatting was out of the question. I clung to the mast for dear life.

With a *whoooom*, the bow crashed down, sending a spray of water over us, drenching me.

It took me a moment to get my bearings, but when I did, I saw the pink underside of a tentacle that could smash the raft and splinter any splinters of log left. There was no time to worry about our positioning. No time to worry about whether Ralrek could get us away from the descending tentacle. No time to even think about my best friend, swimming for his life from a simple error that might rob him of it. There was only time for one thing.

And its name was Creed.

I jerked the double-ax heads up and yelled—because yelling helps me sound tougher than a three-hundred-year-old impling playing ouija with their sibling.

The azure of Hellfire encased the ax heads before I blinked. Before the second blink, the oval of the flame of annihilation had formed a thick, blue beam, thicker than Ralrek's Fire spell. Thicker than any tree, any clock tower. Heavens, it was thicker than a lot of the buildings in Old Towne.

And that beautiful beam of blue tore through the kraken's tentacle, slicing it cleanly. Forty feet of rubbery, suckered appendage flew above the beast. The air was filled with the low, sad moan of the injured Acheron's defender. Half a mile away, the separated tentacle splashed down into the ocean.

I didn't stop there. With my heart pounding in my chest, I ignored the fact we were drawing closer to Bilba and pulled on the turmoil boiling inside me. I thrust Creed forward, shooting another beam of Hellfire, ripping another appendage off the gigantic beast. This second tentacle splashed down somewhere far, far behind the kraken.

Its moan took on a high-pitched cry. I sort of felt bad for the blasted thing. It was just doing its job, just as we were doing ours. All of us, slaves to the whims of those who set the rules to play by.

I pulled Creed back, readying a third attack as Bilba swam away and Ralrek pushed us closer. But the kraken reacted defensively. Done with the fight, it descended, sinking beneath the waves as we pulled our friend onto the deck.

"Goodness," Bilba said as he rolled onto his back, his hands flapping on his chest as he panted. "That was scary."

"You don't say?" Ralrek said, standing over him and smirking—because that's what incubi do when they care about another incubus.

"Come on, sit up," I said, giving him a hand. "What do you say we let you rest until we get to the dock? Hopefully, you have enough left in you to open that Gateway to the Overworld?"

"Why? You want to see your giiiiirlfriend?" Bilba asked, obviously feeling fine.

"Shut up before I toss you overboard again."

9

OLYMPIA

"Wow, that sounds absolutely terrifying, Z-Zeke," Cassie said.

Or at least I think she did. It's so hard to concentrate on words when she's around.

In my hesitation, Bilba stepped forward. "It was. You should have seen it. Do they have kraken in the Upperworld?"

She snickered. A trickle of water flowing over rocks in the serenity of Eve's Sanctuary couldn't have been more pleasant. "No. No, we don't. I'm so sorry you guys had to go through that just to meet me."

"It was worth it," I said before my brain engaged.

"Oh, there he is," Ralrek laughed. "Nice of you to join us."

"Whatever. Listen, Cassie, I don't want to rush anything because it's great to see you. I mean, it feels like forever since we've seen each other. So much has happened. But we've got business to discuss." Lucifer, I was rambling.

"Do we need to give you two a moment alone?" Ralrek asked, nudging Bilba with an elbow. Both of them wore stupid expressions.

"Yes," I said.

"No, that's okay," Cassie replied at the same time.

Bilba and Ralrek's eyes could have been connected, the way they swiveled between me, Hell's reject and possible savior, and Cassie Haniel, drop-dead stunning angel and member of Yahweh's Council.

"Well, I mean, if you want them to leave," she said, turning her crystal blue orbs on me.

Of course, she said that right as I turned to her and said, "If you'd prefer them to be here, I get it."

"You two are insufferable," Ralrek said, dismissing us with a wave.

"I'd say they're gross, but there's something adorable about it," Bilba said.

"I think they'd benefit," Cassie said, searching my eyes. Slow and deep—just like I liked it. Unless it was Cassie. Then it was uncomfortable. Not because she made me feel uneasy or creepy, but because talking to her was like an exercise in learning how to resist completely baring your soul.

"Fine, but no more wisecracks," I said to the pair of grinning incubi.

Ralrek held up his hands in surrender. "We wouldn't think about it."

"Never," Bilba echoed.

"You were lucky to catch me in Olympia," Cassie said, taking a seat at the end of the park bench.

Bilba sat on the opposite end, and Ralrek leaned against a squared pole painted forest green. For the time of year, the day was moderate, and it wasn't snowing—which it rarely did in Olympia—or rainy, which was a literal miracle. I took a seat on the cold concrete near, but not at—I'm not that pathetic—Cassie's feet. I would have been too far from the conversation if I'd sat at the only other bench under the gazebo. Sitting next to her, though, that would master a worse fate—having to listen to Bilba and Ralrek tease me all the way back across the Acheron about my supposed infatuation with the cocoa-haired beauty. So concrete it was.

"So," Cassie said, her face beaming in glorious radiance, "tell me about this weird stuff you mentioned in the note. What's going on, Z-Z-Zeke?"

I gave her a brief run-down of what it was like on the island. Cassie already knew the basics because I'd been quietly sending her notes every other day. Writing to her daily would have come across as stalkerish, and I didn't want to bother her. She was on Yahweh's Council now—man, that's still difficult to wrap my head around—and she's a busy angel. We were already lucky to get this time—my sense, not her words.

Bilba played with his fingernails, and Ralrek stopped leaning against the pole and joined me on the concrete. But when I brought up my chat with Lucifer, things changed. I'd swear, the wind stopped cutting across the empty city park and not a single one of them blinked until I finished recalling the full experience.

"He told you to talk to me?" Cassie asked when I finished. Her permanently horizontal eyebrows drew down, and her small mouth pinched.

"Yeah, I wasn't exactly excited about the fact that He knew about you."

"This isn't good." Ralrek stood and began pacing in front of the pole this time.

"How could He know about me and you guys?" Cassie looked between the three of us. Unlike the other two, there wasn't a hint of nervousness in her eyes. Instead, she seemed curious He'd encouraged me to have another chat with the angel.

"Could be a set up?"

Ralrek snorted. "You don't say?"

"I don't know, guys," Bilba said, looking at a point across the wet grass and tapping his chin. "Why would He go through all that trouble? For what? He's Lucifer, the ultimate arbiter."

"In the Underworld," Cassie said assertively.

Bilba nodded like he'd already realized his mistake. "Yes, true. More to my point, is that He doesn't need to waste time. He could literally do what He wants with us, when He wants. Why go through the trouble of a night-time visit to convince you to bring us here to chat with Cassie? It doesn't make sense. Not when you realize He could have abolished you right there on the beach, strolled to our camp, and done the same to us while we were sleeping."

"You've got a point. He specifically brought up the point that I have questions." I locked my gaze on Cassie and forced myself not to fall into those crystalline pools of blue. "And He told me to start with you."

"Ze-Zeke, I hope you know I'd answer any questions you have."

"I do. So let's start with something you've never answered."

She fidgeted on the bench, making it creak. "Okay?"

"To who does Seraph owe a favor?"

Cassie paused, blinking a couple of times as if she was collecting her thoughts. "Do you really want to know? I don't want the truth to discourage you guys."

"Yes, we want to know. Doesn't matter what you say; we have to prepare. I can't imagine the fracturing of Lucifer's Council has done anything positive for demon and angel relationships."

"And it's not like that would stop Beelzebub and Apopis from carrying out their plans in the Overworld," Bilba added.

Cassie shook her head. "It hasn't. Trust me."

Ralrek stopped pacing long enough to ask, "Gotten worse?"

"Worse than destroying a women's clinic and terrorizing the people who need it, and those who serve it? No, I wouldn't say that. They haven't gone quiet, though, as the Council suspected they might."

"So the Upperworld's Council is still tracking them?" I asked.

"Of course. Why wouldn't we?"

"It makes sense, and you definitely should. Part of me worries about the Balance going out of whack, though. With everyone on our Council interested in doing their own thing, I can't imagine we're operating at full capacity, but I doubt we can say the same for angels."

There was a flicker of something on Cassie's face, an instant reaction she covered at once.

"So if the Upperworld is operating as normal and Hell isn't, it's not hard to foresee a situation where the Balance shifts. If for no other reason than simply because angels are pushing their influence as normal, to be fair. Because demons might not be able to. The Balance could tip, just from that dynamic alone." My thoughts swirled with everything I wanted to ask her. It was difficult, if not impossible, to snag just one. "Maybe you guys should back off for the time being. Let things in Hell settle."

"Back off?"

"Yeah. Give us a chance to straighten out our mess before all of us wake up one day to realize the mortals have had years of angel influence, putting everything in the Overworld out of whack and careening toward the end."

"Ze-Zeke, I don't know what we can do," she said, sitting back. "It's not like we can stop operating in the Overworld until Lucifer's Council gets their house in order. Especially when your own Council members are actively influencing mortals through subversion and outright hostilities."

"But you've got a say, Cassie. You're part of Yahweh's blessed Council."

"Please don't swear."

"Yeah, sorry. Not important right now, though." I scooted

closer, my jeans making a scratching sound on the rough, chilly concrete. "Maybe that's why Lucifer told me to seek answers from you. If He knows an eighth of what we've talked about, then it wouldn't be much of a leap to think He'd anticipate the problems and the advantages of our relationship."

Her eyes widened. "Are you saying you think Lucifer wants angels' help with His own Council?"

Ralrek had stopped pacing. Bilba sat forward with his hands on his knees. I could almost see the wheels turning in his head.

"Why not? He sure as shit can't handle them."

"Zeke might be onto something," Bilba finally said. "The Council is a mess. It's been a mess. According to Azazel, it's only getting worse." I held my groan at Bilba name-dropping the Founder, our source for so much juicy information about the inner workings of Hell's governing body.

"I guess so, guys. I mean, I'd get laughed out of the next Council meeting if I brought this to them without more solid proof."

"What kind would you need?" Ralrek asked.

"That's the thing. I don't know. How can you prove Lucifer is turning to others to help Him deal with His own demons? That's a betrayal, especially if He truly meant for you to come to an angel for help. I can't just drop that on our Council without something."

"Then we need to work on that," Bilba said, sounding determined.

"Do wayward sons have anything to do with that?" I asked, watching for her and Ralrek's reactions.

The tall incubus gave me no sign he had any idea what I was talking about.

Cassie scrunched her face. "Wayward sons? What's that?"

"I was hoping you knew. Lucifer mentioned it, then told

me about seeking answers from you. I thought it might mean something to you, but I guess not."

"Sorry, Z-Zeke. I can't answer that."

I bobbed a shoulder. "It seemed like an odd comment, anyway. But you can help us understand what we're facing because you know who Seraph owes a favor."

"I do," she nodded, dragging out her answer. "She owes Yahweh."

My mouth hung open. I already had a follow-on question, right until she answered my actual question with something I never saw coming.

"Yahweh?" Bilba said as if he'd heard her incorrectly.

With a sigh, Cassie answered. "Yes. She's trouble. I told you guys that."

"Yes, but we didn't know she's indebted to Yahweh," Ralrek said, leaning back against the pole and crossing his arms. "How'd that happen?"

"It's a long story."

He gave her a suspicious look. Ralrek was always the last one to come around on issues of trust, especially with angels. It was in his DNA. "We're in no hurry."

"Down boy," I warned.

Cassie flopped her hands in her lap, staring down into her palms. "Seraph didn't come from a wealthy or influential family. She wasn't well-off. But she was a hustler. Everyone knew that. A dangerous combination, when someone who is intelligent is also willing to work their butt off."

"She's conniving too," Bilba said.

Cassie huffed. "That's not the half of it. A politician to the core. She'll steal the cloak from your back and then convince you it's your fault you're freezing to death."

Yep, that was Seraph. "What did she do to get herself in so deep with Yahweh that she's still indebted to Him after all this time? I mean, she's been a demon now for, what, millennia?"

"Her and Michael being traded to the Underworld for two of Lucifer's Council came about mostly because Yahweh could no longer trust her after she'd risen to power. It was a historic time in Council's formation. A lot of things were still being organized and ironed out. Seraph used that lack of boundaries to her advantage and positioned herself as the go-to Council member for many of the Upperworld's highest order of angels."

"Order of angels?" I asked.

"Like ranks in the military, Zeke," Bilba said. "Angels are born into a specific order. Sort of like a caste system."

"Gross."

"Right?"

"It's all we know," Cassie said noncommittally. "Ironically, it might have been the motivation for Seraph to push as hard as she did. I don't think anyone will ever know for sure."

"It's not like she'd share her story, and who could trust her if she did?" The three grumbled their agreement to my sentiment. "So what did Yahweh save her from?"

"Unscrupulous behavior," Cassie said. "Illegal activities. Taking bribes. Undue influence of mortals. Inappropriate relationships with demons. You name it, Seraph has probably been guilty of it at one point. Some seem to have that magic, to get away with stuff most of us wouldn't dream of trying."

"She's gotten a lot smarter in her time in the Underworld then, I can promise you," Ralrek said, resuming his pacing.

"Now, no one knows she's trying to get away with something until she already has," Bilba said, the tips of his ears turning pink with frustration I think we were all feeling.

"He expelled her from the Council."

"Seriously?"

"Yes." Cassie rubbed the flat of her thumb over her palm. It stopped, pressing against her pale skin, making it paler still. "By rights, she should have had to forgo all her ill-gotten prestige, power, and wealth. But Seraph is smart. Too smart. She leveraged her relationships. She manipulated angels at every turn, including Yahweh, and got what she wanted."

Bilba snapped his fingers. "She's the one who proposed the trade with Lucifer? She gave herself and Michael up?"

Cassie's head bobbed.

I whistled. "Sacrificed Michael to save her own skin."

Even though none of this was funny, Ralrek tittered. "This explains so much."

"You can say that again," I said. "Once she pulled that off, I don't imagine she was in too much of a hurry to repay her debts to Yahweh? What was he asking for that was so extreme Seraph had to plot her escape?"

"To make full reparations. To donate all proceeds to approved charitable organizations for low-order angels. Of course, she'd never regain her political opportunities."

"So, she'd basically have to start from scratch?" Bilba asked.

"Yes."

"Instead, she weaseled her way out of that, taking Michael along with her?" Ralrek shook his head.

Cassie lifted her head, eyeing us. "I don't know what he's like now, but everyone I've talked to who knew him in the Upperworld said he was a good guy."

"Things change," I said, thinking of Michael's mind-prying and how his voting decisions and orders to the Council had impacted my life. That incubus had done me no favors, and I wasn't in the mood to hand out letters of forgiveness, no matter his sad origin story.

"Their families weren't allowed to join them, obviously," Cassie continued. "Seraph wasn't bothered, but it devastated Michael and his family. His wife—"

"Michael was married?" Bilba blurted.

"Yes, married with children. His wife was influential in her own right and could open Rifts. Michael hadn't been gone for a year when she crossed to the Overworld and committed suicide, leaving their children to foster care."

Well, bless it. So much for my apathy toward Michael.

"Disgusting," Ralrek said, vocalizing my internal experience.

"All of this because Seraph cheated and lied her way into power, and then used angels once she had it?" I couldn't believe this. I mean, I could. Thinking nothing was too low for Seraph. Not as long as she got her way. Over the years, I'd witnessed her interactions with the leader of Lucifer's Third Council and known there was more to their story. But this? No way had I seen this coming.

"She'd become almost untouchable," Cassie said.

I cocked my head. "Only because Yahweh allowed it. He should have nipped that in the bud at the first hint she was up to no good."

"I told you, she's smart enough to be subtle. Always moves ahead of others. A very dangerous demon."

"Now, yes. But she wasn't always the Seraph she is today. Yahweh dropped the ball on that one and now we all suffer. At least, everyone in the Underworld. But I guess that's not Yahweh's problem. He's probably still laughing about dumping her off on Lucifer."

Throughout my short rant, Cassie had sat straight. Her small nose flared, but I was on a roll and didn't stop to recognize it. Why would she be upset? We were the ones suffering because of that trade. We got the short unicorn horn. Now, thousands of years after Seraph wedged herself into a new seat of power, the three of us were in our current situation in large part because of her deviousness. If any of the four of us had a right to be upset, Cassie was in last place.

"Yes, well, Yahweh was dealing with other things. Seraph wasn't the priority."

"Obviously," Ralrek snorted.

"Had He dealt with her, maybe He'd have less to deal with ever since He dumped her in Lucifer's lap."

"It's easy to criticize when it's not you sitting in the seat," she said in a ghostly voice, as if the conversation made her think of another problem she had.

"Sorry, Cassie, I know it might feel like we're picking on angels, but we're not," Bilba said, reaching over and touching her shoulder. "We're not like that. You know that. It's just that we've caught the brunt of her actions, so we're a little upset that she could get away with what she did. We're the ones suffering now because of Yahweh's decision. We're not criticizing Him, but we have a right to be upset. If it wasn't for what He did, we might not be exiles."

Cassie didn't respond to Bilba's touch, not even a sideways smile. So un-Cassie-like.

"Just more proof why there has to be an equal influence in the Overworld," Ralrek said. "We'll need to stop and see Virgo at some point, guys, to make sure they're helping keep angels in-check. Sorry, Cassie. Just the truth. Can't trust a Yahweh who's so weak He lets someone Seraph walk all over Him."

"Ralrek's right," I said. "Yahweh got played. Maybe that's why Lucifer wanted us to talk? Because He wanted us to know about Seraph, and Yahweh's lack of judgment, and how that might play into—"

Cassie slapped her thighs. Even covered in jeans, the smack echoed into the ceiling of the gazebo. "Will you guys stop?"

I held up my hands. "Whoa. Sorry."

She pinched her lips. "Just. Stop. Okay?"

"I didn't think you'd get so defensive about Yahweh. I get that you're on His Council and all, but still."

"Because you guys are talking out of your asses. You don't know Him and what He faces. Has been facing. If you had half the strength He does—" She stopped, pinching her lips again and turning away.

But I'd already caught the glimmer of tears in her beautiful eyes. For the first time in this conversation, I got my ass off the concrete. I went to her and squatted at her feet. "Hey. What's wrong?"

She gave a tiny shake of her head and hid her face.

"Yeah, Cassie, we're sorry about that stuff. We don't know Yahweh," Bilba said. "I wouldn't have said it if I thought it'd upset you."

"Y—you didn't," she said behind her veil of cocoa hair streaked with blond. "Ignore me."

"No, Cassie, we are sorry," I said, still unsure just what in the heaven had set her off. "We didn't mean to bludgeon Him."

This was ridiculous. We'd had difficult discussions in the past; about Gemini, about demons and angels, about immortal influence in the Overworld, and she'd never reacted with such ownership. Maybe her new role on Yahweh's Council truly had changed things. Maybe she was too closely aligned to the Upperworld's cause for us to continue sharing openly like this. But then again, Lucifer was the one who pushed this meeting, for reasons known only to Him. Something bigger than picking on Yahweh was happening here.

Then it hit me like a blazeball defender.

"Cassie, who is He to you?" I asked, reaching out. "Who is Yahweh?"

Between sniffles, choked back a cry, and answered. When she did, everything changed. "He—He's m—my father."

10

UNDERWORLD, FIFTH CIRCLE

"Young Ezekial? Did you hear me?"

The aged voice of Azazel hung somewhere in the background behind the cloud of thoughts blocking my meat container of a brain. I had enough crap in there, so crammed full of troubles it couldn't possibly take on a slice of Hell's version of Spam.

We still hadn't made in-roads with any of the four tribes of the Isle. Each time we traveled across the Acheron, we risked dying—by kraken or Council assassins. The one fight we'd had against them turned heavily in our favor, so I doubted they'd come back without a far-larger militia at some point. Those plans were probably well into the planning phase. Ralrek still didn't want to try Gateways and Rifts from the Isle after learning Lucifer could open them there. He feared, probably rightly, with his uncontrollable power, he might swallow the last home we had. Oh, and then there was the minor issue of Cassie being Yahweh's daughter. Yeah, I had feelings for the daughter of the mortal's God. Just my luck.

Now, we were in the upstairs hideaway for the Fifth Circle's rebel cell, led by my auburn-haired, green eye shadow-wearing ex-employer, learning that the Council was indeed fracturing. The time for sorting this mess was drawing short, being cinched closed like a tightwad's gold coin sack.

"Huh? Sorry. I'm distracted."

Dialphio watched me with firefalcon eyes. "Yes, apparently deeply. We need your focus, Ezekial. Give it to us."

"Yes, ma'am. Sorry." Then I dropped the bombshell of a revelation on them.

The pair of older, conniving—for the good guys—demons eyed each other. Dialphio twirled her glasses by the arm, but said nothing.

Azazel, who had seemed to give the news a lot of thought, only said, "This could work to our advantage. I'll think this over. No need to put anyone at risk."

"Don't tell anyone else," Dialphio warned.

I looked down at the table. "No problem. I didn't even want to mention it here."

"Why not?"

"Didn't feel right. Safe. Sorry, but it's too big of news and we can't know where the Council spies are."

"That's very true, young Ezekial," the Founder said. "Though I've taken a number of precautions to keep Dialphio, the cell, and this location safe, we can't be too careful. Still, I agree with my cousin's assessment. No one else needs to know of this."

"I'm not saying a blessed word."

"You two as well," Dialphio wagged her glasses at Bilba and Ralrek.

"We won't," Bilba promised.

Dialphio hummed. "Azazel, you were saying?"

"The Council? Oh, yes. With the Council pulling in different directions, we must find the Horn," he said, his voice cracking with age and exhaustion. "I'm afraid it won't be much longer before Lucifer takes drastic action or the Council itself does."

"What do you expect them to do?" Bilba said, holding a

plate piled with shredded roast and potatoes. He had been popping shreds in his mouth as he made his way to sit down, but had stopped both to ask for clarification.

Azazel's lips moved before he spoke. His goatee was so long I don't think it technically could be categorized as a goatee anymore. There were what looked to be spaghetti stains spotted from the first tufts of hair below his bottom lip to halfway down the mane. He hadn't brushed it in a while by its appearance. "My sources tell me they're moving, individually, mind you, in other Circles."

"As if they're preparing to carve the Underworld into their own states," Dialphio said. She held her glasses by a stem and was rotating them in a circular motion with the see-saw of her finger and thumb. She thumped her finger on a closed copy of The Histories of the Balance. "Remember what I said about a civil war? If this information is even half-accurate, we must consider that a very real possibility."

"Not really our thing to worry about," Ralrek said, kicking his feet up on the table.

Dialphio scowled. Whether at his posture or comment, I couldn't tell. "It's everyone's problem, Mr. Burning. Innocent demons suffer in times of conflict. As always, it's the most vulnerable who pay."

Ralrek grunted.

His family was a broken family. Long before I despised then befriended him, I knew of his troubles. Everyone our age in the neighborhood did. The Burning's shattered home was one of the favorite gossip topics for my mother and her circle of friends. No one even knew his father. That didn't stop them from making up all sorts of reasons why he was never around. Only later did I discover just how broken Ralrek's family was. He barely had more than a few memories of his days as an imp, and nothing of his impling life. The memories must have been bad—not that he shared them—because of the way he always reacted when people asked him about his life.

Someone with a background like that could be a good demon, while not seeing the greater impact of their struggle on an individual level. So I jumped into the discussion before his demeanor and feet set Dialphio off. "We understand that. But I don't know what more we can do."

"For starters, you cannot hide on the Isle," she said sternly. "The rebel cells are busy, and we're growing."

"Around all the Circles," Azazel added.

"But they need to see you, Ezekial, to have faith," Dialphio said. "We'll have to figure out how to do it safely, but your presence needs to be felt. Whether or not you like it, to them, you're the Great Prince. You don't get a choice in how they see you. We're talking about motivating demons to move against the regime. We have to make sure they know you're still around, fighting for them if we want them to fight for the Underworld."

"How? I'm exiled, and we're just trying to survive, Dialphio. Unless you're going to send engineers and farmers back to the island with us so they can help establish a stronghold, we haven't even had time to look for Libra. That's the first task. Unless something has changed?"

"No. No." Azazel shook his head. His goatee swayed to the side and settled in the middle of his shredded roast that filled the room with its meaty aroma. I was thankful for it because Ralrek had heaped a small mound of firehorse radish on his plate, and that tangy stuff was slicing a path through my nostrils. "Finding Libra is still the priority. If he's as skilled as you say he is—"

"He is," Ralrek interjected.

"Yes, yes," Azazel said, now nodding and coating more of his goatee with roast juices, "then he's the priority, because the Horn is the priority. Now more than ever, I fear. With this inevitable splintering, no one can afford Seraph taking the

Horn deeper into hiding. Not if she's partitioning off a portion of the Underworld. Mmmm, I shudder to think of the cost of retrieving the Horn when she's surrounded by loyal henchmen."

"She has it then? You're sure?" Bilba asked.

"I'm as confident as I can be without actual evidence."

That drew a grunt from Ralrek. "None of us would be in this position if these so-called rebels had worked toward a solution instead of talking endlessly about them from the very beginning. We knew what we were facing when you sentenced Zeke after Aries. Yet, they all sat on their asses. They had the perfect excuse to act when he was Abandoned, but how much did they do?"

Dialphio made a sound deep within her chest that reminded me of an ember cat that'd received too much attention from a rambunctious toddler.

"We can change none of that, young Ralrek," Azazel said, rotating his hand in the air. "All we can do is move forward. And forward, we must head. The Balance is swaying. The administrative team tracking it is confused, over-tasked, and pulled in different directions, not only by my peers but Circle administrators and sub-Councils as well. It's a mess, I say."

"And it will only get messier with each passing day," Bilba said, his plate untouched. Blessed roast going to waste.

"We're afraid so," Dialphio said with a sigh. "What can we realistically do to help free you three?"

"Bring Leo's family to the island," I said without missing a beat, receiving confused looks from the older demons. I'd already written to Dialphio about Lucifer's visit and she'd confided that she'd shared the information with her cousin. Azazel knowing took a load off my mind. He might sway things at his level. "Lucifer said he couldn't because of free will. But they're at risk. As Abandoned, they know what the actual game is. They know what happened to Leo, and trust me, they're not stupid. Plus, having that many demons on the island who are on our side will help us get settled, and they'll be safe. There's no way Beelzebub or Apopis could get their hands on them. Not easily. Can you do something about that?"

Azazel's bottom lip pushed up. "Possibly. I'll look into this."

"Just make sure you don't forget about Cancer."

The way he shook his head made me worry instantly. "I won't forget, young Ezekial. But getting information out of the war zone isn't easy. There are too many variables. With my peers manipulating things as I'm sure they are, it's even riskier to poke around about her status." He held up a finger. "Now, that doesn't mean I'm not. But you will have to be patient."

"I have been."

Dialphio patted my hand and gave me a sympathetic smile. I couldn't return it.

"If I do this, if I can work it so the Neto family is approved to travel to the Isle—"

"Not approved to travel, Azazel. I need them, we need them, on the Isle so we can work on everything else you need us to do."

"Finding the Horn—"

"I know."

"We can't read the coordinates," Ralrek said. "We've told you that. This isn't the Overworld where we could take advantage of their Technology Abilities like GPS. The code used for the location you gave us doesn't make sense."

"They did to my source," Azazel said, sounding troubled.

"Then ask him," Ralrek replied.

"He's dead."

Ralrek spread his hands as if saying, "well, that's that."

This was getting us nowhere. "Neto family to the island. We find Libra. Ralrek says he'll be able to read the coordinates."

"Seems like the right fit," Azazel said.

"Meaning?" Ralrek sounded as defensive as a jealous boyfriend.

"I've snooped and discovered he was a resident of the Isle," the Founder said. "A beloved one, from what I understand."

"You're kidding?" I said.

"I am not."

Ralrek flopped his head back, looking up at the ceiling. "So that's where he's been?"

"Not anymore," Azazel said, now waving in the air. "He was too popular with the tribes. Michael found out he was thriving, that he was getting the tribes to work with him. Not with each other, mind you. I don't think anyone but Lucifer Himself can make that happen. But Libra was effective."

Dialphio blew out a slow breath. "And making enough of an impression to get Michael's attention."

"Yes, I'm afraid so. I understand it was upsetting for most of the island's inhabitants."

"Exiles," Ralrek said, still looking at the ceiling. "We're not inhabitants. All of us were exiled. Unfairly."

Azazel sounded rebuked. "Yes. Yes. Exiles. Libra will be an asset once you find him."

"If, you mean."

"We will, young Ralrek. I already have a team working on narrowing down his location."

"How?" Bilba asked.

Azazel's long mustache and beard twitched with his smile. "Michael's records aren't as, let's say, secure as they should be. It won't be long now."

"Good," I said, finally feeling progress. "Now, can we eat while we chat? I'm starving and really looking forward to a meal that isn't berry-based."

We ate until we couldn't eat any more. Dialphio caught us up on happenings around the Fifth, including what we wanted to know about our families. For Ralrek, that meant nothing. For Bilba, Akimon was doing alright. Not thriving. Not suffering. But in danger of slipping into depression over his son's absence. She said she was inviting him around more often to get him out of the house. For me, she stepped tentatively, which was fine. I couldn't have cared less about Kanthor Sunstone. It was Lilith who I worried about. Hearing that she was a quieter member of the neighborhood had me anxious.

"I'll check in with her when your father isn't around and see if she'll come have tea," my ex-boss said. "I'm sorry, Ezekial. I'm sorry you have to go through this."

"Don't be," I said, no longer feeling as hungry as I had moments before. "It's not your fault. Thank you for keeping an ear out for her, Dialphio."

"Of course. I want to make sure you're taken care of."

"We know."

"And we appreciate it," Bilba said.

We cleaned up after that, the momentum and appetites lost. We were just about to leave when I caught Azazel and pulled him to the side. "Do you have a second?"

His aged eyes searched mine. "Of course. What's on your mind, young Ezekial?"

I made sure the three others were still cleaning up and out of earshot. "The other night when Lucifer caught me on the beach, he mentioned a term I'd never heard. I asked Cassie what it meant, and she didn't know either. It seemed like He expected me to know it, and I think it has something to do with Ralrek that is very meaningful."

"What term is that?"

"Wayward sons. Do you know anything about it? Does it sound familiar?"

It did. I knew it in the instant Azazel's tired eyes shot up enough to make his bushy eyebrows flap. He probably didn't notice, just as he likely didn't pick up on the fact that I caught him glancing toward my friends helping with cleaning up duties.

"Young Ezekial, are you sure He used that term? Are you sure you're not mistaken?"

It was etched all over the Founder's face. "Azazel, don't break the trust I've just started building in you. We've been through too much. In case you haven't noticed, I'm not exactly big on Founders, the Council, Lucifer or anyone in positions of authority. What's it mean? Tell me."

"I should go," Azazel said, attempting to step past me.

I'm fast. Azazel is four billion years old—okay, he's not that old, but you get my point. I slid a half step to the side and effectively cut off any route away that wouldn't result in Dialphio becoming curious about what we were up to.

"Tell me, or I'll have your cousin drag it out of you," I whispered. "We both know she will."

He looked at Dialphio. "She most certainly will. A terror since she was an impling, that one."

"Why would Lucifer mention it? Why is it important?"

"This is a conversation best had under different circumstances. At a different time." Again, he glanced at my friends. I don't think he realized what he was doing.

"Azazel, don't fall on this sword."

He drew himself up straighter. "What I do, I do out of caring, not treachery. I thought you'd have realized that about me by now."

Okay, in that instant, I felt chastised. But who knew when, if, I'd ever get another chance to ask. The next time I stepped into the Overworld, Beelzebub and a hundred of his closest muscle heads might be waiting for me. "We're about to head back to the Isle of Dread. We'll be looking for Libra. Trying to save the Horn. We'll have to get to the Overworld again. At any minute, something could happen to one of us." I reminded him of the run-in with the kraken. "Unless you want all of this to end before it begins, I need to know what it means. If Lucifer dropped it on me accidentally, He did so because He's going senile, and that's a problem. Or, more likely, He did it on purpose. Whether because He thought I already understood the context or not, it doesn't matter. Besides the fact that you care, why aren't you telling me? At least care enough to make sure I understand the mess I'm in."

I heard instead of saw—because his chest-length goatee blocked my view—Azazel swallow. "Because you are correct. It pertains to Ralrek, and I'm afraid that if he finds out, you may lose him for good."

11

ISLE OF DREAD/OLYMPIA

"WHAT DO YOU DO WHEN YOU'RE NOT TRYING TO UPKEEP YOUR garden and collect water?" Bilba asked Marijon.

"Nothing, really. I'm so tired of exploring the island. I usually just sleep or work with my Ability. There isn't much else to do. But the farm and garden keep me busy, especially since I'm a one-succubus show." She hovered over an iron pot centered on her fire.

"Where'd you get that?" I asked, indicating the pot.

"Oh, that? In a trade."

"Trade? With who?"

She returned her attention to the water coming to a boil. "The Untouchables."

"Who?" I picked a strand of corn silk from my teeth with my tongue. Kicked back on a blanket, surrounded by wild grass that surrounded Marijon's camp, as thick as Bilba's understanding of how to flirt with succubi, I couldn't have been happier. Well, I could, but that included finding myself at a chicken wing buffet, with excellent beer, and Cassie as a dinner companion—not a date, mind you.

Marijon whipped her head, dipping her chin to her shoulder. "Zeke, the Untouchables. By now you should know the tribes' names."

"I don't."

Ralrek snickered.

"Do you?" I asked my tall friend.

"No."

"Yet you're laughing?"

"I'm laughing because you showed your ass. At least I keep my ignorance quiet."

"Hey," I said, finally craning my neck, "I'm not ignorant. I just lack knowledge of the tribes."

Ralrek closed his eyes, shaking his head. "Literally, that's what ignorance means."

Bilba blew out his cheeks. "Well, you're in a dark mood."

"Yeah, well."

Marijon shoved a thin log into the fire. Sparks kicked up before settling, cracking, and popping. "Everything okay, Ralrek?"

He wouldn't tell her what was bothering him. No way. No doubt. She was still earning her way back into our trust. With Ralrek, she might never get there. I was more forgiving than the jet-black haired incubus, especially when he was in dark moods like this. A dark mood I caused by sharing what Azazel said about wayward sons once we were on our way across the Acheron.

"No."

She looked from him to me. I shrugged. "I've got a tomato salad in the cooling bin if you're hungry?"

"Thanks, but I'm not." He pushed himself to his feet and walked to the edge of her camp. Near the ring of wild grass that reached his waist, he looked out into the forest, putting his hands behind his head like he was about to stretch.

We met eyes, and Marijon mouthed, "Is he okay?"

I shook my head, wishing I'd kept my big mouth shut until I had something more solid from Azazel.

It really was true. Sometimes, most times maybe, no answer was better than half-responses. Who needed just enough information about something that provided hope, promise, despair, anxiety or whatever, without knowing the full context? What good was it? Didn't it always end up causing someone to spend energy filling in the blanks? What a futile expenditure of time. A pointless activity. A path to an unnecessary turn in someone's outlook. I felt terrible about opening my big mouth, and even worse about letting Azazel convince me to let him go without answering.

The silence between the four of us wouldn't distract Ralrek from whatever troubles were tumbling around in his skull. I tried to break the monotony by learning more about Marijon's time on the island. "Have none of the tribes given you a chance to prove yourself to them?"

She was in the act of sitting. My question stopped her halfway through her squat. Her blue spandex pants had a hole in one knee and another on the side of the opposite thigh. "Nope. And I tried hard to prove myself. But what are you going to do when your story has already been told?"

"What do you mean?"

She made a popping sound with her lips. It was so strange to see their true color. All the time we'd hung out with her during our caper to steal the Horn from Taurus Hammerwulf, Marijon had covered her face in makeup. Deep maroon lip gloss. Black eye shadow that'd make Lucifer proud that she'd reinforced demonic stereotypes. The eyeliner had made her eyes look wider than they were. But here on the Isle, she didn't have access to makeup and had probably exhausted her stock long ago—I didn't ask. I liked this natural look. Yes, it made her look less fierce, but that probably helped us reconnect, especially considering how we departed last time. Everything about the succubus made her more approachable.

"When they dumped me on the Isle, I didn't get a chance to tell my side of things," she said. "I don't know if the guards had orders or not, but they spent the entire crossing telling the others about my supposed activities. They were all lies, but since when did that matter?" She used the stick she'd been poking the fire with to draw idle lines in the sand around her feet. "The powerful always get to frame the narrative, don't they?"

"You can say that again," Bilba said. "Did you tell everyone the truth?"

"Didn't get a chance," she replied, still drawing. "The guards forced us to be silent. None of us could speak. Me or them. The idiots said they had permission to throw us overboard if any of us caused a disruption. We were bound. What could we do?"

Bilba's head jutted forward. "They bound you for your crossing?"

"Yes," she said, looking up. "Weren't you guys?"

I shook my head. "Nope. But we came with Azazel. Maybe that made the difference."

Marijon's head dropped. She shook it.

"What?" I asked.

"You guys," she said, flicking the end of the stick out of the dirt, flinging small clumps of brown island toward the rock circle containing the flames of her campfire. "Ever since we met in the Eighth, you've been involved with the Council. I still can't wrap my head around how such normal demons are kicking it with the elite."

I chuckled. "We're not exactly kicking it, and haven't been for a long time. But we have served as kicking bags. Does that count?"

"Punching bags too," Bilba said, trying to be funny. Great guy, that Bilba Ravenous, but rarely one to intentionally elicit a guffaw.

Marijon harrumphed. "Well, we didn't get the luxury of free hands and feet, and the guards looked very serious about their threat. I think they were looking forward to it."

"I'm sure they were. No fault in complying. I'm sure you thought you could fill everyone in on the truth once you arrived on the island." Bilba said that last part with a slight scrunch to his face, like he meant to frame it as a question.

"That's exactly what I thought," Marijon said with a head nod, "but once we got to the island, the tribes' representatives greeted us. I knew they were feeling us out. Honestly, I was a little overwhelmed. I mean, you guys get it. My entire life was turned upside down. I was still mourning for my mother. I was still pissed about what happened and how I was taking the fall." She held her free hand up, still not meeting our eyes. "Don't get me wrong. I helped others, and that was important. But I shouldn't have had to. The Council should have made sure the Eighth didn't fall into chaos. They should have been there."

Tap. Tap. Tap. Marijon was no longer dragging the stick through the dirt, but smacking it.

"They've got a knack for being out of touch with the going-ons around Hell," I said.

"That," she said, tapping, tapping, tapping, "and the fact that they don't care."

"They never have," Ralrek said from the edge of the camp. One of his hands was balled into a fist behind his head.

"Sometime during that whole feeling out phase of our arrival, the incubus who came with me mentioned what he'd heard," Marijon said, returning to her story. "Word spread fast. I'm sure it was quite entertaining for them, but it didn't take much to see, literally, the tribes turning from me. By the time the Grand Chamber was closed and night fell, I was alone on the beach."

Ralrek grunted, dropping his hands and doing something with them in front of his body. From my perspective, it looked awkwardly like he was... entertaining himself.

"Wait." I held up a finger. "You mean to tell me they rejected you just like we were?"

"Yep." She cocked a shoulder. "But everyone exiled since, except you guys, has found a place with the tribes within a few days. Sometimes, within hours."

Hours. We were coming up on closing out our second week. Heavens, I'd saved the lives of thirty or forty of them over their fight for fresh water. Where was our acceptance? Had Marijon been going through something similar? She could have starved out here, and the tribes wouldn't have cared. How many others, now and in the past, had similar experiences?

"I can't do this anymore," Ralrek said, sounding more like he was talking to himself.

I had to agree. This was past the point of tolerance and patience. Too much depended on us getting established on the Isle. Azazel couldn't exactly help without drawing suspicion. Even reaching out to the Neto family might be too risky of a proposition. He—

I stopped when Bilba slowly rose from his seat like I was watching a slow-motion recording. The outer folds of his protruding ears were turning pink with the rush of blood. Marijon had dropped her fire poker, her mouth agape.

"Wha—" I started to ask as I turned in Ralrek's direction and nearly crapped myself.

In the tall wild grass just beyond the camp, a Rift was opening. My brain tried to process what I was seeing, wondering if Lucifer no longer gave a care about making surprise appearances, and how I was the last to notice.

"You—how?" Bilba said in a rising pitch. "How are you—we can't. But—but—"

I was on my feet along with the other two and darting toward Ralrek.

The Rift flashed horizontally, widening to thirty feet. It was as silent as the night without the ocean and appeared just as deep. I'd never seen such a large opening between the worlds.

"Ralrek?" Bilba said with a smack of caution.

"I'm going to the Overworld," he said, not turning to face us.

"Not alone, you're not," I said. Calling to Creed, the halberd flew to my open palm. "You coming, Bilba?"

"Y—yes. But how did you do that, Ralrek?"

I tugged Bilba's arm, pulling him close. "He's not in the right headspace. Can we talk about that later and just make sure his ass is safe for now?"

Bilba blinked out of his stupor. "Yes. Sorry, Zeke. You're right. Let's go. Marijon, sorry, but we'll catch up when we get back. Or... or maybe tomorrow or something."

"Hate to eat and run," I said to the stunned succubus. "Thank you for inviting us and, I promise, we'll check in as soon as we can when we get back. Not sure how long we'll be gone, so I'll ask for a raincheck. Next time, we'll cook?"

"Okay," she said in a distant voice, still distracted by the monstrous Rift.

Ralrek had stopped its growth, not always something he could do. With Bilba, I would have felt comfortable. He created controlled openings. The same couldn't be said of our taller friend. His magic had always been powerful, but he seemed to gain strength with each passing week. The size of this Rift was further proof of that.

"I've never seen one without a border of some sort," Bilba said, craning his neck to take in the opening's height.

"Creepy, how quiet it is," I said.

Ralrek stepped into the Rift without a word.

"Come on," I said, nudging my fascinated best friend, "let's keep him from doing something stupid."

We stepped into the Rift. After a brief spell of disorientation, we came out in the middle of the hangar Virgo's Vigilantes used as a command center. The Rift stretched a quarter of the length of the building. Thankfully, it didn't appear to have disrupted any operations or squashed a mortal or immortal.

Bilba whistled. "Very accurate placement."

"Thanks," Ralrek said, heading for the meeting room where we'd held far too many discussions with Virgo about far too many demonic travesties we needed to impede.

"What are we doing here?" I whispered to the handsome devil who'd brought us here. No one was around to hear us. Every table sat empty. The wide-screen TV was off, and the sofa and chairs, unoccupied. Three vans stood side-by-side at the far end of the hangar, as silent as Ralrek's Rift.

After taking a few unresponsive steps toward the meeting room, I grabbed Ralrek's arm. He stopped. I didn't like his deadpan expression. "Close the—" I was about to remind him he still had an open passage to the Underworld splitting the Overworld air, but halfway through my reminder, I noticed the Rift was already gone. When had he done that? "Nevermind. Are you okay? What are we up to here?"

"I had to get off the Isle, Zeke," he said. His expression remained distant. Cold and concerning. "Away from the Underworld. I can't take it anymore."

"I know, I'm sorry. Whatever you need. But, hey," I said in a rush when he looked like he was ready to walk away. "I want you to know that you're not alone. Don't do shit like this again, okay? Always take me or Bilba along. Preferably both, since I don't trust you two to not get your asses kicked on accident."

"Sure, man."

"Ralrek, how did you do that?" Bilba asked, sidling up to the Fire caster. "How did you open one on the Isle? That's impossible."

"Obviously not," I said. "Lucifer can do it."

"He's Lucifer." Bilba looked at Ralrek. "How?"

"You taught me," Ralrek answered. "You know how to open Rifts."

"Yeah, but the Isle blocks them. No one can open them. Not even the Founders."

Ralrek popped his shoulders up in a shrug. "When Zeke mentioned Lucifer opened one, I thought, 'why not?' and gave it a go."

"Just like that?"

"Yes, just like that." Then Ralrek did something that let me know the true him wasn't too far gone. He lifted his arms, wrapped one around my shoulders, doing the same to Bilba, and pulled us in. Three heads met as one. "I care about you guys more than anything in the Underworld. You are my family. And I'm tired of watching those I care about being messed with. Screw everyone else. I'm tired of waiting on the rebel cells to do something. I appreciate Dialphio and Azazel, but they're not moving things forward, but they demand we do. And I'm done with it. From now on, I'm going to do what needs doing if it means you guys are safe. Come on." He stepped forward, pulling us with him. "Let's see if Virgo is working."

"So it's not getting any better?" Bilba asked the Commandant of Virgo's Vigilantes.

Virgo ran a scarred hand over his shaved head. "It's a mess. The only positive thing that's happened since the last time I saw you guys is that no new countries joined the war."

"Give them time. I'm sure it'll change," I said. "Not exactly positive."

Virgo looked at me with his hard, dark eyes. "That's my point. And it only gets worse from there. Whatever is going on in the Underworld, I'm not hearing much involvement from demons up here. Not in the war, at least. Angels are gaining more influence every single day. Makes our work precarious."

The ex-fighter and member of the Abandoned had taken command of this Overworld vigilante group after Seraph's nephew, Chax Vicu, tried to have me and Leo killed. Chax was a punk, but now he was a dead punk, thanks to Cassie's intervention. Without her, I would have been a permanent part of an Overworld rooftop. In saving my life and defeating Chax and his thugs, she'd given Virgo an opportunity to make better use of his time here. And, boy, had he.

Taking the Abandoned, demons and angels kicked out of their respective immortal realms, he'd led the formation of the group now named in his honor. Though he was thin, Virgo's lean muscle layered his frame. Hard as concrete. Anyone with eyeballs could see how dangerous it might be to cross him. The only thing that softened his presentation was his voice. Normally, smooth and rich, it now had a huskiness I didn't like.

"They can't let the Balance sway too much," Bilba said.

"They don't care," Virgo said as he leaned back, narrowing his eyes. "How bad is it back in the Underworld?"

"Bad," Ralrek said, his feet kicked up on the conference room table.

"We've been exiled to the Isle of Dread," I said.

One corner of Virgo's mouth curled. It lacked humor. "So that place exists, for real?"

"For real."

"Because of the women's clinic?"

"Yep. Seems the Council didn't like the fact that I tried to roast Beelzebub to save myself."

"Go figure." He sat forward with his elbows on the table, placing his forehead in his open palms and rubbing it. "So, this will only get worse unless we get the angels to back off?"

"Seems like it."

Bilba shot his hand up like we were implings back in fifty-fifth-grade school. "Oh. Why not get a message to Cassie? She'll listen."

"Sure, she will. Whenever she can get around to responding."

Virgo pulled his head away from his palms. "You two break up?"

"We were never together."

"Sure," all three incubi said simultaneously.

I groaned instead of entertaining them. "I wouldn't wait on her. Yahweh's Council keeps her busy."

"You're still in contact, right?" Virgo asked. "Because I don't see her around much, even though that was part of the deal between you guys and the Vigilantes. I get that she's busy, but if she can't or won't check in, she'll need someone else to take up her role."

"I'd rather she keep her place," Bilba said. "We trust Cassie. That can't be said for another angel."

Virgo nodded, pushing his tongue against his bottom lip and making it bulge. "Agreed. But we don't have the luxury of waiting for her, especially if she's going to be inconsistent and unreachable. We've got too much going on with The Path."

Ralrek pulled his feet off the table and sat forward. "How's that prep coming?"

"Just started. We've got a lot to iron out, but at least it's moving in the right direction. Of course, we'll work with you on the timing to kick it off."

"Finally, some encouraging news," I said.

The Path was an agreement between Virgo's Vigilantes, us, and Cassie to sneak Abandoned demons and angels back into their immortal homes. We'd devised the plan shortly after the formation of the vigilante group but had to hit the PAUSE button when Beelzebub intensified attacks against Overworld targets.

"It's going to be a lot more difficult to pull this off with you guys exiled," Virgo said. "But we can work that out once I have a better idea how we want to proceed. Again, this is why Cassie needs to be involved."

All eyes fell on me. "Of course. I'll write to her as soon as we get back to camp."

"Good. Maintaining neutrality is hard enough. The war makes it more of a challenge. The fact that I never see her anymore, and you guys are hit and miss, makes it a problem. I'm doing what I can, but I won't be able to do it forever. Not without burning myself out. The network is growing. We're in over a hundred countries now."

Bilba whistled. "You work fast."

Virgo shook his head. "I can't take all the credit. Everyone is pitching in where they can. Steve, you remember him? Great publicist. He deserves the praise."

"That's what I enjoy hearing," I said, thinking of the man I'd bonded with over a fight against bigots in a city park. The Vigilantes had provided him with a vehicle to seek the justice he wanted to see in the world, and I dug that. "I'm not surprised he's stepped up. Good guy."

"He is. Could use more like him. But we'll get there. The attack on the women's clinic helped with recruiting locally. The war has everyone overseas understandably distracted, but those groups are making headway. It's encouraging."

"So now would be a bad time to ask about sending the Abandoned back to the Underworld?" Bilba asked.

This was a new one on me, something we hadn't discussed.

"You want them walking into that mess?" Virgo asked skeptically. "From the sounds of it, the Council would get wind of their return and exile them too."

Bilba's face scrunched, making his forehead ripple in wrinkles. "That's what I was thinking."

"Explain that one to me."

Bilba ran Virgo through our short history on the island,

our isolation in an already isolated community. He brought up Marijon's experience and relayed his concerns about how ours might mirror what she'd been through, and how that would only serve the Council's benefit. "We've asked to have Leo's family brought over, and even that might be impossible. Which is something, when you think about it, because we have—"

"Someone helping us," I said over the top of his unnecessary admission that Azazel was assisting us. "Look Virgo, we're in dire need of help. This runaway train isn't restricted to the Overworld war. Shit is sloshing downhill in Hell. Once it hits the village at the bottom, it'll wipe everyone out. We've got to do our part. If we can't stop it, maybe we can slow it down enough for someone else to pull the brakes. Using The Path might not be the way. Putting demons back in their home Circles might raise the wrong suspicions. But Bilba's onto something. If the Abandoned demons came to the Isle of Dread, they'd already have allies who understand their situation."

"And they'd help us, which will lighten your burden in the bigger picture," Ralrek added.

Virgo's bottom lip jutted out. "Sure, in the end. But sending back Abandoned now, at least the demons, would hurt my short-term work. It'd also imbalance the Vigilantes. I'd only have Abandoned angels and mortals left. I'd be the only Abandoned demon."

"Maybe not all of them, then? Just a few, at first?" Bilba said.

"Let's wait to get in touch with Cassie," I said before this got too far along or we put too much work and time into something that might not happen.

"Yeah. I need time to think about it," Virgo said. "There's already a demonic absence here. Around the entire Overworld. We don't need an Overworld where mortals are only being influenced by one side. That's dysfunctional in the best of situations, nevermind in the middle of a world war. Plus, the next threat from Beelzebub could be a day away. I'll be blessed if he thinks he can push us around. Everyone has to be ready for him the next time he thinks he can come here and terrorize everyone."

He was partially right. Everyone had to be ready to fight. Where he was wrong was thinking it was just Beelzebub we'd have to worry about.

12

UNDERWORLD, FIFTH CIRCLE

"Mmm, spaghetti," Bilba said, snagging a plate like he thought there was one scoop left and fifty demons fighting over who held the tongs. His sense of urgency was palpable, even making Azazel take snippy sidesteps down the table toward the bread rolls.

Dialphio chirped, a sound of being humored I'd heard too infrequently nowadays. "There's plenty. I'm having a meeting with the cell later this evening, when it's safe, and made enough for them. So don't worry. Take as much as you need."

Unlike Bilba, I stopped to hug the bookstore owner before stuffing my face. "How are you?"

"I'm fine, Ezekial." She looked at my arms while rubbing them. "Every time I see you, it feels like you're losing weight. I don't like that."

"Just baby fat."

She chirped again. Two times and still too few. The Underworld, Overworld, heavens, my life, was too absent of the sounds of levity. She pushed me along. "Go. Fix yourself a plate before Ralrek eats it all."

She wasn't wrong. He had a mountain of noodles on his

plate and was now ladling a river of sauce and a landslide of meatballs on top.

I gladly accepted that challenge. Noticing a stack of Tupperware at the end of the table, I asked, "What are those for?"

"You're taking food back to the Isle," my ex-boss and demon-with-the-biggest-heart-in-Hell said.

"We don't have refrigerators." I almost entertained the thought of sneaking them in to the cooling trunk Marijon had, but that was a step too far with as much as hunger twisted my stomach.

"Then don't take the meatballs," she said, stating the obvious. "But you are taking food back, if I have to pack it myself and swim it to the Isle." Dialphio was standing at the table, pressing her hands down like she was trying to squash it into the floor. "I can't do half of what I want to help you boys, but at least I can do this. Let me, okay? I'm working with others who have restaurant connections for other alternatives, but for now, at least you won't be hungry for the next few days."

"Thanks," Ralrek said, shoveling an impressive amount of dangling noodles from his fork to his mouth.

"Yes, Dialphio, thank you. This is very kind." Bilba was a little more polite than the Fire caster with the portion he crammed into his hole.

"No offense, but I'd really like to make sure we wrap up our chat before the cell gets here," I said. "So, why'd you call us, Azazel? Something to do with the powerful fighting each other for more power?"

"Mmmm, you could say that, young Ezekial," the Founder said, concentrating on his plate.

No one made eye contact except for me and Dialphio. I understood the tension. Azazel hadn't revealed the meaning behind the "wayward sons" message Lucifer had given me. Everyone in this room now knew about it, yet it remained unanswered to four of the five. It was outright disrespect for

Ralrek, if you ask me. My patience had run dry, so I could only imagine where Ralrek's head was at.

"There was supposedly a large blowup at the last meeting," Dialphio said, filling in the awkward silence.

"Everyone is definitely working for their own interests. I fear my initial suspicions have been reaffirmed by what I'm seeing," the Founder said after slurping a strand of noodles, spotting his gray goatee with red sauce. "A source relayed a recent real estate purchase in the Seventh Circle. A large compound."

"Beelzebub?"

"I'm afraid so."

Not-so-lucky-guess.

Azazel continued, "Heavily fortified. Belonged to one of the fighting pit's greatest champions. Very wealthy fighter."

"Then the time has come for everyone to stop dragging their feet."

"What I think Zeke means," Bilba said, "is that we recently met with Virgo. He's the incubus, the Abandoned one, in Olympia."

"Ah, yes, the vigilante?" the Founder said in sudden recognition. "I hope their operation is running smoothly."

"As smoothly as it can, given the circumstances. What I was getting at is that we met and are figuring out if we can bring the Abandoned back to the Isle."

Azazel made a series of throat noises, as if a word was struggling to come out, before he said, "Why would you chance doing that?"

"We need a greater presence there," I said. "We need safety and security, Azazel. All it takes is for Beelzebub or Apopis or Seraph to sneak across the Acheron with a few baddies and they could take us out in our sleep. More demons aligned with us means more protection."

"It means we can establish a camp, and we don't have to rely on coming here to get a full meal," Bilba added, briefing

Azazel and Dialphio on The Path and the standing agreement we had with Virgo's Vigilantes and Cassie. "That will free us to concentrate on everything else."

"Mmm, I see the sense in that," the Founder said, setting his fork down. "I like this plan. Very much needed. Indeed, very much needed. My wish is for the three of you to unite the tribes of the island. Would doing this hinder your ability?"

"Nothing will," Ralrek said evenly, more to his rapidly diminishing bowl of pasta than to the Founder.

Azazel stared at the top of Ralrek's bowed head.

"The tribes won't accept us, Azazel," I said, and then ran through our brief history with them, including how they'd ostracized Marijon.

"Well, we can't wait for them," Dialphio said, sounding as frustrated as I felt about the tribes and their isolationist tendencies.

"Libra can help," Azazel said. His mouth twitched under his overgrown hair.

"You found something?" Bilba asked.

Azazel nodded. "I did. I know where Libra is being imprisoned."

"You do? How?"

"My sources are very good at what they do," the Founder said. "And the good news is that he should be relatively easy for the three of you to find." He held up his hand. "Easy to find, but difficult to free, I'm afraid."

"Free?"

"Libra is being held in a prison," Dialphio said, lifting her glasses and resting them on top of her auburn hairdo. "The problem is, it's guarded."

"Why do I feel that's not the full scope of the challenge?" I said.

"And," she said, stressing and drawing out the word, proving my intuition correct, "it's an ocean prison."

Bilba's brow furrowed. "What does that mean?"

"Michael wanted to ensure Libra had no way back to the Isle to influence the tribes," Azazel said, "so he placed him in a cage suspended over the Acheron. You can still get to him, but it will be tricky. You'll need to get close to the Underworld-side dock and travel four nautical miles along the coast. He's about a mile offshore. Because of the austere location, they only keep one guard on him, and that duty on land. Really, they're there to feed him and check the cage. They don't actively guard him outside of that."

I set my fork down even though I hadn't finished my dinner. "But that sounds like heaven. Locked up. Exposed. I don't care how big the cage is. That's cruel."

"He's given water and enough sustenance to stay alive, but he's constantly exposed to the elements," Dialphio said, her emerald eyes gleaming with tears.

"Well, we know where he is, at least. We can scout it and figure out an extraction plan," Bilba said.

"Once we get him back to the Isle, he can recover," I said, snapping my fingers at a sudden thought. "Then the tribes will have to at least consider us. If we walk up on that beach with Libra in tow, if he means as much to them as you think, they'll have to give us a chance. Right?"

"Well, I don't see why they wouldn't," Azazel answered. "Libra held great sway, or Michael wouldn't have taken this step. I have hopes this will lead to a complete unification of the Isle. Lucifer knows we need that."

"Now, more than ever," Dialphio said.

I didn't like the despair I heard in her voice. This was a positive turn. Everything else in Hell might be going to the hellhounds, but this was a glimmer of hope. If everyone needed anything, it was hope.

"I'm afraid it's not all good news, though," Azazel said, fixing his gaze on Bilba even as he squashed the earlier fugacious positivity at the table. "Even before that unfortunate incident in the Overworld between you three and Beelzebub, there was a concerning trend of disappearances around the Underworld. Demons taken from their homes, from shops and stores, plucked right from the streets. Without rhyme or reason, demons simply disappeared. It has only gotten worse. More each day."

"How many?" Bilba asked.

"Though it's hard to pinpoint a specific number. Going off my reports, I'd guess at least three to four-hundred per day from all around the Circles," Azazel said, locking his gaze on my best friend.

Bilba whistled. "That's bad."

"It gets worse, young Bilba," the Founder said. Before I could sense the bad news coming, he delivered it. "I have confirmation your mother is among the missing."

A rim of pink flashed around Bilba's ears. "My—my mother is missing?"

"I'm afraid so." Azazel finally broke his eyes away from Bilba, shaking his head. "Now, I'm doing everything I can to get more information on her whereabouts. I have a very reliable succubus working on eyewitness reports, but the Eighth is a challenge. What we have heard is unreliable. Some even claim angel spies are responsible." From the corner of his mouth, he muttered, "I would like you to ask Cassie to look into that, please."

"Of course," I said, still stunned at the news of Bilba's mother. She'd ripped his heart out of his chest and stomped it more than a few times over the past few years alone. My concern was with him first, of course, but something told me there was a more devious reason for her disappearance. I mean, who bothers with a former flower shop owner with no connections? For now, I'd keep those thoughts to myself.

"Mind you," Azazel said, "we don't have evidence, but I'm not discounting it. Bilba, I'm truly sorry. As soon as I hear something, I'll relay the message."

Bilba's cheeks were as pink as the rims of his ears. I got up and walked behind him, resting my hand on his shoulder, squeezing it, just to let him know I was there.

"Just don't make promises you have no intention of keeping," I said to the Founder.

"Ezekial Sunstone," Dialphio exclaimed, twisting to face me.

"No, Dialphio," I said, not taking my eyes off Azazel. "The fit has already hit the shan, as they say. We're at a crossroads. Virgo is hanging on by a thread. What if we lose him? What if the other Vigilante network leaders wear down? We could have vulnerabilities all around the world. Where does that leave us? We're alone on the Isle. I've asked for Leo's family to be sent to us. Where are we on that? We've told you about the Abandoned and explained how they could help us prepare for what's coming. How long will that take to get movement? How much longer do I have to wait for a definitive word about Cancer? What are the rebel cells actually doing?" From my periphery, I noticed Ralrek had stopped eating and was nodding along with my questions. "It's time. Less talk. More results."

Ralrek grunted.

Just then, I heard it. For the first time since the beach, Crazy Zeke was back. "Who wields, liberates."

A passage from The Histories of the Balance. A message about Creed. The promise that the Great Prince would save Hell.

I didn't have time for Crazy Zeke. He could visit again when I stopped scrambling to put out fires. "Now, Azazel."

The Founder was courteous enough to wait out my tirade. "Do you want the truth? No matter who it hurts, no matter the consequences?"

"The truth is the only way we move forward."

We stared each other down. No one moved, grunted, squeaked, sighed or passed gas.

He wagged a crooked finger at us. "All of you feel the same?"

Bilba and Ralrek said they did.

Azazel said, "Dialphio, is the shop locked up? Lights out?"

"Yes," she said cautiously.

He nodded and slowly pushed himself up from the table in a series of grunts and groans. "Then, young Ralrek, I would like you to wait here." His gaze found me. "The rest of you, I'd ask you to step out and give Mr. Burning and me a moment of privacy."

A MOMENT TURNED INTO TWENTY.

I passed the time idly flipping through books and asking Dialphio questions about the current state of the bookstore I'm sure neither of us cared to address. Tension pressed down from the second floor, where the Founder was meeting with Ralrek. Bilba had moved as close to the front of the store as he dared and stared out at the Fifth Circle patrons of Old Towne. He might as well have been asleep on his feet for as much as he interacted.

When the door upstairs clicked open, we all jumped, even Bilba. Footsteps thumped across the landing, heavy and lethargic, before pounding down the stairs. Too heavy to be Azazel. A single set of steps.

Ralrek's feet appeared. Then, with each plodding step, more of the tall incubus became visible. I stopped moving toward the stairs when I saw how pale he looked.

"Ralrek?" Bilba asked.

"Hey bud, are you okay?" I said in a follow-up.

Everyone watched him descend, chunky step after chunky step. If this wasn't a bookstore, I'd swear it was a library, as quiet as we'd fallen.

When he reached the first floor, he stopped, standing in place. Bilba and I went to him. Dialphio hung back. When I looked at my auburn-haired ex-boss, I could see it in her face. She knew what Azazel had just done to Ralrek. For how long, I didn't know, but she was aware of what my friend faced. Somehow, that gave me a sense of peace.

His far-away look wasn't zeroed in on the here-and-now when he said, "Bilba, can you open the Gateway? I don't want to practice."

Me and my stocky bud shared a look.

"Sure, Ralrek. No problem. Are you ready now?"

"Yeah."

"Okay, sure."

I took a hesitant step closer. Hesitant, not because I feared Ralrek lashing out, but because the handsome jerk looked like he needed physical connection but wasn't sure how to ask for it. I'd never seen him so vulnerable. Not even when I caught him in a loving embrace with a mortal back in Germany. When I put my hand on his shoulder, I swear he might have crumbled into me. "Are you okay? What did Azazel say?"

Ralrek's head wobbled. "Now I know why the Council denied my Passage application." He scoffed. It held a twentieth of his typical attitude. "You can free yourself of any guilt you had about me being passed over. Even if the Council didn't hate me for being your friend, Zeke, I'd still never get a chance to be a Major demon. I'm not even eligible."

"What? Why?"

Dialphio sniffed behind us.

"Because I'm not a demon," Ralrek said, and I felt his weight shift under my hand.

"That's crazy talk," Bilba said, taking another step closer. "You're as much a demon as any of us."

"Literally, no, I'm not," Ralrek said, so detestably my heart ached for him. "You can't be when your father is mortal."

13

UNDERWORLD, ISLE OF DREAD

MARIJON CAME BY AND INVITED US TO HER CAMP FOR BREAKFAST. She'd caught a boar in a snare while we were gone and could only salt and store so much of the meat, apparently. I wasn't complaining. Plus, she said, she enjoyed having us around and her company was growing on me.

"Thank you," I said groggily, absolutely exhausted from a lousy night of sleep. I checked on Ralrek, who was still lying on his side, unresponsive. He'd slept less than me. "Give us a bit to get ready, and we'll head your way?"

Marijon glanced at Ralrek and then back to me. "Oh, sure. Of course. See you guys soon."

"Bye." Bilba waved even though she'd turned away and was already jogging through the tall blades of tropical grass. He leaned over and placed a hand on Ralrek. "We can bring back food if you feel like staying here."

Ralrek only grunted.

Bilba looked at me, and I shrugged, having no idea what we could do for our friend. Even if I wasn't exhausted, my brain fried, I wouldn't know how to help. I think I got about two hours of sleep in total. Sure, the revelation that Ralrek's father was mortal troubled me. The incubus Ralrek thought of as his father, the estranged one, was actually his stepfather. A familial lie held for thousands of years and maintained through the disintegration of the family. I didn't even know it was possible for immortals to have children with mortals. I imagine dealing with that would be difficult enough, even if his family checked in every couple of decades. But they didn't. They never did. As estranged as estranged got.

His family had made him who he was. For most of his life, I'd thought of him as Hell's ass. But that changed during our mission in Germany, when Bilba was still in the Eighth Circle tending to his own family problems. I'd caught Ralrek making out with a mortal, a big taboo, and we busted through the walls of antagonism separating us from becoming friends because of that accident. Since then, we'd only gotten closer. Good thing, too, because I had a feeling the handsome devil curled into a ball on the far side of our platform bed was going to need all of our support.

I'd do whatever I could for him.

Bilba caught me looking up into the treetops. The palmetto trees shielding us from the open sky stood roughly thirty feet high. Tall, but close enough for me to inspect the branching leaves for my midnight torturer I hadn't heard from in a week until last night. "What are you looking for?"

Scanning the trees, I saw no sign or hint of the harpy. "You wouldn't believe me."

He shuffled closer. "Listen, I don't know how to help Ralrek, and I'm feeling pretty crappy about it."

"We just need to give him time." My inspection went to the next tree. If I had to, I'd shimmy up the rough stem and knock the freaking nest down. The half dozen bruises on my legs, showing proudly beneath the hem of my shorts, served as a reminder of her insidiousness if the spray of pebbles all around didn't. "He'll deal with it, and he'll let us know when he needs us."

"But, he's stubborn. He'll try to work through it on his

own." When I didn't respond, Bilba grabbed me. "Zeke, pay attention. This is important."

"I know it is, bud. But we can't force him to talk about it. We just have to be here for him." I returned to inspecting the ball-shaped treetops.

"Lucifer, what are you looking for?"

Bilba rarely cursed, so when he did, it got my attention. I lost track of which branch I was scanning when I looked his way. "When we made camp here, we pissed off a harpy."

"A harpy? Here? But they're only in Lucifer's headquarters."

"That's what I thought too, but apparently not." I pointed up to the treetops. "Somewhere up there, she hides. I was up all night because of her." I pointed at the cloud of pebbles at the foot of the bed and in the dirt just outside of it.

"Throwing rocks?"

"Yep." I explained my run-ins with the annoying gnat, including the fact that we were supposed to have moved by now. "I guess the fact that we haven't pissed her off, because she came back. Honestly, I was hoping she'd have moved on." I squinted, trying to make something out behind a branch of dead leaves, deeper near their tree's stem. It could have been a solitary coconut, but I wasn't sure if palmettos grow coconuts. Definitely not a harpy in hiding. "If I had to guess, I'd bet she plans on coming back until she breaks my spirit."

Bilba laughed. "Then she's in for a rude awakening. You're stubborn as heaven."

"Aw, shucks."

"Maybe we could talk to Marijon about moving to her camp," Bilba said. "That would be a pain, but we'd all benefit. Her included. Would you be okay with that? Trusting her again?"

It was a brilliant idea and told Bilba so. "I'm not sure she'd go for it, though."

"We can always ask. I think she'd be open to it. I think she's lonely."

"Me too."

"Then it's settled?"

"Whoa, sparky. We need to talk to Ralrek." I looked past Bilba to our A-frame shelter. "And right now isn't the time."

Bilba swiveled. "He'll pretend he's not hurting."

"Yeah. I know."

I don't know what devildog crap feels like, but I definitely felt like it now. I'd pushed Azazel on the meaning behind the 'wayward sons' term. I wouldn't let the issue rest. Seeing the impact of truth on my friend, curled up like he was an impling with a stomach ache, this was mine to fix.

The fact the elite looked at him as a "wayward son" because of the taboo of having a mortal parent changed nothing for me. It wouldn't be for Bilba either, because that jovial sack of brain power was a better demon than I could ever hope to be. We just needed to convince Ralrek we could help.

And then fix it. Then I'd find out why Lucifer dropped this problem in my lap. This wasn't done without purpose. He planted that stinking seed, pushing it into my brain soil for a reason. But what?

It took time to convince Ralrek to get out of bed. Even when he did, I couldn't take the credit. I'm sure it had more to do with what I heard his stomach doing than anything we said or didn't say. During the entire walk to Marijon's, he said little. Eating her amazing breakfast, he said less. When Bilba brought up the proposal to combine camps with Marijon, I groaned—because he blurted it out in his excitement, forgetting that we needed to chat with Ralrek first. Ralrek tipped his head. Once.

He wore a distant expression throughout. I wasn't the only one who shifted nervously when stealing glances at him.

Azazel had warned me that if he explained the wayward

sons, we might lose Ralrek. I feared how correct he may have been.

We cleaned up. Bilba detailed the logistics of combining camps. I wasn't sure Marijon had bought into the idea yet, but she pointed out spots she felt would be places for us to settle. They were close, but not too close. I was okay with that, and was already thinking about how the three of us could each take one spot instead of building a shelter together. Look, I love these two, but I don't need to sleep next to them. Bilba snores and Ralrek farts a lot. There was plenty of space for all four of us to start our own tribe, and bless the other four for rejecting her and us.

"We need to go now," Ralrek said after we'd finished cleaning up.

Marijon, Bilba, and I shared a look of confusion.

"No problem, bud, but why the rush?" I asked.

Ralrek's tone was icy. "I want to liberate Libra. Now."

"We... I mean, we just ate," Bilba said, looking to me for help.

"I know."

Crickets chirped somewhere in the tall grass around Marijon's camp. Stalks rustled in the slight breeze. Above us in the treetops, something peeped. For a moment, I had to wonder if the terrorist harpy had followed me to Marijon's.

"Ralrek, we've got to make sure we're—"

"We need to go now," he said. In a strange instant, I thought I saw the skin under his eyes sink with bags.

The strain of the realization of who he was, already wearing him down, was behind this impulsive decision. If he didn't do something with the emotions roiling inside him, he'd burst. I got it. Friends did this for friends, right? Even against our better judgment? We hadn't planned how we were going to rescue Libra. One guard all the way on the shore or not, we couldn't half-ass this.

But Ralrek was in trouble. Going back to the camp would

only shove him to get deeper in his head. Staying at Mari-jon's, listening to us, might drive him to his edge.

Ralrek had covered for me in Baghdad when I needed to find out who Cancer truly was. He testified for me when Seraph tried to lie about my activities during the deployment to protect her family. He'd been there during my Abandonment. Still, after everything, he pushed the rebel cells to do something more, because he saw how close everything was to unraveling. He put aside his feelings of angels for me. Without delay, he'd faced Beelzebub in a battle that could have killed him.

After all that, was I going to turn my back on him, ask him to delay when it was obvious he needed this task to distract him from his personal heaven?

I wasn't alone in this decision, though. "Bilba?"

My best friend nodded.

I exhaled stiffly. "Okay, Ralrek. Let's go."

14

UNDERWORLD, ISLE OF DREAD

"There it is," Bilba whispered, squinting into the distance.

We'd crossed the Acheron in record time thanks to Ralrek's personal turmoil fueling his beam of fire. This time, he put a little more *oomph* in his *oomph*. Even rocketing across the water, we didn't suffer any injuries, and no one took a risky bath. We'd been ready. Almost. His spell was particularly powerful and there were more than a few moments I was sure he'd flip the raft. Once we got up to speed, the raft spent more time out of the water than touching it.

Before reaching the Underworld dock, I manned the tiller, turning us from the automated course. Ralrek provided—literally—the firepower to push us off the predestined destination and parallel to the shore, only tempering his spell when Libra's cage came into view.

"Cruel," I said, taking in the cage and the silhouette of the incubus inside.

Twenty feet above the waters of the Acheron, a rectangular cage hung suspended. Libra had, maybe, a five-by-five cell to move around. Distance made judging the cage's size difficult, but I didn't need specifics. They'd crammed him into a space unfit for the Upperworld's most conniving angel.

This was beyond punishing innocence out of a Founder's paranoia. This was downright cruelty.

Out on the open water, the wind cut through my sweats and t-shirt. I should have brought a hoodie, but I only had one on the island, stuffed in the bottom of my trunk because I never needed it. Until now.

"So cold," Bilba said, as if reading my mind.

"Imagine what he's feeling." I tipped my chin at the suspended cage and the figure inside.

Ralrek didn't even growl, which had me worried. He'd settled his flow of fire pushing us. Our progress felt necessarily sluggish.

"The shore is a long way away," I said.

"Do we just go pluck him? Could be a trap," Bilba added.

I turned to Ralrek. "Are you guys tight?"

He squinted. "Me and Libra? No. But we're cool. We haven't seen each other in a long time, though. But he's the kind of demon who can pick up right where he left off."

"Good, so he won't freak out when he sees us coming for him?"

"Not if he recognizes me."

I turned forward again, scanning for anything that would tip off those guarding Libra to our presence. Nothing but deep water stretched out between our raft at Michael's prisoner. "This is too easy."

"Azazel said Michael took this upon himself," Bilba said. "We know the Council. They're petty. I'll bet Libra isn't the only demon a Founder has caged up somewhere on the Acheron."

"Totally something they'd do."

"If I'm correct, they can't exactly keep everyone guarded, can they? Let's be smart. Use a little caution, don't attract attention from whoever is guarding him onshore, and get out of here as soon as we have our hands on him."

The coast was clear, literally. From this distance, it was too difficult to make out individual demons strolling the beach, soaking in Hellfire rays, but I'd bet the on-duty guard could see us. "They could have sensors or something."

Bilba looked at me like I was stupid. Maybe I was. "Out here?"

"Sure, why not?"

"Because," he paused, raising his arms, "we're in the middle of the ocean. How would they do that?"

"Let's not take any chances."

We continued drifting closer. The anticipation of a fight, the paranoia, deep and unrelenting, that the Council was aware of our presence and waiting to suck us into a trap, was undeniable.

Libra came into detail after a while. He slouched against the flat cage bars. Probably asleep.

Was this rescue operation part of the 'who wields, liberates' calculation? We were about to find out.

Two hundred yards out, Ralrek broke the quiet of our approach. "Libra!"

I jumped, not expecting him to call out. Ridiculous, I know. We were a mile from the shore. No one could hear us. Yet, I couldn't settle the feeling that this wasn't all it appeared to be.

Libra lifted his head, turning slowly in our direction.

He was scrawny, likely because of his imprisonment. His dark hair—black is a popular color in Hell—was matted to his narrow head. I couldn't tell if that was because of the lack of a healthy diet or if he was just an unlucky bastard who nature had toyed with.

Libra turned, wincing and grabbing the cage bars. He tried to pull himself up, but slipped after just a few inches.

"There's a platform under the cage," I said, seeing the flat expanse of wood bobbing in the waves. "We need to lower him to that before we try getting him on the raft. I doubt he'll be able to walk."

"I could open a Gateway on the platform and try shooting him straight back to the Isle? Though I'm not sure it'll work," Bilba proposed.

"Think that's a good idea?"

Bilba had a familiar far-away look of deep thought. "Azazel said Libra was popular on the Isle, so it's not like the tribes would screw with him if they found him alone on the beach. Plus, that would be a lot easier on him than a return trip on the raft. There's a chance it won't work, though."

"How much of one?"

Bilba shrugged.

I groaned.

"He doesn't look to have the strength to hold on with Ralrek propelling."

I nodded. "True."

The plan made sense. A quick extraction, and then back to the island. Maybe a tribe would pick him up and nurse him back to health before we returned. I didn't have any ownership in who Libra hung out with back on the Isle. If he was half the incubus Ralrek and Azazel testified for, we could sit down with him once his strength returned and figure out the problem with the Horn's location. Getting him out of Michael's clutches and back to a vibrant demon was what mattered. "Let's be safe and get closer."

Fifty yards away, and no sign of Michael's henchmen. We might just pull this off easily.

A shaggy beard and thick, unkempt mustache covered Libra's face. His skin was pale and drawn. The jacket he wore didn't hide his thin shoulders.

"Hang on," Ralrek shouted across the divide. "We're going to get you out. Don't move."

Libra's hand drifted in the air, and he opened his mouth, maybe to speak, maybe to cry out in joy.

Twenty yards away, I said, "Bilba, are you going to open the Gateway?"

"I was thinking—"

In a silent flash, a wall of black appeared on the floating platform. A Gateway expanded, stretching well past the platform and far higher than the top of the pole holding Libra's cage, completely blocking my view of the prisoner.

I was about to ask what in the heaven Bilba thought he was doing when two things happened simultaneously. First, I saw a look of shock on my best friend's face. The Gateway wasn't his. Ralrek had opened it. Second, alarms clanged.

There were no speakers or blow horns on the pole. I didn't remember seeing any on the floating platform, either. Magical alarms. Wards against anyone with ambition looking to save Libra.

My arms felt the smooth chill before I saw the first evidence of Water magic.

"We've got to go!" Bilba pointed toward the location where the platform should be if Ralrek's Gateway did not block it.

"We've got to get Libra," the tall incubus said.

"Look, Ralrek!" Bilba put a hand to his jaw.

The water around the platform was turning white as it froze. Not a slow freeze, the sheet of ice was already three hundred square feet and expanding quickly.

"They've got multiple casters," I warned.

"We've got to get him," Ralrek said, forcing each word.

"We're on a raft, buddy," I said, turning the raft's tiller. "I can't shield us if that sheet keeps expanding."

The ice popped and cracked as it stretched out from Libra's location. The sheet rolled across the Acheron, looking like a yoga mat being uncoiled. It was then I understood what the guards were doing. Long before we thought to rescue Libra, they'd already developed a defensive plan. One guard on the shore for maintenance, not defense. A triggered alarm system was their calculated response all along. Sucker someone into thinking they could reach Libra, then kick off the fight.

"They're going to outflank us," I said. "Get us out of here, Ralrek."

Pulling on the tiller did little to turn the raft when we were off the automated course between the mainland and the island. Without a stiff wind of the Fire user's intervention, this would take forever, making us sitting targets.

"How are they doing that?"

"Look at the ice." I growled as I pulled on the tiller, as if that would somehow propel us away without the aid of wind. "They're pushing it out and around. In about twenty seconds, they're going to hit us from all angles. We're on the open water."

"You can shield us."

"Yes, but all they have to do is tip us over. My shield won't do squat for an upside-down raft. We'll be sitting gulls."

"We've got to get him out of there," Ralrek said, jabbing a finger at the spot where Libra's cage, hopefully, hung behind the Gateway.

"Not this time, buddy. We can't save him if we're dead. We've got to go."

"They're coming!" Bilba pointed at the hidden platform.

The popping and cracking ice wasn't coming from thin layers. The sheet expanded out and up. Near the cage, it rose five feet above the water. From behind Ralrek's Gateway, guards split to the left and right, running along the ice. First five, then a steady stream ran to take up positions.

"Ralrek, now!"

He stared down the guards. The raft was perpendicular to Libra's location. So exposed.

"Lucifer dammit. Bilba, take the tiller."

My bulbous friend shuffled along the raft and took my spot. I activated Creed from the side of the raft. Facing twenty guards, I guessed another twenty were at my back. My skin crawled with sensations. Water magic. Fire. Discernment. Deception.

"They're all casting." I refused to fully turn my head over shoulder. This was all about situational awareness. "Get your head out of your ass and get us out of here!"

"Ralrek, please," Bilba squealed from the back of the raft.

My shield burst from Creed, blocking off the guards I faced, before rising in an arc above and around us. It stretched into the waters of the Acheron, preventing the Water spell from encasing us in ice, and connecting underneath the raft. The bubble encased us, but would only last as long as I did.

Ralrek growled in the silence of my shield.

"I'm sorry, bud, but we've got to go," I said as I maintained Creed's shield.

Ralrek raged. He screamed, and I did the smartest thing I could in that moment. I spread my legs, widening my base, anticipating the raw power of his spell.

The raft swung around and Bilba cried out.

I almost stumbled into the water. "Get us on course!"

"I... can't!" Bilba shouted. The forces of the spin pulled him as far away from the tiller as his arms allowed.

"Lucifer dammit!" I stopped Creed and my shield dropped. The field of ice approached. The first tickling inside my head of the Discernment magic teased more menace to come. My skin felt conflicting expressions of Fire and Water magic. The only way we'd survive the fight was by getting away from it. I had to help Bilba and hope Ralrek didn't dump us in the Acheron.

Together, Bilba and I pulled the tiller to set us on a straight course back to the automated channel between the mainland and the Isle of Dread.

We bounced across the ocean's surface. Each time we slammed down on the water, the impact sent a jolt through my arms, neck, and spine.

My skin settled once we were away from the prison, feeling completely normal long before we reached the channel. Once we turned toward the island, the magic connecting it with the Underworld dock took over, and Bilba and I held the tiller only so Ralrek's spell, still as thick as a mature angel oak, didn't dump us into the water.

By the time we reached the Isle of Dread, my shoulders and arms burned, and I just wanted to make for our camp and sleep.

"We're probably going to need to set a watch tonight," Bilba said as we reached the camp.

I nodded, not bothering to look up into the palmettos for the terrorist harpy. "Tonight and every night afterward."

15

UNDERWORLD, ISLE OF DREAD

SOMETHING HIT MY FOOT.

I turned over, trying to ignore the harpy and her rocks. One of these days, I'd set a snare. When I did, I was going to feed her a steady diet of her blasted pebbles.

My foot jolted with another knock.

I groaned, rolling on my back, ready to blast the stupid little creature with a beam of Hellfire if Creed felt like participating.

When I cracked my eyes, I saw it wasn't the harpy who was trying to wake me, but Marijon. I scrambled awake, nudging Bilba.

He snorted, breaking up his incessant snoring. "Wha—what is it?"

Ralrek was already awake, his hands locked behind his head, staring at Marijon as if he'd expected her. He'd taken first watch, and I didn't remember being woken. Had he stood watch throughout the night?

"Marijon?" I scooted to a seated position and rubbed the sleep from my eyes. "Is everything okay?"

"Remember when I told you guys that you'd need to prove your value to the tribes if you wanted to be taken in by a community and not have to live like beggars?" She stood with her arms crossed, towering above us like a dictatorial school master.

"Y—yes," Bilba said, his mouth gaping in a yawn.

"Well, get up. Because now is your chance."

With that, she started away.

Bilba and I shared a look. Ralrek stared at the ceiling of our shelter.

"Do we follow?"

Bilba slid off the platform bed. "I am."

"Me too, then. Ralrek, you coming?"

Without looking my way, he said, "Yeah, sure."

Marijon was already fading into the flora by the time he got off the bed of logs and followed. Bilba and I jogged after her.

"What's going on?" my best friend asked when we caught up.

"They're squabbling again," she said, as if this was the norm.

"I thought they'd settled on the water issue?" I asked.

She shook her head and rolled her eyes. "Not water. Farming rights."

"Farming? They're arguing about farming?"

Marijon put her hands on her hips. "Do you want to sit here and chat about it or show a tribe that you have something to offer if they'll take you in?"

Bilba checked behind for Ralrek, who was plodding through the forest. "Do you think they'll listen to anything we have to say?"

Marimon shrugged. "Probably not. But what do you have to lose? Come on, we've got about a mile to go to get to the meeting. You don't want them to finish before you get there."

We took off at a slight jog, maintaining it until Bilba tired. Our time on the island wasn't doing us any favors when it came to physical fitness.

Ralrek fell farther and farther behind, even though we weren't speeding across the island. We stopped periodically to check on him and make sure he wouldn't get lost. This was unfamiliar territory. The grass was tall; the bushes were thick. When you didn't know where you were, every tree looked the same. He jogged often enough to keep us within eyesight, but he definitely wasn't exerting himself.

Finally, Marijon pulled us out of the jog. "Here we are."

Ahead, the tall grass, cut like someone had taken a sickle to it, gave way to a field. Short enough, you could tell this area was cared for. A longhouse, a single story, sat centered in the open area. Eighty feet long and twenty feet tall, it was the most impressive thing on the island—well, if you didn't count the thousands-feet tall mesa or the perpetual wall of ocean mist that hid the island from the rest of the Underworld.

"The meeting house," Marijon said, answering our unasked question.

"Fancy name," I replied.

"Be nice. Remember, you want them to like you."

"Maybe I should do the talking then," Bilba said, and I think he meant it.

Ralrek loped up behind us, staying three feet back.

"Let's go."

A few demons hung at the corner, ten feet from the door. They eyed us but said nothing. Marijon grabbed the handle and yanked it open. The door banged against the siding. A succubus in the group watching us rolled her eyes.

"Guess we're dropping in unannounced," Bilba said, delaying.

Ralrek strode inside.

"Come on," I said, giving Bilba an encouraging push.

Turns out, the building was a single room. Tables of rough construction were pushed together to form a giant U-shape. I couldn't count how many demons filled the building, but it had to be well over two hundred.

Each passing second, more voices dropped, cutting off at Marijon's appearance. The quiet settled as more demons recognized something had changed, that strangers were in their midst.

If this was a meeting to bring demons together, it had failed, if first impressions were reliable ones. The way each dressed sort of gave it away. I'd noticed it upon our arrival at the beach, and it'd been reaffirmed when we broke up the fight over fresh water. These demons seemed to segregate themselves by outward appearances. Overalls for one group. Demons clad in furs in another. A third, neat and tidy, dressed in gray wool. The fourth, standing apart from the other three as if even they, a tribe themselves, had been rejected by the greater community, were garbed in black. Though these four tribes shared the building and we'd walked into active chatter. Outward appearances told me they weren't here to meet more than they found themselves in the same building to push their agenda.

"What are you doing here?" an older incubus asked from the security of his group of overall wearers.

We waited for Marijon to answer. She told us we needed to prove our worth, but we needed an opening to do that. Forcing ourselves wasn't the best way to endear them to us or us to them.

"We want to help," Marijon said stiffly.

"Help? You?" someone in the back said, adding a scoff for good measure.

"Yes, me." She cocked her body, swinging an arm behind. "Us."

"Why do you think you get a say in our matters?" the older incubus in furs said, stepping forward. He was the one from the water fight, the one who I think appreciated my efforts. Sethel, I think, was his name.

Marijon seemed to straighten, as if she was trying to

appear taller. "I don't think I should get a say. I think we have something to offer."

"Oh? And what's that?" a freckle-faced succubus from the tribe dressed in black said, crossing her thin arms.

"Unbiased opinion," Marijon said flatly.

Probably not in the most politically astute manner, but Marijon might have history with the other succubus. Understandable that she'd have history with all of them. She'd been here a lot longer than us, and she'd been here on her own. Badass, yes, but also motivation to serve any comments with a healthy dose of spite.

The white-haired succubus with narrow eyes stepped forward. Across from the shaggy incubus, she aimed her comment at Marijon, but watched her opponent while speaking. "We don't need outsiders to decide for us what and how we will live."

Marijon flung her arms in the air. "Of course you don't. You're doing so well on your own. I've only been here a year, and I'm sick of listening to you bitch at each other. I'm amazed you haven't torn each other's throats out over something that could easily be resolved if you weren't so stubborn."

Marijon's comments were aggravating an already aggravated meeting. Hardly shocking. In our time on the Isle, the residents made it abundantly clear that they accepted no one until they were ready. Until that time, these demons saw everyone outside their separate communities as less than the other. Lower life forms. Undeserving of effort, help, or empathy. Lucifer dammit, more of the same petty blazebull dung.

The shaggy elder crossed his arms. His thick lips curled slightly, never reaching the full status of a smile. "And you propose you can resolve our issues?"

"No, but we can give you an outsider's perspective, and that might be enough for you to push through this impasse."

I loved hearing the confidence in Marijon's voice. I just

hoped we could back it up. I didn't have the slightest clue how to help. By the way Ralrek stood with his arms crossed and his eyes slowly scanning the two hundred demons, I doubted he cared either way.

"There's nothing to discuss," an incubus from the black-clad group shouted, shaking his fist. "We have our crops in that field. Our crops. You've taken enough from us, and you won't take any more."

Those dressed similarly roared.

The white-haired succubus with narrow arms lifted her chin and the group of demons behind her roared back at the black-clad gaggle.

"This is a mess," Bilba said, leaning in.

Marijon moved closer to hear what we were saying over the din, as now the other two groups joined in the indecipherable shouting. Ralrek hung to the side, watching, observing, analyzing. "They're so stubborn."

"So, how do we fix this?" I asked, pointing behind her. "I'm not getting in the middle of that. This is a fireball, ready to explode."

She waved a hand at the groups. "They're idiots. They always act like this and then wonder why they never move forward on their issues. That's why I grabbed you guys. If you can get them to hear you, to come to an agreement, you'll have a chance to get accepted by one of them."

"Not without you," I said.

"Let's deal with that after they've accepted you. Until then, we're stuck with each other."

"Marijon, we can't leave you on your own," Bilba said, watching the mushrooming argument.

"If they accept you, you can."

He shook his head. "No way."

"I've been on my own." Her light hazel eyes swung across our intimate group. "And I owe you this much."

"You don't owe us anything."

"Yes, I do."

"The past is the past," Bilba said, taking one of Marijon's hands. "We've moved beyond that. We're friends now."

"We are," she said, not letting go of his hand, "but you guys are important. Whatever you're doing, I know you're trying to help others. And what am I up to? Nothing. I sit at my camp and tend to my tiny garden and pathetic farm, and accomplish nothing. I'm going to contribute nothing to anyone's life if I stay on this path. But if I can help you three get accepted into one of these tribes, I'll be able to sleep at night." She glanced at the groups and gave them a stiff shake of her head. "I hope you've got ideas."

Bilba and I glanced at each other, but Marijon spun, raising her hands. "We have a proposal!" Portions of the crowds closest to us glanced our way, paused, then quickly resumed arguing. She raised her voice and filled it with heat. "I said, we have a proposal."

More heads turned her way, and this time, they didn't immediately resume their shouting and arguing and threats of physical violence.

"Have any ideas?" I asked Bilba.

He scanned the crowd. "This is toxic, Zeke. How do any of them think they can work together?"

"Doesn't sound like they care."

"If you don't want to spend the next twenty thousand years at each other's throats, you'll listen," Marijon shouted, drawing more attention.

Like all slow-gathering momentum, with each quieted voice, demons stopped bickering to see what was happening at this end of the long room.

The white-haired succubus turned to her tribe and put a finger to her lips. That silenced them, even if a few demons needed an elbow in the side from their neighbor to get them to comply. As she was doing that, the shaggy incubus raised his hands like he was about to flap wings, and slowly lowered them. His group was less aggressive than the white-haired succubus's, but they quieted just as quickly.

The succubus stepped forward. Her narrowed eyes became slits as she scrutinized us. Clasping her hands at stomach level, she connected her thumbs, peaking them above her interlocked hands. "Well?"

The question of expectation hung in the air.

Marijon turned. "Guys?"

I flared my hands, clueless about what I could say that wouldn't set the mob on us. Ralrek stood with his arms crossed, his expression so apathetic he looked like he was daring someone to make him care. He stared ahead like he was examining the depths of an empty room, one not filled with two hundred demons now looking his way.

Seconds seemed to stretch into minutes. An air of tepid expectation thickened. From the back of the room, someone coughed. Ralrek might as well have stayed outside for as much as he looked like he wanted to get involved. Marijon pushed us forward. She'd done her part, and these demons were obviously jaded to her presence and input. Any solution to this standoff had to come from me or Bilba, and I was fresh out of creative solutions.

"I've got nothing," I whispered.

From the crowd, someone snickered haughtily. That set off a slow-building round of murmuring. A few heads shook. Demons scowled. Chins thrust our way, sending a coherent message that if the Isle had alleys, some of these incubi would meet us in a dark one. Though no one tapped into their Abilities, I wasn't about to lower my guard.

Bilba stepped away from our group, his arms wrapping around his waist, not so much in a defensive posture, but one of someone who was going to take a chance and wasn't sure they should.

I almost pulled out Creed when I saw too many sneers in the hostile crowd.

If Bilba saw those responses, he didn't withdraw. He stopped, close enough for the support of proximity, but definitely now the solitary center of focus.

I readied myself. The funk of so many bodies pressed in a confined place didn't help my mood. The outright hostility shown on the faces looking at my best friend only darkened it. I rested my palm on Creed's knob.

"We know we're new," Bilba started, his voice shaking, "and we don't have a right to tell you how to conduct your business."

"Heaven right, you don't," a youthful voice boasted from the ring of overall lovers. It was the same jerk who thought his poo didn't stink at the fight over water. His comment received chuckles from his peers and replies of "hush" and "shhhh" from the other tribes.

Bilba waited, his shoulders shrinking like he was about to collapse in on himself. Intentional or not, his silence put pressure on the overall-wearing idiot, and he flicked his head at his neighbors, trying to look tough but coming across as awkwardly uncomfortable, before falling silent.

Instead of calling out the bully, Bilba spoke in a gentle tone that forced everyone to attend. "But the thing is, we've seen what happens when demons can't agree on how things should be. You don't know us, and we don't know you, but we," he said, lifting his arm to indicate our small group, "have been involved with Council business for years. We've dealt with Michael, Seraph, Beelzebub, and Apopis." That got the murmur train going again. "They have sent us on missions. They have jailed us. Framed us. Wrongly accused us. I've been stripped of my rights as a Major demon because I wouldn't let them bully us into submission."

The time for murmuring had passed.

"Heretic!"

"Lies!"

"Truth." Bilba unlocked his hands from the self-hug and spoke the words so coolly I couldn't help but be transfixed.

Bilba hadn't backed down. They came at him and he swung back. I grinned—probably not the smartest thing I could have done with the politics of the situation, but after so many millennia of seeing demons treat my friend like chimera dung, I'd take this moment to be proud of him.

"Back in the Underworld, I'm referred to as the Rebel Mage. He," Bilba said, his voice no longer shaking, pointing at me, "is the one everyone used to call the Segregate."

I swear I heard someone murmur "Sunstone" in the mass of faces.

Bilba pinned Ralrek with the next jab of his arm. "He was framed in the Gemini case and was supposed to be put to death in the First. Had it not been for the angel attack, he would have been."

"I saw 'im. It's true!" a voice squeaked from the overall wearers. "Both of 'em. Saw 'em both."

The dark-skinned incubus named Sethel tilted his head as if he was considering something new.

Bilba held both his hands up. "This isn't a boast. Honestly, I'm proud of the fact that we've survived the Council's manipulations long enough to be here, and that we've always done what was right. When we made mistakes, terrible mistakes, we did our best to make amends. We're enemies of the government. Like you, we were exiled. We're not here to spy. They didn't put us here to report back on what's happening on the Isle. Just like you, the Council sent us here to die." He took a step forward. "Despite that, we work to make the Underworld a better place." Slowly turning, he asked, "Do you remember Libra?"

He waited and watched. Flashes of recognition were evident on faces across the collection of exiles. Regardless of tribe, name-dropping Libra got their attention.

"We tried to rescue him." Bilba turned, now facing us. He

lifted and spread his arms, looking like he was giving us a distant hug. "This group. Those you ostracize and ignore. Marijon helped us survive the early period of our exile. Without her, I don't know if we'd have had the strength to try what we did. We may have never had the energy to get to Libra's cage, and we definitely couldn't have fought off the guards who attacked us for trying to rescue him."

In that moment, my trepidation that he'd overshared again, that Azazel was wrong about the adoration the Isle had for Libra, was washed away.

The stoic white-haired succubus dropped her hands. Her wrinkled mouth pursed repeatedly as she tried to form her question. "You... you attempted to rescue Libra? You know where he is?"

"Yes, to both." Bilba faced her. "And we're going back to get him, because he's being abused by the Council. For doing nothing wrong, he's being treated in the cruelest of ways, and we're going to stop it."

The room filled with whispers that grew louder as everyone talked over each other.

"So when I tell you we want to help, that we're not spies, that we're not trying to subvert your communities, I mean it."

The air crackled with change. No longer did I fear they'd pull Bilba into their midst and beat the tar out of him. I slipped my hand into my pocket, away from Creed.

"I think we can help you with these issues, but there's something you must do first if it's going to work."

"What is that?" Sethel asked, his head still tilted.

"Bond."

"SERIOUSLY? BLAZEBALL?" I ASKED, WATCHING THE TRIBES CIRCLE the open field near the longhouse. "Why?"

"Because they're never going to work together until they have a reason to." Bilba smiled as the tribes spread out.

"It was a good idea to have them split up," Marijon said, dipping her head toward the mix of strangers. "Let's hope they don't kill each other."

"They won't," Bilba said confidently, "because Zeke is going to keep them busy learning the rules of the game. At least those who don't understand it."

"I am?"

"Yep. You're the best blazeball player I've ever seen. I can't teach them. I'll end up tripping over my own feet and making a fool out of myself. They need someone who can show them how it's done, correctly."

"But I can't cast," I said, tapping Creed. "And I'm asking him to help. Lucifer knows what he'll do."

"Ralrek can help with that," Bilba said, flicking a glance at the silent incubus.

He sighed. "Sure."

The four leaders of the tribes joined us in the middle of the field, ringed by the demons they represented.

"I hope this works," the white-haired succubus said, shooting Sethel a look.

"My tribe will cooperate, Cantrell," he said.

"I hope so."

They stared at each other before nodding almost simultaneously.

"Your tribes better respect us," a thin succubus from the black-clad tribe said, wagging a finger at the others.

Interestingly and disappointingly, the other three representatives didn't respond.

Bilba cleared his throat. "Remember, this only works if all four tribes are invested in making it work. Everyone needs to pull in the same direction. Even if one of you gives off hints you're not completely supportive, your tribe will pick up on that and everything will fall apart. That won't work."

"I just don't see how games will settle our differences," a large incubus in overalls said in a surprisingly soft voice. Taller than Ralrek, somehow his presence didn't dominate this small circle.

"Because forcing discussions when no one sees the value of others will get you nowhere," Bilba answered. "From what I've seen in our time here, the tribes don't see each other as equals, and that will always be a factor in any discussions. By having a blazeball tournament, we'll strip away some of those differences."

"Not all of us are athletic," the thin succubus said.

"It's not about the game. Who cares about the results?" Bilba said, smiling at me. My buddy knew how seriously I take blazeball. "We're going to create a day of celebration."

"Celebrating what, exactly?" Cantrell asked.

Bilba thrust his arms out. "Celebrating this."

The overalled incubus turned, looking back in confusion. "What?"

"Freedom."

The four representatives waited, as if expecting more from my friend. "We're alive. We're not constrained to meeting the expectations of our Circles. There is no Council here. No guards or patrols. No limitations on our speech. Yes, we're stuck on the island, but I can think of worse places to be."

Marijon laughed. "I'm from the Eighth. Trust me, he's absolutely right."

Bilba lifted his arms in an arc, like he was trying to draw a dome around the sky. "It'll be a day of sports and food. Each tribe will bring special dishes, unique to your culture. We'll bring some too, though we don't have much to offer. If anyone in your tribe plays an instrument, tell them to practice now. Artists too. Sculptures. Painters. Whatever your tribes do."

The overall incubus scowled. "Music. Food. Games. There's work to do."

"It can wait for one day," Sethel said, still examining Bilba. "Let's give it one day and go from there. Who knows? Maybe these strangers are onto something. It's worth a try."

"Agreed," Cantrell said. Turning to the thin succubus in black, she said, "Anayese?"

Anayese watched the other three like she expected them to jump her. Finally, she said, "Agreed."

"Then it's settled?" Bilba asked.

"Fine," big overalls said, holding a finger so thick he could have clubbed someone with it. "One day."

"One day," Bilba said with a beaming smile. "Now, Zeke, can you run everyone through the rules?"

"Not everyone is here," Cantrell said.

"We keep groups back to guard our settlements," Sethel added. "And there are those who cannot travel."

"Zeke will teach everyone, then you can go back and explain it to anyone who missed out," Bilba said. "On the day of the tournament, everyone who can travel should. No reason to guard anything if everyone is here. We'll figure out a way to help those who can't travel long distances."

Sethel rolled his lips. "I have ideas."

"Good." Bilba turned to me, gesturing toward the middle of the field. "Zeke, it's your show."

Though the beginning of my instruction was awkward, I soon found my rhythm. It helped when most of the tribes got into the spirit of the rules. Once I got them to collapse on the field and ran them through the motions of the game, it looked like they were putting aside their differences. When I explained the sticks we'd need to craft, a few of the overall wearers volunteered, excitedly, I might add, to make them. When I brought up the fact that the rules allowed for Abilities to be used, everyone readily agreed that wasn't a good idea. The Isle was technically outside Hell, a place where we could be hurt or worse. Still, the fact there was no resistance from the experienced blazeball players brought a smile not only to

Bilba's face, but to the four representatives as well. Demons from all four tribes volunteered to tend to the field when they agreed they weren't young enough for sport but wanted to be part of the festivities. Even the mention that the game was full-contact didn't discourage anyone or their representatives. I'd miss the body checks. A tempered version of my favorite sport, for sure, but an appropriate one considering the circumstances.

We'd already eaten and were relaxing back at our camp before my mind stopped buzzing. "I can't believe you pulled that off, Bilba."

His goofy smile was adorable. "I can't either. I didn't know if it'd work, but Marijon put us on the spot and it was the only thing that came to mind."

Ralrek grunted. "It was a good idea." He put his hand on Bilba's shoulder, rocking him. "I'm proud of you."

"Thanks," Bilba said, patting Ralrek's hand. "Guys, now don't be mad, but I want to go."

I squinted. "Go?"

"Yeah, I need to check on my mother." He held up his hand, stopping me. "I know what Azazel said, but I've got to see the Eighth for myself. Just to check in around the neighborhood. That's all. Talk to neighbors I met when I was staying with her. See if they know anything. That's all. I promise."

I winced. "I don't know, bud. That's risky."

"The Council can't detect my Gateways." He patted Ralrek's knee now that the taller incubus had pulled his hand from Bilba's shoulder. "And now that we know we can open Gateways on the Isle, there's no reason not to sneak away and settle my mind."

He had a point. I hated thinking he'd put himself at risk for his mother, a succubus who hadn't shown him one-sixteenth of the concern he showed her.

"We can go with you," Ralrek said.

"No." Bilba shook his head fervently. "I don't trust that neighborhood. No one will notice a single incubus by himself, out of place. But three? That's a different story. Especially the three of us. We know that. That's too much risk." When he saw my doubt, he said, "Guys, I can handle myself. I promise. I'll be back before the Hellfire feeds."

I kept shaking my head. "I don't like this."

Bilba was up, standing over me and resting his hand on my shoulder. "Zeke, things are ratcheting up. That was a close call with Libra. We can die here, but we can also die on the Acheron." He looked away toward the ocean. "We're running out of time to close chapters in our lives. I need to do this."

"You swear you'll be back before the Hellfire feeds?"

He crossed his fingers. "I swear."

"Ralrek will open a Gateway for us and we'll raise heaven in the Eighth looking for you if you're not," I threatened, meaning it.

"I know." He squeezed my shoulder. "Which is why I'll be back before you take your next dump."

"Funny, I was just about to head off and do that." I rested my hand on his. "Be careful."

"I will. I promise."

I stood, stretched, and grabbed my demonic notebook. I wagged it at Ralrek. "I'm going to head to the beach and think about closing my own chapters. You good?"

Ralrek gave me the thumbs-up. "Gonna sleep."

I waved at the pair. "Before the Hellfire feeds."

"Yes, Zeke," Bilba said with a slight chuckle that betrayed his attempt at being patient with my hovering parenting.

The beach was silent, providing the chorus of crushing waves that always settled my soul.

My demonic notebook lay open in my lap. I'd written one word.

ZEKE: Mom.

One word, incredibly easy to put down on the page. The

magic of the notebook wouldn't send the message until I lifted the point of the quill from the paper. I had it pressed firmly to the page.

What could I say at this point? It wasn't like I was getting a ton of correspondence from the Fifth Circle. It wasn't like she'd gone out of her way to write.

Maybe she'd lost her notebook? Maybe Kanthor had seen our letters? Maybe she didn't care.

"Liberate your soul," Crazy Zeke said inside my head.

Liberation would only come when I felt peace. Slugging through this letter brought me nothing resembling the emotion I desired most.

I closed the notebook and stretched out on my back. The sand was cool and only getting colder. The ocean mists, blocking off my view of anything beyond the first few hundred yards of the Acheron, swirled. Beyond that wall of white was Libra, imprisoned in a cage. The Fifth, my home for six thousand years. My family. My dear ex-boss. The Council. Lucifer. All my troubles and worries.

Bless it, I needed to talk to Cassie. She'd understand. She'd have something helpful to say. But life denied me even that pleasurable distraction.

I tried to ignore the reality that I was spending all my time helping others and doing nothing to help myself. The longing to see the cocoa and blond-haired angel with the ugliest laugh in immortal history was a growing distraction.

I laughed. Alone on the beach, I let it burst out of me. The one who was supposed to wield Creed to liberate, couldn't liberate a single demon in a cage or himself. How's that for irony?

16

UNDERWORLD, FIFTH CIRCLE

"I'M NOT READY FOR THIS." I GROANED, RUNNING MY HAND OVER the cover of a book titled All Hell's Good Incubi. Snatching my hand away, I asked Dialphio. "When did you start carrying smut?"

"It sells," she said unapologetically. "With everything going on here and in the Overworld, times are challenging. Not tough. Not yet. I'm preparing for the worst."

"By selling sex?" I said, trying to keep my face straight.

"If it funds the cell, why not?"

I shook my head in mock disgust. "If the prudes only knew."

"Prudes aren't fun enough to concern myself with their opinions," Dialphio said, chirping.

"Is everyone here?"

Dialphio finished stacking her daily accounts paperwork, tapping it on the edges to ensure it was flush. "No, not everyone."

Ralrek grumbled from the other side of The Book Abyss. Dialphio stopped making the stack of paper perfectly flush, shooting him a disapproving look even though the half-wall constructed completely of titles she'd never sell separated the two demons.

"We've outgrown the room," she said proudly. "A benefit of selling those racy books you seem fixated on is that it earned the store enough to purchase the neighboring property. I've had a crew coming in at night and gutting it so we can make it a focal point of the cell's operations. To anyone walking around Old Towne, they'd think the store closed, and the space was abandoned or would never be used again. A sad testament to hard economic times. Soon, they'll forget there was a store there, and we'll take advantage of that obscurity."

I scratched my chin. "But your bookstore customers will notice."

"That's why the crew is doing their demolition work at night. Once that's finished, they'll start soundproofing the space and then carving out the new work centers I want installed. It's going to be glorious. They've already installed a hidden passageway between the store and that space."

"Where?"

She raised her arm, pointing and tipping her finger like she was ringing one of those tiny, domed metal bells. "Over there. In the back corner. Behind where I cased the expensive books. Customers don't go back there. Even if they did, they wouldn't notice anything. It's concealed."

"It's genius," I said. "That's going to help me sleep at night."

"Oh? Why is that, Ezekial? Are you worried about me?"

"Always," I said seriously.

She took her time sliding her stack of documents into her center desk drawer. It closed with a thud, and her hands remained upside down on the drawer. "As I worry about the three of you. I hope things have improved on the island?"

I was about to run her through the update when Bilba, fresh from coming through on his promise to return from checking on his mother before the Hellfire fed, interrupted. He asked what we were talking about, then took it upon himself to eagerly tell her all we'd achieved with the exiles. Seems the fact that he couldn't find any news on his mother's whereabouts didn't dampen his enthusiasm over making progress with the Isle's tribes.

"Blazeball, huh? Interesting tactic."

"It's going to work. I can feel it," Bilba said, not one to be deterred.

She drifted past us from the back office, into the store's customer area. "Well, I cannot wait to hear how this goes. I'm sure you boys will pull it off. I just hope no one gets injured. Things are moving too quickly toward a very serious situation, and the last thing any of us need is one of you in a cast, splint, or crutches."

"I won't get hurt," I said, sticking my modest chest out.

"Hmmm."

"I'm way too good of a blazeballer, and we're not allowing magic." I added that second part so I sounded less cocky than my statement might have otherwise conveyed.

"Don't make promises you can't keep," Dialphio said. Now at the front door, she checked the lock, even though she'd closed the store upon our arrival, locking it up immediately. She drew the shade. "Young incubi tend to lose their minds when they get competitive. Just remember why you're doing this tournament thing."

She already knew of our attempt to free Libra and had reported it to Azazel. Supposedly, he'd help us with our next try. We just didn't know what his support was going to look like.

"Okay, we're all locked up and secure," she said as she reached the first step leading upstairs. "Are you ready to see everyone again?"

"Depends."

"On?"

"Whether or not they're going to keep making a big deal out of seeing me."

Dialphio made a sound like *pawwwfftttt*, and waved her hand as if she thought I was being silly. I was actually being serious.

"Zeke just wants to know if they want to see his stick," Bilba chimed in. The rims of his ears turned pink when Dialphio blushed.

"You'll want to watch jokes like that," Dialphio said as she started up the stairs, "unless you want your mentor to think less of you."

"My mentor?" Bilba asked, watching her climb. "Melchiot? She's here?"

Dialphio's hand slid along the handrail as she took another step. She reached it, stopping and looking back at my best friend. "After they stripped you of your hard-earned title as a Major demon, she says she found the motivation to get over her fear of standing up to the Council. I thought you might be excited to see her, even though it's only been a few weeks. But if you're going to just sit down here and chat all day..."

She started up again with a short chirp of a laugh.

Bilba smiled. "Melchiot is here." He bounded up the stairs.

I followed, pausing at the third and watching Ralrek. He circled the display of new hardcover releases. "Are you not coming?"

Without looking up, he said, "I will when I'm ready. Go ahead. I'd rather avoid the ruckus for now." His hand had been drifting over the cover of a book as if he was tracing its design. The hand stopped. "I'm okay, Zeke. I'm just not in a good place, and I can't fake it for them. No. I mean, I won't. It's great that they're excited to see us, but I won't be able to return it. Let them have their moment of celebration without me pissing on the parade. I'll be up soon."

"Okay, bud," I said, and climbed the stairs.

The landing was unoccupied. During our first meetings with the rebel cell, my ex-boss had stationed a faithful incubus here to make sure no one strode into a meeting who wasn't supposed to be there.

"Where's Nostris?" I asked, pointing at the empty chair next to the simple standing table. A single lamp lit the landing, making it take on a gloomy feel.

Dialphio's hand rested on the door handle. "In the meeting, of course. He's an important part of our progress. No sense in excluding him. We're too far along for that, and with Azazel sitting in on the meetings, we have measures in place to keep it as safe as possible for everyone. Come, we have a lot to discuss, and not much time to squeeze it all in."

She opened the room, and the conversations on the other side of the door stopped. It reminded me of the times in the Council's chamber when everyone was collected together for another violation of our rights by Hell's rulers, only for Lucifer to show up and turn the screw. Every time He entered the chamber it was like His mere presence silenced demons instantaneously. This was a lot like that, just on a smaller scale, and without the threat of death by the Lord of demons.

Bilba exhaled. It shook.

"We're good. We've done this before," I reminded him.

"I know. It's the expectations that wind me up."

"Release the old ways," Crazy Zeke whispered. Unlike all the times in the past, I was becoming quite used to his presence and oddly timed interruptions. So much so that I could almost always cover any display of my internal struggle. These demons had enough to worry about. They didn't need to concern themselves with the fact that my brain was turning to mush. Though I had to admit, I slowed my steps, hoping I could decipher what in the hell Crazy Zeke was talking about. Old ways? What old ways? Cultural? Familial? Zeke-centric?

"They're here," Dialphio announced as she stepped into the room, moving to the side to allow us past.

I still hadn't heard Ralrek coming up the stairs, so I formulated a quick excuse to buy him time, pushing Crazy Zeke out of the way. I pasted on a warm smile, not feeling as excited as I thought I'd feel about seeing the cell for the first time since being exiled. After all, they were an anchor, something the three of us could tether to and take encouragement from in the dark moments. Their expansion, and that Dialphio no longer had room to host everyone, were signs that should have set my blood pumping. I was excited, but I was a second away from seeing who was included in this bigger batch, and knew that at least Melchiot was involved. Who else? Anyone else I knew? Anyone who didn't believe in our cause? Spies who slipped through undetected?

Turns out, the room held few surprises.

There were loud greetings and lots of handshakes—and a few requests for hugs—but little else. New names and faces, all of which I'd probably forget before we walked out of the room. Nostris was the first to put me in a bear hug, even though we weren't exactly close. Illis wore another garish outfit, just as she had every time before. Just as dependable as her horrendous choice of clothes was her standoffish attitude. Good for keeping the Great Prince grounded, I guess.

"It's so good to see you," Melchiot said, making a beeline for Bilba.

They didn't embrace. Heavens, they didn't even shake hands. She simply came to him, weaving through the crowd to greet him, and then hit the brakes two feet away. It was a comical reunion to witness.

"I can't believe you joined the cell," Bilba said excitedly, looking like he was forcing himself to not embrace her.

"Bilba," she said, his name mutated with her accent that seemed to cut every word short, "I couldn't stand by and watch those injustices take place."

"But your school? They'll shut it down."

"They already have," she said, her dark eyes darting around, never looking at anyone or anything for more than a few seconds at a time. "Right after your Passage. None of us can be surprised after Apopis didn't allow me to attend with you. They knew I'd be able to help you through it. They didn't want that. Once they stripped you of your title, they decommissioned my school within a day."

"Oh my Lucifer, I'm so sorry," Bilba said, reaching out as if to take her hand and yanking him back. "What are you doing now? How are you surviving?"

Melchiot spread her hands. "The only way I can. Let's discuss this another time, shall we?"

"Okay."

"Everyone, let the boys get settled, and then we'll get the meeting going," Dialphio said from in front of the table of food. Leave it up to her to know how to get demons' attention. "We all have plenty of tasks, and they can't be gone from the Isle for too long. Remember, we raise no suspicions." She looked around the room, taking a survey before turning to us. "Where's Ralrek?"

I jerked my thumb toward the door. "He's coming. Just needs a minute."

Dialphio understood. "Okay, let's begin."

The rebel cell was only a few meeting points into their update when Ralrek pushed the door open slowly and slid into the room. He barely made a sound as he made his way to the spread and built a plate of goodies that would sustain him throughout the night. Plate full, he picked from it in the corner of the room while he listened to Dialphio lead the updates. When everyone finished, I had to admit, and did so, they impressed me with all they were accomplishing without landing themselves in prison.

They'd set up an off-the-grid communication network of runners in case the Council was spying on their messages.

Dialphio had formalized a command structure, not out of authoritarian reasons, but so they could function in case one of them was discovered. They had bug-out plans if someone in authority uncovered this meeting place and planned a raid, though Dialphio admitted they had yet to run through an exercise. They even had a budding propaganda machine to fight the Council's rhetoric. All signs were promising.

"Just be careful, please," I said to the group of thirty, three times larger than the last time we'd attended a rebel meeting. "We know the Council will stop at nothing to punish you and those you love."

Heads nodded, including Azazel's. I had to give it to Dialphio. Here was an ancient incubus, one of the Founders, witnessing our scrutiny of the governing body of Hell, plotting its demise, and everyone in this room obviously felt comfortable doing so. A testament to the safe environment she'd created. Proof that Azazel was ready to take any leap required to secure the future of not only Hell, but the realm of mortals as well.

"What security forces do you have?" Ralrek said, leaning against the wall, still feeding himself blocks of cheese.

Dialphio gestured to a succubus standing in the back of the room. She wore a dark outfit and looked as dangerous as meeting Beelzebub in a dark alley. "Scorpio is in charge of that aspect."

The hard-looking woman stepped forward, down the center aisle between tables. The demons closest to the aisle leaned away, as if her proximity was a physical force field. When she reached us, she shook our hands. Though she had small hands, her grip was ridiculously strong. "Nice to meet you."

"Same," I said, finding the need to swallow undeniable.

Ralrek and this new succubus shook hands for a painfully long time.

Thankfully, Dialphio had the wherewithal to break it up. "Tell them about the progress you've made, Scorpio."

She gave Dialphio a sidelong glance. "I'd rather not discuss that openly. Or with them. Not until I get to know them better."

Ralrek scoffed. "Know us better? Didn't you hear who he is?" He pointed at me.

Oh good, I love being the center of attention.

Scorpio looked me up and down like I was a chimera carriage she was thinking of buying. "I'm well aware of who he is. You too. All three of you. I know you so well, I can count how many security risks you create. Bad enough that you've got scores of mortals wrapped up in this. But it's especially risky while you're sharing mission-critical information with angels."

"Whoa. Whoa." I held my hands up. "Don't know where you got that from. But we're doing nothing of the sort."

"Cassie Haniel?" This new succubus cocked her head like she wanted a challenge.

"This is the first chance we've had to meet," Bilba said, stepping forward. "I'm sure all three of us would love to sit down and discuss our roles in securing the future of the Underworld."

"And you think you're doing that by working with angels?" Scorpio asked.

"Even I have to admit, this makes me nervous," Melchiot said. "There's so much at risk. Not just those of us in this room, but everyone around the Underworld. They don't know what they're facing. Introducing angels makes me very nervous."

"They can't be trusted," Viztor said. An older incubus with a cleft chin, he'd always come across as frustrated by everything whenever we were in a meeting together.

I pinched the bridge of my nose.

Dialphio tempered the conversation before I could get

frustrated. "We've been over this issue, and you won't get anywhere with it. Cassie is essential to our operations."

"Cassie is on Yahweh's Council," Scorpio said testily.

Azazel grunted and groaned as he pushed himself up. It took so long, his effort cut off the burgeoning argument. "I can assure you, we can trust Cassie Haniel." He wagged a shaking finger at us. "The boys are smart. They'll never say too much to her or those working for her." He spoke to the entire room. "This goes back a long time. Years, in fact. These boys have proven themselves time and time again."

"That may be," Scorpio said, crossing her arms. "But as long as I'm in charge of security, I'm going to mitigate risks. Especially with these disappearances. Just because other Circles are experiencing more cases than we are doesn't mean I'm going to overlook what's happening and not take precautions. Our operations cannot fail."

"Plenty of demons suspect angels of being behind the disappearances," Zenas said. She was a younger succubus with big hazel eyes. Innocent and considerate, I'd liked her from our first interactions.

"Could be rumors," Ret said, bobbing his shoulders. I suspected nothing less from the friendly incubus.

"It's not just the Underworld," Bilba said, swinging a finger between the three of us. "We've sat down with Virgo's Vigilantes. Disappearances are happening in the Overworld, too."

"Isn't that where Beelzebub attacked the women's clinic? Might have something to do with it," Arin, the librarian look-alike, said.

Bilba shook his head. "No. Cassie let us know that was taken care of immediately following the attack. Angels aren't involved there."

"That's true," Azazel said. He aimed a finger at Scorpio before she could argue or object. "Our Councils worked together to ensure that happened right away. Cooperation is the only way we avoid catastrophe. As I briefed you last time, the time is coming that the Council will no longer exist as it does today. We have to be ready. We need to hear their experiences so we can formulate our own responses. Our strategies. That's our advantage. We have access my peers, for the most part, could only dream of having. Let's not waste it by playing too close to our chest when all relationships between the Upper and Underworlds depend on mutual transparency. To get, we have to give."

"I'd rather take," Scorpio said, spinning and walking to the back of the room.

"Especially since you're not working with Cassie anymore." Melchiot glanced at Dialphio. "If I understand the recent meetings correctly."

"We don't know that for sure," I said.

I'd written to Cassie the day after sulking on the beach. The only way to get through my malaise was by forcing myself. Since I didn't have much going on, with Bilba sleeping the majority of the day away after his quick trip to the Eighth, I deliberated for a long time about writing the angel.

Thankfully, or not, she had a moment to spare and informed me that the duties of her position were impacting her ability to work with Virgo and the Vigilantes. Virgo was worried about disappearances around the city, not only of mortal civilians, but the word was, some of his vigilante crew were not turning up when they should be. Without Cassie's involvement, it wasn't like everyone was heading off The Path and being snuck back into the Upperworld. Vigilantes weren't showing up for duty, and that was a problem, just not one that was important enough to pull Cassie away from her Council duties, apparently. She ended the letter by letting me know she might have to re-assign her Overworld duties to someone else.

I hated everything about that proposition and made sure my buddies, Azazel, and Dialphio knew right away.

It also didn't bode well for earning Scorpio's trust.

"Until we know something for sure, we won't plan around it," Dialphio said, taking control of the meeting again. "For now, let's run through the rest of the minutes. There's something I still need from the boys before they head back."

The rest of the meeting was uneventful, at least for us. I think Dialphio was trying to get us to see how much the cell was doing. But she couldn't get it unless she lived our experience. When you're exiled and constantly tired, hungry, thirsty, and unbathed, there was only so much brain-space left to care about everyone's problems. Plus, I didn't like the feeling I was getting.

Weeks had passed since the last time we sat down with the cell. We weren't strangers, and time made for weird cousins, but something felt off. The unfamiliar faces didn't help relax me, and I told Dialphio that on the way out.

"They'll come around," she said. "This was the first time seeing you for many of them. Give them a chance."

"How much do you know about Scorpio?" Ralrek asked. He was already on the first floor, waiting for the rest of us and looking like he'd love to be away.

"That she's dedicated to the cause," Dialphio said. "You have nothing to worry about with her."

"What's her background?"

"Ex-guard."

Interesting.

"Calm down," Dialphio said. "Just for the sub-Council. She's trustworthy and all about what we're doing. Azazel screened her himself through his sources."

"Fine."

She turned to me. "Zeke, I need a few minutes of your time before you go. There's... Well, there's something I need you to do. And, honestly, you might not like it."

DIALPHIO DRIFTED TO THE BACK CORNER OF THE FIRST FLOOR. Dust hung in the air here, in the least loved part of the store. A maple and glass case held valuable, irreplaceable books that were thousands of years old and drew a great profit margin when they sold, I imagined. The problem was? No one ever bought them. Customers just didn't care about obscure titles from thousands of years ago.

The lighting back here didn't help.

"I can replace the bulb before we leave," I said, pointing at the sconce where the light coming from the bulb looked more sky blue than the Hellfire's azure.

"No, no." Dialphio shook her head. "I like it this way. Keeps customers away."

I chuckled. "Hardly a responsible business decision."

"I don't want them here."

My suspicions grew. "Why?"

She paused at the corner of the wall. A lazy footstep had been dragged through a fine layer of sawdust.

"Ah, I get to see the secret entrance? Why not Bilba and Ralrek?"

"This isn't about the construction project." She placed the flat of her hand on the wall. "I am doing this for you."

"Doing what?"

She pushed against the wall and I heard something click from the other side. "Ezekial, she wanted to see you. She's heartbroken, and I couldn't deny her. Please be patient. Don't be angry with me."

"Dialphio? What's going on?"

When she took the pressure off the door, it slid open. Dialphio stepped back and her secret chamber opened. "Lilith wanted to do this without your father around. Go. Talk to her."

17

UNDERWORLD, FIFTH CIRCLE

MY MOTHER? SHE WAS HERE? SEPARATED BY THIS WALL?

I glanced over my shoulder.

Bilba had his hands to his chest. "Go see her. We can wait."

I lingered. I don't know why. My mother, my blood. The only blood I had left in the world. She was waiting on me and I was hanging out here, unable to move. Unwilling? Waiting for Bilba to impart wisdom? Maybe waiting for Dialphio to say something that would light a fire and help me see through the hurt, pain, and yes, anger of familial betrayal? Who knew? I know I wanted my feet to work, but they were determined to rebel.

I pivoted in the slowest turn in Hell's recorded history. I think I took a deep breath. Dialphio dipped her thick chin to her chest. Somehow, that's all I needed to take the first step.

I want to say it impressed me with what Dialphio's contractors had done with the place, but I wasn't registering the bare floor and walls stripped to their studs. At the end of the rectangular room, a single table had been set out with two chairs. One was neatly pushed up against the table, across the way from the occupied chair.

Though weeks had passed since I last saw my mother, a

lot in our respective worlds had changed. She looked healthier, somehow, her skin more vibrant. As an exile who was supposed to waste away to nothing on an isolated island designed just for that purpose, I probably looked worse to her.

Her relatively healthy appearance didn't mean she looked at peace, though. If anything, her stresses had been on the assault since the last time we spoke, carving deep worry lines across her forehead. She stood like she was seeing a hellcat on the prowl. I smoothed my expression.

This was Lilith Sunstone, after all. More than the succubus who brought me into the world. More than the even keel that prevented Kanthor and me from rocking the family boat too aggressively over the past turbulent years. She'd been there through everything, up to and including my time working for the Council. She deserved a chance.

"Hi, Mom." My voice croaked.

My mother has a jaw like an undefeated boxer, as immovable as the mortals' perception of demons as the 'bad guys.' Yet, in that moment, it quivered. She clamped it, adorable little balls protruding in the back corner of her jaw.

She stood, looking youthful and hopeful, despite the wear of the stress I'd introduced into her life. "Oh, Ezekial." She crossed the space between us. Had Dialphio been standing there hoping to ease the reunification, I worried my mother would bowl over her. She embraced me. Kissed my right cheek, then the left one. When she stepped back, her eyes gleamed with tears. "I didn't know if I'd ever be able to hold you again."

Hold. How did I feel like an imp again? Six thousand years old, responsible for so much, to so many, and I could barely resist the urge to crumble into her arms and have her convince me it was all going away very soon.

"You look like you're doing well for... Well, you look like you're holding up. I'm so sorry for what you're going through, son. It's not fair. If I could change anything, I would."

"I know." We stood there like that for a moment longer before I gestured at the table. "Want to sit? Dialphio is becoming quite the hostess. Wouldn't want to make her go through all this trouble for nothing."

We sat and stared at each other. I didn't know what to say, and she looked like she was fighting an internal battle to not say too much. Talk of the happenings around the neighborhood and the Circle came up first, of course. Easy kills. We stayed away from any flashpoints until she mentioned their house.

I'd lived with my parents until I went to the university, then moved back in when I couldn't survive on my own because real estate prices made it an impossible dream for anyone my age who hadn't tripped over a fat inheritance. It was supposed to be temporary but went on for several years —far more than was healthy for any of us. That led to a lot of head-butting with my father, which didn't help our already-fragile relationship. Mom played peacekeeper the best she could. When I moved out of their angel oak house, it was one of the better days I'd had in a long time—and my life wasn't exactly going swimmingly then. It only got worse afterward, ironically enough. That they were converting the angel oak into a modern home, something my father swore they'd never be able to afford, bothered me. Nothing had changed in their finances. They still shouldn't have been able to afford it. Yet they had. How?

So I asked.

My mother placed a hand on her chest. "How did we afford it? I—that's an odd question, Ezekial."

"It's important," I said. Something was gnawing at me. After my father's betrayal, though, I guess nothing would sit right.

Mother fidgeted. "I don't know, honey. You know money

is your father's business. Plus, I'm so busy with mine, I don't have time to wrap my head around the refinancing he had to do. Weeks and weeks of paperwork, and going to the bank. Utter nightmare, I swear. But we're finished with the refinancing part, I guess. It's just all the construction. Never ends. They're working upstairs, so I have my kitchen back, at least. Though there's not much privacy during the day. I have to work from the living room, which is cluttered with boxes of product."

I didn't want to tell my mother that the house had always been cluttered with the pyramid scheme crap she bought from those above her and then tried to sell to those in the levels underneath her. She refused to understand how it was a scam, and I loved her enough to continue dropping hints when I could. She'd probably never listen, to be honest.

I tapped the table. "Just seems weird."

"What does?"

"That you guys could afford the work. I mean, nothing has changed, right? Dad still has the job at the Hellfire and you're still doing your business. I'm curious why now? How is it possible?"

She stiffened. "Ezekial, we don't have much time, and this is what you want to discuss? When we have so many other pains in our lives. Our family—"

"After what he did?" I didn't need to specify who 'he' was. "I won't forget that, Mom. And I'm curious if a sudden, and very expensive, home renovation is linked to him lying about us. He testified against us, lied about what Bilba and Ralrek were doing with Gateways and Rifts."

"Well, you know you boys were doing things you weren't supposed to," she said, breaking eye contact. "Dangerous things, Ezekial. Your father—"

"Helped the Council exile us," I finished for her.

She had no response to that. I didn't expect one.

I reached across the table, softening my voice. "Mom, this

is hard. I don't enjoy it. But I won't pretend what happened didn't actually go down." I almost called her out on her ignorance about what life on the Isle of Dread was like, but I couldn't. Not to her. Him? Yes, most definitely. Not my mother. My skin warmed. The walls squeezed in.

"What will make this right with you, son?" She reached for me again.

A swirl of thoughts clouded my brain. As with any time you're in a tempest, separating specifics isn't easy. It wasn't this time, either. Finally, I gave her the most honest answer I could. "I don't know."

Her shoulders slumped.

"I'm sorry, but things have changed." I stood and went around to her side of the table. She shuffled to sit sideways on the chair, her hands rubbing each other in her lap. "I love you, Mom. I'd do anything to fix this."

"Then talk to him, please."

"Except that," I said, stressing the first word. "That, I can't do."

Mom seemed to get smaller.

I patted her knee awkwardly, stood, and wrapped my arms around her. Kissing her on top of her head, I turned and fled the room before she saw the turmoil in my face.

Dialphio waited on the other side of the wall. I'm sure she heard everything. She hugged me. "We'll see you soon. I'll send you a note."

"Okay," was all I managed before being drawn by the undeniable need to get to Bilba's open Gateway. "See you."

I was almost at the shimmering image of the Isle of Dread on the other side of the divide when my ex-boss said, "Ezekial?"

"Yeah?" I answered without turning around. I left my head hanging.

"Don't think you can liberate others if you can't liberate yourself."

18

UNDERWORLD, FIFTH CIRCLE

"THIS IS BAD," BILBA SAID, HOLDING OPEN ANOTHER GATEWAY TO The Book Abyss for another trip back to the Fifth.

"That's not the half of it," I said.

"Better not be another update on the cell," Ralrek grumbled. He almost didn't come when I told him Dialphio had written through the demonic notebook, requesting our immediate presence even though only two days had passed since we met with the rebel cell and my upsetting meeting with my mother. "We've wasted enough time. We still can't get anywhere near Libra. Clock is ticking and I won't reset it to have another potluck with them."

I shook my hand. "Dialphio said we had to come right away. Something's going down. This isn't a meeting."

"Good. We've had enough."

I put my hand to the middle of Ralrek's chest as he stepped toward the Gateway. He looked down at it. I left it there. "Listen, that's not helpful, so drop it."

"What's not?"

"Your attitude. Leave it here, okay?"

"Yeah. Sure." Ralrek pushed past me and stepped into the Gateway.

Bilba sighed and shrugged. "He's got a lot on his mind and he's frustrated."

"We all do and are. No different."

Bilba winced. "It's sort of different, Zeke. He's got the whole thing with his father to consider. Who knows how long he'll need to deal with that? So we should probably take it easy on him." He gestured to the Gateway. "Let's figure that out after we hear what this is all about."

We found ourselves in The Book Abyss again, leaving the Isle and its slow progress behind. The tribes and our bonding event disguised as a festival had to wait. We were almost completely moved into Marijon's camp. Libra still dangled in misery in a cage over the ocean. At least Lucifer hadn't visited again, so there was that.

The street outside in Old Towne was empty. The Book Abyss was sober.

"Did we miss the time?" Bilba asked, closing his Gateway.

"No, we couldn't have. She wrote a half hour ago."

"Something could have happened. The Council?" Ralrek said at the foot of the stairs, his head turned to listen.

"The way things have been going, it wouldn't surprise me if Seraph is at the top of the landing with a dozen of her nastiest friends," I said, privately extending my Senses.

Bilba knew what I was up to. "Anything?"

"How did you know I was Sensing?"

His shoulders popped. "You're as transparent as plastic wrap."

I made a flicking motion with the back of my hand. "Get upstairs. If there's anything odious waiting for us, we're all going to walk into it. Nothing we can do now. Especially if Dialphio is in trouble."

As it turns out, she wasn't. Everyone was.

"The entire thing?" Ralrek said, his voice pitched in the first emotion that wasn't pissed off—yes, 'pissed off 'is an emotion if you've lived six thousand years under the Council's rule.

"Yes," Azazel said, spreading his hand. "The entire thing."

We were alone in the cell's meeting room. Me and my gang, the Founder, and my ex-boss. Good thing, too. I wouldn't want to be Hell's hopeful hero and have anyone but these four see how overwhelmed I must have looked at the news that Lucifer's Third Council had self-obliterated.

"How?" Bilba said, betraying his wonderment, confusion, and astonishment. He's smart, so it was nice to have my similar feelings validated.

"Lucifer is doing what He always does," Dialphio said, pacing at the back of the room near a long table where stacks of The Histories of the Balance stood awaiting their distribution. "Not getting involved."

"But doesn't He have to at this point?" I wondered aloud, watching the auburn-haired leader of the rebel cell.

"Normally, yes," Azazel said. His voice shook, but I wasn't sure if from this situation or a betrayal of just how tired he was. "But without declaring a Council President, He condemned any negotiations."

"Not that it mattered." Dialphio shot him a hard look, sharing something left unsaid.

Azazel stroked his goatee like it was helping him recall the younger, but not necessarily vibrant, Lord of the Underworld. "He's always been like that, even when He was younger. From my earliest memories, actually. When I was just friends with Aries instead of peers, and it was him who Lucifer leaned on. Well, at least in those times He bothered to lean on anyone. He moped often. Shut Himself up in that tower when He wasn't. The rest of the time, He was jaded. At least what I remember of the few times I saw Him before I was selected for the Council. Trusted very few demons. Lucifer could be stubborn back then. Stubborn and far too easy to manipulate. He never saw it. Now? Well, the eons have worn Him down.

That's expected when one sits in that seat for so long. I think He's given up."

Dialphio sniffed. Her head dropped. She pinched the arm of her glasses between her teeth.

"Then He should have given the title to someone else." Ralrek looked as displeased as Dialphio, matching scowl for scowl.

"Perhaps that would have been best."

"A good reason for Yahweh to turn over so often," Bilba said with a little too much gusto for the situation. I know this stuff intrigued him, but read the room, buddy. "Lucifer, the one we know, is the same incubus from the beginning of our time, right? He hasn't changed hands."

"Correct." Azazel nodded.

"But Yahweh has."

Azazel was dressed in a gray button-up and dark jeans. Dark leather shoes had replaced his typical go-to white sneakers. So unlike him. "A few times."

"So it's no shock that Lucifer would become less effective," my friend concluded. "If Lucifer was tired from even a young age, what else could any of us expect now? We could dwell on that, or we can plan. I'd rather do the latter." He turned to me, a smile on his face until he noticed no one else joining him, and then reset his expression. "Maybe this is our chance to position you, Zeke? Isn't that what all of this," he said, waving around at the room and all the materials the cell used and created in their efforts to undermine the Council, "is for? Maybe now is our time?"

"Zeke's not ready," Ralrek said.

"Thanks for the vote of confidence."

Azazel raised both of his hands, waving them. "No, no. Too soon. Not all plans are in place." He wagged a finger at Bilba. "But you're not exactly wrong, young Bilba. We cannot sit idle, hoping Lucifer changes His mind, reconvenes the

Council, and sets all of us straight. It's too late. The Council is defunct, and the others are already playing their pieces."

"Do you know that for sure?" Bilba asked.

"Most definitely."

"They have been positioning themselves, boys," Dialphio added. "Tell them what you uncovered, Azazel."

The sound of something that reminded me of the times Gigi would steam coffee at Chilly Willy's came from the Founder's nose. "Yes, yes. I've long suspected the others of working to carve out pieces of the Underworld for themselves. Things like this are complex. You can stare right at the evidence and overlook it in the blink of an eye. Try as I might, I couldn't find validation of my suspicions beyond possibly innocuous maneuvers like the realty deal in the Seventh I told you about."

"Something tells me you have now?" I prompted.

"When Michael tried to establish himself as the de facto ruler after Lucifer's refusal to stop the fracturing, things became very toxic. Of course, by this time, they had excused everyone from the chamber, but I noticed a full squad of Chamber Guards, more than normal, remaining behind. I had two of my own, of course. But I was still outnumbered."

"Are you saying it could have come down to assassination?" Bilba asked.

"Most certainly. It didn't, obviously. But tensions were high. Michael was claiming his right to have unilateral decision-making authority over the Council, or whatever the Council would become. Of course, we opposed him, but he was hardly concerned once he felt Lucifer abandoned us to our own devices."

"He just left you to fight it out?"

"No, he was there," Dialphio said, tipping her chin at Azazel. "He just didn't care, right?"

"One doesn't know if someone else cares or is apathetic,"

Azazel said, "but it was obvious Lucifer was on the periphery of the breakdown."

"Honestly, I'm surprised Seraph or Beelzebub or Apopis didn't try to yank control away from Michael," I said. "Heavens, or all three of them."

"Oh, they didn't have to."

The ominous tone Azazel used told me the really troubling revelation was about to come. My question came out slowly, torturously. "Why?"

"They've all made moves," Dialphio said, sounding as if she was mad at her cousin.

For his part, Azazel seemed far more troubled than I ever recalled, and I have extensive experience with troubling situations in which the Founder had played a role. "I'm convinced Seraph is hiding the Horn. She's not holding it in Lucifer's headquarters, and must have it tucked away somewhere safe."

"Safe, even when she's not present," Dialphio said.

"Mmmm, I'm afraid that is accurate. She definitely has the Horn in her control, which puts everyone at risk."

Ralrek plopped down in a chair. "It's been missing. That's a risk. Hasn't changed. Why's she keeping it quiet?"

"Because she doesn't possess the power she needs. Not yet," Dialphio said.

"Not yet, but she's building it within her circles, that I can promise," Azazel said, tapping his goatee-covered chin. "So we must move. Beelzebub and Apopis have their compound in the Seventh. It's heavily guarded and protected. My source says they're reinforcing it."

"Already?" Bilba asked.

"Already."

"What's their plan?" I asked.

"We don't know that yet."

Ralrek tapped his foot. "Why not? How much time do you need?"

"These things aren't easy when you're spread thin and trying to cover your tracks," the Founder replied. "With dealing with the Council business. Snooping around on my peers. Ensuring Lucifer goes in a direction we can at least work with. Providing the three of you with as much as I can. Looking for the Horn. Helping Dialphio. Tracking Seraph's use of the horn to sway influential demons. I have my hands full."

Dialphio drifted closer. "He's moving as fast as he can, boys. But he can't do it alone."

"Don't ask us to do more," Ralrek said.

My ex-boss snapped her mouth closed, breathed deeply, and restarted what she was about to say before the interruption. "The cell plans to work with others. Not only around the Fifth to unify our efforts, but the other Circles as well. Azazel will have a trusted source to help move us, so Bilba and Ralrek, you won't have to be involved."

"For right now, the priority is freeing Libra, then going after the Horn," Azazel said.

I shook my head. "If we can find it."

"You still have the coordinates?"

"Yes."

Bilba tapped his head. "I've memorized the code."

"Good. That's all you can do for now, unless you're up for uniting the island. We may need their numbers in the time to come."

Ralrek stretched his neck by placing his hands behind his head and pulling forward. "They won't come together. They're too divided."

"But we're trying," Bilba countered. "The tournament and feast will change things. You'll see."

Azazel nodded. "Seems it can work. Though, as with everything, stay true to the cause."

"That's all we're doing," I said.

Azazel held my eyes. "I know, young Ezekial. But let's all

still hope it pays off. Because it has to. With Seraph gaining power and holding the Horn, Beelzebub and Apopis building an army, and Michael using his political connections, everything is broken and headed in the most dangerous direction." Azazel stopped, stroked his goatee, the tips of which weren't as vivaciously orange as they had been over the past few years. "Lucifer has set up individual Councils for now. Somehow, at least in His brain, they'll be able to keep the Underworld running. It won't work."

I asked, "What does that mean?"

"He created what He thinks are separate but equal groups comprising Circle sub-Councils."

"Sounds like a mess," I said.

"Convoluted and unhelpful. It won't work." The Founder sounded sure. "Right now, they have executive power. The Council, now fractured, are useless figureheads."

"Except that they're ensuring their own utility," Dialphio said warningly.

"Everything will only become more dysfunctional. More rapidly." Bilba sounded haunted by the proposition.

"You're absolutely correct, young Bilba," Azazel said, dropping his head. "We're sitting in a chamber not unlike that which contains the Hellfire."

"And it's only a matter of time before it explodes," I guessed.

Azazel gave us a grim look. "The time to find Libra and get to the Horn is winding down."

19

UNDERWORLD, ISLE OF DREAD

IF I THOUGHT LUCIFER CARED ABOUT GIVING US GLORIOUS weather for a blazeball feast day, He would have convinced me with what we had.

The Hellfire was bright and warm. There was just enough of a breeze coming off the ocean and through the forest to cool the day. A comfortable way to play in the tournament and enjoy the music, artists, and food.

Lucifer, the smell of grilled vegetables twisted my stomach into something that gnawed so aggressively it broke my concentration on the game. Rare. When I play blazeball, I focus. The game is my game. When I was younger, it was my release. I wasn't the smartest in Hell, though I could hold my own, but I did far more than that on the field. Maybe it was the island atmosphere, the way things here seemed a world away from the troubles of a troubled mind. Easier, this far away from the rest of Hell, the Overworld world war, the disappearances of demons around the Circles and even from the ranks of Abandoned fighting to keep the mortal realm safe. Maybe it was the competition. Without magic, there wasn't much in the way of competition. Even if these demons were allowed to use their Abilities, I think I could have handled my own against an entire team. By myself. That's not being cocky, just honest. When you're good at something, it's okay to embrace it as long as you're not bludgeoning someone over the head with your superiority.

Countless demons from all four tribes came out of the festivities. Even the harpies showed up, in a swarm, proving there was more than my personal tormentor nesting in the trees around the Isle. At least now, Bilba and Ralrek wouldn't dismiss my crazy talk of the annoying creatures.

The first hour or so was awkward. The tribes mostly hung to their own areas of the oblong field of grass that was way too tall for a blazeball game, but which would have to suffice —I'm a snob about the game and I readily admit it.

Bilba worked the groups, pulling the four representatives away, having them sit together in an open space where everyone could observe their conversation and shared meal. None of them looked ready to play.

"This is amazing," Sethel said, holding a slice of white goat cheese under his nose and smelling a little too deeply. "How have you managed such a subtle scent in your cheeses? Ours are," he continued, waving the slice in the air like it was a tiny fan, "more ammoniated. I like it."

"Thank you," Cantrell said evenly. "We've learned the nannies emit hormones when the billy goats are kept too near. We do our best to keep everyone separated and behaving, and have found that makes for better cheese."

"Well, you've definitely perfected it. Very nice work."

Cantrell's hard face cracked in a flash of a smile. "Thank you."

Bilba looked pleased at the casual conversation and the sharing of information. He even skillfully rerouted the chat when it got too close to the struggle for farming rights that limited solutions for Cantrell's tribe, who I learned were called the Risers, and their goats. A close call, too. We focused them on learning about their tribes.

The Inceptives were the first demons of the Isle. The first to be exiled. Like the other tribes, they were mixed races and backgrounds. Just as with Sethel, who represented them, the Inceptives dressed in brown furs of hare. They had a 'wild farm' where they raised the hares. A cruel necessity of life on their corner of the Isle.

The Planters were the second tribe of the island. Originally, they made their home alongside the Inceptives, but later broke away to establish more agrarian means of sustainment. By the sounds of it, the Inceptives were doing more of that hunter-gatherer thing. To be fair, as early residents of the Isle thousands of years ago, they probably had to focus on surviving and did what they could to see the Hellfire feed for another day. The big incubus in overalls and a soft voice was nominated as their representative because he yielded the best crops in his first few years in exile. He changed his name to Roy when he was exiled for the 'crime' of stealing back his pigs from an unscrupulous administrator in the Fourth Circle. On the Isle, he overcame his personal crimes and taught the rest of the Planters how to copy his methods. Their influence grew after that.

The Risers, Cantrell's demons, broke away from the establishment to form an independent tribe when they pushed the Inceptives and Planters to create a formal community. I guess they wanted the Isle to feel more like home. As more and more disgruntled demons realized there were others thought like them, they migrated toward each other and formed up. They formed a community, and started building up, literally, thanks to having engineers in their numbers, to save space.

But, as with any community of immortals or mortals, nothing lasts forever, and the ugliness of collective imperfection always rises to a crest. Mixed in with casual chats about cheese, farming, the constantly pleasant weather, we learned the fourth tribe, those donning black regardless of how high the temperature, were the misfits of the island. Unlike the other three, this tribe didn't get the chance to name themselves. Their name was assigned by the other three. These were the Untouchables. The sickly, the weak, cast to the side to preserve the greater good. But they didn't expire. Though the implication was that they had a dark history, this tribe of rejects had survived. By the appearances of Anayese, their representative, I wouldn't insult them by saying they were thriving, but they were present and claiming their seat at this meeting of the minds.

"Looks like everyone is getting along," Bilba said, gesturing with the corn cob at the crowd of demons just now splitting into smaller groups.

"Will you look at that?" Sethel's wide mouth expanded even wider at the sight.

Ralrek was the center of attention, having gathered the players together, and was creating small blazeballs. They weren't regulation size—I'm a stickler, remember?—but they were perfect for allowing the groups to practice.

"I cannot believe he got them to practice outside their tribes," I said.

"This is encouraging," Sethel added.

Cantrell watched the disparate groups like they were toddlers she didn't trust to not run out into the street in front of a chimera carriage. "I'm impressed your friend could do that."

"So fast too," Roy nodded before shoveling more beans into his maw.

The groups, teams of eleven players mixed from the four tribes, broke off to practice individually.

"They'll get to know each other very quickly," Sethel said, shooting Bilba a sly look. "Brilliant."

"I just want to make the island more peaceful for everyone," Bilba said, being blatantly honest. I hoped these four representatives felt that. "If we can learn to trust each other and work together, we all win."

Cantrell had been sipping wine—wine, can you believe it? —from a goblet, but stopped. She tipped it at my friend. "What's your end game?"

"End game?" he asked innocently.

"She thinks we're doing this to get something out of them." I didn't look away when she held my gaze.

Bilba was not flustered. "Peace is built on relationships. Relationships require a give and take. That doesn't mean that one side gives and the other takes. We can help you, as we've already proven. You can help us. Everyone wins." He waved both hands like an annoying vendor was trying to push some overpriced black-market goods on him. "None of that matters. Today isn't about any of the bigger problems. It's about the island community. By the end of the festival, I hope you'll see that I mean what I say."

Anayese pressed her lips so firmly that she created speck-sized dimples in her flat cheeks. Around his fat cob of corn, flecks of yellow skins sticking to his cheeks, Roy bobbed his head. Sethel appeared more analytical; Cantrell was more skeptical.

"Well," I said, wanting to avoid any butting of heads, "let the games begin, shall we?"

The representatives, along with me, my two buddies, and Marijon, presented ourselves to the circle of exiles. They tried their best to stay off the field as I'd asked, wanting to preserve the integrity of the game and prevent anyone from snapping an ankle during play because the already-questionable field had been trampled before we even started. After running down a reminder of how the tournament would go, and inviting the teams not involved in a game to enjoy the festival atmosphere around the field, we kicked off the first match.

To say it went smoothly would be an understatement. Though there aren't a lot of rules, especially with no one being able to use their Ability, most of the twenty-two players in the first game still seemed confused. Play had to be stopped every few minutes as the referee explained the rules. One incubus cross-checked another so hard he flew off the field of play. Normally, cross-checking with the flat blazeball bats is allowed. But this wasn't a normal game, and Bilba was smart enough to know that such physical intensity wasn't likely to help the tribes bond. Thankfully, this 'learning opportunity,' as my friend categorized it, didn't result in anything more than grass stains and temporary tension.

The game carried on the best it could. All the teams in the tournament watched that first one, more to make sure everyone who'd never played blazeball understood the rules than for the entertainment factor. Honestly, the one succubus playing a kazoo to a delighted crowd of six was more entertaining than this spectacle. Once that torture was over, the team with younger demons winning, the tournament continued at a faster rate.

Before I'd finished my first coconut pie—I can't play on an empty stomach—the second game was over. This time, a shocker. By the luck of the draw, one team seemed to pull all the bigger demons from the tribes. Eleven hulking incubi and succubi. If you don't know the game, you'd think they'd give them an advantage, but it didn't. The field, normally, is a hundred and twenty yards long and seventy yards wide. Like I said, a big field. This one wasn't nearly regulation size. The island didn't allow for that, but it was still too big for a bunch of large demons to easily cover ground. I thought they'd get their asses handed to them, but they won by a landslide. Their strategy of keeping their best shot closer to the goal at the end of the field did the trick.

I missed the next few games when I had to take a leak. The longhouse was close to the field, but didn't have indoor plumbing like I heard the tribes had in their own communities. It was a hike to get natural privacy to answer the call of said-nature—an oversight in the festivity planning, but one

Bilba could be forgiven for considering how successful the day was.

"There you are," Bilba said when I returned, looking like he was nearing panic mode.

"Had to piss."

"Your game is starting. They're waiting for you. Hurry. Go. Go."

His urgency was questionable. The teams had taken the field. Mine, all ten, turned in short, jerky movements, trying to spot me in the crowd. Bilba was my buddy, but he was mostly definitely taking this day too seriously. I appreciated his passion, but the future of the island didn't hinge on this day's festival. As long as an all-out brawl didn't develop and demons didn't start throwing around spells like boxers fling insults in a pre-bout weigh-in, we were good.

I took the right-forward position after the team brief. Usually, I played center-forward, but that would have put me in a position to receive the blazeball too often, and would turn this from a bonding contest into a rout. None of us wanted or needed that.

Ralrek came out to the center circle to join me and my two fellow forwards and the three from the other team. "You ready for this?"

"You know it."

He rolled his hands like he was massaging a stress ball. "Just take it easy on them."

"We've played before," an incubus from the other team said.

"Sure," Ralrek said with a smirk. "But not against Zeke."

"This is a friendly match." I inched toward my teammates as a subtle reminder that I was as much a part of a team as any of them, and that's where the attention should stay. "Plus, there's nothing wrong with having a little fun."

"Let's hope you remember that when it gets competitive," Ralrek said, still rolling his hands to form the blazeball. Once it reached regulation size, about the size of a mortal volley-ball, he set it on the ground and started away. "Don't break anything."

"Alright, let's kick this off," said the young succubus, prob-ably around my age, serving as the referee. Putting her fore-finger and thumb in her mouth, she whistled for the match to start.

The three from my team charged. Our opponents did as well. We nearly collided, and would have if this was a normal blazeball match. The newer players seemed unsure if they should hit the others. Those who'd played before remem-bered this wasn't the same game they were used to. Collisions were avoided, and the pause gave me a chance to swat at the blazeball with my bat, knocking it past the three forwards.

Scooping it up, I kept it bouncing on the flat of my bat while I dodged the first opponent. She swung her bat, attempting to knock mine down. Had she been successful, I would have dropped the blazeball and turned over posses-sion, because there was no one on my team close. She missed by an Overworld mile.

Seven more opponents stood between me and the goal, but half of them were on the other side of the field, holding their positions. Unless they broke their formation, opening the rest of the field to my teammates, they weren't a factor.

The next incubus tried to jostle me, ostensibly to allow his teammates to join the defense. I was around him in a blink, popping the blazeball up with a slight knock. Before the last defender got close, I swung, sweetly hitting the blazeball with the flat of my bat. It shot toward out in a streak, passing through the center of the goal atop the eight-foot pole that was more square than round thanks to the non-existent manufacturing facilities on the island.

The referee whistled, signaling the point.

Scorekeeping isn't a thing in blazeball. Well, it is. But the point of scoring is not the, er, point, if you will. Whenever a player hits the blazeball through the opponent's goal, the team conceding has to take a player off the field. The game continues until one team is out of players.

Our opponents were down to ten.

Play restarted with the ball charge. We won that—okay, well, technically, I won it. I was through the defense again, this time nearly walking the blazeball to the pole before hitting it through the goal.

Down to nine. We had a two-demon advantage now, and used it well, scoring two more times.

"Let's take it a little easy on them," I said as we walked back to the center circle after our fifth goal. "Give them some fun."

The score was eleven to six. A romp. None of us wanted to embarrass our opponents, and I definitely wasn't interested in undermining Bilba's plan to help the tribes bond by humiliating anyone, so we toned down our efforts.

In the end, we conceded three goals before running the other team out. I promise, we weren't bullying them. They exhausted themselves trying to score. Down several players, they couldn't keep up. It would have been worse if we didn't try to score. Everyone would know we were allowing them to stay in the game, confident we could win it. I know that'd piss me off if I was in their position. So we finished them and returned to the festivities a little sweatier and ready to enjoy the food and music.

"How's it going?" I asked Bilba when I found him again.

He had been sitting with the representatives all morning, but now that the tournament was in full swing, he made his way around the festival. He checked out the artists, watched a painter, listened to the Planters band playing in the far corner, and was now with a group of elderly demons sitting in the shade.

He joined me in my quest to find something to eat. Leaning in, he said, "This is better than I could have expected.

Just a few minutes ago, I sat with succubi from all four tribes. They shared stories of their tribes' respective histories. They talked about their spouses and children." He grabbed my wrist. "They even talked about their hopes for the future. Do you know how important that is? It's significant, Zeke. It really is!"

I couldn't help but laugh. "Yes, it is. That's awesome." We stopped to get in line for a desert the Risers swore was the best in all nine Circles. A berry tart, it proved their claim true.

Bilba used his pinky to scoop his bowl clean. "This is amazing."

We stood back from the food stalls. The clumps of demons sitting in the grass together, getting to know one another, the teams stretching for upcoming matches, the musicians, magicians, and even the old incubus weaving straw into animal forms for the youngest in attendance kept the atmosphere lively and light.

"Island life wouldn't be so bad if it was like this every day." I wrapped my arm around his shoulder. "You've done well, buddy."

Bilba sighed contently. "This has to work."

I squeezed him closer. "Don't put pressure on yourself. It'll happen, but it has to happen in its own time. Look at what you've done. Everyone is together. The tribes helped set this up, cook, entertain, and build this atmosphere." I held my arm horizontally, moving from left to right. "Walls have been broken down, buddy. All because of you. Some of them have been here for thousands of years and have done nothing like this. We haven't even been here a month and you've pulled it off. Be proud and enjoy what you've created."

Under my arm, I could feel his shoulders lift as he filled his chest with a satisfied breath. "I guess you're right. Thanks."

"We should thank you."

A whistle from the field signaled the end of another match, and with it, the end of the first round of eliminations.

"Down to eight teams," Bilba said, watching me from the corner of his eyes. "Are you going to behave, or are you looking to lift the trophy?"

"There's a trophy?" I said with mock enthusiasm.

"No." He laughed. "Lucifer, you're ridiculous. I'm surprised you haven't checked out the bracket board to see how everyone else performed."

"I was thinking about heading that way, to be honest."

"Of course you were."

I denied the temptation throughout the first quarterfinals match. Bilba had moved off to continue meeting demons and making connections. I'd listened to a band playing a type of music that reminded me a lot of the Overworld's grunge. When they finished their set, I couldn't put off the need to see what the results from the first round had been.

Most of those matches were close. Some were blowouts. Ours was the second-most non-competitive final score. A team calling themselves The Islanders, as if they represented our entire island community, had won their match with a perfect eleven-zero score.

Well, that wasn't cool of them. I'd have to remember The Islanders if we faced them in the final.

As it was, that would have to wait. We had a quarterfinal match against the Squatters. Weekend beer league-type stuff, I tell you. But the match was fun. My team asked me to play center-defense because I'd apparently had too much of the blazeball in the first match. Still, even starting in defense and playing the entire match there, I scored four times. We won that match at a canter. Actually, it was over so quickly I didn't even have time to get hungry again.

I still ate though—don't judge me.

"You act like you're starving," Ralrek said from behind.

I turned to see him holding two plates of potatoes. They

were slathered in butter and chives to spice up the typically bland food. To a demon who'd never left Hell, they'd think he was nuts for 'destroying' good food like that. But demons didn't know good food. The Overworld had it in abundance, and only those fortunate enough, or those sacrificed by the Council, to go to the mortal realm could understand. "You're one to talk."

He lifted his plates. "Oh, these? Do you know how much energy it takes to maintain that blazeball through all these games?"

"Why can't someone else do it? Give you a break."

Ralrek made a low humming sound. "What else do I have to do? I've eaten almost everything there is to eat. Who knew they could grow so much good food? Not so bad here when we get to eat like this."

I chuckled. "Was just saying the same thing to Bilba." I patted him on the shoulder. "Let's enjoy the day. Just don't work too hard."

"Holding a blazeball spell is the easiest thing I've done in a long time with my Ability. Plus, it helps me work on my control."

"Lucifer knows you need all the help you can get."

He gave me a playful shove. It was nice to see his character coming back. "Don't you have a tournament to win?"

I made a pew-pew gesture with my thumb and finger that I'd learned from watching mortal children in the Overworld. "Yes. Let me return to the games while you work. See ya."

"Good luck, asshole," he called out after me.

"Thanks." I waved at him with my middle finger extended —a gesture I picked up, again, from a mortal in Seattle that wouldn't mean a thing in Hell. That wasn't important. What was, was that Ralrek would understand.

His guffaw was my confirmation.

The oldest incubus on our team went down in the next match. Twisted ankle. The injury happened early in the match. The spirit of the tournament wasn't to have big teams so we could have substitutions, which meant we were down a player for the rest of this game and the championship if we moved on.

This game was more of a challenge, as it should be for a semifinal match. Our opponents, ironically named the Turtles —ironic because they were a quick team to the player—were smart. They must have had some experienced players, because they knew the beauty of blazeball was not only its fluidity, but that it also involved strategy. Instead of concentrating solely on attack or defense, they took advantage of the laws of the game within the boundaries of the rules set out for our version here.

Use of Abilities was outlawed, but that didn't mean they couldn't use the other rules. Players were allowed to tag an opponent by hitting them with the blazeball. The Turtles, we discovered when the match was at five-four, with them on the losing end, were holding this allowance close to the vest until they needed it.

The first of my teammates they took out was our weakest player. Not a big loss for the game, but they really went for the easy target, and that wasn't cool. The poor guy had turned to chase a player and slipped. Face down, he never saw the opponent bat the blazeball back to a teammate standing over my prone teammate. She swatted the blazeball on the first contact, shooting it straight onto my teammate's back. He howled until a spectator used their Water Ability to put out the blossom of flames that caught on his shirt.

The referee had to call for a timeout while she recruited and stationed four Water users around the field to prevent any further injuries. Thankfully, Ralrek hadn't made his ball blazing—this was a toned-down version of the game after all. No one needed to lose clothes here. Materials were hard enough to come by.

After he was taken care of, it might be easy to say I went a little overboard, but I couldn't help myself. They ticked me off. Sure, what they did wasn't against the rules, but it wasn't in the game's spirit either. So I may or may not have stepped out of my role as a dedicated defender and eliminated the rest of their players by scoring the first goal that took them back down one player. Once that happened, the floodgates opened, and I tore through what remained of their team. We finished with our four, for a final score of four-zero. It was the least they deserved.

"Nice game, bully," Ralrek said with a wink when I passed. He was hanging out with a guy from the Risers. They looked to be getting chummy.

I couldn't have been happier for him. But when I was almost out of his earshot, he had one more comment that rang true.

"Try to tone it down for the championship, okay? This is about bringing everyone together, not dishing out ass-kickings. Save that for the Council."

A timely reminder, just as my adrenaline was dwindling. Someone, a group of someones, deserved my best efforts, and it wasn't the demons I shared my exile with. Not hundreds of demons, but four. And those four were going to get everything I had.

20

UNDERWORLD, ISLE OF DREAD

"I want to win," Holy—yes, not 'Holly'—said.

"Me too," our best defender, Bennet, said. He pumped his first to deliver the message with more gusto.

I held up my hand, careful to not assume the role of captain. This was a team, and there's no 'I' in team, except for 'wInnIng team," and winning wasn't what we were here for. A mental image of Bilba's floating head hung over my shoulder. Its presence, constant. Damn, Bilba. Asking me to temper my competitiveness was the cruelest of cruel, even though he literally wasn't here doing it. Did he really have that kind of effect on me? The big old, intelligent, lovable jerk. "Remember, we're here for the fun of it."

"And to win the championship," Bennet said and winked like we shared an inside joke.

"Coming together," I said.

"To lift the trophy," he said. Another wink.

"Wait, why does everyone keep saying that? Is there seriously a trophy?"

Bennet clapped like he was trying to smack a fly. "Don't we wish? We'd shove that in the Untouchables' faces."

I was pretty sure the lanky incubus who played wing for

us was an Untouchable because of his black garb. The flash of annoyance he showed helped—I'm not exactly a sleuth. None of that mattered. Bennet was missing the point of the game. "I don't want to be 'that guy,'" I said, knowing I already sounded like him, "but the purpose of this is to have fun. If we win, great. If we don't, life will go on. We just hope, when it does, it's a little better than what the Isle was like before."

The lanky guy—I really needed to learn his name—grumbled his agreement.

"Okay, can we round up and figure out how we're going to play?" Holy asked, going into game mode.

We did as The Islanders—yes, they capitalized both words in their team name—strutted out of the forest surrounding the field at the last minute. Supposedly, they didn't trust us to not spy on their game plan. Whatever it was, it involved a lot of yelling and far too much chest-pounding for something that was supposed to be a friendly match.

"They're going to be tough," Bennet said, eying the athletic-looking team as they huddled one more time on their half of the field. They threw in a few head butts for good measure.

"They're just trying to get in our heads. Don't let them." I moved toward the center circle, raising my arm and encouraging my teammates forward. That drew a few confused and skeptical glances. "Come on, guys. It's the final. We've earned this."

Typically, just the forwards enter the circle to fight for the blazeball. Pulling everyone up showed solidarity and unity, and a distinct misunderstanding of the nature of the game. If The Islanders won the scuffle, they'd have a wide-open backfield to attack into. Bilba's big-eared monstrous head remained floating in my mind's eye. This was about togetherness, not wins.

I repeated the message all the way to the center circle. The three Islanders forwards watched us, showing more than a modicum of humor.

"Hey guys," I said without hesitation.

All three were bigger than me, but that wouldn't intimidate me or my sense of the purpose of the day. Not because I had the rest of the team around me, but because no one in blazeball intimidated me. This was my game. I mean, I was never a professional, but that's more to do with the fact that I lacked the discipline to train throughout my childhood. I just wanted to play. Had I been serious, had a coach in school, or a father who wanted to spend time with me and run me through drills at night and on weekends, maybe I would have become something in the sport. Maybe not. No, three overstuffed burritos holding blazeball bats weren't intimidating.

My teammates' steps quickened. I hoped they sensed my confidence, of which I had more than a fair share.

The referee came to the circle, gave the size of our contingent a double-take, and then went through the motions of briefing us on the rules even though we'd heard them before each match.

An Islanders forward extended his finger, rolling his hand. "Yeah. Yeah. We got it. Let's kick this off."

He smacked bats with a dufus to his side in a show of overstocked testosterone, and the ref set the blazeball at the center point.

"We ready?" I said, turning to my team.

I saw a row of smiles. We had the right mindset. Already, that put us ahead of The Islanders and their stupid insistence on capitalizing the T in their name.

Who does that?

When they won the scuffle for the blazeball and passed it to a sprinter in our backfield, scoring within the first ten seconds of the match, we might have been winning in attitude, but we were definitely losing on the scoreboard.

"I'll go," Janey said, raising her hand. She'd played all four matches, looking more tired with each one. I wasn't surprised she was the first to raise her hand. Before walking off, she shook a fist, and just for a flash, her pale skin deepened with blood. "Go get them!"

It was the weakest rah-rah speech I'd ever heard, but it was charming and friendly.

The Islanders won the blazeball again, but this time we were set in our nine-player formation—three forwards, three midfielders, and three defenders. We slowed them down, but couldn't do much when one of their forwards ran into our right defender, knocking him down. The opponent put his non-bat hand in the air to plead his innocence. The referee bought it, and the Islander passed the blazeball backward. I saw what was coming before it happened.

The midfielder swatted the ball into the air to slow it, let it come back down to rest on the flat of his bat, and propelled the ball into our felled defender. Because of the earlier use of the tactic, Water users were still on standby and put out his fiery clothes, but we were down another player.

Eleven for the Islanders—oh, excuse me—The Islanders. Eight for us.

This wasn't about winning. This wasn't about winning. This wasn't... oh, who was I fooling?

I won the next faceoff. I took the ball through their defense with two moves, one dodge, and a hop over a bat that was swung way too high and swiftly for the opponent to claim he wasn't going after my body. I felt a deep sense of satisfaction when my strike sent the blazeball sailing through the goal.

Ten for the Islanders. Eight for us.

Again, the next faceoff was mine to win. They tried to stop me by guarding me with three players. Smart to slow me down, but pretty insulting to my teammates, considering this was supposed to be a friendly match. A bad move. I passed the blazeball to Holy.

She dropped it and The Islanders almost regained possession. But Holy, complete with a grim expression, squatted and scooped the blazeball onto the flat of her bat. She twisted her wrists and sent it to the lanky guy, calling out, "Catch, Simeon!"

He took it and scampered forward five yards before an Islander confronted him. The succubus took a wicked swing at Simeon's bat when he tried to dodge past her. The problem was, his appendages were so long that when he extended them, he gave her plenty to aim for.

Simeon's bat collapsed, and the blazeball tumbled away.

He went to reach for it and was shouldered out of the way by the succubus. He yelled out. She laughed. Another Islander, this guy about the size of the mesa standing watch over the Isle, lurched to scoop up the most valuable asset in the game. He started—well, calling it 'racing' would be an injustice to anyone who has ever raced in their lives, including schoolyard challenges—toward our goal.

"Not on my watch." I growled as I sprinted past the sole Islander between me and the giant incubus.

From my perspective, it was funny watching the cocky sneer slide off the incubus's face. He was exerting, but there was no way on his best day and my legs tied over my head, that he'd outrace me. What had been a cocky jaunt toward our goal suddenly turned into a harried runaway wobble when he saw me barreling down. He was using all his brain-power to concentrate on not dropping the ball, leaving nothing to direct his pumping legs and arms.

I could have swatted his bat with mine. He would have dropped the blazeball, no doubt. Heavens, he was almost dropping it now that I had him so unnerved. The ball rolled and swayed on his bat, and nearly toppled with every island-pounding step.

But I didn't want to swat the blazeball out of his hand. I wanted to remind the Islanders—no, I wouldn't use their full name—that you don't dish out what you can't take. That was the problem with this place. Too many demons thinking they had a right to do what they wanted, whether that perceived entitlement was hogging the water, or the fertile farming land, or betraying the spirit of friendly competition. The purpose of today was to bring everyone together, or at least try to. Yet, here we were in the finals, and this team still didn't get it. Someone had to drive home the message.

I did that by driving my shoulder into the big guy's flabby side. It felt like jumping into an oversized marshmallow.

The speed of my approach worked wonders. Got to love physics. The big guy rocketed sideways, landing in a heap, dropping his bat and the blazeball. We were close enough to the boundary to hear the 'ohs' and 'ahs' from the crowd, along with plenty of giggles. The big incubus rolled for another five feet before his momentum slowed. By then, I'd balanced the blazeball on my bat and I was zipping through the Islanders' defensive ranks. A couple missed swings and shoulder charges later, I was at the step of the pole, just outside the no-shoot-zone spanning a ten-foot radius around the pole's base, and rocketing the blazeball through the loop.

I hit it so hard it flew into the crowd behind the goal, dispersing them in a panicked moment.

I used that time to rejoin my team, not even acknowledging the obviously frustrated and definitely pissed-off opponents as I passed them.

Nine-eight.

"Nice one," Holy said, beaming.

Simeon was still rubbing his shoulder as we touched bats. "Thanks for that, Zeke."

"No problem, man. We're a team, right?"

"Blessed right, we are."

Bennet nudged his chin in the direction of the center circle. "Will you take the face-off, Zeke?"

"Someone else should get a turn."

"Let's worry about that when we're level again," Holy said with a fierce fire in her eyes.

"Okay," I begrudgingly said, taking my place in the circle.

The Islanders adjusted when they saw me approach, adding two more forwards to the circle. Three-on-one. Nice.

The referee blew the whistle. One Islander made a beeline to me, bowling me over and knocking me to the ground. His fat ass, almost literally, sat on me while stuff happened all around us.

He looked down, grinning with a dot of saliva in the corner of his mouth. "Fuck you, Speedy."

A roar went up from the Islanders.

Nine-seven.

Okay, now I was officially done. Bilba could figure out another way to bring the island's tribes together.

I wish I could provide details, but everything became a blur.

Once he got off me to celebrate with his teammates over their dirty goal, mine helped me stand. Words were said. They could have been asking if I was okay, if I'd take the center again, or if I'd quit it all and find the nearest Over-world chicken wing hotspot. Every sound blurred into a deep, flat rumble. All I could hear was the thumping of my heart as it slammed against my protective rib cage.

This was war and I was the Lucifer-blessed general leading the troops—because, you know, between the Over-world world war and my battle against Lucifer's Council, I didn't have enough strife in my life.

The whistle cut through the blur. The Islanders moved toward the blazeball. Time to act.

I won the face-off, beating the three of them. I zipped and dodged through their defense, once flipping over a lateral swing that reminded me of one of those Overworld baseball players. I'd mention that I didn't even drop the blazeball, but that would sound like bragging.

Eight-seven.

I won the next face-off, repeating my strategy. This time, on the right side of the field.

Seven-seven.

Again, hell hath no fury like a demon bullying bullies.

Seven-six for the good guys.

But I wasn't done. The score was down to Seven-four for us when I felt it. Someone was tapping into their Ability. I was slow to react because I was in the middle of a blazeball game, nearly single-handedly taking the game to the jerks. Hot and sweaty, I could have been forgiven for not noticing the warmth glowing on my arms, my neck, the rims of my ears.

As I neared their goal, about to shoot the blazeball through and give us a two-player advantage, the post and loop warped. The head wagged around like a cobra. As the blazeball flew, the loop swayed like a boxer avoiding a punch. The blazeball sailed past it. Miss.

I've been in awkward situations in my life. That's commonplace when you're the only demon in the history of Hell without magic. Oh, and those awkward years between two thousand and about five thousand years—mortals would call those the teen years—when there isn't anything in life that isn't awkward. Even those times would have had difficulty comparing to what happened when that wooden pole and squared loop goal bent to prevent me from scoring. A hush fell over the crowd, flowing out toward the comedians, artists, culinary masters, and even the bands playing at different corners of the festival.

The referee put her hand to her mouth, connecting her thumb and finger at the tips, and blew a weak, almost tentative, whistle.

Bilba excused his way through the crowd, joined by the four tribes' representatives.

I held my hands up. "I didn't do it."

"I know." Bilba rounded up the representatives, referee, and players. "What do we do now?"

Sethel inhaled, his broad nose expanding. "This is touchy. That was a stupid thing to do." He held up a gnarly hand, cutting off any potential arguments. "No, I won't hear any defense for it. I don't care which tribe you're from. Whoever did that is in the wrong. I'm sure you'd agree?" The other three representatives, even Cantrell, nodded without hesitation.

"We can't let this continue," Anayese said.

"It's the final," Roy said, wagging a half-eaten corn cob in the air. "Everyone needs to see it finished."

"For what reason?"

"Need a champ."

"I don't think that's the priority here," Cantrell said. She folded her hands, pressing them against her stomach. "We don't have time for games, and now this has added another problem. Whoever did that should be ashamed of themselves."

Feet shuffled. Someone cleared their throat. I watched the players from the Islanders, trying to pick out the guilty party while pushing my Sensing out to make sure they weren't still holding their Ability.

Bilba made direct eye contact. He knew what I was up to. Ah, best friends. Being able to communicate without saying a word. Excellent stuff.

Whoever had screwed up the day by the taboo tactic hid now. I didn't want everyone to know I could sense magic, so I simply told my friend, "We're good."

"We won't let this ruin a great day. A mistake in the heat of the moment. That's all. No one got hurt. A misjudgment." He stopped, turning slowly to address the circle. "Let's not forget why we're here. Everyone has worked so hard to make this a festive occasion. When was the last time you felt community like this?" He waited. An uncomfortably long time passed.

Everyone knew the answer. "I don't know all of you or the reasons for your exile, but I'll bet everyone not born on the Isle got screwed by those in power. There is no greater reason to unite. If we all come together, as we've proven today we can, we can build something great. If we do, every day can be like this."

"A festival every day?" Cantrell scoffed. "Hardly can afford the time away."

"I liked it," Anayese said, her mouth tucked toward her shoulder. "It was fun."

Roy waved his corn cob again. "I agree."

Bilba waved his hands like he was trying to clear beach sand from a buried treasure. "No, no. Not like this. But working together, sharing resources to make a safer, more secure future for everyone. Honestly. When you see something like this." He stopped, angling his arms so they formed a V above him. "Doesn't this make you think of what it could be like, so far away from the Council, if we were to build an island community of togetherness?"

"Not without my children and grandchildren," Cantrell said stiffly.

"The day may come when we can reunify families," Bilba said, and I swear, the island air stilled as everyone waited for him. "We've traveled through the mist wall when we tried to rescue Libra. One day, maybe we can do that for reunifications?"

Roy held his corn cob in a dangling arm. "But no one can get past the mist."

"We can. And have," I said, firm but friendly. "We will again. And if everyone here would stop fighting each other over stuff and start working together, we could do more than punch through the mist, because that goes both ways."

Anayese craned her neck. "You could really bring our families?"

"Let's not get too far," Sethel said, tipping his head. "This is encouraging, but we cannot think about that until we discuss what these young incubi have been saying since their first day here."

"But our families—"

"Bringing our families here would only exacerbate our problems," Sethel stated calmly. "Once we have a workable solution where everyone—"

"In every community," Anayese cut him off.

Sethel bobbed his head. "Yes, everyone in every tribe. Once we all believe we're pulling in the same direction as a single island community, maybe then we should have a conversation about our families."

"As much as I hate to agree," Cantrell said, her voice cracking for the first time. Kudos to her for keeping herself as hard as the mesa. "Sethel is correct. Tension mars our history. That's not a situation to bring our loved ones into. Let's straighten up our mess, then open our arms." She looked at me. Her high cheekbones dominated her face. With a stiff nod, she moved on to Bilba. "And you. You are very impressive. I think the four of us should sit with you and agree about fair use of resources." She eyed her peers. "Anyone disagree with that?"

Roy shook his head while returning the corn cob to his mouth. His top lip formed a sharp angle just above the cob. "No, ma'am."

Anayese wrapped her bony arms around her thin waist. The movement cinched her black garments tighter, showing just how frail she was. Were all the Untouchables like this? "I just miss my family. But, I agree."

"Okay," Bilba said, like someone had just offered to take him for devilhorn cake. "Let's finish the championship, and then we can kick off the celebration." He winked at me. "I asked Ralrek to cook up a surprise." They started clearing the field, but not before I heard him tell the representatives he also hoped they had time to chat about teaching others Gateways and Rifts.

I left that alone. Let the bigwigs handle the important stuff.

And you know what happened? The pause to cool off worked. The Islanders and us batted the ball around. We chased each other. No one swung a bat to knock the ball free. Every time one side went down a player, the other followed suit. The game went down to a one-on-one duel, me against the succubus who kicked off the nastiness.

At the center circle for the last face-off, she smiled. It was an attractive smile for someone from the Isle who probably hadn't had proper dental care since her first step onto its dock.

"Ready to get beaten?"

"You have to score first," she said, the smile never slipping. She might have been flirting, I don't know.

She was a handful, but in the end, I could have put the game away ten times. I chose not to. Not because I wanted to draw out her torture, but because of the reaction the crowd was giving us. One section by the veggie kabob table started cheering for Slash—yes, she insisted that was her name. After that, the crowd across the way cheered for me whenever I picked up the blazeball. This went back and forth, growing louder with each turnover. Then all sides began cheering for each advantage gained, like they didn't care who won.

The goodwill lasted as long as we kept them entertained. But then the crowd grew as tired as us and the referee agreed to a shootout.

"First one to miss after both have shot for the round loses," she said. "We'll start out at twenty yards and increase by five yards each hit."

Even that lasted too long. At fifty yards, we were allowed to use our Abilities to assist our shots, and to distract, not harm, our opponents. Turns out, Slash had Water magic. Two things came out of that. First, she wasn't guilty of cheating earlier with the goalpost debacle. Second, she had firm control over her Ability. I discovered that the first time I missed, and she went second with her shot.

It looked on target. Since Abilities were now allowed, I called Creed from where I had him stuck in the grass on the sideline. Demons ducked even though it was in front of them and coming my way.

I caught it and took aim. "Knock that shit down, buddy." I fired.

Creed zipped through the air, splintering her ice-encased blazeball and sending it toppling into the grass.

She stuck out her tongue. "Nice stick."

"Thanks. A lot of ladies say that."

"Do you always go wagging it around like that in public?"

I nearly choked on my spit.

My next three throws were crap, but that was Slash's fault. Her Water spells were powerful streams that kept knocking the blazeball off target. I still had the wherewithal to knock her ever-weakening ice balls out of the sky each time she shot. She wasn't steady on her feet at eighty-five yards. Nearly collapsed at ninety.

"Please," she panted when I caught her, "just score. I don't have it in me to go another round."

I almost made a 'that's what she said' joke, but I think that's copyrighted. "Are you sure?"

"Yes." She pushed herself off me. Not in a 'I'm repulsed by you' way. More like a 'I'm literally going to pass out if we try to carry on' manner. "It was fun, but not anymore. Honestly, I'm freaking hungry."

A succubus after my own heart.

"Okay. If you're sure."

She bent, placing her hands on her knees. She lifted her drooping head. "I'm sure."

"Okay," I said, lifting Creed and aiming its wavy dagger at

the blazeball. "Do you have enough left over to encase that in a solid ice ball again?"

"It's your shot."

"I know, but I need something to stick my halberd into. Plus, as tacky as it sounds, it'll be a way for both of us to be part of the winning goal."

She raised an eyebrow. One corner of her lips slowly peeled up. "You're right. That is tacky. Let's do it."

"You sure?"

"I'm sure that I'm starving and ready to ransack that kabob stand," Slash said, lifting her arms and dangling her fingers.

The sensation of a cool, smooth stone lightly drifting over my skin followed. A sheet of white ice seemed to swell from within the blazeball, neither melting nor putting out the flames. It cracked and popped as it thickened.

"There you go. Finish this."

"Nice work." I jammed Creed's dagger into the ice. I pulled Creed up, its magic negating the weight of the ice-encased blazeball.

A murmur oozed from the hundreds of demons watching the final event, I hoped, of the tournament.

"Stay true, buddy," I told the halberd. It buzzed quietly.

Creed shot through the air when I thrust forward. Demons in the crowd shouted 'oooohs' and 'ahhhhs' as Creed sped toward the goal. True to my instructions, it pierced the wooden goal, and a cheer went up all around us.

I turned and high-fived Slash. "Let's go eat."

The festival turned into a party after the tournament. I met so many demons I'd have been lucky to remember three names tomorrow. Throughout the evening and into the night, as one community, we chatted, joked, listened to the musicians, and sang along to a string of Hell's old-time favorites. We laughed along with the stand-up comic and even broke out into flash mobs of dancing.

Much later, Bilba threw a heavy arm around my shoulder.

"This is awesome, Zeke. I think we even came to an agreement about land use."

I patted him on the back. "Congrats, bud." Waiving my hand in the air at the festivities, I said, "All your doing. I hope you're proud? Because you should be."

"I am." He went silent for a moment and smacked my arm. "Oh, I've got to get Ralrek."

I looked, half expecting to see that a brawl had broken out just from the urgency in Bilba's voice. The Hellfire had fed, a deep purple held the sky. Torches had been lit during a show, lighting small areas of the field with a deep azure. "What's the problem? Everything okay?"

"Yeah. Yeah. I had asked him for a fireworks show to bring everything together. I guess we should get him to do it now, before the tribes head back."

"I've got to see this," I said with a smile I couldn't hide. Just seeing Bilba's excitement and pride swelled my heart. Humble to a fault, this was a guy who'd become a Major demon earlier than anyone, and still hadn't seen his accomplishment as something to brag about. He'd never changed. He never would.

Ralrek was at a campfire, being forced to sing a traditional campfire song. He looked so happy to be rescued by Bilba.

"Are we doing this?" he asked.

"Do you have energy left after keeping that blazeball alive all day?" I had to admit, he looked as spry as if he'd just woken.

"I'm good."

Bilba waved his hands over his head, signaling the crowd nearest us. "Come on. To the beach. We have one more surprise for you. Pass the word. Bring your drinks and food."

The buzz prickled my skin. I felt re-energized by the collective enthusiasm. The smiles, the breaking down of borders, different tribes walking with new friends, and the light steps in the sand. All of it, magical. All of it because of Bilba.

We spread down the edge of the line between forest and beach at Ralrek's direction.

"What are you planning?" I asked.

"Watch and see," he replied before making a shooing motion. "Back with the commoners, peasant. This could be risky."

"Just don't blow yourself up."

"I make no promises," he said as I rejoined the crowd.

We stilled as Ralrek began his movements to build a Fire spell. For such a handsome devil who has every physical attribute in his favor, he is actually quite reserved, both in terms of how much he speaks and how outgoing he is. Ralrek doesn't draw attention to himself intentionally. It just happens. So I was a little surprised by how wild his arms swings were. I'd never seen him put himself out there like this. It was like he was trying to slam closed an invisible barn door that belonged to giants. Then he swayed to the other side and did the same.

Ten feet in front of Ralrek, a line as thick as one of the palmetto tree trunks raced out in both directions. Flames, twenty feet high, roared skyward. The heat made me turn away and shield my face. More than a few demons screamed in surprise, but fear laced some. Understandable, since the fire way was now thirty feet high and ran eighty feet down the beach.

The flames merged into balls as if being sucked up like spaghetti noodles by an invisible mouth. Forty balls of roiling flame hung in the air over the beach, spread out as if they were soldiers standing sentry. Bright flaming balls. Even though they hung on the edge where the ocean met the beach, far away, they still illuminated the first rows of curious observers.

"Whoa," an impling, who couldn't have been more than

seven or eight hundred years old, said beside me, her mouth agape.

I smile down at her. "Whoa is right."

The first fireball on the far left shot into the air, zipping out over the ocean. It soared so high I lost the sound of its roar. The night air went silent, as if every demon, harpy, every critter and crawling thing, and even the night itself waited to see what would become of Ralrek's impressive trick.

Heavens, I couldn't imagine what it took to hold these forty balls, especially after keeping the blazeball going through more than twenty games. I was already impressed. Now he had a line of blazing balls as big as boulders, holding them aloft, and shooting them into the darkened sky. Anything else he did was just the fire in the furnace.

It seemed like everyone held their breath. Rustling of palmetto leaves reached the crowd as we waited for the ascending ball to shrink into a point the size of a tip of a pencil.

Just when I thought this was the extent of his trick, the ball exploded, showering the sky with trails of burning oranges and reds.

"Ohhh."

"Ahhh."

"Boom."

This crowd was on their game.

Another ball shot skyward. Now that we knew what Ralrek had in store, demons lowered themselves into the sand for the show, laughing and chatting happily. Parents held their small children, pointing upward and sharing in the merriment. With the second explosion, no one jumped and cried out in anything but glee.

"This is really touching," someone said beside me. Sethel had joined me at one point in my distraction. Without taking his eyes off the third fading ball of flames, he said, "The three of you have a lot to offer the island. It's a shame we didn't give you a chance before. Regardless of our reasons, we were wrong. I hope you have it within you to forgive us."

Boom went the third fireball.

"We have too many enemies to make more. I'm glad to hear you're seeing through the barriers to us becoming part of the island. But we're a package deal." I bent around him and looked down the row of seated demons to the brown-skinned succubus who I once wanted to exact revenge on and now felt so much sympathy for. Marijon's eyes sparkled in Ralrek's orange light. "Our fourth has just as much to offer. She's carved out a nice home here, all by herself. She's just as much a part of our group as us three."

Sethel turned Marijon's way. Since he and she were to my left, I couldn't read his reaction. Maybe that was for the best. I wasn't budging on this and knew neither Ralrek nor Bilba would. Rejecting us because of her would go against the spirit of the day, the purpose for the festival, and would definitely set a marker down for what kind of incubus Sethel was.

Boom! Boom! The double percussion was awesome. Now, three balls went up simultaneously. Who knew Ralrek could be such a showman?

Sethel watched the triple explosion. After the air stopped echoing, he said, "Even if it wasn't a package deal, we have amends to make. This day has taught me that. My peers feel the same. What do you say we enjoy the rest of this show and make time tomorrow to see what we can do to help the four of you settle?"

I nodded. "Sounds good."

We followed through on our agreement, which was easy to do. Ralrek ratcheted up the excitement, steadily increasing the rhythm until the grand finale, when he sent the last ten fireballs up together. As if it wasn't overwhelming enough when the fireballs exploded simultaneously, turning night into day, Ralrek had one last trick up his sleeves.

Standing tall, facing the ocean, he brought his arms down

to his side and back as far as he could reach. His fingers splayed, Ralrek went rigid for a moment before sweeping his arms forward.

A swirl of beach sand was blown into the air by a rolling tube of fire laid down by my friend. I don't think I swallowed as I watched the tube of fire quadruple in a breath and roll toward the ocean.

The sand sent skyward cascaded down to the beach, twinkling like tiny stars. The older imps loved it. A lot of the couples and succubi seemed entranced. But just as many stared as the rolling tube of flame smashed into the ocean waves.

A wall of steam rolled into the sky, thickening. Ralrek held his arms forward. Unbelievably, his tube only grew thicker and higher as it rolled atop the waves and out into the Acheron.

The mist created by the heated tube striking the water became impenetrable, so thick, I lost sight of Ralrek's creation.

Bilba sidled my way, keeping his shoulders square on the scene unfolding in front of us.

A couple hundred yards from shore, the wall of mist grew so thick I couldn't make out the glow of the fire tube. "Did you have any idea he was this strong?"

"I... I mean, I knew he was strong," Bilba said, his arm drifting up and back down as if a string controlled it.

"Should we help him, like you did when you taught him Gateways?"

"I'm afraid of what will happen to him if I interrupt." He took a tentative step forward. "Let's just be near him. Just in case."

"Okay."

Two steps behind Ralrek, we stopped and waited, watching him keep his arms extended. They shook like he was trying to hold up two-gallon jugs of water.

I couldn't hear anything over the sound of the waves. The

fireballs above us had long died out. The twinkling sand had fallen back to the ground or into the Acheron. Whatever had become of Ralrek's fire tube, we wouldn't figure it out now.

The night was dark again. The thick wall of mist churned, but held the secrets of what lay beyond.

I shrugged when Bilba met my eyes. "Maybe it was a dud?"

Ralrek dropped his arms and wobbled. I caught him, helping him down to the sand. "You alright, bud?"

"Will be. Just need to..." He didn't finish the sentence before his head hit the sand and his eyes closed. The snore that followed was almost immediate and sounded inspired by a horror movie monster's growl.

"Do we let him sleep here all night?" Bilba asked as the tribes drifted closer to check on the demon who'd just given them one heaven of a show.

"He's safe. Let's help clean up, and then we'll carry him home if we have to."

Clean-up went well, which is a testament to what Bilba had achieved, as anyone who has ever had to pick up after a party knows. Everyone pitched in, and we had the area returned to a respectful state before everyone passed out from exhaustion. The only thing we had to finish was tearing down the small stage, blazeball goals, and food stands that had been hastily, yet safely, constructed.

"We can finish tomorrow," Cantrell said. "We're all tired. Let's not ruin the feeling we've created today. Nice work. We'll see everyone in the morning."

Turns out, 'everyone' was not the only thing we saw the next morning.

21

ISLE OF DREAD/LUCIFER'S HEADQUARTERS

"YOUR SPELL DID... THAT?" I ASKED, STILL NOT BELIEVING WHAT I was seeing.

"I guess so," Ralrek said, his voice hoarse with exhaustion.

The Acheron was open to view, at least for now. All thanks to the quietly confident incubus I'd known for thousands of years.

When we woke and met the tribes to finish cleaning up the festival site, a demon had run to the ocean to let their implings play. She scurried back, reporting the news that the wall of mist perpetually circling the Isle was carved open. At first, no one believed her. But she swore she could see the open ocean, that the towering mist that extended from the surface of the water to the highest reaches of the sky had been sliced open.

As one, the volunteers raced to validate her claim. And you know what? She was telling the truth.

A big old gaping piece of the mist was cut away. Wide enough to fit an airplane through without the wings touching the sides, the wall was open. Exiles who'd been stuck on this island from the day they were dropped off were finally getting their first clear view of the ocean.

Ralrek's final trick last night ended being the furthest thing from a dud imaginable.

Some demons gasped. Others whimpered and cried. Most exclaimed joy. One incubus from the Risers shouted that he no longer felt like a caged animal. Everyone wanted a piece of Ralrek.

I have to admit, after thousands of years of knowing him as the asshole of Hell who had everything, the right huskiness to his voice, the height, the dark hair and eyes that seemed to suck you in, just the right amount of shadow to his mustache and beard whenever he didn't shave, it was nice to see him finally get—harmless—attention he wasn't comfortable with. Served the tall jerk right.

Demons crowded around him. Incubi patted him on the back. Succubi hugged him—the older ones seemed intent on kissing his cheeks. Imps, too insecure in their age, gave him appreciative but still cool nods and winks. Implings, not yet possessing the attitudes of what mortals would think of as teenagers, hugged his legs and pulled on his hands, even though most of them were too young to understand the significance of what Ralrek had done.

"Will it stay like that?" I asked when the crowd had finally let him loose from their clutches as they spread out around the beach with their loved ones to enjoy the view.

"I have no idea." He took a quick look from side to side. "Honestly, I didn't mean to do that."

"Oh?" I chuckled. "And what did you mean to do?"

His lips curled. "I meant to shoot up towering curls of flames at the grand finale."

"Well, this ended up being a cool mistake then." I rocked my fingers like a pendulum between the demons stretched out along the beach. "Plus, look at the joy this is bringing them. Much better than a big flash. I'd keep that little mess up to yourself and claim this victory, my friend."

"Yeah, guess so." He ran a hand through his thick hair like a shy school-aged incubus being flirted with for the first time.

I patted his shoulder. "Let's get back to work before this goes to your head."

The cleanup went later into the day than anyone had planned. No one's fault. It happened because we spent most of the early part of the process sitting on our asses on the beach and simply enjoying the sense of freedom that came from an opening in the wall of mist. The impression I got was that no one cared. We wanted to enjoy this sight. Who knew if it was going to last. If you've ever been on vacation to a new location and had a thick fog choke off your view of that once-in-a-lifetime thing you've always wanted to see, that might be a tenth of the frustration everyone on the Isle had felt since their exilement. What Ralrek had done was profound, beyond Bilba's understanding even, and everyone was going to enjoy it while they had it. Guilt-free.

By the time we finished cleaning up, returning the area around the longhouse to its previous condition, everyone was worn out, ready to bathe and eat, and not necessarily in that order. I'd eaten and jumped in the ocean to clean away the grime of the day long after Ralrek was asleep in our new home at Marijon's camp. She and Bilba were still up, excitedly talking about what the tall incubus had done—I think my buddy was really struggling to wrap his head around Ralrek's accomplishment. That left me with my new stretch of beach to myself.

I hadn't been relaxing on the cooling sand for more than five minutes when Creed buzzed.

"Embrace," Crazy Zeke said. The interruption was so sudden, so unexpected, I jumped.

Twenty feet away, a Gateway split the beach air open. I was on my feet and slowly inching back and to the side before it formed. I couldn't make out what was on the other side, but it didn't look familiar. Too formal to be any place I'd hung out before.

A booted foot stepped through, a black robe sweeping out with that first step. The incubus's hem and seams were embroidered in red. The sign of the highest station in Hell except for the Big Man's. I didn't know this incubus, but he had to be as old as Azazel, maybe older.

When he completely stepped through the Gateway, he scanned the beach. Aged eyes, though they may have been, betrayed intelligence. A smile fluttered on his lips when he found me. In a cracking voice, he asked, "Ezekial Sunstone?"

"Yes?" I said, making no attempt to hide the fact that I held Creed. Anyone opening a Gateway on the Isle of Dread, looking for me, was someone who'd know what Creed was. Plus, he might be connected, and maybe even powerful. Even though he didn't appear particularly dangerous, I wouldn't chance it.

The elderly incubus trod forward, looking like every joint hurt. "I'm Baphomet." He stopped, verbally and physically, as if he expected a reaction.

"How are you doing?"

I had no idea who Baphomet was, but the robes of Lucifer and the fact he opened a Gateway on the Isle were enough to tell me that if this incubus were a poker player, he'd sit at the high-stakes table. Those in the know might fall at his feet, but not me. I wasn't falling for his station or ploys. I didn't have to. Abandoned to die once, multiple attempts on my life, and now exiled to rot, I'd been knocked down so many times that I was numb to it. Default reverence was never my strong suit, but that was especially true now.

When it was obvious I wouldn't give him more than that, Baphomet cleared his throat. He looked at his hand, and a scroll slid from inside his sleeve and into his open palm. He extended it. "This is for you."

"From?" I reached for it. My Sensing would allow me to

feel if he was about to tap into his Ability. Right now, I felt nothing.

"Read the scroll, son," Baphomet said as if I were his annoying child.

I did, looking up at the high-ranking messenger when I'd finished. "Now?"

"He waits for no one." I didn't miss the emphasis on the first word.

"It's been a long day."

"Then I'd recommend not making Him make it longer." Baphomet turned. Something—a knee?—cracked, but didn't slow him.

I jerked my thumb over my shoulder. "I should probably let my friends know."

"He has called you to attend to Him. You'll return before they notice your absence. You have His word."

With a sigh, and a small dose of nervousness I kept well hidden, I followed Lucifer's errand boy.

After a short-but-dizzying ride through the Gateway, I stood on a landing made of wide, gray stone. Behind me, a stairwell wrapped in a tight, steep circle down to a lower level. "Where are we?"

Baphomet winced when my voice echoed down the steep stairwell. "Please keep your voice down. This meeting needs the utmost discretion." He moved to the door, resting his hand on the bronze knob. The lines around his mouth and cheekbones deepened, but his lips remained level. I couldn't tell if that was a smile or if he was doing his best impression of a hellhound seeing a new chew toy. "And try to be respectful of His time. Lucifer has many things on His plate that demand attention."

"Sure thing." I didn't even know why I was here except that the leader of Hell wanted me to be. Who was wasting whose time in that scenario?

Baphomet turned the handle. The springs inside the mechanism creaked torturously. The hinges did as well when the elderly incubus pushed the door opened and stepped inside.

I waited a second because that felt like the right thing to do. I mean, as many issues as I had with the most powerful demon in creation, you just didn't disrespect someone's personal space.

Baphomet crept back into the frame, his hands cupped. "He will see you now." He dropped his hands, one swaying out to the side, and moved aside to give me breadth to walk into Lucifer's chambers unobstructed.

Hardly impressive. I mean, this was the ruler of the Underworld we were talking about here, and His room was gloomy and pretty nondescript. Tight, actually. Small, definitely.

A four-foot round table, upon which stacks of papers sat, occupied the front of the room. Two piles, one to the left, the other to the right. The papers in the left stack were disheveled, a few were rumpled, and definitely the victims of a reading by Hell's Lord. The stack on the right obviously waited for His attention. Twice as tall as the left stack, Lucifer obviously had His work cut out of Him. I hadn't seen a stack of paper that thick since my first week on the job in The Book Abyss, and at least Dialphio had an excuse as the sole owner and operator of her store. Lucifer had teams of demons working for Him. Surely, someone could take a bit of the work off His plate?

A blood-red curtain hung across a rounded arch, cutting off whatever room lay behind this one. The floor was gray stone. I smelled dust in the air. In the corner, a wide bookcase with two drawers on the lower half was filled with old books whose paper had browned long before Kanthor Sunstone ever thought of having a failure of a son. In that spirit, the books looked as unloved as Kanthor's son.

The Lord of the Underworld sat hunched over a paper. He had thrust a wrinkled hand through His hair, separating in finger-wide rivers. He lifted the quill and wagged it at the chair opposite. "Sit, Ezekial. I'm almost done."

My body moved as my mind swirled. With Creed hanging from its loop around my waist, I felt as confident and calm as possible given the circumstances, which wasn't saying much since this was apparently Lucifer's blessed office and bedchamber. I didn't sense any magic being touched, but again, I couldn't pick up on His ability to do that. A smarter demon would be nervous.

"Yes, almost done," He said before scribbling something on the paper and grunting to himself.

I took my seat and waited, trying to find anything to stare at that was appropriate. Over Lucifer's shoulder, Baphomet stood by the door, still cracked open. He wasn't looking at Lucifer either, instead pretending to analyze the room while keeping an eye on me.

The ruler of Hell pulled the quill away suddenly after a flourish, sat straight, still staring at the paper, and said, "Baphomet, you may leave."

"Yes, my Lord." The elderly incubus nodded, slapped his hands to his sides, and stepped out, closing the door behind and leaving me alone with Hell's most powerful demon.

Lucifer stared at the paper until the door clicked closed. Then, He looked up, His blue eyes finding me and almost glinting in... What was it? Humor? Relief? Intrigue? As disguised as His magic was, so too were Lucifer's emotions.

"I'm glad you could join me," He said. "Behind that pillar is a stand with iced water. Please fill two cups. I'm parched. One for you as well."

I stood without really challenging the command.

I almost stubbed my toe on a pair of boots sitting near the water stand. The light in here was poor. Two sconces burned Hellfire on each opposite wall. A lamp atop the bookcase cast off the strongest Hellfire azure, but with it placed atop the seven-foot-tall case, it hardly helped me see the blessed trip-ping hazards.

Lucifer didn't react, so I doubted He witnessed my stumble. I made it to and from the water table without further incident, setting the two glasses of iced water near Lucifer but not close enough to create a situation where the condensation would wet his papers.

Once I sat, He said, "I dislike calling you here. I know this was unexpected, and trust me, I'd much rather have visited you on the Isle." He sat back, tipping His head and crossing His arms across His chest. Dressed in a short-sleeve shirt that matched the mood of the room, He looked like He wanted nothing more than to disappear into the background. "I hate this place," He continued as if reading my mind. "It's stuffy. It stinks. Dank. Dark. Oppressive. Don't you think?"

What was He going for here? Did He want me to insult Him? "Yeah, sort of."

Lucifer's small eyes narrowed as He looked toward the far wall. A solitary window, shuttered, was the only thing to break up the expanse of smooth stone. "A prison, Ezekial. That's what this is. A prison."

A silence fell between us. I took a sip of water to fill it, not knowing what to say or do.

Lucifer, His arms still crossed and staring at the wall, tapped His triceps with a finger. Over and over. Tap. Tap. Tap. Finally, He unlocked His arms, and grabbed the edge of the table. "The Overworld is a mess. That world war is wreaking havoc on millions of poor mortals. Did you like your time in the mortal Army?"

"Not particularly." What was the point of lying? What was He going to do? Make me serve again?

"No. No. I don't imagine it was enjoyable. War is always so... How do you even begin to describe something that robs so many of so much?"

"I'm not sure."

"Good answer. Those who claim to know war are those I hold in high suspicion. No one can know war. One war is not like the next. One conflict, one army, one soldier. Even the same soldier in different situations isn't the same. Then or when all is said and done. I hate it. What the war doing to mortals and immortals alike."

"Me too." My thoughts drifted to Cancer and what she was up to. If she was safe. Where she was. I knew nothing, having not heard from her since I hugged her goodbye outside our Olympia apartment. I missed her almost as much as I worried about her.

Then it hit me. I was sitting across a small table from someone who could give me answers about a lot of my concerns. Preeminent among them, I wanted to know about Cancer. I needed to know.

"I'm not a big fan of immortals or mortals having something forced upon them that they didn't decide and can't control."

He slowly turned to look at me. Pressing His lips together, He definitely didn't give off the impression that He was interested in interrupting.

"Honestly, it was pretty shitty to force demons to serve in the Army, but I get it. Without us there, side by side with the mortals, angels would have had unfettered influence. That helps no one. Well, except them." I chanced raising my finger to make a point. "But here's the thing. Most of them don't care about swinging mortals to their side. Just like most demons who served didn't either. Heavens, we were just trying to not have our heads blown off when we weren't looking for a quiet place to take a shit."

That got a tired chuckle out of the king of demons.

"I lost friends over there. Good people. I saw the price paid by those who didn't want any part in it, by those who lived through the fighting in their backyards. I still have friends over there." Sorry, but I have trust issues. That comes with having a father who was only too happy to betray his own son and his son's friends to curry favor with Lucifer's Council. I wasn't about to name Cancer. "I worry about them every day."

"Understandable."

"Is it?" The words were out of my mouth before I realized I'd opened my lips to prove I was very ballsy or a complete idiot. I swear Lucifer stopped breathing for a second. "Because a lot of demons don't get that impression. I certainly don't." My heart thumped in my chest. But I'd been called here for a reason. Which reason was beyond me, but it was there, under the quiet demeanor of the ruler of this realm. "My entire life has been a testament to the fact that I don't think you get what it means to care. Not that I want to make this about me. I'm a big incubus. Life sucks and then you die. I know that. I don't even care about all that Segregate stuff. That's in the past. What matters is stuff like with Leo."

I waited. If He could play the silent-but-strong type, so could I. Youth and time were on my side, even if He had the power of the Hellfire behind Him and nearly eternal life. What happened to Leo, what Lucifer approved and ensured was carried out, didn't sit right with me. It never would.

Lucifer could have stopped it. Instead of pushing us on, the ruler of Hell could have gotten his ass out of his oversized chair in the VIP section of the stands and called it off.

"You let them force Leo and me into fighting. You let him die," I said, only realizing until after the fact that I'd jammed a finger into His table. "You don't, you can't, understand. I have a friend in Iraq somewhere. I worry about her every minute. She was there, helping mortals during my deployment. The Council, your Council, Abandoned her because she told the truth about what happened between her family, Chax Vicu, and Seraph." I stopped when I saw an obvious cloud of confusion pass over His face. I shook my head. "You don't know one of your own Council members is manipulating events in the Overworld." Sad. Truly sad. "I'm sorry, but you don't understand what it's like."

All went quiet. Though His chamber door was thick, I swore someone shuffled around on the landing.

"I wish I could tell you how your friend is doing," Lucifer finally said. His voice was soft. Whatever my rant had done, it hadn't pissed Him off. "But I cannot. Even if I had the energy, which I don't. I'm spread too thin." He waved at the stacks of paper forming two towers on His cluttered desk. "The Underworld is just as difficult a challenge as managing our influence on the Balance. It's shifting. The war drains our resources, but with the Council fighting each other, we've been unable to manage it effectively. I've assigned that to a few elders I trust. They're doing the best they can. But we're still bleeding here."

I watched as Lucifer slowly stood, wincing. Unlike the times I'd seen Him in the Council's chamber, where two attendees made sure He didn't fall getting up or down the stairs to the Council's riser, He was on His own here. Even getting out of the chair looked like it required more effort than me cleaning my bathroom on a pleasant Saturday—well, when I had a bathroom to clean. He hitched His stride all the way to the shuttered window and pushed it open. A blast of fresh air punched the workspace, and I breathed deep.

Staring out the window, He said, "The Balance has shifted. The angels have the advantage. We're so busy fighting ourselves, we can't even worry about that. The Council." Lucifer sighed. His head dropped, and He gripped the window's ledge. "I don't trust my agents. I don't trust the Council members. Even splitting them, hoping it will cool tempers and bring everyone back to the table eventually... even that doesn't guarantee success. We may be too far gone." As His words drifted away, He swayed back and forth. "I've been tired for a very long time, Ezekial. The members of my Council grow stronger, maybe with the exception of Azazel.

Stronger than me, soon, I fear. The Upperworld isn't interested in working with us. Yahweh is dealing with personal issues, and those representing Him struggle to honor the agreement He and I had. That is creating problems."

My throat felt rusted shut. I cleared it. "Problems? What kind?"

Lucifer looked out over His kingdom. "Assassin activity has picked up. They have a few who worry me, but there's one in particular I'm trying to keep a close eye on, among other..." He stopped and waved a sightless arm toward His desk. "Demands."

"Like what Beelzebub, Seraph, Michael, and Apopis are up to?"

He nodded at the Underworld sky. "Yes. Azazel too, though to a lesser degree. Azazel is... He and I go way back. It's different for us. I've come to see that over the ages." Lucifer turned suddenly, keeping one hand on the window ledge to brace Himself. "I have a task for you. One that will require you to reach out to your friend and see what she can tell you about the Upperworld's plans." He must have seen the instant reaction of panicked resistance. He pinched His lips and held up a hand. "My apologies. That was sudden, I realize. The Underworld needs heroes. Heroes act with courage, and we need someone with true courage, now more than ever. Cassie trusts you."

"I won't betray her," I said again before I thought.

"I'm not asking you to."

"Then what am I supposed to do?"

His lips spread in what I think was an attempted smile. "Just information. I don't ask for anything more than that. All in the interest of the Balance. Nothing more. Cassie will understand that, and coming from you, she's our best bet at slowing down what could be a runaway shift."

I shook my head, feeling thick, like I'd just chugged a vat of ice cream and got walloped with an epic dose of brain freeze for my troubles. "I'll see what I can do. But in order to do that, I need to get off the Isle. Without," I said, really laying into the emphasis, "being attacked or even watched. Can you help with that?"

"Discretion is key," He said, rolling His lips. "But, yes, I could. However, you and Bilba and Ralrek will have to take greater control of your paths. Don't ask of me what you can do for yourselves."

"Meaning?"

He stopped His approach, giving me a sly look. "You're smart enough to know what that means. Just make sure the other two hear it as well. Bilba will know what to do, even if you and Ralrek struggle."

I think He was trying to be funny, but one thing He wasn't was that. Did anyone expect that of the great Satan?

"I mean, I'll see what I can do, but right now, we're fighting at every turn."

He passed the far wall and the Hellfire burning in the two sconces lowered, regaining their vibrancy only when He'd moved on. He stopped two steps past the second sconce. "One last thing before you go."

"Yes?"

He turned and raised His hand like He was about to reach out for the flame. The Hellfire rippling in the sconce lowered until it looked like a pilot light. He pulled His hand away, and the flame leaped to its original height. "Control of the Hellfire is a rare Ability. The rarest, actually. Until recently, only one demon has had the gift of tapping into and controlling the Hellfire. Me." He turned toward the table but didn't take another step. When He lifted His palm, three tiny columns of flames danced upon it. "When my friend Aries gave you Creed, he changed that."

The weight of the halberd hanging from my hip felt heavy. "Now I can?"

Lucifer rolled His fingers into a fist, collapsing the small flames. "Yes. And before things get too far, you will need to understand what you can do. Learn and perfect."

"I can't..." The words jumbled in my head. "I can't draw on the Hellfire. Creed does."

"The weapon is a conduit, designed for the one who can use it." He lifted His finger, the tip turning a rich azure. "One has designated you as worthy of being the weapon's master."

"Don't let him, err, Creed, I mean. Not One. But... anyway, don't let Creed hear you say that."

As if He didn't hear my murmur, Lucifer said, "Within you is the power to touch Hellfire. It is yours to command. For the sake of everyone you care about in the Underworld, and those you don't even yet know, I hope you accept that soon. Aborning events give us little time. Give you little time. Learn to command and control the Hellfire, Ezekial. We may not have the time we think we do."

22

OLYMPIA

"ARE YOU EXCITED TO SEE HER AGAIN? BET YOU ARE." BILBA grinned in the goofy way that always disarmed me, even when I'm in a bad mood.

I wasn't now. I couldn't be. We were readying ourselves to head back to the Overworld as soon as the Hellfire cracked the sky, only hours after Lucifer informed me I could command the Hell's life-giving force. Admittedly, my mind was still a blur. Bilba, Ralrek, and Marijon had listened as I told them what had transpired. It was nice to spread the shock around. Really helpful, you know?

Turns out, Marijon was the coolest head in the bunch. She got us away from talking about the awe-inspiring possibilities, implications, and ramifications of my conversation with the leader of Hell and onto our next step. I'd already written to Cassie when I got back to camp—there was no way I could fall asleep after that meeting—and the angel had agreed to wait for my message in the morning, Marijon had suggested writing again to see if she could meet.

Cassie accepted. Hearing your name dropped by Satan would have that effect on anyone, angels included, I imagined. For her, this was the second time in a brief span, and she was still cautiously curious when He brought her up.

I was finally going to see Cassie again. It'd been too long. Way too long. Work or not, this unexpected twist in the tale was giving me the chance to hang with the coolest angel in Heaven.

As we secured the camp and Bilba moved off to the clearing Marijon had cut out of the forest before our move to her place, he called me over.

"What's up?"

He checked on Marijon and Ralrek, quietly making sure everything that could get damaged from a chance rain was packed away. "I know you're excited to see Cassie, but I want to respect you and her enough to know that I'm going to ask her about my mother."

"Your mother? Why? What would Cassie know?"

He shrugged. "I don't know, but nothing came out of my visit to the Eighth. No one there had answers. Most avoided the topic of disappearances altogether. It's a strange place now. Everyone's walking around in self-preservation mode, Zeke. Plus, I'm tired of waiting on Azazel. If angels are behind the disappearances, she could help. Maybe she knows something already?"

"I mean, maybe? I don't know, Bilba. But hey, if you need that, I get it." I gave him a friendly shove. "Plus, don't make it sound like I've got some school-age crush on her. Cassie is just... I mean, she's..." Oh boy, I was not helping my cause, and my best friend's widening grin only exacerbated the issue.

"Let me save you." He put a hand on my shoulder, shifting topics. "There was something cool. Interesting. Maybe that's a better way to put it. When I went back to the Eighth to look for my mother, I ran into that homeless guy. The one who always hung out on the street corner. You remember him?"

"Outside the convenience store where that asshole worked?"

Bilba snapped his fingers. "That's the one."

The poor incubus. I remembered him clearly. The Eighth is a terrible place. A personal heaven for a lot of demons. Tough streets. Uncaring populace. Being a homeless beggar was probably at the bottom of the list of desirables in a Circle full of them. Now knowing Marijon's story and what became of the place after I killed Taurus, I wondered how much harder it was for demons like the beggar. I'd given him snacks and coin every time I saw him. Nothing significant. I'd intended to help more, but never saw him again after the Horn mission. Maybe I should, now that my buddies could open Rifts and Gateways on the Isle.

"Is he okay?"

Bilba tipped his head side-to-side. "He's pretty much in the same situation as before. Seems that even though the Eighth has gone to heaven in a wheelbarrow, his station hasn't gotten much worse. So, I don't know if that's good or bad. Not like he's still not begging. Anyway, when I was in the neighborhood, looking for my mother, I stopped to help him out."

"Thank you for doing that."

"Of course. Why wouldn't I? Anyway. I stayed for a little while and asked how he was and if there was anything I could do and stuff." Bilba swallowed and waved his hand like he was about to cough. "Here's the thing. Though he seemed grateful for the coin, he wouldn't let me leave until he could share a message he said was for you. It was weird. I don't know, but I just couldn't walk away. I think I was a little perturbed, maybe paranoid, that he remembered me and our association. Creepy, right? No matter how crazy it sounded. I didn't think about telling you because, well, you know?"

"Know? Know what?"

"Come on, it's not like it's a secret that you've been different, in a slightly weird way, ever since you came back from Abandonment," Bilba said, chuckling but without the heart, like he was forcing levity into the conversation. "We've never really talked about it, not that we've had a chance to with all the craziness. But I know something has been going on with you. I get that you're keeping to yourself about it. That's fine. But what he said might help. It might hurt, too, which is why I've said nothing."

"What did he say, Bilba?"

"Don't hate me if this sounds nuts. I didn't want to insult him by saying so, but it does."

"What did he say?" This time, I put a little more force into each word.

Bilba's gaze danced across my face. "He said, and I quote, 'listen to the voice. It is. Oh, and thank you for the chips.' That was it. But he put a lot of emphasis on the 'it is' part." He scanned my face for a moment. "Told you it was nuts. I feel bad for him, being in the situation he's in, so I hope it doesn't sound like I'm picking on him. But that's just weird. Sorry. I'm sure he meant well. Seems like a nice guy in a crappy situation."

Listen to the voice. It is. Bilba had no idea what that meant to me. I had no idea about the full meaning behind it. How would a homeless incubus in the Eighth, who I had never met and only interacted with a couple of times while trying to help him, know about any voices? Was it because he's as crazy as I had been feeling since stepping through Azazel's Rift to come back to Hell from Olympia after my Abandonment? A bond between the two of us? Both hearing Crazy Zeke—or at least, him hearing his version of Crazy, whatever his name was. That was the only explanation. Right?

The problem with that thinking was that I hadn't heard Crazy Zeke then. That was before my Abandonment, before coming back to Hell to be bullied by the Council and forced into a fight for the death.

"Anyway, are you ready?" Bilba said, breaking up my thought train into Crazytown.

"Huh? Oh, yeah."

"Get those two stragglers and I'll get the Rift open," he said, turning away to get to work.

We were in the Overworld before my mind stopped spinning about the connotations of the cryptic message from the homeless beggar. I pushed aside those troubles when I saw the other immortal who had played a similar beggar role when I first met her.

"Hi Z-Zeke," Cassie said, hugging me.

I wrapped my arms around her and the troubles of the Over and Underworlds, those in my mind, and those we were about to discuss, ceased to exist. Though it hadn't really been that long, it might as well have been an eternity since I last got to share words with her that weren't conveyed through demonic notebooks.

Standing in the middle of the hangar Virgo's Vigilantes used as their strategic center, we caught up on all the things that didn't have to do with Lucifer and Yahweh, angel and demon spies, the Balance, or anything that wasn't just two immortals who'd connected through mutual troubles and overcame them together without sparking off a celestial Armageddon.

"Can you two knock it off? We have work to do," a deep voice echoed across the silent hangar.

Virgo hung in the opening of his meeting room, his arm resting on the jamb. He wasn't smiling warmly in greeting, but Virgo was incapable of smiling. This was about as friendly and warm a reception as anyone was likely to get from the ex-fighter-turned-Abandoned-militant.

We bumped fists—it's an incubus thing—and said our hellos. Virgo was all business and wouldn't spend a lot of time on light conversation, even when he liked someone. It was good just the same. We all needed this.

"Hey, good looking."

I grinned, not at Virgo, and turned to meet the mortal behind the soft voice.

Steve threw his arms open. "Come here, you lug. How are you?"

We hugged, and then he did the same to Bilba and Ralrek. "You guys are the talk of the town." He punched my shoulder. "Who knew when we first met that I'd be kicking it with such important players, huh?"

"We're not all that, trust me," Ralrek said with a small smile. "Especially Zeke."

Everyone had a good laugh and then headed to Virgo's meeting room. Before we split ways, I nodded to Steve. "I'm still looking for that bag of patience you told me to find."

He patted my arm. "Keep looking, my friend. It'll be worth it. Just hope I'm still alive to see it." He winked. "I'll see you around?"

"You bet!"

Everyone was getting set at the table. Unlike times in the past, we didn't split based on immortal alignment. Angel on one side. Virgo at the head. Us three hell-bound demons opposite the angel. Not this time. Bilba took the chair next to Cassie. He stuck his tongue out at me when I stopped, recalculated, and pulled out the chair next to Ralrek.

"Glad we can knock this out," Virgo said in his sultry smooth jazz voice, getting us focused on business immediately. "Cassie, what do you have for us?"

"Before we get to that," Bilba said, holding up a finger and turning in his chair to face the angel. "Cassie, can I ask you something? And, if you don't know, that's okay, but I'm hoping you can help."

"Sure, B-B-Bilba. Ask anything."

"Well, I'm not sure what the disappearances are like in the Upperworld," he started, his eyes moving from Cassie to Virgo, "or here. But they're bad in the Underworld." He quickly, for him, explained his history with his mother in the Eighth, leaving out the personal and painful stuff, and what he knew about her situation leading up to her disappearance. "No one in the Underworld knows anything."

Ralrek snorted. "If they do, they're not offering."

Bilba hadn't turned away from the corner of the table, but side-eyed Ralrek. "Yes. But those we trust, who have access to more information than we do, are at a loss."

"It's that way with the Abandoned, too," Virgo said.

Cassie bit her thin bottom lip. "In the Upperworld, as well. Though, from what I've gathered, we haven't had nearly as many as the Underworld. Probably a tenth of what you've seen. I'm not sure what I can do to help, though."

Bilba's head dropped. He looked miserable.

I had to wonder what it'd be like to have a heart that big. To be so upset about someone who'd spurred you every chance she got, who turned away from her own child, multiple times, was something that didn't click with me. I rarely thought about my father. Maybe that was because he was still supervising the final touches of the conversion of their new model home. No mysterious force had wiped him clear from society as Bilba's mother had been. But I had serious doubts that I'd miss him if he followed a similar fate. Call me corrosive to the adhesion of the family unit, but I solidly believe even though you don't get to choose what family you're born into, you most definitely get the ultimate say in the family you spend your life loving. For me, that was my mother, Bilba, Ralrek, and Dialphio. Bilba was different. Somehow, someway, he still cared enough about the succubus who didn't care about him. Good guy, that Bilba Ravenous.

"Honestly, Cassie, I was hoping you had information about, well, that..." Bilba blew his cheeks into puffy balls of skin. The release was slower than Hell's tax department paying out refunds at the end of the year. "I didn't know if all the angel activity had anything to do with it."

Her face scrunched. "Angel activity?"

"The Upperworld's spies and agents," I said, not wanting to use the word Lucifer did because it might sound inflammatory to call Cassie out on their assassins in the Overworld. I respected her too much. I gave her a rundown of my conversation with Lucifer, sanitizing the details only for efficiency. Hiding information from Cassie and Virgo was not on my list of things to accomplish today. My alignment was to those I loved, the demons of the Isle, and these two and their charges. It was not to Lucifer, no matter how chummy he seemed to want to be lately.

When I finished, Cassie mimicked Bilba's cheek blowing and his slow exhale. "That's a lot to take in. I'm not sure where to start."

"Disappearances in the Upperworld?" Virgo said. "You've had them, you said?"

"Too many for our liking, but nothing close to what you guys are saying. Our intel says it's demonic agents."

"Not shocking," I said.

"Both sides do it. We all know that." She reached over and took one of Bilba's hands in hers. "I'm sorry to hear about your mother. I don't know anything, but I promise I'll check when I get back." She rolled her eyes. "And get time. The Council has me swamped with work. But I won't forget, B-Bilba. I promise."

He squeezed her hand. "Thank you. I'm sorry to be a bother."

She gave him a reserved smile. "You're not. Not at all. That's what friends are for." She looked at each of us in turn. "I want you guys to know I appreciate your continued trust. Tensions are rising, the war is plowing along, and I'm sitting on the other side of the fence from you."

"I'm on no one's fence," Virgo said. "I'm Abandoned."

Cassie pinched her eyes and nodded. "Yes, I know. I'm sorry. I didn't mean to imply you were on the opposite side.

None of you are. We're in this together. Us, and those who support us." She lifted her arm, pointing at the closed door that led to the hangar. "Like all of them out there. Each one of them is important to our cause."

Ralrek, who'd been leaning back in his chair and playing with his fingers, finally looked up. "What cause is that, though, Cassie?"

"Meaning?" she said carefully.

"If what Lucifer said was half the truth, angels have their hands deep into the Underworld's business and are putting demons' lives at risk," Ralrek said. His dark eyes held her crystalline orbs. "Abductions. Assassination threats. Messing with the Abandoned."

"Forgive him," I said, shooting Ralrek a warning look. "He's got stuff going on."

"No, Zeke." Ralrek sat up, thumping his elbows on the table and leaning toward the angel. "My business is my business, and it has nothing to do with the angels not backing off operations in the Underworld or here. Cassie, this isn't at you. This is about the structure. We're all just pawns. None of us mean anything to those with the real power. You're no different from us in that way, I know. But you also have more sway than all four of us at this table combined." He raised his arm, dropping a finger toward the table, and made a slow looping motion to drive the point home. "You have a say. Spying is one thing. Assassinations? Not sure how the Upperworld justifies that, but it won't help if your assassins are successful. And even more than that. The Balance. We all know how precious it is to keep. Was Lucifer correct? Does your Council know about the shit going down in the Underworld?"

"We do. Yes."

"Yet you're not backing off?"

"From what, Ra-Ralrek?

"Influencing events here, for starters. Backing out of the war."

Cassie was silent.

Bilba cleared his throat. "We all realize the sensitive nature of this matter. And we're not asking you to put your neck out, Cassie. But Ralrek isn't wrong." I opened my mouth to interject, to tell my friends to back off, but Bilba soldiered on and I didn't need to play protector. Cassie could more than take care of herself if any of us in this room overstepped. "With the way things are in the Underworld, with the direction they're headed, and the world war, demons will have ever-decreasing influence in the Overworld. We all know what that means. For eternity, demons and angels have maintained the Balance. Until we get our house in order in the Underworld, we need the Upperworld and the Abandoned to work with us."

Virgo rocked his head, but said nothing.

Cassie took a slow breath. "The Upperworld isn't doing anything the Underworld isn't. We just don't have the structural chaos you do. We know that. Guys, I promise, we're not trying to take advantage of the situation."

"Yet your operatives keep pushing in our realm and here," Ralrek said. If it wasn't supposed to be a verbal punch, it didn't come across as benign.

"Don't be a dick," I said.

"Don't get distracted," he said, just as sternly. "I'm bringing up a point. It doesn't matter if their aim is to take advantage of the mess we're in. Just by continuing what they're doing, the Balance is being affected. It doesn't matter if they want to see our Council crumble or not."

"They're doing that themselves," Bilba said with an air of disapproval.

"And," Ralrek said, leaning into that word hard, "angels aren't helping."

"What can we do?" Cassie asked.

"Pull your troops out of the mortal armies, for one," Ralrek said, flipping a hand. "Literally, it's one of the easiest things to do that will have a tremendous impact."

"Cassie," Bilba said, now taking her hand, "if nothing else, it could buy us time. Zeke already has Lucifer's ear. There's something big coming. Changes of some sort. Whatever it is, we need time to be ready. If there's anything you can do, we'd appreciate it. Everyone does."

"All I can do is try, guys," Cassie said, not letting go of Bilba's hand. "I'll think about how I can propose something to the Council they might bite on. Speaking of. I've got possibly bad news."

"Oh boy," Ralrek grumbled.

I kneed him under the table before asking, "What is it?"

"With everything going on, I'm swamped with work, which is why I haven't been too accessible. I feel horrible about that, but I'm the newest Council member, and I'm learning. A lot." Her shoulders slumped, and in that moment, she seemed to age a century. "It's not easy, upholding expectations of… well…" She sighed, her shoulders drooping lower. "Imagine, with my father, the expectations put on me. My work requires more focus and energy than I could have imagined at first. Now, you guys are bringing me this. Believe me. I want to help. I will help. But doing that will take more of my time. Just understand that, okay?"

"So I'll hear from you less than I already do?" I asked, hoping it didn't sound as pathetic to everyone at the table as it did in my head.

Her head dipped toward her shoulder like someone had yanked her by the ear, and my skin flushed with a smidgen of humiliation. Cassie had the good taste to recover quickly and address everyone, even though, I swear, I saw a flicker of sadness before she did. "I don't want to over-promise. You can't be at my beck and call. Neither can you wait around for word from me, just as the Vigilantes can't wait for me when they need something from the Upperworld, whether that's for the Path or something else. So I've set something up so none of you have to wait."

"What?" Virgo asked carefully.

"A contact to take my role here. To work with the Abandoned and you." She looked at me, but her gaze slid away.

"We'd have to be careful," Bilba said. "We trust you, Cassie. Don't get me wrong. But we can't work with just anyone."

"He's not just anyone. You guys know him."

I'm not the smartest incubus on the Isle. I'm not even the smartest in my small group of friends. Even before I asked, I knew her answer. "Who?"

The corners of her eyes turned down. "Gemini."

23

ISLE OF DREAD/UNDISCLOSED

"Change comes," Crazy Zeke said, making me drop my roasted seal herring into the campfire, which hissed angrily at the invasion.

"Lucifer bless it!" I said, snagging the end of the cut and holding the fish up for inspection. Ash covered it. The smell of charred meat served as evidence that even my instant reaction had been too slow.

Thankfully, Bilba was off bathing in the Acheron and Ralrek was in the forest taking care of bodily functions, so neither witnessed my fumble.

"You might be able to save it," Marijon said around a mouthful of ash-free fish. She stopped chewing. "Ezekial?"

"Zeke," I corrected absently, staring at the figure making his way through the palmetto trees and toward the camp. He wasn't here for a withheld dinner invitation. I pointed.

Baphomet slowed his shuffling steps at the edge of the camp. "Ezekial. You need to come." He glanced around the split logs we used for seats. "Where are the other two?"

"Taking care of things," I answered as I stood. There was no way I was involving my friends in anything Baphomet had planned until I knew what game Lucifer was playing. "Where are we going?"

"Azazel," Baphomet said, already turning back to the forest and, presumably, his Gateway. "He's been attacked. Beelzebub. Hurry."

Shit. I dropped my plate, herring and all, to the sand. "Marijon, please find them. Let them know."

I was at Baphomet's Gateway first.

"Where is he?" I asked, approaching near panic when I turned to see Baphomet fifteen feet behind me.

The elderly incubus was moving as fast as he could. "The Council chamber. He tried to make it to his office," he said, panting as he pulled up to the gate, touching his Ability.

The hairs on my arms rose. Construction magic. I pulled Creed free, activating it. The double-ax heads popped from the wood with a clang even as the wavy dagger thrust itself into the soft forest floor from the bottom.

"Out in the open room?" I asked.

Baphomet swallowed hard, nodding.

I wasn't sure how much help the incubus could be in a fight. He was aligned with Lucifer. He was here, seeking help. Maybe the king of demons was on His way to the chamber too, and I wouldn't be stepping into a harpy nest all alone.

"How many?"

"Beelzebub and some of those aligned with him." Baphomet rolled his arms like he was trying to entangle them with twine. "I didn't have time to count."

"Apopis?"

"Nowhere that I saw, but don't plan for that." He looked behind, ostensibly hoping to spot my two friends. "We have to go. We can't wait."

"Wasn't playing on it." I turned to face the Gateway. "Step back."

Baphomet did, and I spun Creed. The petrified cherry haft weighed less than the banana I'd eaten earlier. The magical halberd had many amazing traits and its weight was just one. The shield formed, a ball-sized dot at first, and then expanded eight feet into the air, arcing around me and the elderly incubus.

Lucifer had told me I needed to learn to command, control, and perfect the Hellfire. I hadn't had time since my chat with Him to think about how to do that. Now wasn't the time to learn. Azazel was in trouble and needed rescuing from the Prince of Demons.

We couldn't be successful without the ancient Founder. He was integral to so much. Beelzebub might know that. This attack might be his reaction to something he suspected or even learned about Azazel's activities. The splintering of the Council. The separation of powers. All that might have been the precedent to something Beelzebub had planned long ago, well before I witnessed him threatening to kill Azazel in front of me, my friends, and the entire Council.

"Will this hold against him?" Baphomet asked, his voice sounding slightly strained.

"It better. We don't have another option." I stepped toward the Gateway, lengthening the shield so that it stretched to include the incubus. "Let's go."

A short tumble later, I stepped out of the Gateway and into Azazel's Council chamber room. Papers were strewn across his desk, many scattered on the floor. His coat rack leaned against the nearby corner. The chair was cocked at an angle to the coffee table that hinted someone had knocked it out of place.

From outside, deep booms and crashing sounds signaled that the fight was still in full flow.

I pulled the door back, not expecting anyone in the middle of a fight to notice. Life and death struggles rarely imparted an insightful level of attention to detail to the combatants. Typically, you're just trying to save your ass. Cracked doors were just one in a litany of things that went unnoticed.

Azazel was on the far side of the chamber, backed into a corner and hiding behind a pillar.

To the front of the room, Beelzebub sheltered behind the Council's long jade table that sat upon the four-foot riser.

There was an open Rift just to the front of the riser. I didn't recognize the Overworld location rippling behind the veil between worlds.

Azazel was pinned down not only by the Prince of Demons, but by three ruffians spread around the room, attacking from various angles as they sought a breakthrough.

A small puddle of water at Azazel's feet told me he'd tried to cast a shield or build a wall of ice to help protect himself, and it had failed colossally.

Along with the dancing hairs on my arms, the battle raked at my skin with conflicting effect. Azazel's Water magic against Beelzebub's Fire. The three ruffians were Fire users as well. The Fire scratched my skin; the Water was a smooth cold stone. My skin; irritated by the inundation of magic.

Creed was too long at six feet to keep obscured, but that might not matter. No one had noticed me yet.

I leaned back away from the cracked door and looked at Baphomet. "I'm going to keep you shielded, but I need you to cast the first attack and buy me time. Can you throw up obstacles between me and the three goons?"

Baphomet looked around the small office. "There's not much to work with in here, but I'll see what I can do. Once I'm out in the chamber, there's more raw material to pull from."

That didn't help. "Is there anything you can do to block one of them from scorching my skin? I only need a second." I looked at Creed. "I think."

The halberd vibrated softly. Hardly reassuring.

Each hair on my arms twitched as Baphomet dangled his fingers at Azazel's desk. The poor thing never saw it coming, collapsing into a pile of boards. The pile pulled apart, each separate piece of wood floating in unison like a fighter jet formation.

"I could throw up a wall with that," Baphomet said, curling his finger and moving the floating wood pile closer. "It won't last, but if you only need a second, it will have to do."

"Do it."

I looked down at Creed and mumbled, "Buddy, don't fail me now."

Creed thumped twice in my fist.

I had no sooner put my hand on the knob, ready to pull the door back and step outside for Baphomet to fling his wood wall at the closest goon, when Creed burst to life. Blue flames, dancing on all three blades, silently swayed and flickered. Creed had come through in an instant, even though I'd done nothing to command the Hellfire as Lucifer decreed.

I dragged the door open. Once it was wide enough, Baphomet stepped forward, peeked out of the office, and wagged his finger. The floating wood pile glided through the air, stopping over my head at the doorway.

The elderly incubus looked my way. I gave him the okay, and he flung the pile forward. It shot into the chamber at the closest incubus in hiding, taking potshots at Azazel. The wood slammed to a silent halt in front of the demon and stacked in rows upon itself. Only two feet wide, it reached over seven feet high, creating enough of an obstacle that the demon would have to step around it to get a shot at me.

I lunged, shooting Creed forward in an attacking thrust.

I wouldn't waste my first unexpected attack on the goon. No one knew I was here. I'd get one chance to hurt Beelzebub. One chance only. Once I fired, the element of surprise was gone. I had to take the chance now.

Even if I was successful in hitting him from this far away, it wouldn't kill him. We were in the Underworld, and demons couldn't kill other demons here without Lucifer's approval. We didn't have that. One shot at glory.

I took it.

This time, there was no need to scream in pain or anger, no reason to tap into my rage. Beelzebub's name was permanently etched on my shit list, one of four steady entrants. I'd fought him before, and he'd narrowly escaped. He couldn't this time. He just couldn't. I might not have a better chance.

The smooth petrified haft melded to my hand, an extension of my arm. I let go of the shield surrounding me and the elderly incubus. A ball of azure Hellfire radiated at the double-ax head. In a flash, it was the size of a carriage wheel.

I couldn't see Beelzebub beyond the ball of flame. It'd grown too big, too fast for me to adjust. I knew where he was hiding, firing on Azazel. Though the Hellfire raging at the end of Creed blinded me to him, I was about to ruin his day based on the size of this spell.

Lucifer I focused on the Hellfire, trying to form a connection that would direct its course. Nothing registered. The ball of flame throbbed around the double axes, but I couldn't feel it. Even though Creed came to life much easier this time, as it always seemed to do in intense situations, I was still as powerless over the Hellfire as the first time I'd accidentally tapped into it.

With a thrust of the haft, a beam of Hellfire burst from Creed. It roared across the room, blindingly bright. Something exploded. There was a roar. From the flame of annihilation itself or Beelzebub, I couldn't tell.

The beam flashed away and the room slowly took on color and dimension again.

Everyone was on their knees except for me and Baphomet. Azazel wobbled and almost face-planted. The jade table, long the symbol of the foundation of Hell, had toppled and split in the attack. On the ruined edges, the remnants of the hole Creed had punched through the table were the only hints of what happened. Chunks of jade littered the riser. Creed's Hellfire had bored through the back wall, the edges of which flickered with small flames of azure.

I couldn't see Beelzebub. Either he was behind the toppled table or on the floor behind the riser.

My skin tingled with the sudden presence of Fire magic. Beelzebub's goons were regaining their awareness and had probably spotted me.

"Get back into the office," I shouted at Baphomet as I started in Azazel's direction. "Help how you can."

I wanted to build my shield again, but I also wanted to live long enough to build it. Running across the chamber, I lowered Creed at the closest goon, a succubus of about forty thousand years, and blasted her into the back wall. She hit it and crumpled to the ground, unconscious.

At Azazel's side, I threw a Hellfire shield around us.

"Young Ezekial," Azazel said in a croak. "Very good to see you."

"Come on, old man," I said, bending and scooping my arm under his and lifting. There was a lot of dead weight. "You injured?"

A fireball slammed against my shield. It fell to the stone floor in ice cream scoop-sized balls that fizzled out.

"Hurt. Not bad."

We limped toward his office. Baphomet had opened a Gateway inside.

I kept my eye on the toppled jade desk. The two remaining hench-demons weren't a threat to us as long as my shield held. Without Beelzebub able to jump into the fight, we were safe as long as we got through the Gateway before he came around from his little nappy-poo. Each fireball flung by his failing friends did nothing worth worrying about to the shield.

Azazel leaned on the door frame.

"Got to go." I watched the jade table as I urged him toward

escape.

"Need breath," the Council member said, holding his side. It was only then I noticed his Council robe was wet underneath his hand. Blood.

"Baphomet, get him into the Gateway," I said, holding Creed's shield in front of me. I stepped out of the office.

"Where are you going?" Baphomet asked.

"Hold the Gateway for thirty seconds once you're on the other side," I said, focusing on the touch of the Hellfire.

"If you don't come through?" he asked, sounding far away.

"Then close it." The Hellfire swelled on Creed's double-ax heads.

"Are you—"

"Go!"

I didn't wait to make sure Baphomet followed orders. None of us had that luxury.

The way the smooth wood ground into my palm helped me focus on the power I felt vibrating down the haft. I raised Creed, which throbbed as if my grip on it was the only thing holding back from detonating. My arms, aloft, shook with tension, even though the magical weapon was lighter than my wallet.

I slammed Creed into the stone floor. A thick crack opened, arcing away like lightning. The crack widened at Creed's base and along the route it took toward the nearest pillar. An inch. Two. Four. Eight.

I stepped back into Azazel's office.

Stone groaned. Something outside the office popped. Shattered. Tiles fell from the ceiling right outside. A fragment broke off one and flew my way, cutting my shin. The one time I didn't travel in jeans. Lucky me.

Tile slammed to the floor in bigger chunks and something above me rumbled, a sure sign that I had no interest in remaining here. The racket drowned out anything the demons on the other side of the collapse were going through.

I jumped into the Gateway and tumbled through inter-dimensional space, landing in a tumble back on the Isle of Dread.

"Thank Lucifer you're okay," Azazel said, holding his side and wheezing.

"He has nothing to do with me being okay."

"He sent me," Baphomet said with a modest bite of defensiveness that betrayed his long-time affiliation with the Underworld's god.

"Fine. Fine." I stood and brushed myself off. My bloody shin turned the dirt to mud. "What in the heaven was that about?"

Over the shoulders of the two old incubi, three demons rushed down the trail toward us.

Bilba's cheeks were flushed. "What's happening? Zeke, are you okay?"

I nodded, pointing at Azazel. "But he's not."

Marijon kneeled at Azazel's side to look at his wound. Her assessment didn't last long. "I've got bandages at the camp, but they won't stem the bleeding."

"What do we do?" Ralrek asked.

"Sethel is a shaman," she answered. "We need to get to him."

"I'll go," Ralrek said. "Just tell me how to find him."

Marijon shot to her feet. "No, it'll take too long. I know the island. I'll go."

"Will they listen to you?"

"Sethel will," I said before we wasted any more time. "I'm sure of it. Marijon, meet us at the camp. We'll get him back and try to make him comfortable."

She was already bolting away when she said, "Use my hut. He can rest there."

Marijon disappeared behind forest shadows and palmetto trunks as we eased Azazel to her hut.

He winced as we slowly positioned him on her cot. It

wasn't a straightforward thing to do with an elderly incubus in cramped quarters. Bilba and Baphomet had to wait outside. Once we had him settled, I squatted in one corner. Ralrek stepped outside to allow Bilba in.

My buddy kneeled beside the Founder. "Why was Beelzebub attacking you? What happened?"

Azazel smacked his trembling lips.

"Get him water," I said.

Ralrek moved outside the hut and was passing in one of Marijon's carved wooden cups just as the Founder was beginning his run-down of events in Lucifer's headquarters. "The Council... has... fallen apart. Lucifer did..." Azazel drew a deep breath.

"Lucifer split the Circles," Baphomet said as he leaned into the hut's archway. "The Council was completely dysfunctional. Inoperable. His decision to split the Circles among the Founders proved to be ill-planned."

"Wait. What?" Ralrek said, squinting.

"The First and Second belong to Michael," Baphomet said, holding up two fingers. "The Third and Fourth, to Seraph. Apopis has the Fifth and Sixth. Beelzebub, the Seventh and Eighth." His gaze fell on the injured Founder. "He has the Ninth and the Isle."

"But the Isle is outside of the Underworld," Bilba said. "That gives Azazel only one Circle while the others get two each."

"Four, when you realize Beelzebub and Apopis are tag team buddies," I said.

"That was a stupid move." Ralrek slammed his hand against the hut, rattling it. "What was Lucifer thinking?"

Baphomet watched the tall incubus as he turned away to pace the flattened dirt around Marijon's home. "You'd have to ask Him." Lucifer's executive assistant pointed at the prone Founder. "He's the one who convinced our Lord."

Ralrek stopped. He approached the hut and leaned in,

eyes and words aimed at Azazel. "Why did you do that? You've just given those assholes all the power they need." His head snapped at Baphomet. "Why didn't you stop Lucifer from agreeing?"

The incubus shook his head. "If you knew your Lord, you'd understand, and not be upset by this."

"I had my reasons," Azazel said in a weak voice from the cot.

"We don't doubt you do," I said, "but this hands almost half of Hell to the two Founders who shouldn't have a say over how much sauce to pour over a chicken wing. I don't even want to think what Seraph will be up to in her two Circles. Complete control, Azazel. They now have complete control over large portions of Hell. We're talking tens of thousands of demons in each Circle."

"But so do we," Azazel said, and coughed. It came out hard. He winced, putting a hand to his chest. "We won't be bothered in the Ninth or here. So I hope you've been... able to..." He coughed again, this time in rapid succession. "Been able to bond with the exiles. Time is short."

"We're making headway, but we need time," Bilba said. "That doesn't address the fact that even if we're safe here, everyone in the other Circles falls under the control of the other Founders."

My mother. Dialphio. Bilba's father. They and everyone in the Fifth were now the riffraff of Apopis. Surely, he'd treat them as such. What a nightmare.

"We can't let this happen," Ralrek said, still pacing and almost stomping in the dirt.

"It was... the only way to keep you safe," Azazel said between coughs as he rolled his head to look at me. "They were plotting to set you up on your next attempt to rescue Libra. Coordinated effort. All available... All available resources. Including..." He coughed and hacked. "Including my peers."

"The Council was going to wait to ambush us? Are you seriously saying that?" Ralrek nearly spat.

Azazel's chest rose. "Not ambush. We were to be on standby. When you three approached Libra again, we'd be notified and combine our efforts."

"And Lucifer was going to stand by and do nothing?"

Baphomet held up a hand. "Hold on. Our Lord was unaware of this plan."

"He seems unaware of a lot."

"Ralrek. Please," Bilba said calmly. "Let's solve this together."

"They planned on killing you, young Ezekial," Azazel wheezed as Bilba took a wet cloth from Baphomet and began cleaning around the Founder's wound.

The smell of iron hung heavy in the air in the small hut.

I felt everyone's focus drop on me. I didn't know what to say. Everything inside me wanted to rage. Long ago, I'd dropped the worry of whining about my course. Even though I'd never asked for any of this, I was here. Had been. Fighting fights I wanted no part of. Being a pawn in games I didn't want to play. Making enemies of demons I never wanted to engage with. Asked to lead when all I ever wanted was to drop into the background. None of that was going to change. Whining wouldn't make a difference. Acting hadn't either. If anything, trying to get and stay ahead of the Council seemed to set them on a determined course. This wouldn't end. I'd never be safe.

That didn't mean I had to put others at risk.

"So that's why you proposed splitting the Circles to Lucifer," I concluded.

Azazel took another sip of water before answering. His swallow was audible. "Yes. I had to protect you from them. Michael wants to be the next Lucifer. He'll do anything to get the title. Yes, Beelzebub and Apopis now control almost half of the Underworld, but they can't get to you. Seraph has the

Horn. We can't forget that. But this should help distract her from her local interests. She has far more connections to the Upperworld than any of us, even more than you have with your girlfriend, Ezekial. Devious, that succubus." The moment was so serious, I didn't even bother attempting to correct the Founder about my relationship with Cassie or the extent of her connections to the biggest player in the Upperworld. "As she builds a power base, we can develop our strategy for getting the Horn from her. Right now, we have to keep you alive."

The air grew thick with tension until Bilba snickered. "After all, you are the Great Prince."

"Shut up," I said. Azazel tried to laugh, only to wince again. "Is that why Beelzebub was fighting you, Azazel? Because he suspected you were protecting me?"

His mouth moved like he was swishing around a big gumball. "Yes. Even though I've been careful over the past few years, always trying to maneuver you away from their clutches, Beelzebub isn't stupid. None of the Founders are. He suspects everyone, and I don't think it helped that you survived every situation I helped put you in. He's suspected me for a long time, and has been waiting for his chance. Today, he had an opportunity to remove me, and he took it."

"And throughout it all, Lucifer has stood by, doing nothing." Ralrek crossed his arms.

"Doing so would have kicked off a civil war," Baphomet said. "A war he's too tired to fight."

Azazel turned his head so that it was laying flat on the pillow. He looked directly at me. "So you must prepare for that fight, because it's coming, young Ezekial. All three of you must be ready. The exiles must support you. Soon. The next time, Beelzebub might not fail. The Council is no more. Each will yearn for more power. I... I can no longer protect you. We are out of time."

24

OLYMPIA

TIME.

It took time for Marijon to return with Sethel. The shaman didn't come alone. A few incubi and succubi from the Inceptives accompanied him, and they got to work on Azazel. With nothing to do that would help the Founder recover, we used the time to head to Olympia, after I wrote Cassie about the need to update her.

That took time, too.

We wasted more waiting in Virgo's hangar. Most of the crew were home with their families, at their actual jobs, or out on patrol. Virgo was on edge. Updating him took time, but it was time we could afford since Cassie hadn't shown yet.

When her Rift from the Upperworld opened on the gray concrete floor, we took more time reviewing what we'd already covered with Virgo.

"If that's the case, things will be a lot more unpredictable," she said when Bilba finished the run-down.

"Yep." What else could I say? We didn't know what was going on with the other Founders on the best of days. Now, with the complete disintegration of the governing body, the splitting of authority across the nine Circles of Hell, and the injury to our one true source with insight into the Council, we would be moving in the dark.

"We need to take the lead," Ralrek said. He clenched his hands, and I could only imagine what was going on in his head. He already had enough to deal with. Events were coming fast and thick, daily, it seemed. He still hadn't had the chance to process what it meant to be a Wayward Son. That had to be a catalyst for his return to this gruff and hostile personality. The Ralrek of old. The Ralrek I'd hoped he'd left behind forever, but could be forgiven for not abandoning. At least not now.

That, too, would take time.

"I agree," Virgo said, taking his seat at the head of the table once we were back in the meeting room. "We can't keep reacting to them. Here, or in the Underworld. It's time we took the fight to them. Now, more than ever."

"I'm really concerned, guys," Cassie said, fidgeting in her chair even though she'd just sat. "We can expect them to act. B —B—Beelzebub and A-Apopis already were with their recent attacks in the Overworld. How does that change now? That's concerning."

"Guarantee, you pissed him off at the women's clinic," Virgo said, straight-faced.

I think everyone at the table understood that a world where Beelzebub and Apopis had even less accountability to Lucifer was a dangerous world.

Lucifer was right. I needed to learn to command Hellfire. Had I last month, Beelzebub would have been nothing more than a big slab of demonic jerky. I didn't have a choice now. But perfecting command of the Hellfire would take time. Time we didn't have.

"Z—Zeke, you need to be careful," Cassie said.

Looking into her angelic eyes, my heart beat like a heavy metal double kick drum. "I know."

"I'm serious."

I swallowed. The other three incubi in the room disappeared. "I know."

"So," Bilba said, breaking the sudden awkwardness I felt at my vision tunneling to a focal point that only included Cassie. "We need to figure out our approach. I think we're all in agreement that we can no longer sit and wait to react to the Council?"

Around the table, head nods greeted the statement.

"I have to report this back to the Council," Cassie said. Her tone was darker than normal. "This is going to be problematic."

"How so?" I asked.

"They'll want to establish proactive measures."

Bilba rubbed his ear. "What would those look like?"

Cassie dragged her head to the right before shaking it quickly. "I don't know. But the one thing that helped keep every other aspect of the Balance balanced was the security that came from formalized governing bodies who could be reliable. If Lu—Lucifer has split the rule of the Underworld among the five Council members, there's even more guarantee of rogue operations, regardless of any centralized component for the Overworld's management on the Underworld's part."

"Has," Ralrek said coldly. "Not 'if.' Lucifer has split up the Underworld."

Cassie bent over the side of her chair, reaching for something on the floor. "Yes. And that's going to get a reaction from the Upperworld. What type of reaction? I don't know" She sat straight, placed a small leather-bound notebook on the table, and flipped it open. Scribbling quickly, she tore the piece of paper out and folded it. "The Council will react, guys. It might even overstep."

"Can't you influence that?" Virgo asked.

Ralrek scowled but said nothing.

She lifted the folded paper that was now no bigger than

the head of a fork. With a flick of her wrist, the note radiated with white light and puffed out of existence.

"What was that?"

"I sent a message to Gemini. He needs to be here."

"Okay." I couldn't hide the caution in my voice.

Gemini was someone Ralrek and I came to know through a mission years ago. An angelic spy. A tough cookie to crumble. His planned execution at the hands of the Council led to the attack on the First Circle by an angelic hit squad that resulted in the deaths of over three hundred demons. Though we'd started our relationship with mutual distrust and dislike, Gemini wasn't a half-bad angel. But in Ralrek's current state of mind, I worried how this would go. We already sat on a powder keg of problems. Gemini might just be the struck match.

"Let bygones be bygones," Crazy Zeke whispered suddenly in its typical voice, neither masculine nor feminine. Usually, I'm conditioned enough to the voice that it doesn't surprise me, but this conversation had far-reaching implications. Caught off-guard, I jolted in my chair. Everyone looked at me like I was the incubus who crop-dusted the table during an evening out with friends. I cleared my throat. "I'm good. Ignore me."

"Sorry guys," Cassie said, not sounding sorry at all, nor did she sound interested in appeasing us. This was more about etiquette. "Like I said last time, my focus has to change. I've got to get better at it, too. I'm not blaming you. All of this, here? It's important. You guys are, too." She found my eyes, held them for a second too long for everyone's comfort, and looked at Virgo. "Supporting the Vigilantes, ensuring they have what they need. Making sure the Path stays open once we agree to move angels and demons home again is important. But I have to be where I'm called. The Council needs me, and honestly, it works in all our favor if I am there and not here. I'm not disappearing, and we'll stay in touch, but I have to be involved in everything they're doing if I'm going to influence decisions and how they're made. We can't keep meeting without Gemini."

As if on cue, someone knocked on the door. An unfamiliar voice, muffled by the barrier, said, "Virgo. There's a new guy here. An angel. Says you're expecting him?"

In his deep, smooth voice, Virgo commanded, "Let him in."

The door cracked open, and I caught a flash of the Vigilante playing door guard. A burly, older mortal with thick arms. Gemini replaced him. The angel stepped into the room and closed the door behind him without turning away from the immortals at the table.

I stood before anyone else.

Gemini was dressed in a pale green rain jacket. He'd cut his black, curly hair close to the skin. His dark skin shone with the zest of life. When we last saw each other, he'd been imprisoned and abused by the Council, and it'd shown. No longer was he ashen and riding a run-away train to starvation.

We shook hands. His smile was as cautious as mine. After all, our last interaction involved his near death and escape, paid by the blood of over three hundred of my kind thanks to Angelfire. "You're looking good."

His thick lips spread. "Been working out. You look a lot better when you're not in shackles."

I held up my arms, showing my free wrists as if they were expensive new watches. "Been thinking about adding them as accouterments. Bilba keeps talking me out of it."

"Come on over, Gemini," Cassie called in a paradisaical voice. "Meet everyone."

Ralrek stood. "Gemini." He was sitting again before Cassie rounded the table.

"Hi, I'm Bilba." My best friend pumped Gemini's arm like it was a water well pump. "Nice to finally meet you."

There was an awkward moment where everyone in the room analyzed his greeting. But this was Bilba, and this was how he interacted with everyone who wasn't a threat to life, limb, and safety.

As we took our seats again, Cassie said, "Gemini, why don't you take the lead and brief them on our operations in the area? Get them up to speed on what you've been doing."

Gemini took about ten minutes to run us down on where the angels were in this part of Washington, and what their goals were. Nothing antagonistic. No oversteps. In fact, according to Gemini and not countered by Cassie, they had withdrawn several operatives in this part of the world.

"I don't have any say in anything outside the Pacific Northwest," Gemini said, "but I promise, we're not pushing for advantages here. That's not our direction."

"And it won't be," Cassie added. "Gemini, do you know anything about the disappearances in the area?"

His already dark skin deepened as if a shadow had passed over it. "Rumors. Nothing more."

"Rumors that say what?" Virgo asked, leaning forward. When Gemini didn't answer right away, the leader of the Vigilantes pressed. "This affects my people. I need to know. If we're going to trust each other, we can't hold anything back. What do you know?"

"The Vigilantes haven't acted out against angels," Gemini started. "That has left a positive impression on your work, V-V-Virgo, I've got to say."

"I don't need compliments. I need information."

The air thickened as the two stubborn immortals waited on the other to blink first.

"Okay, guys, let's focus," Bilba said firmly. "Gemini, we trust Virgo."

"Easy to do. He's a demon."

"We trust Cassie." Bilba put a lot more emphasis on the angel's name. "Though I haven't met you, I will not start off not trusting you. There's no reason to. It's silly. The Underworld can't afford an Overworld that is out of Balance. The Upperworld can't either. All around our realms, demons and angels are working to keep things even-keel. In the Underworld, we have rebel cells across the Circles, putting themselves at risk to defy the Council's unethical behaviors. We're doing this for them. I'm sure plenty of angels in the Upperworld are worried about the events in our realm. They'll never know for sure, and hopefully they never will. They don't need a hint about how fragile the Underworld has become, or how much of a threat to the Upperworld it can be." He stopped, scooting forward in his chair. "Peace can't be maintained without us. We might be few, but we have to try. If we don't, who will?" He wagged his finger between Cassie and Gemini. "If the two of you can keep the Upperworld from overreaching, then we can focus on taking care of business on our end. Virgo can too. We have to do this, because we might be the few barriers to things getting out of control. None of us wants a time where peace has to be enforced through magic. At that point, it won't matter whose magic is at play."

Heads dropped around the table. Lucifer, bless it, Bilba was amazing. Taming a room full of young immortals with far too much responsibility in a celestial power struggle wasn't a simple task. He handled all of us with ease. All of us. A leader of vigilantes, whose concept was spreading around the globe. The most powerful untrained demonic caster I knew of. The Great Prince himself. Two angels, including one who served on Yahweh's Council and whose father was the Lord of the Upperworld. Bilba had brought us all back down without breaking a sweat.

Time. We spent the next few hours updating each other on what everyone agreed needed to be discussed about each of the three realms. We not only swore to conditions that would put our necks on the line. Virgo was in the line of fire should he come across a demon or angel who thought he was impinging on their right to sway the Balance. The two angels placed themselves squarely at odds with their realms' objectives for this new reality. Still, we laid out conditions and responses. One of the most vital agreements was a provisionary agreement that our allegiances had to be to this small group, above all else. For right now. Every single one of us understood that in time, that would change. Because time changed everything.

Virgo's Vigilantes. Gemini's crew. Yahweh's Council. The exiles and Hell's conniving Founders. If any of us could regulate those actors for the greater cause of influencing the maintenance of the Balance, we were committed to doing it.

"All of this changes if the Horn comes back into play," Cassie said darkly.

"We're working on that," Ralrek said.

"Good. Because there's no margin for error with that artifact. Especially if it's in Se-Seraph's hands." She shared a look with Gemini that didn't need an explanation. We already knew Seraph still had contacts in the Upperworld and couldn't be trusted any farther than I could chuck a planet.

Bilba briefed us on the Horn and Halo, even though Ralrek and I had heard this before. Cassie nodded along. Gemini rolled his lips repeatedly. Virgo's intense gaze hardened.

"Could it really mean the death of the universe?" Ralrek asked. Not Bilba. This time, he aimed his respectful question at Cassie.

She nodded, almost reluctantly. "Yes."

A heavy weight pressed down on us six immortals at that one-word answer.

When we broke, mentally drained and ready to decompress so we could recommit in the morning, we walked back into the hangar to open our Rifts to take us our separate ways.

"Ze-Zeke?" Cassie said before stepping into the Rift she

held open. Gemini had already said his farewells and left. Virgo said he needed sleep, trusting us to be alone in his hangar.

"We'll wait at the Isle, Zeke," Bilba said as Ralrek waved and stepped through the Rift.

"Thanks, bud."

My friend walked into the rippling void and was gone, his Rift remaining open for me.

"What's up?" I asked the angel, grateful for a moment alone with her. Even though we'd spent hours planning and plotting, the chance to have a few minutes with her re-energized me like mainlining caffeine.

She reached her arm out. "I'm going to miss you."

I took her hand. Soft. Warm. My skin tingled. "I'll miss you, too. Please be safe."

She squeezed my hand. "You too. Don't go getting your head taken off your shoulders. I like it right where it is."

My heart raced as she squeezed once more and let go. Our fingers stayed connected a moment longer, and then she was gone. Her Rift blinked out right after her trailing foot disappeared into the other realm.

With no one in the hangar except for one guy in the far corner who looked like he was practicing how to break down and rebuild rifles, the hangar was cold and lonely.

I stepped to Bilba's Rift to return to the Isle of Dread. Time to win.

25

UNDERWORLD, ISLE OF DREAD

I SIGHED. RALREK GROWLED.

But Bilba stepped forward into the circle of exiles. "Listen. Listen. Hear us out."

The morning after returning from war planning in the Overworld with the Vigilantes and two angels, we'd set our next steps in motion, calling together representatives of all four exile tribes. Bilba had explained the need to come together to support one another, and how that now included Azazel.

Though the Founder was physically in the clear now, he was socially struggling. The resistance to accepting him on the Isle was strong.

"It's not that we don't feel for your plight," Sethel Jury said, deep into the discussion. The wind, carrying the scent of salty sea air, whipped his thick brown and gray braids. He was the only one at the camp who refused to pull the hood of his cloak up. "But I just don't know if the rest of the Inceptives will accept you, even with what these young incubi have done for us." He waved his hand at me and Bilba and Ralrek.

Cantrell tapped her broad cheekbone. "This is a sensitive situation. Sethel isn't wrong about what they've done for the

Isle. The community bonds are stronger than I ever remember them. The Risers are ready for more discussions with the others, and many look forward to the next event Bilba has planned."

"They do?" My friend's mouth hung open. Bilba had planned nothing further for the exiles. We had a prisoner to free and a security plan to execute with two angels and a group of vigilantes. Party planning just wasn't on the agenda.

"Absolutely," Cantrell said. "You left quite the mark with that event. Plus, this one," she said, tipping her thumb at Ralrek, "made one heaven of an impression with his fire display. Carving open the mist wall? He's endeared himself to my tribe for life. We never go to that side of the island except to witness arrivals. Now, we have demons wandering off to see the hole every free minute they have. They even ask me to set up a rotating daily schedule to assign someone to check on it."

Ralrek's forehead wrinkled as he leered. "Why?"

Cantrell rocked her head. "It gives them hope."

"It's just a hole. I get it feels less claustrophobic, but hope?"

"Maybe you wouldn't understand. You've only been here for a short while." She raised her arms, holding them out at the three other representatives. "But for the rest of us, that wall has enclosed us for tens of thousands of years."

"Some of us, for our entire lives," Anayese said.

"Everyone has been happier at the farm," Roy said, picking his teeth with a dirty fingernail. "I don't think we've ever produced as much as we have since the festival. Everyone's working hard. Not going to last without hope of something bigger."

Marijon thrust her finger in our direction. "Haven't they already given you that? You've all admitted the festival changed things. I can see it too. Everyone is more open to the other side now. Finally, there's momentum toward building a true island community. Are we going to halt progress because of what is happening with the Council?"

No one met Azazel's eyes, even though he was included in the circle of demons around the campfire. Laid out on a hastily-built cot, he was still part of the conversation, but between his position and his state of recovery, the Founder served as more of a peripheral figure.

I felt for him. After all, it was his fate on the line. If the exiles rejected him, where would he go when he recovered? Here, he was safe. Well, as safe as we could make him after the representatives agreed to put a watch on the dock, so we'd have fair warning whenever another Founder attempted to land. Only Lucifer could reach Azazel instantaneously, and after the rescue operation facilitated by Baphomet, I doubted Hell's numero uno wanted any part of hurting Azazel further.

I'm not saying I trusted Lucifer. It'd be a cold day in, well, you get it, before that happened. Azazel wasn't being left out to dry by the King of Demons, but he wasn't fully being supported, either. Azazel would only be safe if he were protected. Just as the other Founders had done in setting up their own territories, now he would have to. And soon.

That's what we were trying to accomplish with this meeting of the minds.

"If I may?" the Founder said weakly from the cot. No one answered, interjected or interrupted, so he continued. As he spoke, he waved his hand in the air. It flopped side to side. "The Isle has been assigned to me, but I'm not here to force myself on you. That helps none of us. I'm not asking to be allowed to stay on the Isle. I could do that if I wanted, regardless of what the tribes say." Around the fire, demons fidgeted and adjusted. Ralrek was stoic. Azazel was coming out swinging, and I wasn't sure that was the best approach. "But is that how you build a community? No. Most definitely not. I'm not here to take what you've established. For too long, the

Council has mistreated you, and I will not perpetuate that injustice."

"An injustice you were part of," Cantrell said, meeting his eyes evenly.

Prone on his back, Azazel nodded, which only pushed his long goatee into his chest, making it form into a bulge of white and orange tangled hair. "The Council has set policies and procedures that dictate how it operates."

"Operated," Ralrek corrected. He slouched against his log seat, tracing lines in the dirt.

"Yes, young Ralrek. Operated. One of the safety features in our guidance was that no single member could have too much say. Thus, there was little one of us could do with individual displacements. We could try, and occasionally, a stay would be granted. Those were rare. No one Council member could do much."

"You almost make it sound like the Council fought for demons they knew or liked to not be exiled," I said.

"There were times. Such is the nature of politics."

Ralrek grunted. Across the circle, more than a couple of demons shared scowls. A common reaction when one finds themselves thrust into a struggle for control of their own fate.

"This is how things are done."

"Shouldn't be," Ralrek grumbled.

"I ask that you don't take this personally," Azazel said, changing tactics. By the scowls and head shakes he received, I doubted this fresh approach was going to work, either.

"How can you say that when it's personal?" Roy asked. "We're here because of you. Might not have been you directly, but you was involved."

"And suddenly, you want us to hear you," Cantrell added to the end of Roy's comment. "You're vulnerable, and now you seek a relationship. Where were these offers in the past? Over the past forty thousand years, I've suffered on this island, away from my family. Do you know what it's like to not see your own children grow? To wonder if you have grandchildren? To miss their first centuries of life. Their first steps. The moment they discover their Ability? Tell me, Azazel, can you even fathom what that must feel like?" The Founder wisely remained quiet during her challenge. Cantrell leaned forward, taking in the three other representatives. "We can. Though you can't see our scars from the decisions you had a part in making, they're very real."

I looked down at the dirt, unable to watch Azazel suffer. Maybe he had to go through this. These were his victims, too. I couldn't absolve him of the part he played. Facing that reality was something they had a right to demand of him, and if he truly sought refuge among the exiles, he'd do better for himself by meeting them where they were.

"It pains me to know I've caused harm," Azazel said cautiously, like he was measuring each word. "No matter how much I wish I could have done something then, or now, that would have changed the course of exilement, I cannot. Like you, I can only deal with what lays in front of me. My situation has changed, yes, but that doesn't mean I see you differently. Any of you. I never enjoyed the fact that we exiled demons. I never agreed with it."

"Yet you did," Sethel said. "Regardless of the limitations on your power, you participated in those actions."

"Just as he did with me and Leo." I didn't mean to jump in. I wasn't even defending the Founder. But there was a greater context here everyone was missing. From across the fire, Ralrek sat straight. Next to me, Bilba inhaled deeply. "Leo and I didn't want to fight to the death. They made us. Azazel proposed it."

"So you condemn him further?" Sethel said, his eyebrows furrowing.

"We have a lot of quiet time here," I said, gesturing up at the trees with a finger, meaning to include the entire island. "Time affords me a chance to think. Trust me, I've done a lot of thinking. I know what Azazel was trying to do. In a perfect Underworld, he wouldn't have had to plot like he did, using me and Leo." Now I looked Azazel's way and met his eyes. Eyes that glistened with... What? Sadness? Regret? "But here's the thing. I didn't recognize it until much later. Well, maybe I recognized it, but I didn't appreciate it. I'll never be okay with what happened to Leo, but he volunteered to fight me. By doing that, he saved his family. His entire family. Azazel facilitated that. He helped Leo save his family while deflecting any scrutiny from the other Founders. A hard balancing act, if you ask me." I stopped to swallow. This was difficult to share. The memory of Leo was still fresh. Raw. "If he were here today, he'd tell you he gladly put himself in that position to save his family and that he owed their safety, their futures, to Azazel."

"That's great, and I get it," Roy said, holding up his hand and waving it. The gesture reminded me of mortal movies where congregants in a Baptist church were really getting into the sermon. "But what—"

"No, I don't think you do," I said, scooting forward on my stump.

"Zeke?" Bilba whispered. "Be careful."

I waved him down, scowling. "I am." I raised my voice. "Not only did he save Leo's family, but he put his neck on the line to do it. But that's not all. I was on a fast track to being annihilated by the Council. Without his proposal, I wouldn't be standing here now. He saved my life. A few times."

"In what other ways?" Cantrell asked, sitting up slightly.

"Ways I don't think are proper to discuss," Ralrek said. He glanced around. "Not now. Not until we settle this matter."

Sethel stood. Somehow, it didn't come across as an aggressive move. "Though I can't speak for everyone, I've known these representatives for thousands of years. I trust their judgment, even though we don't always agree." He took a deep breath. His wide nostrils spread. "Politics has never interested me, but I understand them. My role on the Isle is a reluctant but needed one. So I do my duty." He shifted toward the Founder. "I believe you have as well. To hold true to one's duty in the face of injustice is something I don't know if I could manage, so I don't know if I should praise or condemn you."

Azazel said nothing, but watched Sethel with soft eyes.

The shaman rolled his shoulders and spoke as he rotated to speak to all of us at once. "For tens of thousands of years, we worked hard to establish a peaceful settlement on the Isle. It has come at a price." He extended his arm toward Bilba. "Thanks to these young incubi, we've seen the destructive path we were on. We can't afford to slip. We've only just begun to make progress."

"Our new policies haven't even been tested yet," Anayese said, rubbing her chin. "If we were to change the course we're on, the exiles might not accept it any longer."

"Might stop working together," Roy said. "Then where do we go?"

"We can ill afford to make the wrong decision here," Cantrell said, watching Azazel.

Sethel drifted back toward his seat. The campfire swirled around him. "Who says we have to decide at all? At least now? This has to be thought out."

"Why rush? Especially when there's so much work to do?" Roy asked.

"Because if we reject him, what does that say about us besides that we've already taken a step back?" Marijon said. Her nose flared, and it wasn't benign, like Sethel's.

"We?" Cantrell challenged the other succubus with a snap of her head and a sharp look. "Is it 'we' already, Marijon?"

Even though she never explicitly admitted it, I knew how much Marijon hurt at the exiles' constant rejection. Wanting to avoid a test of wills, I said, "If you don't allow Azazel to live here, he'll have to live in the Ninth."

"Okay," Roy said, as if it wasn't a problem.

"He'll be vulnerable there," I said with enough heat to help the farmer see through his ignorance. "And if any of the old Council members get their hands on him, we lose the one ally we have who is close to Lucifer."

Roy snorted so hard he almost lost his balance and went over the back side of his log. "Allied with Lucifer."

"Heretical," Cantrell said, scowling.

"Truth," Ralrek said, stopping all conversation. "Zeke is the Great Prince. You've seen what he can do with his halberd." He stopped to rub his face, leaving behind rivulets of dirt. He didn't seem to care. "I'm so tired of everyone not seeing the problems right in front of them."

"How so?" Sethel asked.

He jabbed a finger at Marijon. "You've treated her like shit ever since she showed up. You did the same to us until we showed you what we're capable of." His finger stabbed at me now. "You've got the one demon the Council has tried to kill and can't, and that hasn't moved you." Now Azazel. "You've got a Founder sitting right there, asking to be protected. Someone who'll help us. We know the Council is falling apart. The Underworld won't be far behind." Now he dedicated his scowl and flippant wave to the exiles. "And here you sit, spending more time explaining why you'd reject yet another demon to spite yourself and your future. Let me be straight up with you. If you don't allow him to stay, the Ninth will collapse. The vacuum will lead to more violence. In time, those you care about back home will be put in harm's way."

Bilba stood. When he spoke, he did so without Ralrek's fire. "We're out of time. Without allowing Azazel to remain, I fear for the future. We can instill a more democratic governance so that you never have to fear Azazel assuming control of the Isle."

"How would that work?" Sethel asked.

Bilba grimaced. "Off the top of my head?"

"Why not?" Cantrell said, her prominent cheekbones set as if she was already convinced she was asking the impossible.

"Well," he said slowly, probably buying himself time. "We could establish a representative government, much like you already have. For each issue requiring a vote, the disparate groups would present one to three options. We'd conduct rounds of debate and voting until we had our last two options, then put it to the population for a majority vote. That way, no exile is over-taxed, but everyone has a say in how their lives are governed. We leave no one out. No demon could rise and assume power for themselves."

Sethel puckered his mouth, thinking. Cantrell stared at Bilba but didn't challenge him.

"I know my way around a hoe, but this stuff gets to be too much." Roy dug at the dirt with his heel. "The Isle could use you to do this more often."

Bilba's forehead scrunched. "Do what?"

"Explain how all this works. Don't think a lot would get what you're saying until you say it. If that makes sense."

"I guess. But I couldn't do that."

"Yes, you could," Ralrek and I said simultaneously.

Cantrell looked at Sethel. "We could definitely use someone like you to advise us. Where did you get these ideas?"

"Probably read it in a book," I said with a chuckle.

"Actually," Bilba said, with a finger pointing toward the roof of the Underworld, somewhere thousands of feet above the mist and the mesa, "I observed and learned about it during my time in the Overworld. Mortals don't do well with democracy, but they've got great ideas. I figure we could take those and make something better."

"Make it our own," Anayese said hungrily.

"Exactly." The tips of Bilba's ears turned a shade of pink.

"Guided by the Rebel Mage and the Great Prince," Sethel

said, his wide mouth leveling out. To Ralrek he said, "What do we call you so we can formalize this triumvirate?"

His head dropped. "I'm just me."

Bilba filled the awkward silence. "I just want to help."

"Same," I said.

"I can see my tribe following you. The appeal of listening to the Rebel Mage would be too much to deny," Anayese said to Bilba, and I swear, her ears turned pink. She caught me looking. "Though some would like you, I guess."

"Thanks," I said awkwardly.

Roy clapped his hands. More than a few around the fire jumped. "Are we all in favor of hashing this out?"

The circle resoundingly answered his question with a "Yes!"

And we did. By the end, Azazel was going nowhere.

26

UNDERWORLD, ISLE OF DREAD

THE BEACH WAS BROAD AND DEEP, CARVING INTO THE ISLAND hundreds of yards from the ocean. A slice of paradise amid denial and repression, along with a dose of temptation for good measure.

It didn't matter that it was a mile-plus walk from Marijon's —our—camp. On this slab of sand, I could: focus my thoughts about Cassie, concentrate on proper forms with Creed, attempt to draw on the Hellfire, wonder what Cassie was up to, remember what chicken wings tasted like, temper my hatred for all things The Council, wonder if Cassie had a boyfriend, plot which of Creed's forms I could spring on Beelzebub to catch him off-guard. Remember the way Cassie smelled. And more.

The beach was solitude. The beach was peace. My happy place.

Except when it wasn't.

Hidden in the island's forests, harpies launched pebbles and—assuming they worked into conjunction with each other —the occasional coconut. I swatted a few back, sending one particularly good swing sailing so deep into the forest I lost sight of it and never heard the resulting impact.

Once the pebbles, rocks, and coconuts stopped arcing down on me, I moved through my forms. Rising Dawn to High Sun. The slow, steady movements stretched my arms and shoulders while loosening my back. With Silencer, things picked up. This was my weakest form. Why? I don't know. There's just nothing sexy about low blocks and sweeping cuts. Sure, if I could ever pull it off against a foe, it'd look great. The problem? I didn't practice it enough. Since its required movements always felt awkward and sluggish, I spent a tenth of the time on this form that I spent on the others.

Frustrated with it, I moved on to the next form, Frigid Bite. This one, I really liked. When I say I liked it, I'm talking, blue-eyed, cocoa-haired angel level of likes. Yes, it's that cool. From bottom-up or top-down, the diagonal slashes felt so powerful. Each swing of the halberd, thanks to laws of physics I didn't understand, glided into a rotation and turn. From there, I could block or swing again, or move into another attack form. One thing about Frigid Bite; whenever I was in the form, I felt indestructible.

I'll bet if someone was watching, they'd be impressed. That's how good I felt. Have you ever felt that way? The way your jeans fit? The one time you did biceps curls and looked in the gym mirror and realized that you actually had chords of muscle bulging at just the right spots? Or when you're singing, even in the shower, and you opened your throat and you just... Hit. That. Note? Yes, that's what Frigid Bite did for me. The fact it was an impractical form for the upcoming rescue didn't matter. Frigid Bite was epic.

Sure, I went through the rest of the forms, doing my best to enjoy the warm rays of the Hellfire and the cool breeze coming off the Acheron. The ocean air brought the sickly sweet smell of salt and bio-fumes of life under its waters. Nothing came close to the power I felt shooting—pulsing—through my arms, down to my fingertips, when Creed was in my hands and Frigid Bite on my mind.

During one of my upward sweeps, cutting through the beach sands and arcing the double-ax head blade high, I felt something. I don't know what it was, nor would I presume to claim to know. But it was there. A spark. A zing. A Lucifer-blessed razmataz. The Hellfire. Creed's blades flashed azure. Not blinding like it had when I was fighting for my life. In that upward sweep, I didn't see Creed's cold steel flash past my eyes because it was already encased in the fiery facade of the flame of annihilation.

I dropped the halberd.

Creed hit the sand with a thump and lay still. The Hellfire fizzled out in a sputtering, pathetic death.

"Holy shit."

Creed buzzed.

"Same, buddy. Same."

I retrieved the halberd. The petrified cherry was still in my palm. I tipped it this side to that, aware of the *Fa' Hersei* lettering inscribed on the haft, but ignoring it. Dialphio knew the dead language. She'd given me a guide to interpret it, but I'd rarely used it before losing possession of it in the last Great Adjustment in my life. The saying, Who Wields, Liberates, was meaningless. At least to me. To others, I'm sure it'd give great hope. To me, the halberd had saved my skin too many times to count, but that didn't equate to liberating. Creed saved me because of its inherent power, not anything I'd drawn on. If the Great Prince was a liberator, he came in the form of his magical stick, not in an incubus who had to straighten his back to legitimately call himself five-foot-eight.

I was a prisoner on the Isle of Dread. My friends were prisoners. Four hundred demons we shared the island with were prisoners. Now, we could add a Founder to that total. Dialphio was soon to be a prisoner of Apopis now that he ruled the Fifth Circle. My mother too.

Couldn't forget Libra. None of us could do anything to change our situations. None of us could except the three incubi shoved off to a corner of the Isle of Dread, hoping someone would take them in.

Speaking of, it was time to head back to camp.

I strolled through the forest. Working the forms with Creed had made me sweat, but I hadn't thought in advance and didn't bring a change of clothes or any of the soap she'd traded for. A bath in the Acheron would have to wait until I made it to the camp, and then only if I felt like heading back down the trail to the water's edge. Right now, that was still up in the air. I really just wanted to sit down, drink half the well of water, and gorge on whatever Marijon had in the pot. In her time on the Isle, she had come a long way in mastering austere culinary processes and meal preparation.

But any decisions I was going to make about my night were already made for me before I made it back to camp.

Sethel Jury sat to the side of the fire pit atop a stump, bent and in deep discussions with Bilba.

I nudged Ralrek. "What are they up to?"

He'd been 'busy' flinging small fireballs into the pit. "Talking magic."

"What kind?"

"Gee, if they were only right there," he said with some force, flinging an orange ball of fire about the size of a mushroom a few feet shy of Bilba. "Then you could ask them yourself."

"Lucifer, stop being a dick," I said, leaving him to his fire flinging, but regretting my biting comment. Ralrek had crap going on that he hadn't dealt with yet. He needed supportive friends, the type who'd tolerate sulking and the occasional combative disposition. I hoped he found them soon, because I was failing and needed to get better.

Thankfully, the brief exchange didn't wake Azazel. His recovery was vital to our next steps, so he needed all the rest he could get.

Marijon tended to the garden. I'd learned that was one

thing she truly enjoyed doing. Her back was to me as she hummed an unfamiliar song. I left her undisturbed and pulled a stump over to my friend and the representative of the Inceptives. "What's going on?"

"Hey, Zeke," Bilba said with an excited smile that split his face.

"What are you two up to?"

Swinging his finger like an upside-down pendulum between himself and Sethel, Bilba said, "We were discussing Gateways and Rifts, and how to open them on the Isle."

Whoa. Okay, I wasn't expecting that. Sharing all our secrets now, was he? "Can demons in the exiled tribes open them?"

Sethel pursed his thick lips. "Don't believe so. No one in the Inceptives can, that's for sure. I wouldn't mind testing it. If I can, I can teach others."

I watched the two of them. Neither seemed perturbed by the possibility of a couple hundred demons flitting all around Hell and the Overworld. "You guys okay with that?"

"Well, it's not like everyone could do it, Zeke," Bilba said, as if my implied concern was ridiculous. "But imagine if… I don't know, twenty or thirty of the demons on this island could at least open Gateways. Maybe not Rifts. We'd have to chat about that. But Gateways? They could visit their families. Check in on them."

"Bring them to the Isle or stay in their Circle," Sethel said.

I wagged my finger. "See, that's the problem. Hell won't be safe for much longer. Not that it is, not for anyone exiled. But the splitting of the Council, each Founder taking absolute control of two Circles. None of us know what that means for the residents of those Circles, and I wouldn't trust them to over-extend on their authority."

"They might not," Sethel said. "We have to consider if that's something we would use to restrict the free travel of the exiles. Some of us have been here for fifty, sixty, even longer than seventy thousand years. You heard Cantrell when she confronted Azazel about missing her children, not knowing if she has grandchildren. With this, we could give everyone a new lease on life." Sethel rocked back, cupping his bent knee with both hands. "Imagine the statement that will make to everyone, Bilba. That you could help us learn how to travel? They would ask you to rule the Isle."

A pink hue shrouded the rims of Bilba's ears. "Oh, I wouldn't want that. I'd just be happy if everyone could live more fulfilling lives. If traveling helps with that by ensuring safety of their loved ones, then I'm happy."

"I still don't know if this is smart," I said cautiously. Our relationship with Sethel seemed to be the strongest of the representatives. From our first intervention over fresh water usage, he seemed more open to listening to us and entertaining the thought of us being a part of the bigger island community. Still, he was an exile of just one tribe. One of four. The island's residents hadn't become a single community. No one expected miracles. We'd just had the festival. But he was here, without the other three representatives, and if we were really going to have this conversation, it needed to be a unified decision.

"This is what we've been fighting for," Bilba said in a timid voice. "Remember, Zeke? We've talked about this forever. You have even talked about how much you disliked the Council controlling everyone's movements."

"I'm not saying I didn't."

The Inceptives representative stopped rocking. "Yet you are resistant to this? Why?"

"Simple. I don't trust the Council, or, or whatever it's called now." Was I really the only one who saw the danger in them having full control of Circles? Beelzebub, Apopis, Seraph, even Michael, allowed to do whatever they wanted to the residents of their individual realms? "On the Isle, everyone is as safe as they can be. Even safer than if they were in the Overworld. Only Lucifer can change that, and He hasn't bothered to leash his Founders. Demons opening Gateways across Hell, popping in to see family, checking in on grandparents, bringing loved ones here to protect them? What happens when word spreads? What happens when Beelzebub is lying in wait, and jumps through an exile's Gateway and lands smack-dab in the middle of our next festival? Do we want to rely on Lucifer blocking that from happening? So, when you two talk about demons popping in and out of Gateways all over Hell, I get nervous." I looked at Bilba, sharing a deeper connection. "Even if it's something I've always said was a demon's right. Now just isn't the time, buddy."

"I'm not saying it is," he said, each word measured. "Even if we ran off to the groups now, I couldn't possibly teach them today."

"This will take time," Sethel added. "I must first have conversations with the other representatives." Well, there went that worry I had about the Inceptive making a unilateral decision. A point for Sethel. "We can't move forward until everyone agrees. Even then, we'd have to identify who has the potential."

Bilba flicked a finger. It stood firm above his fist. "Then there's the training." He added a second finger. "Then practice. We can't just expect them to learn the technique and do it. Some of them might open Gateways in the middle of the Acheron, for all we know." He dropped his hand. "It's going to take time, Zeke. We're not rushing into this. Though, we can't forget how long it would take to achieve effectiveness. That has to be part of the calculation." His eyes widened. "Plus, Sethel promised to help us, too. If Ralrek would ever get off his butt and come over here."

The tall incubus going through a personal heaven grumbled something from where he slouched.

"What are you offering to help with?" I asked.

"I can teach these two about listening wards and silencing spells," the elderly exile said, as if he told me he'd escort them to the beach.

"Say what?"

"Yep!" Bilba exclaimed. "Isn't that great? Imagine if I understood them. What that could do for us and everything we need to accomplish?"

"I am." I looked at Sethel. "Can you really do that?"

"I can."

"Phenomenal," I said, smacking my thigh.

Oh, how this would upset the Founders. If Sethel taught Bilba and Ralrek those tricks, assuming they could cast them, we could safely operate around the Circles in more ways than just my buddy's undetectable Gateways and Rifts. We could protect Dialphio and the rebel cell when there were meetings. With demons using Gateways, once Dialphio learned of this new skill, she could invite neighboring cells to join hers, and we could meet under the protection of the listening ward.

Finally, we were leveling the playing field. A moment too late? Possibly. But this was also another step in the right direction.

Bilba seemed to read my mind if his goofy grin was a hint of his perceptive skills. "Awesome, huh?"

I couldn't lie. "Yeah."

They moved out into the clearing. Ralrek reluctantly joined. I watched, since I'd asked Marijon if there was anything I could help with, and she told me I was helping by staying out of her way.

Sethel did most of the talking, and there was very little actual casting happening. At one point later, Bilba walked him through Gateways and Rifts and I drifted off. When I came to, the sky showed the first signs of the Hellfire fading, but the three magic users were still at it in the field. Bilba listened to the shaman intently. Ralrek, in a big swing, was a completely different incubus from the one I remembered when I fell asleep.

I understood why when I heard Sethel say, "Having been on the Isle for... I don't even know at this point. Close to seventy-thousand years, I'd say. My Ability has altered. The Isle does that to everyone. It will to you, as well."

"Altered?" Ralrek asked, looking down at his hands.

"Do you mean it'll strip us of our Ability?" Bilba asked worriedly.

"Maybe."

Bilba gulped. "Maybe?"

"To be honest, there's no way of knowing. Not for sure. But it will change it. Some demons lose their Ability completely. Others become stronger. For the rest, their magic changes." Sethel lifted his arms, palms toward the ground. The murky sensation was immediate. I knew what was coming. He brought them down in a circular motion, his hands now at waist level and his palms pointing skyward. Though his mouth moved, I didn't hear a word. A Listening Ward.

After he finished, Bilba and Ralrek turned my way. Bilba shouted something—I could tell because a vein popped up on the side of his throat. Ralrek flipped me off even though he didn't need a ward to get away with that bad mortal habit we'd all picked up while in the Overworld. I blame the Army. I picked up most of my bad habits and all my cuss words during my service.

Sethel reversed his motion and Bilba's laughter burst through the nearby forest. He clamped a hand to his mouth.

"That was amazing," he said, a little quieter but just as excited. Turning to me, he asked, "Did you feel anything?"

I nodded. "Saw it coming a mile away."

Sethel gave Bilba a confused look.

My friend explained my skill at sensing magic.

Sethel's bottom lip jutted out. He looked impressed. "Is there nothing you three can't do?"

"Cook." Marijon whooped. "Clean up after themselves. Find girlfriends who'd marry them and take them away." She returned to her work, chuckling.

When I stopped laughing, I said, "I felt you pulling on your Abilities to form the ward. But yours feels different."

Though he was replying to me, Sethel faced Bilba. "That's the taint of the island I was telling you about. Everyone, well, those who still have their Ability, says the same thing. The Isle changes us to our cores."

Bilba put his hand to his chin. "This could be beneficial. If our Abilities change, if the Isle mutates them, maybe the essence of the magic is too."

"How's that beneficial?" I asked.

Bilba came back to the fire, and Sethel followed him. Ralrek remained in the clearing, practicing. Bilba took his stump and emptied his jug of water before responding. "Well, if our magic changes on an elementary level, anyone opposing us, planning on stopping us, whether that's rescuing Libra, helping the rebel cells, or anything else, will plan their response based on their understanding of demonic magic. But if the island changes what our magic is at its core, then we'll already have an advantage. I mean, we would need to test this, of course, but on a theoretical level, it makes sense."

Sethel stretched, looking up at the sky. "I have to return home soon, but I must say, I'm impressed with your knowledge of magic."

Bilba blushed. "Thank you."

"I think the only thing about magic he doesn't understand are curses," I said, sharing a look with my friend. Sethel's scrutiny lingered as I explained who Cancer was to us and what her familial situation was.

"Curses are an interesting form of magic," Sethel said once Bilba finished.

Attention grabbed, I blurted out the question begging to be asked. "They're real?"

"If not, they're the most effective Discernment spell I've ever heard of," Sethel said, too casual for the circumstances. "I can't know for sure. My Ability is Manipulative. I encourage you to continue your research. If you have time when you're off the Isle, but even on it. I know of two Discernment users in our tribe, and I'm sure the others have someone among them with the Ability. Maybe we can help you understand it."

"I'd really appreciate that."

"Of course." Sethel gave me a broad smile. "We're all in this together."

For the first time, I believed.

27

OLYMPIA

VIRGO SHOOK HIS HEAD. "ABSOLUTELY NOT."

Bilba blinked. "Why not?"

The Commandant leaned to fill his bottle. The dispenser spat and sprayed water all over his forearm. He yanked it away and flicked the water off. "Because sending someone through your Rift to test if the Underworld can detect their movements is dangerous. It puts them at a lot of risk, and I'm not willing to do that."

"What if they volunteer?" I asked.

Virgo looked like he didn't appreciate the question. He nodded to the meeting room door. "Let's talk about this in there before any of these crazy bastards," he said, raising his voice and his chin at the smiling Vigilantes watching our conversation, "get any crazier ideas than they already have."

Once in the room, he closed the door and leaned against it. "Guys, you can't do that in front of them."

"Why not?" Bilba asked.

"Because it puts me in a bind."

"How?"

Virgo cocked his head. "Come on. Seriously? Demons and angels have dragged this group over the fires. If they're not looking for a fight, they're looking to escape this shit. You just handed them both chances at once. Without asking me." Virgo is intense, but I never thought of him as angry, even when fighting him in Leo's MMA cage. Now? I couldn't say that. I swear, his pupils shrunk. "The Vigilantes have needs. Demons are a mess. Angels are doing things I'm not thrilled about."

"Like what?" I said, feeling too defensive for such an innocuous statement.

"Doesn't matter right now," Virgo answered.

"Why not?"

"Because I don't have proof that the abductions are any worse," he said. "They're definitely not better."

"The angels aren't upholding the slowdown?" Ralrek asked.

"I don't know this Gemini guy," the leader of the Vigilantes said, rubbing his hands like he was warming them up for a fight. "So I won't trust him until he earns it."

"Gemini's good," I said.

Virgo frowned. "Might be. Still needs to earn my trust. Especially until these abductions dry up."

"Give them time to work their angle."

"We don't have time. They'll earn it when they earn it." By the way he set his jaw, I knew pushing the point would be useless. "I can't use the Vigilantes to investigate or patrol the city. We're being hit too. Even if I could, we're stretched thin. I can only assign so many of them to so many things. Most of them have jobs and families outside of this."

Bilba stuck his chest out—a little. It was cute. "I just wanted to test the Rift's undetectability with someone to see if we are ready for the Path whenever we agree to start it."

Virgo sighed heavily. "I know, man. Just ask before you offer in front of anybody next time. Okay?"

"Okay," Bilba said. "But we still need to test this as soon as possible. I think I've—"

Virgo's hand shot up and his gaze shifted as if he heard something none of us did. "Hold that."

"Everything good?" Ralrek asked, watching Virgo intensely.

"Yeah," he said, but moved like an ember cat to the podium tucked in the corner of the room.

From where I sat, I couldn't see what had his attention. Whatever it was, it couldn't be good.

Bilba, Ralrek, and I glanced at each other and waited. We didn't have to wait long.

"We've got to go." Virgo was dashing around the podium and out of the meeting room, yanking the door open so violently it crashed against the wall and bounced back.

"What the heaven?" I got up and was the first one out in the hangar behind the leader of the Vigilantes.

He was calling them to gather.

The hangar woke in a rush. A chair fell over somewhere. One guy—a mortal, as evidenced by the lack of smoky emissions Abandoned immortals gave off—shouted into the bathroom for everyone to "tie it off and get out here."

After Virgo ordered the woman who served as the Sergeant-At-Arms to start a recall, I interrupted. "What's going on?"

He started for the lockers that stored the Vigilantes' firearms. "Cassie wrote. Said there's a group of her angels under fire from Beelzebub and Apopis." He stopped and looked at me. "She's there."

Gear, medical kits, and weapons were loaded faster than most of the dumps I took. Once ready, we were racing down Capitol Way within minutes.

The night was dark and blustery, typical of the Pacific Northwest at the turning of the year. The Olympia Farmers Market was where Cassie had said the attack was happening.

I cursed myself for not bringing my demonic notebook with me, but I rarely did when in the Overworld. When we came here, we came with a purpose, and any meeting with Cassie would have already been organized. A notebook would have just been one more thing to lug around. Plus, I didn't want to look like a dork. That was Bilba's role, and he played it well. Deep down, I selfishly hoped she hadn't tried writing to me before Virgo. Disappointing others was something I learned I did quite well since I was old enough to understand Kanthor Sunstone's outlook on the world. Cassie Haniel was the last immortal I ever wanted to disappoint.

The market was an extensive structure, split into two wings with a central, two-story hub. Each wing was nearly eighty yards long. Maybe longer. I'd been inside the building during my Abandonment, and it was a cool place to peruse the wares of local artists while catching tasty treats. This time of year, it was closed. Good for innocent immortal civilians, bad for the market if the flashes I saw and the racket bleeding out was a hint of the fighting going on inside.

As the Vigilantes unloaded from the van and geared up, I activated Creed.

We'd parked in the southwest corner of the parking lot, next to a restaurant where I'd always wanted to eat and never got around to visiting—mostly because they didn't have chicken wings on their menu.

Glass shattered from a window at the top of the central hub of the market, spraying outward and raining down on the sidewalk.

I took off.

"Don't run into it yet!" Virgo shouted behind me.

I didn't stop.

Bilba called my name. Ralrek hurled an insult. But Cassie was in there. They could curse me all they wanted after I got her out of this mess.

Creed's haft pulsed in my palm.

"Let's do this," I said to the magical halberd as the shield bloomed around me.

I was at the west wing before the Vigilantes were slamming magazines into their rifles. A few weeks ago at the attack on a women's clinic, too many Vigilantes fell. I had to spare them from paying the price again. Virgo was good about playing the tough guy role, but the attack and deaths had hurt him deep. He seemed harder now. Not that he was numb to the immortals and mortals who served the cause, but almost like the toll of this growing struggle had him resigned to the cost of violence.

Lucky for him, I was in coupon-clipping mode.

A decorative sliding barn door was cracked about six inches. In the fighting, Beelzebub's troops must have not noticed. I sneaked to it and peeked inside.

During the season, vendors and their products filled the stalls. The market had been closed for months, and would be for months still. Any table or stand that wasn't permanently bolted to the floor, like the one for the flower vendor and the bakery, was pushed into the middle of the concrete. The temporary stockpile afforded the battle plenty of space to unfold and only a few centralized obstacles to hide behind.

From my quick assessment, this wasn't the battle I'd expected. I didn't see Cassie or any angels, but Beelzebub and Apopis were in plain sight. They walked in my direction down the center aisle. Too confident and cocky, but with good reason.

Twenty yards in front of them, fifteen demons blasted the pile of stalls that had been stacked for the winter. Flashes of spells fell on the pile or manipulated the wood furniture into devices the demons used against their targets. They set the stuff on Fire. They bombarded it with water. Someone pulled stalls apart and built a wood giant that stood nearly as tall as the ceiling's cross beams.

Formed, it went on the attack. Each time the wood giant's arm came down, it smashed an entire section of the collection of stalls.

A beam of white burst from behind the stalls just after I felt the first sign of an oncoming migraine—my reaction to Angelfire. Between the Fire, Deception, and Water Abilities used by the demons and now this angelic version of magic, I was a walking irritation. Every inch of my skin felt slimy and scratchy at the same time. The blossoming migraine wouldn't help my focus.

Call it a self-fulfilling prophecy, but it might have slowed me.

Once I had a clear shot on Beelzebub and Apopis, I dropped the shield and pushed my thoughts into Creed. Lucifer's encouragement to learn to control the Hellfire was digging around somewhere in the back of my mind. However, the moment Creed's blades flashed azure, and I tossed the barn door open, leveling the halberd and taking aim, a massive jolt of sharp pain fried the back of my skull.

One moment, Beelzebub and Apopis were strolling down the center of the market, the next, Hellfire burst from Creed's double-axes.

I winced against the migraine caused by powerful Angelfire. My beam of Hellfire scorched the air, but missed the two Founders. Because of the power of Creed's attack, I couldn't make out the two Founders from the box of match sticks I created when the Hellfire tore into the side of the building.

I tumbled behind a stack of whiskey barrels that had been sheared in half to make decorative flower pots. They exploded when a ball of fire struck, shooting a stack of sticks against the walls. The smell of burning wood was immediate.

I rolled to safety.

Stacked railroad ties served as my next shelter. They were about eight feet long and over half a foot thick. Three rows deep, it'd take a powerful spell to topple them.

I got up to my knees and scanned the scene. To my right, twenty yards away, two angels hunkered behind a wall of sizzling wood. I didn't know them, but I knew the third angel. A former spy. Someone who'd posed as a beggar to earn her way closer to Lucifer's Third Council. Now, a member of Yahweh's Council herself and the daughter of the Upperworld's Big Cheese.

Cassie sat on her rear, braced against the wall. Four feet from the other two angels, she was at greater risk. The way she gripped her right shoulder, she'd been injured in the fighting.

Beelzebub and Apopis's crew fired on the pile as the wood giant smashed it. Soon, the angels would be out of places to hide.

At the open barn door, two Vigilantes peeked in. Within seconds, they would try to secure a firing position. Not long after that, Bilba and Ralrek would join. None of that needed to happen.

I could race to the angels and shield them, pull Cassie out of the fray, and to safety. That was my priority. But if I did that, the demons would follow. Beelzebub and Apopis would have a wonderful chance to batter my shield, and my friends and the Vigilantes would have to get into the scrum to ward them off.

If I used a shield, I involved everyone in the fight.

So I did the best thing I could with the limited power I had. I whistled in Cassie's direction.

Thankfully, I'd done so right in the middle of a pause in the destruction and spellcasting. All three angels looked my way. I put up my hand like I was stiff-arming a blazeball midfielder. They stayed hunkered.

Drawing a breath, I tried to listen for any hint of Beelzebub and Apopis's location. They were the key. Get them, and all this went away. Double-get them in the Over-world, and they wouldn't live to see the re-opening of the Grand Chamber in the morning. Four Circles of Hell would be freed from their tyranny before they felt its first oppressive measure.

Creed thumped in my fist.

"You looking for a fight?"

It thumped once, strong enough to leave a thick red mark.

The wood giant, constructed from stalls and chairs and miscellaneous two-by-fours, arced another chair-sized fist down into the barrier. Wood sprayed outward, slamming into the back wall and splintering, smashing a window, and tumbling down on the angels in hiding.

Fireballs arced over the barrier from the three demons in the goon squad.

Whenever the angels could, they took potshots. Blind as they were to the demons' location, the attacks did little.

Hellfire swelled around Creed's double-ax head and dagger blades. I stood, scanning the length of the market for the two Founders.

Shielded by a corner that jutted out from the wall, an office, the pair weren't as safe from the fracas as they thought. I leveled Creed just as Apopis's form disappeared behind the wall.

Creed loosed, sending a thick beam of Hellfire through the office. Completely. When I say that, I mean it. The walls on the near and far side. The desk that sat in between. Even an innocent office chair evaporated in the attack of azure.

I dragged the second shot across the office, from left to right, hoping I could catch them pushing farther back into a corner to save their asses. Wood cracked and splintered. Glass clattered and shattered. Something in the building groaned.

I continued pulling the beam across and through the office, carving a three-foot wide horizontal split in the wall. When it lashed through the last part, the office collapsed, all three free-standing signs at once. The outer wall bowed out, slowly at first, and then shot like a spring freed of its tension when the ceiling collapsed.

The two side walls fell outward: the nearer in pieces, the farthest as a whole. The weight of it coming down would crush Beelzebub and Apopis.

I grinned, lowering Creed at the wood giant, who smashed its way closer to the angels in hiding.

Creed vibrated. The connection, deep. Through my hands, into my arms and shoulders, filling my chest. Not a well-spring, but gurgling brook. The power, according to Lucifer, and in line with my own desires, I needed to command.

The double axes bobbed up and down. I pinned the haft to my side, tucked under my arm. Swelling, the bubble of Hell-fire around the blades turned white with heat.

The wood giant never stood a chance. The beam of Hell-fire took it in the chest, blowing right through it. In a way, it was funny to watch what transpired. One second, the giant was raising another blocky fist to do more damage, and the next, it had a fraction of a second of gravity defiance. The broad chest, shoulders, and head were separated from its waist, suspended in air after the Hellfire extinguished its gut. Then the upper torso came crashing down on the lower torso. Popping, cracking, shrieking. The wood giant obliterated itself.

One of Cassie's angels took out a demon hiding in the rafters. The succubus was blasted backward, flying thirty feet before hitting a support beam and flopping to the concrete floor.

The battle stilled. I crouched and listened, keeping an eye on the Vigilantes, who had secured the door, allowing Bilba and Ralrek to sneak in and get cover. Virgo was with them, directing his forces.

I scowled. Try as I might, I couldn't finish this before my friends and the Vigilantes joined.

But then, I also didn't hear anything from the demonic forces. We had Beelzebub and Apopis neutralized, maybe injured. Maybe dead. This was the Overworld, so I had to recognize the possibility. The glorious possibility. Their deaths would create chaos in the Underworld, but that was Lucifer's problem to deal with. This was His fault anyway. It'd take a few months of inconvenient adjustment as the rulers tried to figure out who was ruling what over a future that included those two holding power over four Circles.

Cassie adjusted, looking like she was trying to stand.

"Psst." I motioned for her to stay where she was, grateful when she slumped back against the wall.

None of the attacks had come close. She didn't need to move and take a chance of one of the remaining demons seeing her. Even if it was dumb luck, her doing anything but what she was doing now introduced risk that didn't need to be in the conversation.

I moved along my barrier, trying to outpace the Vigilantes, who were slinking through the market with military precision. The problem? They were on the other side. Destroyed office or not, I didn't trust the two Founders to not be dead under a pile of office wreckage.

Bracing myself, I scanned the parts of the market I could see, finding nothing, and dashed to the angels.

Cassie glared when I settled next to them against the barrier, my back to it so I could look at her.

"What?" I whispered with a smile.

She tried to look upset, but it didn't last. Her mouth crooked. "You shouldn't have done that. The Vigilantes are here, right?"

"Yep."

"Yet you're the only one I see."

I jerked my thumb over my shoulder. "They're over there. Plus, I wanted to finish this before someone got hurt. Well, before any of us got hurt. I don't care about Beelzebub and Apopis or their goons."

"That was Be-Beelzebub and A-A-Apopis?" an angel, a stocky woman, said.

The other, a man with a hooked mustache, stared at Creed, saying nothing.

"Yeah, unfortunately. But I think I got him." That part—I hoped it didn't sound like bragging—was for to Cassie. "You okay?"

"I will be," she said. "Got hit by flying debris."

"Caught her square in the shoulder," the man said.

I nodded. "Let me make sure the demons are taken care of. Can you open a Rift and get home? Get your injuries looked at?"

Cassie shook her head. "Not as long as you and the Vigilantes are here."

"Cassie, go take care—"

"No. Once I know everyone is safe, I will. Not until then."

Stubborn woman. "Fine." I looked at the other two angels. "Stay with her, but keep an eye out for any nasty surprises sneaking up behind me, will you?"

"Of course," the woman said.

I slunk along the barrier. At the far end, the spot closest to where the demons had been attacking, I searched for any sign of the enemy. My kind; the enemy. A demon, Hell's Great Prince, fighting to defend angels. What in the heaven was happening to the world?

I really didn't want more death or destruction. The mortals who owned the market wouldn't be happy the next time they threw their doors open to kick off the season, only to find what we left behind. But, as is too often the case, I didn't get much of a choice.

"Zeke! To your right!"

Cassie's warning came just in time. I reacted out of instinct, diving and rolling forward as a fireball tore through the barrier. Out on the open floor, I swung Creed around in the direction I thought the attack had come from, and sent a beam of Hellfire cutting through the rafters.

I'd love to say I looked as badass as the mortals' Hollywood stars who can tumble through the air, blasting their 9mm blindly into a crowd, only hitting the bad guy right before he detonates the bomb. Instead, my shot sheared off the I-beam brace, causing things in that general vicinity to lean.

A demon toppled down the beam, scrambling to stop the fall. He clung to it like a baby koala to its mother. So I shot the other brace, and the beam crashed to the concrete. The demon never felt a thing. It was pretty gruesome.

Gunfire from the other side of the market drew my attention. I peeked around a pole to see the Vigilantes pinning down the last demon. She didn't last long. Ralrek shot fire daggers like a marketing intern blasting out free merch from a t-shirt gun.

Silence settled over the market. Soft scuffing steps were the only thing I heard as I flanked the collapsed office. If any goons were hiding, they weren't looking for a fight. Nothing moved but the good guys.

From the other side of the office, I lost hope. The collapsed wall lay flat. Unless it completely squashed the two Founders when it fell, I hadn't been as successful as I first thought.

The Vigilantes helped lift the wall. When it came away in chunks, my fears proved accurate. The Founders had escaped. Again.

In the instant after realizing the goons were taken care of and the two Founders had gotten lucky through cowardice, every concern save one disappeared.

I sprang for Cassie.

Kneeling at her side, I was vaguely aware of the Vigilantes coming our way, and of the two angels watching me. I didn't care about Virgo or his squad, my friends, or the two voyeurs. The only thing that mattered was that Cassie was safe.

My hand was on her shoulder before I thought about my next move. Her hand was under mine, and my fingers slipped between hers. "I'm so glad you're okay."

She snorted. There wasn't a sound in the world as wonderful as her ugly laugh. "Me too. Dad will appreciate what you did."

"Ha, wouldn't that mess with the mortals' heads? Yahweh being cool with a demon."

Something flickered in her eyes. A temporary loss of relief? In a flash, those cool blues sparkled again. "He's a lot more fun than you might think."

"Has to be to have a daughter like you."

I don't know why, and didn't want to question it either, but I felt a draw. Right now, my only desire was to move closer. As close as she'd allow. The two feet separating us were three feet too far. I leaned in. Her smell overpowered the dusty aftereffects of the fight. Her eyes erased the market, the recent visions of two Founders I wanted to deal with, and the death and destruction. Pull. Pull. Pull. Drawn in without a whisper. The world blurred. Only Cassie's eyes and her small, thin lips. All that existed. Now. All I wanted to explore. Closer.

She rolled her lips. Nervous? Wetting them?

I tried to swallow. I couldn't.

Closer.

Her eyes locked on me.

Inches away.

"Hi, Cassie!" Bilba exclaimed, uncomfortably close. "Are you okay?"

She jerked back, blinking. A courteous smile flickered on her lips as she looked up at the dufus who'd just ruined the moment. "Hi, Bi-Bilba. Yes, I'm..." She found my eyes again and my brain went numb. "Everything is absolutely perfect."

28

UNDERWORLD, FIFTH CIRCLE

DIALPHIO SPREAD HER ARMS. "WHAT DO YOU THINK?"

I was speechless.

"I love it," Bilba said cheerily. He soaked in the neighboring property my former boss had bought. She said she got it on a steal because the incubus who owned the small woodworking store sold it under the impression that doing so would give him a better chance to court her. An overly optimistic business decision, to be sure.

"Thank you, Bilba," she said, drifting to the back wall to show off the whiteboard hanging there. "One member is an electrician, and she wired this to the Hellfire. Watch." She tapped the whiteboard twice and then dragged her finger in big loops across it. A small trail of azure, as wide as her finger, followed, remaining lit.

"Nice," Ralrek said.

When she finished writing LISTEN TO DIALPHIO, she turned and spread her arms. "Tada!"

Bilba's mouth hung open. "It stays like that?"

"Yes, until I do this." She tapped the inner part of a small square shape in the bottom corner of the whiteboard and the letters disappeared instantly. "All gone. Just in case we ever have unanticipated company."

"Smart," I said, impressed. "The cell is coming a long way."

At the back of the room, the handful of rebels I'd previously met played host to ten demons I didn't recognize. Dialphio had told us the cell's recruitment was paying off, but that the recent events had driven membership far faster. Seems that when leaders create chaos, they can expect the populace to respond. The Fifth Circle was definitely responding.

Tipping my jaw at the socializing demons, I said, "You've got to be happy about this."

"Not happy that it's necessary, but happy that demons are stepping forward," Dialphio said.

Ralrek mumbled. "Finally."

"Building this will take time and courage," Dialphio said. "We have to be patient."

"Sure. As soon as we have that luxury."

I nudged him toward the long table covered in plates of food. "Let's get something to eat and mingle. Nicely."

He grunted but allowed me to escort him away.

Nostris hovered over the cheeses, looking at the variety as if he didn't understand what they were, but yearning to explore all the opportunities they provided. When he saw me approach, he fumbled with his plate and almost dropped it. "Oh, hi, Ezekial. I didn't see you coming." He tried to wedge his plate into a spot on the crowded table and it nearly fell off when he pulled his hands away, wringing them.

"Calm down. He shits just like the rest of us," Ralrek said, before snagging a plate and filling it to the edge with thick slices of pepperoni, salami, prosciutto, and about ten types of cheese. The blessed incubus didn't even have to snag a clump of grapes or a few slices of apple in an effort to pretend to eat healthier. Lucky bastard.

I left him to drift off and learn how to be a good boy by practicing cordiality while I caught up with Nostris on the side. He seemed overwhelmed. By the growth of the cell. By the developments in Hell's governance. By my presence.

Should I worry? For being Dialphio's muscle, this guy really got unsettled easily.

Viztor and Arin stood in a corner, quietly talking. I stopped to say hi, but quickly moved on when it appeared they were in the middle of a debate I wanted no part of. This was supposed to be a social function to welcome the newest rebels. The last time I got wrapped in the rebel's debates, it turned on me, our work with angels, and the group's need for me to push for the title of Lucifer. None of which I was interested in discussing right now.

We were here to help the growing team bond. Time for squabbles and debates had long passed. This group needed to get to work. Here at Dialphio's request, she believed this group introduction would bring the others on board and help with recruitment once they carried word back that the Great Prince himself was in attendance. If she felt that was needed, we'd do it. We had to. With Beelzebub and Apopis already showing their hand the same week Lucifer gave them control of four Circles, Libra's rescue was even more imperative. We had to ensure the strength and safety of these rebels in case something went bad in the rescue operation.

Zenas caught me as I was on my way to say hi to Melchiot. Bilba had her and Scorpio in the corner and I'm sure they were talking magic, technique, and all sorts of business chat that shouldn't be brought up at a social event. I wanted to rescue his mentor. Zenas made that impossible.

"She's trouble," the large-eared succubus said, subtly casting her head forward, stretched in Bilba's general direction.

"Who? Melchiot?" I said. "She's a little strange, but nothing to worry about unless something has changed in the few weeks we've been on the Isle."

"A lot of us old-timers are worried about all these new

recruits," she replied, pulling her cup to her mouth and sniffing her drink. The cinnamon hit me in the face even at this distance. "I'm not so sure about her, but the other one. She's even more trouble."

The "other one" was the succubus I'd only met recently. Scorpio, if I remembered correctly. She was a straight shooter who didn't leave any lasting impression other than her demeanor being rougher than burlap. Not a fan of me, I imagined, since she wasn't happy about the risk of working with angels.

Join the queue.

"Why do you say that?" Again, I wanted nothing to do with drama.

Like I'd already read the script, Zenas said, "Because you guys are working with angels." She sipped her drink noisily, her eyes on Scorpio and Melchiot the entire time. "I don't know, Zeke. I know it's not my place. But you're the Great Prince. Someone has to be truthful, so might as well be me. If no one else is going to speak up, I will."

My knowledge of how succubi addressed conflict was extremely limited. So instead, I said, "Is it really that bad or are you maybe being careful? Which," I said, putting a hand up, "I'm totally okay with. Trust me. We're facing enough risk."

"No, I swear," Zenas said, "I'm not making it up. I get why Dialphio has her in charge of security. That succubus is all over every little detail. I mean, it's made us better, for sure. No stalactite left unturned." She huffed, doing a full-body turn to me as if she was on a stool and someone had just spun her. "Here's the thing. Something's wrong."

"Gut feeling?"

Zenas looked more frustrated with herself than anything else. "I know it sounds crazy, but I don't trust her any more than I like her, and that's not much. The other one isn't much better."

I almost choked on the chunk of cookie in my mouth. "Who? Melchiot?"

"Yeah."

Talking around my mushy cookie, I said, "I know she can be... eccentric."

"Weird?"

I met her halfway. "Strange. But she's got the best of intentions."

"She's got serious," Zenas said and then rubbed her thumb and finger together, the universal sign to refer to someone's wealth, "and connections."

"Her Passage school is, was, very popular," I said in Melchoit's defense. She deserved it. Bilba trusted her. Though he could be naïve, he was still a decent judge of character. After all, for four to five thousand years, he was really the only one to give me half a chance. Only when I had Creed and the attention of the Council did others see my potential. Bilba saw it all along. But that wasn't the only reason Melchoit deserved my support. She had never wronged Bilba. If anything, she defended him. Pushed him. Stood up for him. Stared in the face of Apopis and demanded he allow her into the Passage, a place where she could have been hurt or killed, because she didn't believe my friend was ready for his test. Of course, Zenas wouldn't know any of this, but I couldn't let her ignorance inform her decisions. Too many immortals and mortals already did that. No sense in adding another. "She knows what she's doing. She stood by him," I said, pointing at my best friend, "when no one else would. When it could have cost her everything. Even when it did."

Zenas made a sound between a purr and a buzz. "Just." The word faded like an eighties song.

"Just what?" I shuffled a quarter step closer. "We don't know each other that well, but you've already put a lot of faith in me. More than I deserve, probably. More than I'm comfortable with. Definitely. If you're feeling something, tell me. Lucifer knows, my feelings have saved my skin more than a few times."

"Just be careful, please. We all need you."

Dialphio stole the attention from anything I could have said in response, which was good, because I didn't have anything Hell-shattering to share with Zenas. I appreciated her candor, but it gave me nothing to work with. Who knew if her feelings were grounded in suspicion or personality? For now, I'd note it until something validating came along. I could give it no more attention as my ex-boss clapped her hands, asking the group of rebels to gather around.

I moved to Ralrek. "Nice to see, isn't it?"

Taller than me, which wasn't saying much, he had a better view to examine the crowd. His arms were crossed. "The numbers are encouraging. Now, let's see what they do with them. That's what matters."

"Give 'em a chance."

"Ticktock, Zeke. Tick-freaking-tock."

"Though it's wonderful to see everyone together and enjoying themselves," Dialphio said once everyone quieted, "I wanted to apologize for hosting you in such a mess."

Soft music played through speakers set in the corners of the long room, stretching sixty feet. The air smelled of flowers and pepperoni. The room was on the bright side of intimate. Sure, the drywall was unfinished, but the flooring was done and we were warm and safe from the prying eyes of the Council—well, from whatever Apopis was calling any governing and law enforcement bodies helping him run the Fifth.

"This is fantastic." Bilba held up his glass. Dark soda sloshed over the rim. A few giggles later, he was cleaning up the spill while Dialphio centered everyone on the reason for the get-together.

"This is only the beginning of what we hope to accomplish," she said. "Significant challenges lay ahead. I think you all know that. Today, we don't live in the Underworld we've always known." A smattering of grumbles and aggressive sounds of agreement from the rebels told me she'd hit the mark with several in the crowd. "The disappearances we've experienced here in the Fifth aren't the only ones in the Underworld. Across the Circles, demons have disappeared. The concern is that it will continue."

"Because no one has done anything about the angels," a voice said from the back of the room.

Heads turned in that direction. Ralrek, able to see over almost everyone, grumbled, "Scorpio."

I leaned, picking her out between the bodies. One leg was straight, bracing her. The other was bent, wrapped around the corner of the table she kept half her rear on. She'd crossed her arms. Her pock-marked face dared anyone to contest her challenge.

I'd never seen anyone with the fortitude to stand up to Dialphio, but if anyone could, Scorpio was definitely in the running.

Dialphio pulled her glasses from her face, letting them dangle from their white pearl strap. "There's no evidence angels are involved in the disappearances, Scorpio, and while I appreciate you keeping us focused on the risks, this isn't the time."

"We shouldn't pretend, Dialphio," the head of security for the cell said.

The air crackled. Newbies looked at the strangers around them like they suddenly realized they might have walked into a snare. The experienced rebels stiffened, watching the two succubi as if they knew what was coming but couldn't look away. Zenas, now across the U-shaped crowd, looked at me. When I found her, she widened her eyes in an 'I told you so' sort of way.

Dialphio's intonation was measured, not combative, but definitely one of someone who held authority. She stepped close to the center of the crowd, slowly turning so that she spoke to everyone, not just Scorpio. "I can promise all of you that no one here is pretending. More than anyone in the Fifth, this cell knows the dangers of our reality. Every single day, at any minute, we could be arrested for what we've done. What we are doing. With Apopis running the Circle, no one," she stressed, now finding Scorpio, "knows the future. We cannot be too careful. Scorpio is right. Every day, each one of you will have to be diligent. Aware of your surroundings at all times. Even when you're not working for the cell. By doing this, you're risking everything, but it might be the most important thing you'll ever do."

"It's worth it," an incubus said from somewhere in the gaggle.

"Definitely," Ret shouted from the side of the room, raising a fist in the air. Other fists soon joined his solitary one.

No one in the room knew how dangerous or important their future activities would be. Everything in Hell was unpredictable now. Until Azazel was fully back on his feet, they were under the leadership of a bookstore owner without connections to the higher levels of government. An island nation in the middle of a hurricane named Apopis.

His rule of the Fifth was an incipient threat, one that would be fed and watered daily to grow into a fearsome tribulation for his enemies, innocents of the Circle, and those who acted against him.

Yet here were the Fifth's most courageous. They weren't imps driven by hormones or underdeveloped prefrontal lobes. These were grown-ass demons who knew the lives they lived, and were about to live, were not what they could be. What they should be. They knew, in order to change their course, they had to act. No one would do it for them.

The heroes of the Fifth.

A slow hand clap hushed everyone. If clapping hands could sound sardonic, this was the perfect example.

Scorpio had unlocked her arms to draw attention with the clap, but hadn't moved otherwise.

Dialphio's mouth shrunk in a pinch. "Do you have something you'd like to share?"

She frowned, raising an arm and flipping her hand like she was royalty, dismissing an annoying court jester. "We can rah-rah all day long, but as long as we're not prioritizing angels, we're setting ourselves up for trouble."

"What trouble do you expect to face?" I asked, unable to listen to her bitching any longer. The cell was just gaining momentum. If she continued, she might give more than a few of the new members hesitation about their decision to join. Some might never return to another meeting, never again engage in one of the cell's activities. Some of those might think a better guarantee for their future would be to rat out the cell, bringing Apopis's forces around. Plus, Lucifer bless it, Dialphio deserved better.

"You of all people should know," she said, meeting my eyes and not looking away.

She was a hard succubus. Old Zeke might have crumbled under that glare. But she wasn't dealing with him. That guy had been left back in Olympia in Abandonment. That guy had been lost until Cancer helped him see. He'd been weak until Cassie showed him what true strength was. Had been a whiner until Leo taught him what it meant to love so deeply that you'd give anything for it. I was new-Zeke, and I wasn't going to break. For her. For any of the ex-Council members. For Lucifer Himself.

"What I know," I said, stressing the last word, "is that whatever agenda you have, it's not helpful."

She scoffed. "Agenda? What makes you think I have an agenda?"

"Because you're doing this," I said, flicking my hand in her general direction. "Winding everyone up. You talk about the angels as if you know them and what's going on. But you don't. I promise."

"You would say that, Zeke," Scorpio said, her ambiguous message full of implication.

"His name is Ezekial," Ralrek said stiffly. "What's your problem?"

"My problem is that we're putting our lives on the line for this cell while demons all around the Fifth are disappearing," she said, finally gliding off the table. "We're flying blind and having parties. This isn't impling play. This is the real deal." She stepped toward, but not into, the center of the half-circle. "You asked me to take charge of the security of the cell."

Dialphio nodded. "You're very qualified."

"Then let me do my blessed job."

"What would you have us do, Scorpio?"

"For one, stop all associations with angels. Every single one of us."

She didn't have to name me, Bilba, and Ralrek. Scorpio was so tough she didn't need to hide behind nuance and ambiguity. I wasn't the only one who understood the target of her comment. Plenty of heads turned in our direction.

"We have responsibilities that require us to work with angels," Bilba said, speaking far more calmly than I could have ever managed in the situation. "Without their help, we wouldn't be able to do what we're doing. Not only for the Fifth, but for the other Circles, for the exiles on the Isle of Dread, and for those Abandoned in the Overworld."

"I don't care about any of them," Scorpio said, her lips thinning as she nearly growled. "I care about the Fifth. My family is important to me."

"We don't have that luxury," I said, not bothering to hide my annoyance in the name of protecting her ignorance.

"Scorpio, I'd love to sit and discuss this with you at some point," Bilba said. "Then I might be able to help you see why we've got to work closely with them, for everyone's sake."

Her head dropped like someone had tugged it down with an invisible string. She shook it, speaking to her feet. "You don't get it. None of you do." She snapped her head up, addressing everyone. "Am I the only one who remembers the First?"

No one spoke. Demons watched her. They glanced at each other warily. I didn't see defiance. No anger or despondency. No indignation or irritation. The mention of Hell's worst recent tragedy sucked the air out of the room.

"I was there," she said, her voice cutting through the repentant aura of what was supposed to be a joyous celebration of the evolution of the single entity that would stand against Apopis. "I remember it well. Unlike these two," she said, aiming a finger at me and Ralrek, "my head wasn't on the block." Her finger moved to Bilba. "Unlike him, I saw with my own eyes what the angels did. Innocent succubi, incubi, imps, and implings. Angelfire tore them to shreds. Where they stood, they died."

A succubus bleated. Tears rimmed the eyes of more than a few who Scorpio had drawn in with her argument.

Her jaw twitched to the side, her bottom lip wrapped over her teeth as her eyes took on a distance that told me she wasn't here with us. In her mind, she was back in the First on the day of Gemini's planned execution that ended with three hundred dead demons. She was reliving the horror of that day. Her voice croaked when she spoke. "I was in the back. We got there late."

A single foot brushed over the dirty floor. The scraping sound, clear in the silence.

The rims of Scorpio's eyes burned red, but she held back her own tears. "My sister and niece went with me. A day trip. My sister... She always ran late. Never on time." Scorpio had stopped turning to include everyone, yet there wasn't a rebel in attendance not focusing on her story. They couldn't break away even if they wanted to. "My niece was mad at her."

Scorpio laughed, bitter and hard. "Feisty, that little succubus, let me tell you. My sister put her on her shoulders so Anatilia could see. Her weight bothered my sister after a bit, but they'd just brought the spy up on the platform, so Ioana sucked it up. She was doing it for her daughter. Beautiful, beautiful Anatilia." Scorpio drew up straighter, setting her jaw. "I hit the ground with the first blast. I tried to pull Ioana down, but she panicked. I... I tried to grab her, but when the second blast came, she ran. I... she... Anatilia was still on her shoulders when... The third..."

Dialphio had moved closer throughout Scorpio's recounting. She slowly lifted her hand and put it in the middle of Scorpio's shoulder blades. The younger, fierce succubus didn't swat it away, didn't crumble into a heap, didn't even acknowledge that she wasn't alone.

Instead, Scorpio hooked her tongue on her bottom lip, pulling it farther into her mouth, her eyes narrowing. She looked up at the enraptured throng. "I saw it all. The Angelfire shooting down into that packed square. The windows shattering, the stone and wood splintering. None of it compares to seeing demons being blasted apart. Demons... like my family." Though her eyes shimmered in a lake of pain, Scorpio didn't blink. The pools remained as she scanned the far wall as if she was searching for her loved ones there. "I've been living the horror of what those angels did every single day since. Unless one of you lost someone in that attack, don't talk to me about understanding the First. You can't possibly know what it's like to lose two treasures because our leaders turned a blind eye to the angelic threat." She slowly turned, now squaring on me, Bilba, and Ralrek. "I won't. I'll never give them that chance. I'll never forget what they did. And I will never forgive."

Turns out, Zenas knew what she was talking about. Scorpio was going to be trouble.

29

ACHERON OCEAN

No wind. A still day. The bright Hellfire highlighted every feature of the Underworld. I could see the black dot that would transform into a dangling prison cell the closer we drew. That meant anyone on shore looking our way probably could pick out the raft as we drifted across the Acheron. The conditions were not in our favor, but since when had they been? We were here to rescue Libra and, if we were successful, set the wheels in motion to regain Lucifer's lost power. Well, if we didn't die. Someone had to be watching Libra, and that meant we wouldn't pull alongside his cell, pop him out, and scurry back to the Isle without a skirmish. We were as ready as we'd ever be.

"Once we get closer, I'll propel us," Ralrek said, "but you guys know I'll have to pull that back to cast if we're attacked?"

"Of course," I said. "Azazel was clear that they're watching the cell. We can expect intervention."

"We just don't know what to expect," Bilba said. Sitting toward the bow. Tapping his chin, he never turned away from the spot in the distance that was Libra's cage. Beyond that, the shore, complete with a lookout manned by those aligned with the Founders.

He was up to something. I could tell by the way he tapped his chin. "What's on your mind?"

"Just thinking."

"Hmmm. Don't like the sound of that."

Bilba's voice was distant, a prisoner to his thoughts. "I don't like how light it is. We have to be ready for long-range attacks. At this point, I'm not sure anyone cares to spare Libra."

"Why do you say that?" Ralrek asked as we crept across the water, salty drops raining down in a constant spray every time the raft slapped the ocean's surface.

Bilba's shoulders bobbed. "Azazel said this arrangement, imprisoning Libra like this, was a favor for Michael. The entire Council voted on it. A statement about Libra defying them."

"They do that to everyone they don't like or want to suppress," the Fire caster said.

"Yes, but Libra's different."

"How so?"

Bilba pressed his hands to the raft and turned, looking displeased. "Ralrek, I know you're going through stuff and it's crap. I really feel bad for you. Zeke does too. But you've checked out." That wasn't a lie. "I don't want to sound insensitive, because I care and worry about you, and I want to help. We both do." That was true as well. "But until this is taken care of, we can't do much to help. We don't even have time to sit down and talk to you about what you want to do about your situation."

"Who says I want to do anything?"

"We do," I chimed in. "You've been a miserable bastard since Azazel told you about your true father."

"But," Bilba said, drawing out the word, "we love you and

we'll stand by you throughout this. For now, though, we need you present and focused. Had you been around, you would have heard Azazel tell me that Libra was marking ley lines between the maintained Gateways and Rifts. He started in the Fifth and grew out from there. I guess he was already marking in other Circles and that's what got him exiled to the Isle."

"Libra was? You sure?" Ralrek said, looking skeptical. "He's just a hippie-dippy who likes to get lost exploring the Underworld. I'm not sure he was into all that."

"Why would Azazel lie?"

Half of Ralrek's face scrunched. "Man, I don't know. Maybe Azazel got bad info. Who knows? The other Founders screwed with him all the time. Maybe he's wrong? I mean, Libra is smart. I'm just not sure he'd be down for marking ley lines for Gateways. Why?"

Bilba shrugged. "So demons could know where they are. So we could travel more easily around the Underworld, maybe even without the Council's knowledge?"

"Yeah, that would make anyone an enemy in their eyes," I said, amazed by this turn. "No wonder he got their attention. He's lucky they didn't fry his ass."

"Probably," Bilba said, "but maybe they had plans for him."

"Like what?"

His hands flailed out. "Heaven if I know." He pointed at the dot slowly taking the form of a cage suspended above the water. "But if they're willing to do that to him, they must have had plans. Now? I'm not so sure. Everything is up in the air. So much so that I'm not sure if they care anymore if he lives or dies."

"We have to get him out of there," I said, looking toward our goal.

"That might just be the antecedent of his demise," Bilba said, turning forward again.

I reached between my crossed legs to where I kept Creed. The halberd, in truncheon form, was propped against my ankles. I clutched it.

I hated being out here on the water. A vast, open nothingness that limited my ability to do much. Here, I'd be forced into a defensive mode. Without room to run around, leveraging my agility and speed, they could focus their attacks on the raft's finite space. Bilba and Ralrek were less agile, more vulnerable. The raft was twenty feet long and half as wide, but two hundred square feet did not a viable defensive posture make. We would be sitting geese, ripe for the picking for whoever cared about denying us access to Libra or killing us—or killing two harpies with one stone.

As we rocked across the Acheron, pushed now by a small stream of Ralrek's Fire, I thought about what was to come. For the first time in a while, I realized I was scared. This wasn't just about me. Bilba and Ralrek could die here today, too. None of us deserved that, and part of me even recognized the harm that would come to the Isle, to Hell, to relations between demons and angels in Olympia if we fell. I'm not saying we're all that, but if I was the Great Prince, a heavy weight sat upon my shoulders. A weight that would pull me to the bottom of the Acheron if I fell.

"Guys, if something happens," I said once my hazy thoughts coalesced into something tangible, "I want you to know that it was a heaven of a ride. There aren't another two demons I'd rather have taken it with."

"What do you expect?" Ralrek said, overly cocky.

Hiding his fears, too, I realized. Good. None of us needed an overconfident Ralrek.

Bilba reached over and patted my arm. "We've got this."

The last thing I wanted to highlight was just how few options we had. "Just be ready, bud."

I don't know how long we chugged across the surface of the Acheron. Being a blazeball player throughout school, I understood the benefits of hyper-focus. A lot like meditation, just in 'oh, I'm going to set my heart rate to racing' sort of way. That experience paid dividends now.

With each rise of the raft's bow over yet another crest of spraying ocean waves, I fell deeper into my focused zone. The presence of the wind, the salt in the air, the thunk-thunk-thunk from the underside of the raft as it fell atop the water, all fell away. So, too, did my best friend and Ralrek.

Creed was ever-present. Maybe for the first time since making his arrival, I missed the silence of Crazy Zeke.

This was something big. Something that could be the beginning of the turning of the tide. That moment had almost come in Olympia, outside the women's clinic, when I was a second away from giving Beelzebub a Hellfire colonoscopy. Just because I missed then didn't mean the moment would forever deny me.

This rescue attempt felt like that now. I doubted any of the Founders would show, but if they did, I'd be ready. I didn't know how or if the three of us could take one of them on, but as long as we stayed on the Acheron, they were vulnerable to never taking another self-centered breath again. Should that gift come my way, I'd snatch it. Bilba and Ralrek's safety came first. Libra too. But...

At some point, I heard Ralrek shout just as I toppled backward. I came out of my focused state, my hands swinging wildly for purchase. One found solid wood, the other splashed into the cool water before finding a rounded beam.

I clung to the raft as Ralrek shot us across the water.

The spot that had been a dot grew into a blob, then a ball. Into form, then distinction. The platform. The cage. An incubus within.

"Anyone see anything?" Bilba shouted over the roar of Ralrek's column of fire billowing out behind us, pushing the raft and its passengers across the ocean's surface.

"Nothing!" Ralrek stood, legs spread as wide as those long appendages could stretch, shouting in response.

I could. "There's nothing but him, the cage, and the platform!"

"Not good!" Bilba replied.

"A setup?"

"Probably."

It was.

At fifty yards out, Ralrek pulled back on the power he was pushing into his spell. The raft's bow slammed into the water at the loss of speed.

Bilba shot forward. I snagged him by the waist of his pants, my fingers scraping across more skin than I was comfortable touching. I yanked back and let go.

As soon as the raft moved under the speed of "oh my Lucifer, we're going to die!" I stood and jolted Creed.

The truncheon transformed into the three-bladed halberd, possessing the properties of the All, safeguarded by Aries, and held for me as determined by One—if you believe everything I've been told to this point. The blades clanged open. Music to my ears. Confidence. Power. Lust to hurt those who had hurt so many. All of it and more surged through me.

"No remorse. No repent," I whispered to Creed.

It thumped in my hands.

And I no longer doubted.

I wouldn't say I commanded the Hellfire. That'd be a lie. The sensation wasn't new. I'd felt it before. Rare, but not unknown. Growing strong all the time.

Creed swelled with the power of the Hellfire. Every sense I had responded. My vision became clearer. I now saw details about Libra, his cage, the platform that I didn't see before. The way the platform bobbed in the water, it was obviously anchored. Even from this distance, closing but still too far away for even a demon with good eyesight to pick out, I noticed the two slide locks, split by approximately three feet.

In the cage's corner, a growing patch of rust spread up and out.

Hellfire pulsed in Creed's haft.

I glanced at the halberd. Never had I felt it inside the petrified cherry wood that was older than the formation of Earth's continents. Now, I did. Like when you've sprinted two hundred yards farther than you should have—or taken that amusement park ride you just weren't-ready-for-kind of heart-thumping. That was the connection between my palm and Creed's haft.

This wasn't about fooling myself. This was me being pushed. Not a command. But connection.

Activated, I willed the shield into Creed. The azure of Hellfire bubbled around the raft, spreading out ten yards beyond the wood.

"That's a big one, Zeke," Bilba said, with a slight hint of awe in his voice.

"That's what she said," I said in full-stereo monotone.

Ralrek grunted, moving from the stern closer to us. "Focus. This isn't impling play."

At thirty yards, before we called out to Libra, who was still slumped against his cage bars, it all kicked off.

A horizontal line of sizzling white split the air above the platform underneath Libra's cage. The poor bastard in the ocean prison didn't even move. I hoped he was in a deep sleep or unconscious. That way he could wake to newfound freedom on the Isle—assuming we pulled this off.

The split widened until it stretched forty yards to either side, pulling up as if someone was peeling the backdrop away to reveal nothing but a black curtain. Then, at once, demons rushed from the blackness. Ten, twenty, thirty demons poured into the opening in the sky across the impossible magical platform that didn't need the support of Libra's tangible one.

"Will your shield hold?" Bilba asked, standing, his hands already moving.

"We're going to find out." Though I didn't give him a definitive answer, I knew in my heart that it would. As crazy as it sounds, Creed told me so. I just didn't want anyone getting overly confident. Not here. Not in this.

This was going to be a statement.

I held the shield as demons continued pouring from the gap in the sky. Sixty now. No sign of a Founder. Cowards.

"We can't shoot through your shield," Bilba said. He held his hands still, but looked over his shoulder at me.

"Give me a second."

"Can you open it for us?" Ralrek asked.

The raft bobbed up and down in the waves now that he'd cut off his spell. His hands were ready to cast as soon as I dropped my shield.

If I did, this became a sixty-on-three battle. Twenty demons for each one of us. We wouldn't win that fight.

Command it, Lucifer had said.

I forced everything out of my head. The anxiety I felt about being isolated on a raft in the middle of the ocean. The worry prodded me to believe Libra would never make it out of this alive. The gut-wrenching fear that Bilba and Ralrek would pay for being aligned with me. The ache raked at my heart that, should I fall, I'd never see Cassie again.

All of it. Away.

In the space provided in that freedom, I found my answer.

The shield was a bubble around the raft. From early on, almost from the minute I could use Creed as a weapon, I'd been creating shields. Early on, I didn't know what I was doing. I just did what came naturally. But that wasn't the case anymore. I'd tapped into the Hellfire. I'd tasted it. I knew it. Me. Creed. Hellfire. Connected.

"Now," I groaned to the pair as I pushed my will into the shield, opening separate holes in front of them.

"The shield," Bilba protested.

"Open. For. You. Just. Shoot. Straight." The toll was

immense. The strain, much like the times I'd bench pressed a little too much weight, usually to impress a succubus. There's something visceral that triggers when you have a lot of weight above you, a spotter to help lift it, yet still you fight against the mental monster that the weight might crush you in the end. Survival instinct, maybe. Whatever it was, in those times, it fed my muscles, pushing them beyond something they were previously capable of. That's what this felt like. As I pushed against the Hellfire, poking two separate holes in it and then widening them, it seemed to resist.

Without this, we wouldn't win. We wouldn't rescue Libra, and we wouldn't survive.

I ground my teeth together and pushed against the resistance, past the blockage, tipping the fulcrum.

The resistance snapped, and the Hellfire responded to my will.

"Go. Now!"

"Awesome!" Bilba's shout contained a healthy dose of joviality.

"Burn, motherfuckers. Burn!" Ralrek growled.

My skin itched as his stream of fire swept across the farthest edge of the platform, erasing it right under the feet of the incubi and succubi sprinting down its length.

Bilba's Deception spell covered my skin. He took longer to conjure, but it was worth it when he finished.

Large blocks of ice formed over the enemy platform, suspended high over their heads. From this distance, I could only estimate their size, but they had to be at least four feet wide and just as high. If they were solid, they were going to do major damage.

From what I could see, the demons along the platform didn't notice their presence. Spaced out every six feet, Bilba created ten before he put them into action.

The blocks dropped in unison. A couple fell directly on the demons. Others clipped arms or legs. One guy took it directly to the noggin. Even the blocks that missed individual demons still wiped out the platform, sending nearby demons into the Acheron.

With their first attacks, my friends had taken thirteen enemy troops out of the fight.

Someone on the other side had Construction magic and began forming a wall in front of their platform to protect the forty-something remaining fighters. Ralrek assaulted it, but the wood took longer to burn than it took to build.

"We need to close that Rift." Bilba was working on his next spell. "That's the only place they can get the raw materials to build defenses."

"Any ideas? How we can. Do. That?" I said, wishing I didn't have to ask the question. Holding the shield around the raft was one thing, but holding it while it was being assaulted by Deception, Fire, Water, and almost every other type of demonic magic was quite another. Who knew if there was an Underworld record for the greatest number of deflected and denied spells, but if there was one, I was close to breaking it.

Fireballs and beams smashed against the shield. One caster held his beam in the same spot for what felt like hours, though could have only been minutes. The shield around the target held the same nearly transparent azure as the rest of the bubble, meaning his concentrated attack was a waste of energy. Maybe it was a distraction from their real probe into the shield's vulnerability. Who knew? The ice shards that bombarded the left side weren't as focused as that fire beam. The ocean bubbled on the right side. A Water user or two tested the shield's bottom.

All the while, the raft drifted closer to Libra's cage. Almost close enough to wrap the shield around him and his prison. Once I could reach out with it and snare him, Ralrek would get on the platform and bust Libra to freedom while I held off whoever remained. The problem? Who knew how long I could hold the shield, if the enemy didn't have a secret weapon in waiting, or if one of the Founders—or all four who opposed us—would make a guest appearance. Quick and dirty. That's what this operation needed.

The raft rotated in the ocean's current.

"Zeke, my hole is aimed in the wrong direction," Bilba said. His forehead was beaded with sweat. "Can you make another over here, or move it?"

"I don't know."

Ralrek shifted to the back of the raft again, casting a small column of fire into the water. It steamed.

"Be quick," I warned. "Don't need this bubble filling with that and blinding us."

"Just hold on." Ralrek pushed the beam into the water, thickening its width. The Acheron hissed and steamed, boiling around the spot, now three feet wide, where the spell sank into its depths. The raft cranked around, and he cut the beam off.

My arms shuddered, and Creed vibrated as fire and ice spells struck the magical barrier, probing, testing. Casters, recruited by the most powerful demons in Hell, concentrated their spells. The beam of Fire still pushed against the shield. The Fire users had to be one determined son of a billy goat. By keeping his spell focused on that one spot, I couldn't just ignore him, no matter how innocuous his constant attack was. But these weren't school bullies or street thugs. The casters moving against us were agents of the Council. They wouldn't be here if the likes of Seraph and Beelzebub didn't think them capable of killing us. The beam was a distraction. Something to keep me occupied. A test for something later.

The water around us rolled. The waves came quicker now, lifting and dropping the raft in their wake.

"They're pushing us away." Ralrek snarled. "I'm going to have to use the spell to push us closer."

I lessened the power into the barrier, opening a hole in the dome's crest wide enough for someone to stick their noggin' through, but that was all. The hole would allow Ralrek to combat the Water spell and bring us closer to Libra without introducing substantial risk.

Steam began to fill the bubble again as he cast.

"Can you make it bigger?" Bilba asked. "I can't see much, but I'm sure they have no problem picking us out. We're one big floating ball of mist in the middle of the ocean on a clear day. This isn't working."

"What do you want me to do?" I asked. When you hold a shield of this strength against a constant barrage of strong casters, there wasn't a lot of energy left over for mental flexing. Any answers to our dilemma would have to come from the smartest of the three.

Hey, I wasn't against knowing my place in this calculation.

Bilba turned to Ralrek. "Can you get us to him?"

"I'm putting a lot into this just to move us inches. Unless Zeke opens the shield, I'm limited."

Bilba turned again, looking for the enemy forces to Libra's cage. "I think they're using multiple Water casters. They have to be, to counter you so effectively."

"We have to get to Libra soon," Bilba said, his face drawn. "Ralrek can't keep this up, and for all we know, they might be holding back their strength."

"Meaning?"

He pointed to the black rip in the sky, where the blue looked like it had been opened with a box cutter and peeled back. "They could have an entire squad of reinforcements in that Gateway. What we're facing might just be the preliminary force. We have no way of telling, especially now that Azazel is out of the picture. We have to move for him now."

"Get me close and I'll wrap the shield around him," I said. "Then we can get him and get the heaven out of here."

"We have to be ready for anything," Bilba said, sitting down on the raft and reaching for something to hold on to. "They're going to respond."

"Any idea how?" I asked.

"I'm ready if you guys are," Ralrek said, spreading his legs to brace himself.

"I don't know, Zeke," Bilba said, sounding frustrated. "Can you pick up on anything?"

"From my senses?"

He nodded.

"No, not with everything going on. I feel everything at once. Not every type of magic, but enough. Mostly Fire and Water. Some Construction and Deception."

"Okay, I say we do it. Ralrek, you tell us when, then blast us to him. Zeke, you wrap him in the bubble, and then we break into the cage and get him out of here and back to the island."

"He's going to be weak. We'll have to do all the work," Ralrek said.

I spread my feet. "Ready."

"Okay, hang on."

Ralrek cast. I stumbled backward, and Bilba toppled onto his back. The bow lifted out of the water and we skipped across the surface, aimed just to the seaside of the thick pillar sticking out of the ocean that supported Libra's cage.

We closed fast. My pulse skipped along with the raft. Waves smashed on its underside so hard I feared the beams would splinter.

Bilba yelped when the raft gained air and crashed against the water. I would have too, but I was too busy holding my breath, waiting to be jettisoned into the Acheron.

When Bilba had said he expected the Founders' troops to respond, he wasn't wrong. They did. In a big way.

Distance was impossible to gauge on the open water—at least for me. The only reason I knew the coast was a mile away was because that's what we were told. I didn't know if from fact or fiction. What rolled across the ocean was much, much closer.

Not a beast. Not the kraken. The ocean itself rose. At first, nothing more than a small, unnoticeable ripple in the distance that lifted from the relatively calm surface. The wave grew to two feet high. The height doubled by the time I knew something was wrong, before Bilba noticed, before we even started discussing alternatives, of which we had none.

"It's going to hit us," Ralrek growled from his position.

What would happen to the shield when it did? "Get us to Libra."

"Go! Go!" The loose skin on Bilba's chin wobbled. From the bouncing of the raft or the fear of anticipation of this aquatic disaster, I couldn't tell.

"He's going to get hit!" Ralrek thrust the raft forward.

'Him' was Libra. He was between us and the growing wave that was over ten feet tall now.

I pushed more of my will into the shield, hoping doing so would push it outward. Though I was tiring from holding it for so long, against so many attacks, I extended its reach. Not fast enough. "It won't reach him in time."

Twenty feet high, the tsunami swelled and rolled over Libra's cage. Before it hit, I wasn't even sure if he'd seen it coming.

I winced as I watched the collision and then the cage and him disappear behind the wall of water that still rolled in our direction.

"Get ready!" I pushed everything I had left in me into the shield as the wave swelled above us. Creed's brightness blurred the world, which was probably for the best. The roar of the water coming down, the screams of my two friends, my cry firing focus into the halberd's force; all of it made me forget the forty-something demons taking pot-shots at my shield. Every ounce of me went into holding what I had for the next few seconds. The Fire spells, the Water magic of those casters not involved in building this tsunami, the Deception magic; protecting us from any of those wasn't a priority any longer. It wouldn't matter if a thousand allies of the Founders poured through the gap if I couldn't hold the shield until this wave passed.

Funny thing about being a young incubus you might not understand if you're not one; we tend to feel invincible. Okay, most of the time. Demons give guys my age a lot of crap about how much we think we can handle. It was at a time like this, staring up at a wall of ocean about to tumble down, that I realized those demons might be right. An older incubus or any succubus would have been smart enough to have seen this trap coming before plunking themselves down in the face of it and daring it to take the first swing.

We came to rescue Libra with three. We held our own against sixty. Right there, a smart demon would have turned and scampered away to count their lucky stars and fight another day. But no, not us. Even when we introduced eighteen of the Council's forces to the bottom of the Acheron, we kept pushing. Duty. Honor. Righteousness. Stubborn pride. Whatever pushed us to face odds that were easily recognizable as superior, guys like me pressed on.

Looking up at the incomprehensible weight of water that was about to hit us, I realized how stubbornly reckless this was.

Where was everyone else? Where were the armies to defend Libra? Where was Azazel? Everyone had a reason for not being here, sharing this raft and the end of their immortal lives. Not us, though. Here we were, floating across the deep blue, exposed to the elements and forces of the unscrupulous Founders and a couple of slabs of wood held together by tar and twine, thinking we could do it all. We could save Libra without being hurt or killed. We could convince him to help the greater cause. With Libra's help, we could find the Horn before Seraph set the universe into a tailspin.

Wisdom is wasted on the young.

In the white swirls of air caught in the water, the cresting and tumbling of the wave that was thicker than I was tall, I wanted to say so many things to the two idiots who shared the raft with me. But we didn't have time and I couldn't think of anything to shout that wouldn't come out sounding like a squeak.

In seconds that could have spanned mortal lifetimes, I couldn't think straight enough to even say goodbye to the two poor bastards who'd been through so much while always staying by my side. I wanted to, but when you face death, your brain does this little trick of narrowing your focus to a pinpoint. I guess it has its own way of going down into survival mode.

Just before the tsunami hit, I felt completely alone.

As the last few feet separating my shield from the tsunami evaporated, I screamed and held Creed above my head. I didn't think about it. I just did it. And the weirdest thing happened.

The shield thickened, dulling everything outside.

The massive wave hit. Land. Sky. Enemy forces. Everything disappeared as we were shoved under the water. Bubbles and swirling water, forced down by the crashing wave, caressed the shield. Daylight disappeared. Deeper and deeper into the Acheron's embrace.

Utter silence became our world.

We looked at each other in disbelief. A brief sanity check. Then, when we realized the tsunami attack hadn't killed us, we did what could expect of all demons filled with testosterone and surging adrenaline.

"Fuck yeah!" Ralrek gave me the hardest high-five I've ever felt—and I've been to war with the American Army.

Bilba leaped into my open arms, hugging me. "Lucifer bless it, Zeke. That was amazing!"

When he stepped back, I raised my middle finger in the direction of the ocean's surface, and toward the general direction of the Founders' troops. "Suck my ankles, asswads."

Bilba and Ralrek's faces fell.

"Suck my ankles, asswads?" Ralrek asked before his mouth curled up and he broke out into laughter.

"Okay, okay. That's something I have to work on. I admit it. But I'm kind of distracted and… Shit, that was awesome."

Bilba looked up—well, at least I think it was up. Hard to tell up from down with as dark as it was. He squinted. "I think we're getting closer." His arm thrust out. "Look! You can see the tsunami moving out."

"Keep watching it," I said.

"Why?"

"Because, if that thing doesn't come back, it means whoever cast it doesn't think we survived."

"You think they're going to be lax?" Ralrek asked, tipping his head in short, rapid nods. "They won't expect us to pop back up."

"Exactly." I lifted Creed, aiming the double axes at the roof of the shield that acted as an impenetrable bubble. "And I'm a little pissed off. If they're still up there, they're going to be very sorry."

Ralrek rubbed his hands.

"What do you need from us?" Bilba asked.

"Just watch my back and make sure Libra is okay." I swallowed. "Make sure that tsunami didn't take him out. Besides that, be ready."

"For?" Bilba asked.

I scrunched my face and shrugged. "For if my plan works."

That took a little of the fun out of the air. I doubted any of us wanted to recognize it was a possibility. We'd have to deal with it if the time came.

The ocean above us cleared as I told them what I thought. The deep azure of the sky was pushing back the deep ocean dark. Two hundred yards out, I saw a school of fish. Maybe three hundred of them. A cloud of unseen life.

Countless fish schooling to survive. Doing what was necessary.

Creed pulsed. *Thwomp. Thwomp. Thwomp.*

The first cracks of waves on the surface came into detail.

"Be ready," I said, exhaling deeply.

The bubbled shield drifted closer to the ocean's surface. Even if we wanted to, we couldn't stop its rise. Our only choice was to wait and prepare for what happened once we broke the surface. Our only advantage was ambiguous, at best. If the Founders' forces thought the tsunami had killed us, then we'd have a chance. But if they suspected we might still be alive, the chance we were about to take could blow up in our faces.

I was near exhaustion and we were running out of time, though. The chance was necessary. I'd been holding the shield since our approach. Time and the magical attacks I'd held off up to this point had taken their toll. I smelled of funk from my exertions. My arms and shoulders burned with an ache. Fatigue tremors were on the horizon. No, once we broke the surface, we'd have to go on the offensive because the enemy far outnumbered us and my tank held only fumes. We'd never get away if we didn't go at them.

Now or never, and all that.

Ralrek drew on his Ability. The scratching sensation made its presence known as soon as he tapped into his magic. Bilba was a little slower on the draw, but his Deception magic's stickiness coated Ralrek's effect. Lucifer, I loved being the only demon in Hell who could feel someone pulling on their magic. Such a wonderful skill to have.

That's sarcasm, by the way.

We were ready. The ocean's surface was close. Just up and to the right, a dark rectangular shape gave away the location of Libra's platform. To the left of it, a longer rectangle blurred as it stretched away. That was where we'd find whatever

Founders' hench-demons still hung around to make sure we were dead-dead.

"I'm nervous, guys," Bilba said, sounding every bit.

"We've got to do this," I said. "I can't hold on for much longer."

"I understand. I'm sorry we can't do more to help."

I looked at him. What I really wanted to do was reach out and squeeze his shoulder, but he was on the other side of the raft and I was too tired to take the chance of shifting my balance as we closed on destiny.

The interior of the shield stilled as the daylight pierced the ocean in hazy beams all around us, twinkling off the ripples.

My breathing came rapidly and with force. The crust of the Acheron rolled away from the shield's curved top. Salt-water clung to the shield in bubbles before rolling off the sides to rejoin its greater body.

"Moving too slow," Ralrek said with a fierceness that could have been driven by nerves.

We weren't floating in the water like a fishing bobber, but we weren't exactly shooting up out of it, either.

"Come on, come on, come on." My urging was aimed at the shield.

Creed *thromped* rapidly, harder now. Either it was raging or my palm was bruising, because now each pulse jolted deeper in my hand.

The water line was at eye level, revealing the secrets of the situation.

Libra's cage was still in its place. Water rained down onto the platform from its bars. The dark rags covering his thin frame hung down, dripping streams of ocean water. His brown, unkempt hair was matted to his skull. A single arm had flopped outside the cage bars.

I didn't have time to worry if he was alive or dead. The Founders' troops still littered the platform. They stood in small clumps, chatting. Others were carefully sliding across the platform toward either Libra's cage or the Rift. What they weren't doing was looking our way.

I looked at my two friends as we continued to rise out of the water. "Ready?"

"More than I'll ever be," Bilba said, moving his hands in swift, circular motions. The air grew sticky as he pushed more into his next spell. Once again, he proved how amazing of a caster he was when twenty small black balls suddenly popped into the air, hovering close to him.

I didn't have time to ask what they were. We'd been lifted high enough out of the Acheron to engage before they noticed us. "Now!"

I let go of Creed's shield, exposing us to anything and everything the forty-some-odd casters could throw together once they realized the tsunami hadn't done its job.

Talk about gratification when they had a split second between recognizing our reemergence and what was to come. In that breath, their laughter ceased, their cocky smiles slipped, and I loosed Creed's power.

All the force he'd been building up while we were underwater was unleashed when I lowered the double-ax heads at the Rift.

The beam I shot from my halberd was the thickest, brightest azure I'd ever seen. When it left the blazing blades, it was three times as wide as them. That six feet of awesomeness expanded as it split the day. Cutting above the ocean, the water underneath the beam sizzled. Hazy tendrils of rapidly evaporating water trailed behind the beam. By the time it struck the Rift, the beam was thirty feet wide. The Rift itself wasn't even that big. I could have toppled Seattle's blessed Space Needle with what I'd created.

The azure flashed white when it hit their escape. A roar sounded from within the Rift, like a giant zipper being yanked closed from the end of a long jacket, right toward my ears. The white flashed brilliantly and a horizontal ring about four feet thick rocketed in all directions.

The concussive wave flung demons, water, and rafts alike. Even as I enjoyed the sight of forty-plus demons being tossed through the air, I feared for Libra as his cage rocketed up in a swing. The significant weight of demon-plus-steel didn't seem to stand a chance against the ring of white ripping demons' open and exploding across the ocean.

When the ring struck us, my need to draw breath distracted me from noticing how far from the raft I'd been thrown. I hit the water somewhere past Bilba, who had the advantage of already standing at the edge of the raft and probably fell into the water before the concussive output of the ring struck. I wasn't so lucky. Once I resurfaced after the blast passed, I started on my long swim.

Bilba hung from the raft, its beams locked under his armpits. He wiped his face with his palm without unhooking himself. "You okay?"

I pulled myself up on the raft, sitting on my butt and swinging my legs up. "Yep. You?"

"Yeah." He took my hand and we sort of pull-rolled him to safety with late-arriving help from Ralrek.

"How about you?" I asked once we'd dragged Bilba on board. I offered the tall incubus a hand, and he took it.

Once on the raft, he pushed back his black hair with a hand, smoothing it. I swear, he could have been a model in a succubus magazine. Ridiculous. An intense fight against a small army of the Council's best, catapulted into the Acheron, and he still came out looking this good? What. A. Jerk. "Good here. Better than them."

I turned to where he pointed. "What?"

Bilba got up and stepped toward the far side of the raft. "Where are they? Where is the Rift?"

"I don't know," I answered honestly.

"What did you do? What was that spell?"

I spread my hands. "Don't know that either."

"Whatever it was, he wiped their asses and their Rift out." Ralrek chuckled.

The disturbing bit about it all? I might have just killed forty-odd demons with a single spell. All allies of the Founders. And I didn't even feel bad.

30

ACHERON OCEAN

"ALL I WAS TRYING TO DO WAS SCREW WITH THEIR RIFT. I DIDN'T expect that." Creed's haft was cool in my hand. No more life within, reflecting the lack of it all around Libra's prison. The enemy Rift, the demons trying to stop us from freeing Libra, and the platform upon which they launched their attacks. Each part, vaporized in Creed's wrath. What was left behind was three stunned incubi and a single platform, floating next to a thick pillar holding a suspended cage.

"Come on," Bilba said, pointing to the cage. "Let's see if he's okay."

Ralrek pushed us to the platform. I don't want to make it sound like we were reckless. We weren't. We were tired and wary. Another Rift could open at any second. On guard, I wasn't about to finish this rescue operation under an umbrella of naivete. I mean, unless someone on-shore was watching the fight, there was no way the Founders would know what happened.

We were almost away free.

The lack of movement coming from the cage was disturbing.

Behind me, Ralrek grumbled something I was sure I

didn't want to hear. He was friends with Libra, though they hadn't seen each other in a while. But this might have more to do with the general lack of answers Ralrek was getting from every aspect of his life. If Libra was dead, Ralrek might never get the chance to seek his own answers.

His Fire spell carried us forward, with no outward sign of trouble. Of course, if someone was watching from the shore, it would take a moment for the Founders to open a second Rift and send through another cast of characters looking to make a name for themselves.

Time and security were luxuries.

Ralrek cut off the spell just as he turned the Raft to dock. Bilba grabbed the platform and wormed his way onto the soaked surface. When he stood, he waved his arms wildly and shuffled his feet to keep his balance. "Whoa. Far less stable than it appears."

Impressive that he didn't dump his ass in the ocean after half a minute of finding center gravity.

Bilba reached up and grabbed the bottom of the cage when a stiff wind whipped across the water. "Whoa!" he cried out for a second time when his hand slipped and he flopped onto the platform, hit it with an *oomph*, and then rolled off into the water.

I leaped onto the platform, not losing my balance—thank you very much—and waited for my best friend to resurface. When he did, I grabbed his hand and pulled him up.

"When you're... done," a dry voice rasped, "would you... mind... getting me some... water?"

"Libra!" Ralrek nearly jumped off the raft to join us until he realized, as he lifted his foot to stretch for the platform, that he was the one mooring the raft. He stayed put and grinned.

I waved to him. "Switch with me."

Ralrek accepted, showing a smile and swiftness of such

alacrity that I almost did a double-take. He gripped the cage bars. "Damn, you're scrawny."

Libra's head cranked up away from the bar it'd been resting against. I saw his face for the first time. I swear, his goofy, weak smile took up a third of the space. Large, crooked teeth filled his mouth. With his rags for clothes, unkempt appearance, and frighteningly thin frame, Libra looked like an incubus in need of help and happy to take it from anyone who offered. "You're... uglier than I remember."

Ralrek reached his hand through the bars and the two clutched each other. He offered the prisoner a tender smile. "We're getting you out of here. Move back."

Libra had little space, but he shifted as far as he could, causing the front of the cage to tip up as he sat near the back.

"This is going to be tricky," Ralrek said. "Zeke, do you think Creed could help?"

I didn't need to ask the halberd for its opinion. Somehow, after the fight where it, yet again, showed me a new sign of its potential, I knew Creed was due for a coffee break. "I'm done. Finito."

Bilba raised a finger. "I've got an idea."

Ralrek tapped the bar. "Hang on, Libra. We'll get you out." He moved out of Bilba's way as the kick-ass Rebel Mage stepped forward.

What felt like a light layer of glue coated my arms before Bilba's spell manifested into a glowing gold key. The key hung in the air in front of the door. It looked brass, though molten. Small gold driblets plopped onto the platform.

The key floated forward into the keyhole. The post and bit pushed into the slot. What didn't fit simply melted around the hole like hot butter in a pan as Bilba pushed the key deeper. Halfway up its shaft, the key stopped.

Bilba concentrated. A small line of sweat beads formed on his upper lip. "This is the tricky part. Tiny margins for error before it cools."

"If it does, I could reheat it," Ralrek said.

I scanned the area around us, my gaze constantly flicking back to the shore. While Bilba worked his magical key into the lock, I used the little energy I had left to push my Sensing out. I didn't know if this would work or not, but it was worth a try. Sensing the shore would help anticipate another Rift or unwelcome kraken visitor.

My sheer wave rippled out toward land, covering a mile in seconds. I felt its empty echo before the cage lock clicked open.

No perceivable threat and a prisoner about to step out of the cage for the first time since Michael's cruel effort to break Libra.

"Bilba, switch. Let me help," I said when I saw Ralrek carefully pulling Libra, who was too weak to move on his own, toward the cage door.

We swapped spots, but I only moved away from the raft once Bilba was on his knees and gripping the prison platform with both hands. Still, he almost let the raft slide away from the only solid footing we had out here.

"Hold on," I said, turning my attention to getting Libra out of the cage.

Legs-first, we inched him out. As soon as his backside cleared the bars, he fell to the platform like a soaked stuffed animal, even though the two of us tried to hold him up.

"Hang on, big guy," Ralrek said as we draped Libra's long, thin arms around our shoulders. "We're going to scoot to the raft."

"Don't know... if I can..." Libra tried to move, but his bare, filthy feet flopped forward and only ended up getting caught underneath him.

Ralrek seemed to understand the struggle at the same time. We shifted to hook our hands under Libra's knees so we could support his upper and lower body.

Libra was a mess. Another example of the danger of giving too much power to the unscrupulous.

The raft rocked as we awkwardly loaded him. Bilba clung to the prison platform, at one point lying out completely to spread his mass. Team player, that guy.

Loaded, we pushed away. I stayed on guard for any last threats from the Council or mysterious undersea guardian. I don't think anyone's posture relaxed until the cage was nothing more than a blur in the distance.

We managed Libra's water intake carefully. He wanted to chug. I understood. We all did. But we didn't need him blowing chunks or introducing us to a medical emergency. We were still on our way back to the channel between the Isle and Hell. Ralrek couldn't push us too fast because he was as tired as the rest of us, and Libra didn't have the strength to hold on even if he wasn't. Without pursuers, there was no reason to push our luck and undo everything we'd finally accomplished.

"I owe you guys," Libra said when we were back in the channel and headed to the Isle, hovering in the distance.

"No, you don't," Bilba sat, turned away from our destination to face Libra, who we'd propped in the middle of the raft against the mast.

"If it wasn't for you…" When his voice drifted

"We're in this together," Ralrek said. He seemed to consider something else, then said, "Bless it, I missed you."

"You too, my friend." Libra swallowed. His scrawny throat bobbed. "Sorry. Still feeling lousy."

"Totally understand," I said. "We'll get you back to the Isle, then get food in your gut."

"A cot too," Bilba offered cheerily.

Libra closed his eyes, his wide mouth stretching in a smile. "That sounds wonderful. But seriously, we have a long trip still ahead, if I remember correctly and if that mesa is the

Isle." He pointed at the humongous flat mountain rising above the Acheron's water.

"It is," Bilba said.

"Then tell me how you got suckered into saving me?" He aimed his question at Ralrek. "The last time I saw you, you were flirting your way around the Fifth."

"He still is," I said before Ralrek could defend himself.

"Yeah, well, a lot has changed since the last time we had beers," Ralrek said, tipping his square jaw at Libra. "You good enough to hold on so I can get home faster?"

Libra patted the raft. "The sooner I'm on solid ground... even if it's just sand, the happier I'll be. I'll never take it for granted again."

Ralrek pinched his lips. "Okay. Hold on to the mast. We're going home."

This Fire spell was much weaker than his previous. Still, he pushed us along the channel at a better pace than the ocean breeze or the magical current between the mainland and the Isle. Bilba and I enjoyed the trip, catching up on our rest while trying to stay awake. Ralrek briefed his friend on the last few years of his life. I noted my friend left out the part about being a Wayward Son. I swore to myself, once I could think again, I'd sit down with him and make him ask for help.

"Damn, so the Council really did not like me?" Libra said, giving us a crooked-toothed smile.

"Join the club," Ralrek said.

The raft skipped across the water with a little more oomph than he realized he was putting into his stream of fire.

"Is it true?" Bilba asked. "Did you really map out ley lines between the permanent Rifts and Gateways?" I gave him the 'are you kidding? You're bringing up work now?' look, but he just shrugged. "What? We've still got a way to go, and it's interesting. Significant too. If he... Well, we'll worry about that another time. But, did you?"

Libra had been trying to sip more water. At Bilba's question, he coughed, spitting out a mouthful. Droplets clung to his long mustache. "Yes. I did. Not all, though."

"How many?"

"Can't remember now. Not for sure," he said. "They took all my notes. Before I got exiled, I had probably fifteen or so between Rifts and Gateways. Nothing impressive."

"Nothing impressive?" Bilba asked after he re-hitched his jaw. "That's amazing. That could make all the difference in the world." He leaned to swat at me and missed. "Imagine how this would help with all those things we talked about. And if there was one on the Isle—"

"There is," Libra said. "I just couldn't get to it before they dragged me off the Isle. It's on the summit of the mesa."

Bilba's jaw hung open for the second time.

"Do these ley lines," I said, flipping my hand in the air as I tried to come up with an accurate word, "things extend to the Overworld?"

"He has them to Rifts," Bilba said. "So they'd have to connect with the Overworld. Right?"

Well, color me stupid for not understanding advanced quantum physics or whatever this was.

"Yes, they do."

"See, Zeke?" The way Bilba said my name meant he was trying to tell me something. I didn't make the connection, so he helped, giving me the sledgehammer of a clue in the same suggestive tone. "Cancer?"

Oh, my Lucifer! I almost reached out and snagged Libra by his rotting wool collar. "You have one of these lines to Baghdad?"

Libra eyed me warily. I just helped him escape the Founders' clutches, but we still didn't know each other and I might have been guilty of coming on too strong.

"He's cool," Ralrek said with a small snort. "The Great Prince, if you listen to everyone back in the Circles."

Libra's mouth twitched. "Cool. Cool. But yeah, there's one

in Baghdad."

"Shut your fae mouth!" I smacked my hands. Of course, that did nothing to put this stranger at ease. "Sorry. I've got a dear friend who I need to check in on and she's there."

"It's a big city."

"I'm stubborn."

"Let him recover first," Ralrek cautioned.

The Isle grew more prominent, but we still had a long stretch of ocean to go. Once we got there, Libra would need to eat and rest. He'd be surrounded by those he knew, and those curious about the incubus who'd only been a story to them until we delivered him home. Once Libra was stronger, Azazel would want time with him, no doubt. There would be security needs, too. Surely, the Founders wouldn't stop. Not now. Not after we broke him out from the Acheron prison. Not now that we knew what they knew about his skill at mapping the Underworld.

Peace and quiet wouldn't be quick in coming. Though we were tired and he was experiencing freedom for the first time in a long time, we had to take advantage of the privacy we had. Hell wasn't the same, and it wouldn't wait. We couldn't either.

I ignored Ralrek and explained the desires Bilba and I shared about freedom of travel for all demons. I caught him up on the dissolution of the Council and the threats we faced from its individual members.

Instead of looking exhausted, the conversation seemed to not only intrigue Libra, but re-energize him. His spine straightened. He adjusted and the rags nearly fell off one shoulder.

When Bilba jumped into the topics of the missing Horn, the indecipherable coordinates Azazel had given us, and what it could mean to everything we knew, Libra looked like he was ready to swim to the Isle if we didn't get him there soon.

He didn't, but he seemed confident that he could find it once we validated the coordinates with Azazel and everyone recovered. "I'll even be your volunteer to test this undetectable Abilities thing if you need one."

"Don't worry," Ralrek said, pushing us along faster now that he looked convinced of Libra's vitality, "wherever it takes you, I'll go too."

"Cool. Cool."

As Libra stared up at the hole in the wall of mist in amazement, Bilba rocked on his butt. "Imagine when demons can travel between Circles. We could map everything, guys. And once I practice Sethel's trick for wards, and study the impact of the Isle on my Ability, we're going to create headaches for the Founders. This is going to be epic."

Libra thrust his head forward, his thin neck giving even more prominence to his Adam's apple. "What?"

"Yep." Bilba explained the new structure in Hell as we drifted through the mist, bringing the full picture of the Isle into view. The dock bell clanged to announce our arrival.

When he finished, Libra whistled. I wasn't sure if it was on purpose or a result of his poorly aligned teeth. "What a mess. Good thing you guys didn't die saving me."

We got in a good chuckle before pulling up to the dock, even though, seriously, it wasn't a laughing matter.

Already, swarms of exiles moved toward the dock from the forest.

Libra's gigantic eyes grew larger.

"Not expecting this?" I asked.

He scratched at his throat, a third of it covered in scraggly hair. "Everyone. All four tribes. Together? Cool. Cool. Something I never thought I'd see. You guys really are breaking up the establishment."

I leaned out to grab the dock and pull the raft closer. "You have no idea."

31

UNDERWORLD, ISLE OF DREAD

THERE'S NO REST FOR THE WICKED. APPARENTLY, THERE'S NO REST for demons named the Great Prince, either.

We'd just made it onto dry land, which Libra truly took glory in, and shared a joyous but brief celebration with a beach full of exiles when we needed to get him to a cot. All four of us, actually, needed a cot. Rest and food, and maybe in that order. Had we let the exiles have their way, Libra would have re-lived the festival Bilba created, and none of us had the energy for that.

Marijon graciously hosted Libra, giving up her shelter for him, just as she had for Azazel. He refused. She pushed. We helped him understand the futility of fighting the succubus. She was fresher, determined, and stubborn as a bat in a belfry. He gave in and was snoring before I'd shoveled my first fork full of roasted cabbage into my pie hole.

"Embrace," Crazy Zeke whispered in my ear, nearly causing me to drop my plate.

I tried to blow it off, to deal with the secretive meaning when my stomach was full and my bladder empty.

I was still eating dinner when the air buzzed.

"Shit." I groaned as my head, now feeling like it had three bowling balls attached to it, lolled forward.

Baphomet hung at the edge of our camp, wagging a hooked finger at me.

I sighed, standing. "I'll be back. Soon, I hope."

Ralrek grunted.

Bilba walked me to the Rift. "Be careful. Remember, we don't know His end game."

I patted his shoulder. "I will be."

When I started away, he snagged my arm, forcing me to look at him. "Promise?"

"I promise, bud." I tipped my head at the campfire. "Now, go get some food and rest."

"Okay," he said, but lingered until I stepped through the magical divide.

Let's say I wasn't exactly shocked when I stepped onto the cold stone landing outside Lucifer's chambers. The Big Man had need of me so soon? Or was I here to answer for possibly killing, almost single-handedly, sixty demons? The next few minutes would tell.

Baphomet gave me no encouragement, remaining quiet before and after the Rift trip.

"Nothing for me this time?" I prodded.

"He has His own ways," the aged incubus said, obviously holding something back. "They're mysterious to me, so I don't ask."

I sighed. "Fine. Guess I better get this over with then."

"Good luck," Baphomet said as I knocked. When Lucifer called for me to enter and I started inside, I swear I caught a glimmer of contentment on Baphomet's face.

Lucifer was at His small work table. The same candles and sconces burned bright with Hellfire. The same books and mountain of paper crowded the same space they had the last time He called on me. The air was just as stale.

Lucifer looked up when I closed the door. His long hair

hung in His face. He pulled it back with a hand, keeping His head cocked to the side so the hair didn't fall back into His face. His skin was pale, and I had a sudden urge to tell Him to get outside and take in a few hours of Hellfire, or I'd shove vitamin D pills down his gullet.

Smart demons probably didn't tell Lucifer what to do or that he looked like crap. I didn't either. Guess you can teach old devildogs new tricks.

He stretched, pointing at the empty chair. "Have a seat, Ezekial."

I made my way around the table, glancing at three scrolls on the cold stone. "Should I pick these up?"

Lucifer frowned. "No. They're fine where they are. Better in the garbage."

I straightened and pulled the chair out. It scraped across the floor. "I can toss them?"

He sniffed. "You're not here to serve or clean up after me."

"I figured," I said, trying to get comfortable in the stiff chair that had to be older than me. "But I'm not really sure why I'm here either, and to be honest, I'm too tired for a chat. Even a social one."

"Let's get down to it then, shall we?" Lucifer sat back, folding His hands on His stomach.

"Okay." I tried to sit back, projecting an image of comfort, and couldn't get comfortable in the blessed chair. I ended up switching from ass cheek to ass cheek, leaning back, then sitting forward, and finally settled on my original posture. "What's up?"

The Lord of the Underworld looked at me through squinted eyes as if I humored Him. "How are you feeling after today?"

"Tired."

"I imagine." He drew a nasally breath. "A shame. But a necessary move."

"How much do you know about it?"

"Enough to have ordered the kraken to stand down so you could finish your work," He said with the briefest of flickers of a smile.

I snapped my fingers. "I wondered why it didn't bother us the times we went a little off-course."

"The least I could do. Especially after the long day you had."

"Well, you're not wrong. It has been. I was looking forward to eating and crashing out early. Hope that's still going to happen. I'm not good company when I'm cranky."

Looking toward the shuttered window, Lucifer said, "You've given a lot already, Ezekial. Maybe more than your fair share. Throughout your life. Not just in these past months and years. Your road is long and winding."

"And covered in chimera dung."

Lucifer looked away again. Not at anything in particular. I wasn't even sure He heard, which would have been a real waste of an extemporaneous one-liner. After a moment's thought, He said, "Few see it when they're in the moment. I know I didn't."

"See what?"

When He blinked, His eyelids seemed to smash together. I sat quietly while He repeated the physical tick for an interesting few seconds. "The sacrifices that are necessary for growth." Another drag of time passed before He looked my way. "You've been making them from the beginning. Though those times must have been hard on you, they've made you the incubus you are today. Don't underestimate the benefit of that."

"Might take a few centuries for me to get around to believing that."

"We don't have time." Crossing His arms, hands underneath, Lucifer tapped an elbow with a thick thunk, thunk. "Were you able to get any information out of Cassie?"

The shift was so swift, I stuttered through my answer. "She

has been hard to contact. There's a lot going on." Screw it, I decided. For too long, I'd operated by questioning and doubting, never trusting. Dialphio, Bilba, Ralrek, Azazel. They all taught me to work through that inherent blockage. Here was my biggest hurdle. I could cling to all the old junk in my head that caused my headaches and heartaches, or I could push myself into uncomfortable territory for the sake of everyone else. Literally, if the stories were to be believed.

The stories about me. Stories about Lucifer. Those that said I was the Great Prince, the one who'd challenge the incubus across the table for the title of the ruler of Hell.

Would that demon not do everything necessary? Blessed right, He would.

"You know your boys, Beelzebub and Apopis, attacked her in the Overworld, right?"

His face showed no signs of... well, anything. Like the news didn't surprise, shock, or please Him. In a voice rusted with age, he replied, "I'm aware."

"So that's how Cassie is," I said, not bothering to hide the bite. "She's had to hand off her Overworld duties, so she's never around. When she is, she gets attacked by two of Hell's Founders. Hardly a smart way to keep the Balance."

"We definitely have our challenges. That's why I asked you to keep working closely with her."

"I tried, but I don't get to set her priorities, as I'm sure you know."

"That's true, but," He stopped, squinting toward the window again. "We've got work to do. Plenty of work, and very little time. I'm going to need you, Bilba, and Ralrek to keep your travel schedule open and secretive. I trust you'll be careful about how you proceed with helping others to travel?"

Yikes. "You know about that?"

One corner of His lips curled up. "Yes. That too. Just put your heads together and proceed with caution. I cannot control the Founders any longer. We need Cassie's help. Once we understand if angels are involved in Underworld disappearances, we can plan more accurately. Though I suspect Azazel is already doing his fair share of that."

"Maybe once he's fully recovered," I said. "Another victim, don't forget."

"Again, why we need movement with Cassie. Abductions and their intentions in the Overworld. Try to get it straight from her, and not whoever she has covering her duties in the Overworld. Not that I couldn't trust other angels, but Cassie has a direct line to their Council. Plus, you trust her."

"I do."

Lucifer pushed Himself off the back of the chair and placed His elbows on the table. "Change is coming, Ezekial. We have to ensure you're prepared. Rescuing Libra was a big slip-up for the others. They'll be upset, and they will react. There can be no doubt about that. I will need to mentor you through the next phase."

"Mentor? You?" Oh boy, if Kanthor Sunstone could see me now. What would a perpetually disappointed father say about his son sitting at the side of Lucifer and receiving His mentorship?

He quirked an eye. "Do you have anyone better suited in mind for something that involves Founders far above your station, a close alliance with angels, and an impact on the Balance? Not to say, someone has to guide you on the use of Hellfire. Name them, if so."

I think, I can't stress that enough, Lucifer was poking fun at me. Hard to tell with someone apparently so jaded by His existence. But I suspected that's exactly what He was doing.

"Nah, I think I'll stick with you. You seem to know what you're doing."

Wow, even that only got a prolonged lip twitch. Imagine being so tired, so stretched thin, that you found nothing humorous. And here I had been whining about being Hell's

Segregate only a few years ago. What would it be like to be this miserable? For eternity?

I kind of felt bad.

"You know about Cassie's father?" He asked.

"I do."

"How much has she told you about Him?"

Okay, we might be bonding and all, but I had my limits. Ruler of Hell or not, He had to give a little more before He took. "She's careful about what she shares. Understandably. I mean, for all she knows, your Founders could torture me for information. Or you."

He raised a hand to His mouth, rolling His fingers on His upper lip. Suddenly, He stopped, lifting one finger. "That tells me something there."

"What?"

"She might know as much as I expected. You see, her father and I were close once upon a time. Long ago. Far longer than..." He paused, blinking hard again like He was seeing memories barreling down. "Far longer than any of the Underworld's problems. The Upperworld's too. Back then, we had a lot of fun. He is the one who came up with my nickname. We were meeting over a cookout. We'd been drinking, and He called me the 'fallen one.' It stuck." Lucifer stopped again, blinking. "Complexity ruined that. But we were young and unprepared. Well, younger. That guy, such a shame."

What was He talking about? What shame?

Lucifer wasn't even looking at me, but it was like He knew what I was asking. "Even though He's millennia younger than me, we get on really well. We have many common interests." Lucifer flinched as if struck by a painful thought. "I'll let Cassie share her father's situation with you, but suffice it to say, it's important that you work closely with her and be by her side. She'll need you soon, I fear." He stabbed the air with His finger. "But until that point, we have to take care of our business and keep those channels to her open. With the

Council split, we're in an even more precarious spot with the Balance. Meaning, the three of you, along with Azazel, of course, must be more diligent. I fear, this isn't your time to relax, Ezekial. For you, that time may never come."

Lucifer's hands smacked the table. He pushed away and stood, walking into the small alcove. When He spoke again, it came out as a growl. "Those two, Beelzebub and Apopis, have been a thorn under my toe for too long. Never trusted them. I should have listened to Aries." I shook my head, wondering if I heard Him name-drop correctly. "They're building armies. That's the intelligence I have. The numbers they're gaining are frightening. Beelzebub is leaning on his royal lineage and using wealth and family connections. A challenge to be dealt with." He disappeared behind a support pillar. His shoes clicked on the stone floor. "Michael maneuvers, but time has been as harsh on him as it has been on me. He won't be the primary focus, but disregarding him is a fool's errand." Now at the window, Lucifer pushed open the shutters.

I inhaled the fresh breeze as soon as it flitted across my face.

"Then there's Seraph," He said, speaking to the realm outside His narrow conical-shaped window. He leaned on the sill. "I'm glad you rescued Libra. Don't let the opportunity go to waste. Move on the Horn before she does something."

I wanted to gasp.

"She has to be stopped. Everything I've... everything we've worked for will be lost if she is successful."

He said that last bit like he'd just lost his favorite devildog. I looked around. The office was only a portion of this space. The alcove He stood in was empty of all but a bookcase—and yet another stack of scrolls—and what looked to be a pile of discarded clothes. I noticed more this time, though. The curtain to the other room was pulled back, revealing His high, four-poster bed. The comforter and sheets were tussled. It looked like no one had made it in years. A tray of unfinished food sat on top of a pillow.

This poor bastard's entire existence, was contained in these three hundred square feet.

I scoffed. I didn't really mean to, but this was ridiculous. "A lot of pressure to put on the only demon in Hell without magic."

I've seen it in Hollywood movies and re-lived it now. Intense, awkward silence. Like a record scratching in a country bar when a leather-clad biker with assless chaps walks in.

Slowly, Lucifer pushed Himself away from the ledge, stretched to stand straight, and turned.

"Does that bother you still, after all this?" He asked.

In that moment, I didn't see the devious ruler of Hell. What stood on the other side of the room was an incubus beaten down by life. Not in my 'oh, stop calling me the Segregate' kind of way, or the 'my dad hates me unfairly' way, either. Lucifer was a spiritless husk.

How did I respond when that's who I was answering?

Too few honest demons in Hell, so why not be one? "It's a big deal."

"Only if you make it one. Listen," He said, moving back toward the table and keeping His eyes cast at the cold, gray stones. "One day, you may find your answers. But what you seek is beyond even me. No one in the Under, Over, or Upperworlds can lead you to them."

"Great," I said. "Where do I magically 'find' them, then?"

Lucifer stretched out His arms. The t-shirt he wore hung loosely. His pale arms were nearly hairless and thin. "From One. They are the only way to find the answers to your questions." Lucifer pointed in the direction, though blocked by the table, of Creed hanging at my hip. "On you is the most powerful item anyone could possess except for the combined Horn and Halo. You're hardly helpless. It's not a coincidence that the only demon without magic is also the only one who can possess that halberd. Good thing, because you'll need it."

"For?"

"The Founders won't accept this," He said. "Both you and I know that. Everyone with access to this information knows that. Before long, they'll devise plans to address what happened today. And," He said, pausing behind His chair, gripping it with fingers that looked like skin-covered bone, "what they've wanted to do with you for years. Ever since my dear friend Aries gave you the halberd." Lucifer turned, drifting toward the door with His hands clutched and raised to the middle of his chest. "The measures I could take to ensure your safety are already in place."

"What measures are those?"

"The Isle is now the safest place in existence for demons like you," Lucifer said. "I've closed off the channel. Now, there is no way on or off the island except for Rifts and Gateways from the Isle. I'm the exception to that, of course. Best inform your friends. Yes, it will raise some issues, but better than the alternative."

"That means whoever isn't on the island can't get to it?" I asked, needing to check my sanity.

"Exactly."

"Even the Founders?"

Lucifer nodded.

"Holy heaven!" I said, leaning back and smacking my thigh. "That's great!"

"For those who would be put in danger should any Founder come for you? Yes." Lucifer now paced back toward His nearly empty alcove. "For you, the burden of responsibility falls."

"What do you mean?"

"Well, I couldn't just remove access to the Isle for the sake of it."

I dipped my head and voice. "You want something in return?"

"Of course, Ezekial. All existence, everything, is about Balance. On the grandest scale, and," He said, stopping, waving around at his quarters/office/retreat from Hell, "even here. For something to receive, something else must give. It's not inherently right or wrong. It just…"

"Is," I finished, Dialphio's lessons coming in handy.

"By providing you with protection, I've granted you the space, freedom, and peace of mind to carry out the tasks Hell needs of you."

Hell, all of it, needing me and my friends to save it. The Segregate, a social outcast, and Hell's asshole, turned into its heroes. What was the Underworld coming to?

"Without your efforts, the future isn't just bleak, Ezekial," He said, moving in front of the narrow window once more. "It's non-existent."

I sat, staring at a stack of scrolls I had no interest in, while the Lord of all demons did whatever He was doing in His alcove. His thinking was leading to more thinking on my part. Each word, another aspect of my future to consider. Not just me, but my two friends as well. Marijon and Azazel, too. They were wrapped up in this. The demons of the Isle; they couldn't be left out. In the span of a few short weeks, I'd gone from Hell's newest exile to a major player in its future.

Who said I was ready?

"Come here, please," Lucifer said, dropping His arm to His side, the flat of His hand toward the wall and His fingers splayed like He expected me to take it like a lover.

I pushed my chair back, my thoughts swirling. All I wanted to do was snag Libra, because I'm a good demon, and bless it, good demons act when others need them. Right now, Hell was out of stock of one Lucifer and a goatee-sporting Founder. If not us, who? If not now, when?

I moved to Lucifer's side. We stood there, ruler of the

Underworld and His magicless sidekick, looking down at the demons and creatures who went about their lives so far below they were nothing more than smudges on the Underworld's tapestry. Poor bastards. Each unaware of the monumental affairs happening high above them.

"This is what it's for, Ezekial."

This close, I smelled the funk typical of the elderly. Apparently, even Lucifer wasn't above the ravages of time.

"Look upon them. Now, and when you're back on the Isle. When your friends open those Gateways to different Circles. When you see them for who they are, when you see the struggles they face, you'll understand why those who can affect the Balance must sacrifice as much as necessary. Sometimes more." He inhaled, and I risked glancing over to catch Him closing His eyes.

With that advantage, I examined Him more closely. So many feared Him. Heavens, He made Beelzebub shut down. He set Michael to quaking. Seraph lost a sliver of her abundant confidence anytime His name was dropped. Apopis slunk in His presence. Yet now, all I saw was a demon who would have gladly drifted away like dust on the wind.

"Since the dawn of the Underworld, I have carried the mantle," Lucifer said, but kept His eyes closed. "For so many generations. Millennia. Eons. Ages. I'm tired, Ezekial. Very tired." He opened His eyes and looked out over the kingdom far, far below. "They say the Hellfire is the flame of annihilation. Have you heard that?"

My throat felt rusty. I broke its grip. "Yes."

A hard blink later, He said, "It's not. It's the flame of rebirth. Just as an old forest needs a fire to spur its rebirth, so do we."

What was He getting at? He couldn't mean... Could He?

"There have been three Yahwehs in my time. Three." The word came out so forcefully it sounded like it almost repulsed Him. "I've outlasted each. It used to be a point of pride." The wind whipped through the narrow window, tussling His long, white locks. "But not anymore. Now, I'm ashamed that I've hung on for so long. We have too many challenges. Challenges I don't have the energy to face." His nostrils widened as he breathed in slowly. "I haven't had energy in hundreds of thousands of years. My guilt will shadow me for the rest of my days."

Time seemed to still as the God of devil spawn turned away from the window and locked eyes with me.

"I can't fix those mistakes, but I can stop myself from repeating them," He said. "This conversation we've been having? I'm not mentoring you. I'm blessing you with the last thing you ever wanted."

No, please Lucifer, no!

"Embrace," Crazy Zeke whispered for the second time in the past hour.

Lucifer's eyes searched mine, almost like He had heard the voice. "Do you recognize what I want of you? What the Underworld needs of you? Do you understand what I'm about to offer you?"

My mind wanted to scream 'Yes, bless it, and you can keep that harpy dung away from me!,' but my stupid mouth said, "I think so."

Lucifer, the Lord of the Underworld, laid His hand on my shoulder and squeezed. Even in the weak grip, His fingers shook. "Ezekial Sunstone, I want you to take my place. I want you to be the next Lucifer."

At my hip, Creed thumped so hard it bounced off my leg.

Crazy Zeke tittered inside my skull.

I tried to swallow the blazeball-sized bulge in my throat. My voice cracked when I said, "When do I start?"

THE END

WHAT'S UP NEXT?

Zeke as the next Lucifer? Surely, whatever remains of the Council won't idly stand by and allow this to happen? The target on Zeke's back has grown larger than a super-sized order of chicken wings.

Find out in the next chapter in Zeke's story. Book 8, "Secrets of Scorpio," will be released in 2023.

NEVER MISS OUT!

Get the latest news, special deals, exclusive stories, first looks at book covers, and more by signing up for Paul Sating's newsletter!

Sign up for Paul's newsletter to follow all the news and special deals for upcoming novels, and to catch up on the latest regarding his podcast at http://www.paulsating.com.

EXCLUSIVE CONTENT EVERY WEEK!

More stories! More exclusive Paul Sating fiction, including free audio books, in podcast form!

Get more stories each month by becoming a Patron! New exclusive fiction each month!

Become a Patron & enjoy more content!

ALSO BY PAUL SATING

FICTION

Urban Fantasy
The Zodiac Series

The Fall of Aries (Free for newsletter subscribers)

Bitter Aries

The Horn of Taurus

The Gemini Paradox

Cancer's Curse

The Pride of Leo

Virgo's Vigilantes

Libra's Liberation

Rev Carver Series (Same Story World As Zodiac)

Angel Assassin (2023)

Angel's Creed (2023)

Epic Fantasy

Battleborn Books

Bloodborn (Free for newsletter subscribers)

Battleborn Trilogy

Fireborn

Rageborn

Battleborn

Bonebreaker Trilogy

King of Bones

War of Bones

Breaker of Bones

Crown of Thieves

Birth of a Thief (Free for newsletter subscribers)

Horror

12 Deaths of Christmas

The Plant (Free for newsletter subscribers)

Suspense

RIP

Chasing the Demon

Nonfiction

Novel Idea to Podcast: How to Sell More Books Through Podcasting

Podcasts

Audio Fiction Podcast

(Free for Patreon supporters!)

ACKNOWLEDGMENTS

Between the sixth Zodiac book and writing this one, I wrote and published six other novels. The *Battleborn* books are much different than Zeke's adventures, in many ways, and it took a while, not only to write them, but to get back into our favorite demon's head.

I was reluctant to start it, mostly because there's another fantasy series that has to get out into the world, sooner rather than later. Though writing Zeke is intuitive, they're still long books—which takes time, and jumping into another character's head, especially this intimately, takes time. Zeke is needy like that.

Thankfully, I had a bunch of supportive people in my life who helped me keep my blow holes above water long enough to type 'the end' at... er, well, the end.

First and foremost, Maddie. What is a life lived alone? I never want to discover that answer. My pillar. You know what my fears were coming into the writing of *Libra's Liberation*. Without your strength, who knows how long this would have taken. Thank you for being a rock.

My daughters, Nikki and Alex. Thanks for continually bugging me about getting back to work on the next adventure!

Louis Jackson has been a godsend for many years. Now, you're involved in a more formal role. I feel so bad for you. Thank you for shooting straight and braving treacherous waters.

Fellow urban fantasy author NM Thorn. The days of writing are cold and dark, and full of terrors. As you know, it's wonderful to have a friendly face to journey with!

ABOUT THE AUTHOR

Paul Sating is an author, podcaster, and self-professed coolest dad on the planet, hailing from the Pacific Northwest of the United States. At the end of his military career, he decided to reconnect with his first love (that wouldn't get him in trouble with his wife) and once again picked up the pen. Years on, he has published eight novels and he hasn't even screwed up his podcasts, which have garnered over a million downloads.

When he's not working on stories, you can find him talking to himself in his backyard working on failed landscaping projects or hiking around the gorgeous Olympic Peninsula. He is married to the patient and wonderful, Madeline, and has two daughters—thus the reason for his follicle challenges.

Find out more about his other books and free podcasts from his website: paulsating.com.

CONTACT PAUL

How to Contact Paul Sating

Published by Paul Sating Productions
    P.O. Box 15166
    Tumwater, WA 98511
    paul@paulsating.com

Follow me:

- Twitter: @paulsating
- Instagram: @paulsating
- Facebook: www.facebook.com/authorpaulsating
- Pinterest: pinterest.com/paulsating